"Quentin?" Brandi's eyes widened with wonder.

"What?" His fingers threaded through her hair, discovering its familiar texture for the first time, his entire frame of reference shattering and reshaping all at once. Nothing was as it had been, or perhaps it always had been and he'd just never seen it.

His mouth found hers before he could think, before he could recognize the madness and resist it. "Sunbeam . . ." His voice was hoarse, drugged with an incomprehensible yearning, and he pressed his mouth against hers again and again, until he knew his control was about to snap.

Battling his way to sanity, Quentin forced himself to think about what was happening, to emerge from this staggering, mind-numbing inferno—before it was too late.

"No . . . don't." Feeling Quentin's withdrawal, Brandi's arms tightened, and she shook her head, refusing to release him. "Don't pull away. You can't." Her words were breathy, a reverent whisper against his lips. "I think I've waited for this all my life," she confessed, flushed and dreamy with discovery. "I never knew it until this moment, but I have. All my life."

"Kane meters the growth of the romantic relationship with a maestro's skill and fine-tunes it with humor . . ."
—*Publishers Weekly*

THE LAST DUKE was so enjoyable that even as I'm thinking about it, I'm all ready to reread it!"

—*Kerene Seratzki, Booked Solid*

"I love all her books! Every customer that asks for a great author gets Andrea Kane!"

—*Lisa Wright, The Book Nook*

"THE LAST DUKE has been a delicious pleasure—the stuff dreams are made of!"

—*Koren Schrand, K & S Paperback Exchange*

"I couldn't put THE LAST DUKE down. Andrea Kane is a remarkable storyteller!"

—*Kevin Beard, Journey's End Bookstore*

"Andrea Kane just keeps on writing books that are as wonderful as her first! THE LAST DUKE made me want to put my arms around Daphne and Pierce and absorb them into myself to make me a better person."

—*Diane Kirk, Rose Petals & Pearls*

"A true love story. The passion and respect between Daphne and Pierce is what every woman wishes for! Beautifully written."

—*Jackie Skimson, Pages Etc.*

Books by Andrea Kane

My Heart's Desire
Dream Castle
Masque of Betrayal
Echoes in the Mist
Samantha
The Last Duke
Emerald Garden

Published by POCKET BOOKS

ANDREA KANE

Emerald Garden

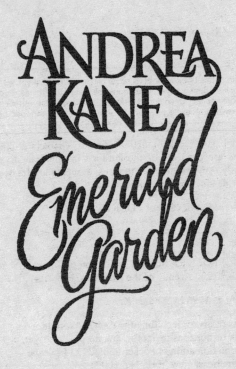

POCKET BOOKS

New York   London   Toronto   Sydney   Tokyo   Singapore

This book is a work of fiction. Names, characters, places and incidents are products of the author's imagination or are used fictitiously. Any resemblance to actual events or locales or persons, living or dead, is entirely coincidental.

An *Original* Publication of POCKET BOOKS

POCKET BOOKS, a division of Simon & Schuster Inc.
1230 Avenue of the Americas, New York, NY 10020

ISBN: 0-671-86509-9

First Pocket Books printing January 1996

10 9 8 7 6 5 4 3 2 1

POCKET and colophon are registered trademarks of Simon & Schuster Inc.

Front cover illustration by Brian Bailey

Printed in the U.S.A.

To happily-ever-after, and to all of us who, by believing in it, make it possible.

Acknowledgments

To my brother-in-law-but-more-like-my-brother Bob, whose scientific knowledge, and patience in sharing it with nonscientific me, made *Emerald Garden*'s mystery possible

And to my sister Myrna and niece Sherri, for their ongoing love and pride. (By the way, Myrn, you still owe me the Japanese talking yo-yo you promised me when I was ten!)

Prologue

"I thought I'd find you here."

Lord Quentin Steel mounted the steps of the white lattice gazebo, pausing beside the bench's occupant. "I stopped by your estate first. But, as I expected, your father said you'd left Townsbourne just after dawn. So I rode directly to Emerald Manor."

"Where else would I be at a time like this?" Head bent, Brandice Townsend's mournful reply was swallowed by her lap. "Emerald Manor holds my happiest memories. 'Tis only fitting for it to hold my saddest ones as well."

Tenderly, Quentin ruffled her cloud of cinnamon hair, smoothing it back to coax her chin from her chest. "Smile, Sunbeam. The world hasn't ended."

"Yes. It has." Without raising her head, she scooted over, silently inviting Quentin to sit beside her.

He complied, unbuttoning the decorated coat of his uniform to settle himself, gently taking her hand in his. "I won't be gone forever."

"That depends upon your definition of forever."

"Look at me, Brandi." Hooking a forefinger beneath her chin, Quentin forced her gaze around to meet his. "I'll stay in Europe only until we've defeated Napoleon and ended the war."

Brandi's dark eyes misted. "That's hardly a comfort. The war is interminable and throughout its countless days you'll be right alongside Lord Wellington, at the very heart of the fighting."

"That's where I'm needed," Quentin acknowledged quietly. "The lieutenant-general cannot lead us to victory if no one is able to successfully decipher French messages."

Brandi nodded, her slender brows knit with worry. "For once I wish you weren't so brilliant. Then you could remain in England, safe, rather than Lord knows where, endangering your life with every battle." She caught her lower lip between her teeth. "I'll miss you."

"You'll scarcely notice my absence," Quentin assured her, his knuckles caressing her cheek. "You have a legion of others to spoil you—your father, my parents . . ."

"Desmond," she added with pointed derision.

A shadow crossed Quentin's face. "I realize that my brother's more"—he paused, searching for the right word—"traditional nature upsets you."

"Traditional?" Brandi reiterated. "Desmond is a relic!"

Quentin's lips twitched. "I shudder to think what that makes me. After all, Desmond is but three and thirty, a mere seven years my senior. Do I border on antiquated as well?"

"Never." Her denial was immediate and fierce. "You and Desmond are as unlike as a knight and a dragon."

"Ah, but which am I, knight or dragon?"

Brandi shot him a don't-patronize-me look.

"Very well, Sunbeam." Abandoning all attempts at diversion, Quentin reverted to a candor he seldom required, save with Brandi. "I won't deny your statement. Desmond doesn't understand you, nor can he fathom your unorthodox behavior. But, in his defense, he *is* concerned about your future, albeit in his own way."

"Everyone is concerned about my future!" Brandi burst out, vaulting to her feet. "Everyone means well. Everyone is anticipating my impending coming of age—everyone but me." She crossed her beloved gazebo, clutching its entrance post and gazing restively over the vast manicured gardens of Emerald Manor, the fairy-tale cottage that, though built and owned by Quentin's family, had become Brandi's haven over the years. "As for understanding me, no one understands me but you. Not Papa, not your father, not even your mother. I adore them, Quentin, truly I do. Heaven knows they try to make allowances for my unruliness. But your parents are the Duke and Duchess of Colverton, and Papa, the Viscount Denerley. For generations, their families have thrived on the same rigid values. So it follows suit that they share Desmond's opinion that, as a soon-to-be woman grown, I'm to adopt the role of a proper lady."

Quentin stifled a chuckle. "Well, you are nearly sixteen. 'Tis only natural for your father to expect—"

"The Season after next he plans to bring me out," Brandi interrupted, her small hand tightening its grip on the post. "Then my life truly will be over."

"Aren't you being a touch dramatic?"

"No." She pivoted to face Quentin. "I'm not. And you know it. The moment I make that magical Court appearance, all I adore most will be wrested from my grasp. No more fishing in the cottage stream without stockings, tearing through the woods astride Poseidon, or honing my shooting skills. Instead, I'll be transformed into a pianoforte-playing, needlepoint-stitching ninny, a procurable prize to be flourished before the *ton.*"

Throwing back his head, Quentin shouted with laughter. "You certainly make it sound dismal, Sunbeam. Although, if your description is accurate, you'll need every bit of these next two years to prepare. Currently, your needlepoint is abysmal and your pianoforte playing, obscene."

"Neither of which I plan to rectify." Brandi's retort was adamant. "I've dreaded my coming-out for as long as I can remember. My only consolation, until now, has been the knowledge that you'd be here to comfort me in my misery."

Quentin rose, sobering as he met her gaze. "I'll return

to the Cotswolds the instant I'm able. I wish I could promise—"

"Don't," Brandi interrupted. "Don't promise. We've never broken a pledge to each other, Quentin. Don't alter that by offering me a vow you might be unable to keep."

Whatever Quentin intended to say was cut off by the sound of his carriage driver calling out to a coachman, and the horses whinnying their impatience.

"Is it time?" Brandi asked, a lump forming in her throat.

"Soon." Abruptly, Quentin reached into his coat pocket and extracted a pair of intricately carved pistols. "But not quite yet."

"Quentin!" Her anguish temporarily forgotten, Brandi's eyes widened with surprised delight. Impulsively, she darted forward, reverently touching one polished barrel. "How exquisite! Did you just purchase them? You must have. I've never seen them before. Where did you ever find them? The workmanship is magnificent!"

With an indulgent grin, Quentin offered her a closer look. "I discovered them last week when I was in London and, keeping us both in mind, I purchased them on the spot." He pressed the pistol Brandi was caressing into her outstretched hand. "Go ahead, take it."

Brandi needed no second invitation. Her trained fingers closed around the ornate handle, exploring the weapon while carefully avoiding its sensitive trigger. "It truly is splendid," she breathed, stroking the gleaming wood and brass.

"Might I interest you in a farewell shooting match?" Quentin inquired with a knowing twinkle.

Instantly, her head came up. "You might."

"Choose our target."

Cheeks flushed with excitement, Brandi walked down the steps and into the garden, pivoting to survey the surrounding woods. A resolute tightening of her jaw told Quentin her decision was made. "That towering oak," she instructed, pointing. "The one standing alone."

"Quite a distance, Sunbeam," he drawled, strolling down

to the garden and squinting to assess the designated target. "You're proficient at spans of nearly fifty feet, but that tree must be ninety feet away. Are you certain you don't want to reconsider?"

"I'm certain," Brandi returned, eagerly embracing the challenge. "Whichever one of us cleanly strikes the center of the oak's trunk—shall we say, just below the first row of branches—will be declared the winner."

"Agreed." Grandly, Quentin gestured for her to proceed. "Ladies—" A teasing pause. "Pardon me. Hoydens first."

"On the contrary," she teased back. "Soon-to-be-great war heroes first."

"As you wish." Quentin cocked and raised his pistol. An instant later, his shot rang out, whizzing through the air and striking the oak a mere inch or two from the designated spot.

"Excellent," Brandi commended. She appraised the tree before raising her own weapon. "But I'll surpass it."

"Such faith in your skill, Sunbeam."

She tossed him a saucy grin. "No, my lord. Such faith in my instructor." Taking careful aim, she fired.

Her bullet flew to its mark, piercing the oak a fraction to the right of Quentin's shot—dead on target.

Triumphantly, Brandi turned to her opponent. "Well?"

Quentin whistled his appreciation. "It seems your instructor is worth his weight in gold."

"Oh, he is." With a sunny smile, she offered him her pistol. "In fact, he appears to be a better instructor than he is a marksman."

Laughter erupted from Quentin's chest. "Touché, my victorious pupil." Still chuckling, he began cleaning his own gun, ignoring her outstretched hand. "What will you claim for your prize?"

All humor vanished from Brandi's face. "Your well-being. 'Tis all I ask."

Quentin ceased his task, raising his head to regard Brandi with gentle understanding. "I'll be fine, Sunbeam. You have my word, contest or not." His gaze fell to her proffered weapon. "Now, as for your prize. It must be worthy of that imposingly accurate shot of yours." He pretended to ponder his dilemma until, all at once, he appeared struck by a brilliant notion. "Your pistol!" he proclaimed. "'Tis the perfect prize." So saying, he pressed Brandi's fingers more tightly about the handle, urging the gun toward her. "It's yours."

"Mine? To keep?"

"Yours. To keep. As I shall keep its mate."

Brandi turned captivated eyes to her gift. "Oh, Quentin. I don't know what to say."

"Say nothing. You won our match—and the pistol." Savoring Brandi's exhilaration, Quentin was abruptly seized by a sense of impending loss, an innate perception that all he loved would be somehow changed when next he walked English soil. Silently, he admonished himself, fighting off the unsettling premonition, dismissing it as a reaction to the imminent bloodshed that loomed ahead.

Still, it persisted.

"Keep the pistol close beside you," he instructed, focusing on something he could control. "Then *I* can be assured of *your* well-being during my absence."

"Oh! That reminds me." Oblivious to Quentin's emotional turmoil, Brandi sprang to action, leading him back up to the bench and carefully laying aside her cherished prize to gather up a small parcel. "This is for you." She placed the box in Quentin's hands. "A going-away gift."

"You didn't have to—"

"Yes, I did. And you'll soon see why." Brandi's grin was impish. "I have a feeling my motives and yours are much the same." She gestured impatiently toward the package. "Open it."

With a puzzled expression, Quentin complied. A moment later, he lifted out a thin, exquisitely crafted knife.

"You're an incomparable marksman, my lord," Brandi explained with a maturity as disconcerting as it was atypical. "But guns alone cannot protect you. What if you should be caught by surprise, attacked at close range? No pistol is

6

small enough to remain unerringly concealed. A proper blade is. Especially one as thin as this. I had it fashioned just for you. Keep it with you at all times, hidden in your boot. Then, no one can harm you, whether in battle or out."

"'Tis the finest blade I've ever owned." Quentin stared intently at the onyx handle. "Thank you, Sunbeam."

"Now both of us will assuredly be safe, will we not, Captain Steel?"

He found his smile, sliding the knife inside his Hessian boot. "Indeed we will, my lady."

"Lord Quentin?" The coachman stood at a discreet distance, calling out to Quentin and pointing at his time-piece. "Forgive me, sir, but your ship leaves at half after three. We must be off."

"Thank you, Carlyle," Quentin acknowledged with a wave. "I'll be along straightaway." He turned back to Brandi, twining a lock of cinnamon hair about his finger and tugging gently. *"Adieu,* Sunbeam. And remember, safeguard your new pistol. For I intend to demand a second chance to beat you immediately upon my return, even if you've already traversed the dreaded portals of woman-hood."

Blinking back tears, Brandi nodded. "Agreed. And *you* remember, always keep your blade close beside you lest you need it." She rose to her toes, giving Quentin a fierce hug. "God speed."

He brushed his lips to her forehead, then released her, descending the gazebo steps and crossing the lush rectangular garden for which Emerald Manor was named. Halfway across the sculpted lawns, he turned, gripped by a compelling need to capture a memory, to take with him something neither time nor change could erase.

Leaning against the gazebo's ivied post, Brandi waved, her burnished hair blowing in soft wisps about her shoulders, a blanket of violets and wild geraniums at her feet.

Resplendence stretched before her; a lifetime loomed ahead.

Heavy hearted, Quentin returned Brandi's wave, smiling

as she held up her pistol, its polished barrel glinting in the sunlight. In return, he patted his boot, indicating that his blade was securely in place.

At half after three, Quentin's ship left London, transporting him to the European mainland and its awaiting war.

With him he carried Brandi's knife and an unrelenting premonition.

One that four years later was destined to become a reality.

Chapter 1

*B*randi sat back on her heels with a triumphant whoop. "There! I've completed the entire section of geraniums surrounding the gazebo."

"And not an instant too soon." Tucking wisps of dark hair from her cheeks, the Duchess of Colverton rose from the flower bed to lean wearily against the gazebo post. "It's grown so warm; why, it was downright brisk when I left Colverton."

"That's because we've been immersed in our gardening for nearly five hours now," Brandi informed her, pointing toward the sky. "Look at the sun. 'Twas barely peeking over the hills when we arrived at Emerald Manor. Now it's directly overhead. It must be half after noon." She came to her feet, wiping perspiration from her brow . . . and decorating her nose and chin with smudges of dirt. "Why don't we take a much-deserved respite and enjoy the refreshment Mary brought?"

"I need no second invitation." Gracefully, Pamela sank down on the garden bench, pouring two glasses of recently made fruit punch. "What time does Ardsley expect you home?"

Unceremoniously, Brandi flopped down beside Pamela, accepting the proffered drink. "Knowing that I'm at Emerald Manor? Father probably won't expect me until nightfall." She pressed the glass to her lips and, contrary to Pamela's dainty sips, downed her punch in five spirited gulps. "I'd rather be here than anywhere else on earth," she declared, refilling her glass.

"I know." Pamela's answer was reflective, her brows knitting in heightened concern.

A small round object dropped from the tree overhead, landing in Brandi's drink with a loud plunk. Punch flew in the air, drenching Brandi's gown with wide stains of pink.

"Not again!" Brandi set her glass down firmly, tilting her head back to scowl fiercely at the branch above. "Lancelot, I am not amused. That's the third gown you've ruined this week. What do you suggest I tell Papa?"

The red squirrel stared back, evidently unconcerned with Brandi's dilemma. Snatching up a berry, he turned his full bushy tail and scampered off.

"And to think I raised that ungrateful wretch from infancy," Brandi muttered, dabbing at her skirts. "I should have known the second I spied that white, quizzing-glass circle about one of his eyes that he'd be as arrogant as every other nobleman of my acquaintance."

Pamela's lips twitched. "So *that's* why you named him Lancelot. I thought perchance you saw some hidden valor in the scamp."

"Hardly. The only motivation Lancelot would have for rescuing me is if I held a nut in my hand."

"He's very adept at ruining clothing," Pamela noted, battling the laughter that threatened to erupt. She dipped her napkin in water, trying, unsuccessfully, to wash the stains from Brandi's gown.

"Oh, dear." Brandi shook her head, rolling her eyes to the heavens. "This time Papa is bound to lose his patience."

"I doubt it," Pamela reassured her. "Ardsley will forgive you just about anything; least of all a soiled gown."

"Perhaps." Brandi cast a self-deprecating look from herself to Pamela. "Still, even if we disregard the outcome of Lancelot's prank, how is it that you manage to look coolly elegant after four hours of garden work and I look like a dirty, pathetic kitten who's just emerged from a violent confrontation with a ball of yarn?"

Pamela could no longer suppress her mirth. "Oh, Brandi, you're anything but pathetic," she said, laughing. "You're a beautiful, vibrant young woman." Seizing the companionability of the moment, Pamela broached the very subject that continually plagued her. "Kenton mentioned that, according to Ardsley, that very handsome Lord Gallister has been calling on you daily."

"Hmm? Oh, Lord Gallister. Yes, he's visited Townsbourne several times." Her mind already racing onward, Brandi abandoned the cleansing of her gown, squinting at a point beyond the gazebo. "Do you think we should suggest to Herbert that he add another layer of those lovely white stones to the rock garden? I noticed that some of the current ones are beginning to lose their luster."

"That could be because you're always drippin' stream water all over them," came a gruff nearby voice.

"Oh, Herbert!" Brandi sprang up and rushed over to the manor's head gardener. "I'm so glad you overheard my suggestion! What do you think of the idea?"

"That depends." Herbert scowled, his rankled tone belied by the affectionate gleam in his eyes. "Are you gonna keep fishin' and wreckin' my rock garden with stream water?"

Brandi attempted a sheepish look. "I'll try not to."

"Humph." Herbert dragged a hand through his unruly graying hair. "All right. I'll collect a few more of those stones you like so much. But only a few! If you ruin this batch . . ."

"Oh, thank you!" Brandi hugged him.

"Does Ardsley know you've been frolicking in the stream again?" Pamela interjected tentatively.

Herbert's gaze darted to Brandi's anxious one. "The fact is, Your Grace, that rock damage could have been caused by lots of things," he hedged. "Rain, sun—"

"I understand, Herbert." Pamela sighed. "How very well I understand."

"Pamela, please don't tell Papa." Brandi gripped her friend's hands. "He'll be terribly upset. I've finally convinced him I'm trying to become a lady."

With a cough that suspiciously resembled a chuckle, Herbert ambled off.

"And are you, Brandi?" Pamela asked softly. "Are you truly trying to become a lady?"

Brandi lowered her gaze. "Honestly? I don't think it's possible."

"But why, darling? You're lovely and warmhearted and vivacious. And I'm far from the only one who thinks so. Even *you* can't help but notice the way gentlemen stare at you, the admiration in their eyes. Why, 'tis more than two years—indeed three Seasons—since you made your debut, yet men continue to fawn at your feet."

Brandi shuddered as if she'd just swallowed a worm. "They disgust me."

"For what reason? Ardsley says they all behave like proper suitors when they call. And my own eyes tell me that many of them are utterly charming, not to mention handsome and thoughtful. Surely one of them—"

"Proper. Charming. Yes, they are that," Brandi interrupted. "And they want someone equally proper and charming on their arm. I can't be that someone." Brandi looked beseechingly at Pamela. "I just can't."

The duchess's eyes clouded. "Brandi, you're twenty years old. You can't remain a frolicking child forever."

"Unfortunately, that's true."

Gently, Pamela smoothed Brandi's downcast head. "Why is the thought of growing up so abhorrent to you? You're brimming with love and life. Surely you want a home and children of your own."

A mournful sigh. "I do. But not at the expense of relinquishing all I find such joy in savoring."

"You make it sound as if you'd be imprisoned! You needn't relinquish everything, darling. Oh, I imagine you'll have to forgo such activities as splashing in the stream without your stockings. But your gardening, your riding—albeit with a proper sidesaddle rather than astride—those things you can still do."

Unappeased, Brandi stared contemplatively at the ground. "Why did you marry Kenton?" she blurted at last.

"Pardon me?" Pamela blinked at the sudden change in subject.

Sitting up, Brandi turned uncertain, anguished eyes to her friend. "Pamela, I never knew my own mother; she died in childbirth. In all ways but blood, you've filled her role, and I love you as if I were your natural child."

Pamela's eyes misted. "You're the daughter I never had," she managed. "Your happiness means as much to me as if I'd borne you myself."

"I know that. Just as I know you. We're very different, you and I. However in several ways—boundless devotion to those we love, a deep attachment to Emerald Manor—in ways such as that, we are much the same. Both of us being women, we were raised with the knowledge that we would someday marry and bear children. And, both of us being tenderhearted, we each had dreams of the man who would one day share our life. What I'm asking you now is, how did you recognize Kenton as that man? What reason—other than duty—made you choose him as your husband?"

A tender smile. "That question requires no pondering. I wed Kenton because I was desperately in love with him. And, one and thirty years later, I still am."

"Kenton feels the same way. He adores you; 'tis obvious in the way he looks at you. Just as your love is obvious in the way you come alive when you're beside him. You're two halves of a whole, Pamela, and the love between you is very special and quite miraculous."

"I won't disagree," Pamela said in a quiet, fervent tone. "Kenton is my heart and my soul. Without him, I wouldn't want to live."

"Precisely as I would wish to feel were I in your position." Brandi's lips trembled. "But I'm not. No man has ever awakened my heart as such. Not Lord Gallister, nor any of my other gentlemen callers. I feel absolutely nothing when I'm with them, not even a flutter. So how can I take the step Papa wants me to take—consider marriage to a man I don't love and know inherently I never will? The answer to that is, I cannot." She lowered her lashes. "I'm sorry, Pamela. Truly I am. I loathe disappointing you, Kenton, and Papa. But evidently, between my unorthodox pastimes and my unfulfilled romantic notions, I'm destined to remain alone."

Pamela studied Brandi's burnished head thoughtfully, assailed by a relentless suspicion—spawned long years ago—that stubbornly refused to be silenced. "You said you had dreams. Tell me, what sort of man did you dream of?"

A small smile. "One who reveled in my spirit and rejoiced in my unladylike diversions. One whose passion for challenge matched my own. One who loved me for who I am, not for the fictitious creature he yearned I become."

"I see."

"You *see,* but can you *understand?*"

"Better than you realize," Pamela responded evenly, with the barest hint of a twinkle. "Brandi, contrary to what you've concluded, I promise you are not destined to remain alone. The man of whom you dream does exist—I can see him as clearly as if he were standing before me. And he *is* someone special, someone rare. All that remains is for you to discover each other, which will happen in its own time— a time I suspect is not too far off."

"How can you be so sure?"

"Trust me, darling; I am." Pamela stretched, glancing idly toward the stables. "It just occurred to me that you haven't exercised Poseidon today."

Brandi's head came up in a flash. "I completely forgot. Of

course! Quentin would never forgive me if I neglected his stallion!"

"Knowing my son, I suspect that's true," Pamela concurred, her gaze once again fixed on Brandi. "Which reminds me, you've still received no further word from Quentin?"

Joy fled Brandi's face. "Not since that letter I showed you last month. The poor mail-coach driver—I badger him each time I see him. But, thus far, nothing."

"Letters from the mainland have been erratic, at best," Pamela murmured aloud, consoling herself and Brandi simultaneously. "I only pray . . ."

"Quentin is fine." Brandi knotted her fists in her gown. "I'd know if he weren't. He'll be home any day now."

"We can't be certain of that, darling. Just because the Duke of Wellington is returning to England doesn't mean Quentin intends to accompany him."

"That's exactly what it means. Quentin vowed to stay away only until the war was over. Well, Napoleon is safely at Elba. Therefore, Quentin's arrival in the Cotswolds is imminent." Shoulders squared defiantly, Brandi gathered up her skirts and rose. "I'd best exercise Poseidon. It's already past noon; soon the sun will be too strong for us to indulge in one of our breakneck gallops."

"Of course, darling, go ahead." Feigning innocence, Pamela waved Brandi off, more certain than ever that the wondrous possibility she was contemplating did indeed hover on the brink of reality.

Now it was up to God and fate.

Colverton Manor

Gone.

Desmond stared down at the empty drawer, his hands shaking with the shock of discovery.

How could that be? he thought, wildly groping for an answer. No one knew of its existence.

Like a man possessed, he began flinging things from every corner of his nightstand, not pausing until it was empty.

He slammed the final drawer to the floor, his breath coming in shallow pants, sweat beading his forehead. There had to be a logical explanation for this. There *had* to be.

"You won't find them, son."

Kenton Steel, the Duke of Colverton, leaned back against Desmond's closed bedchamber door and regarded his first-born through tormented eyes.

"Father?" Desmond's head snapped around, and he fought to control his mounting terror.

"Why, Desmond? Why in God's name would you do such a thing?"

"I don't understand."

"Don't insult me. I'm not guessing; I have proof. The only facts missing are why and with whom?"

Kenton's final query struck home, and Desmond's eyes narrowed. "What do you mean, 'with whom'?"

"You're not clever enough to have managed this alone. Who assisted you?"

"Oh, I see," Desmond returned with biting sarcasm. "I'm apparently not even a praiseworthy scoundrel."

"Praiseworthy?" Kenton's fists clenched at his sides. "Are you mad? What you did was despicable!" His appalled gaze raked Desmond, searching for a man who didn't exist. "And even now you evade my questions, refuse to explain your duplicity. Well, it matters not. There is no explanation you could give that would alter my decision."

Desmond went very still. "What actions do you intend to take?"

"You've shattered my faith—along with the few illusions I had left, where you're concerned. To be blunt, I cannot confer my holdings or my legacy to a man I do not trust."

Resentment pumped hotly through Desmond's veins. "As opposed to a man you *can* trust, like your beloved Quentin."

A muscle worked in Kenton's jaw—his only overt reaction to Desmond's barb. "I intend to ensure that you're helpless to indulge in such reprehensible behavior again. Not only while I'm alive, but after. I'm changing the terms of my will."

Colors exploded in Desmond's head. He uttered a vicious oath, kicking the nightstand drawer from his path. "Changing your will? In what manner, or need I ask? Quentin will now inherit everything—just as your precious Pamela has always prayed he would."

"Quentin has nothing to do with my decision."

"Don't expect me to believe that!" Desmond stalked across the room, flinging open the door with such impact that it struck the wall, leaving its imprint on the plaster. "Quentin might be in Spain, but his ghost is here. Every hour of every day. Haunting me with his presence. I give up. Change your bloody will. Leave it all to Pamela's son. I don't give a damn anymore."

He strode into the hallway, colliding with Bentley, Colverton's long-standing butler, just outside the room.

"Pardon me, my lord," Bentley murmured at once, smoothing his impeccably crisp uniform. "But I heard a commotion and—"

"It doesn't matter, Bentley," Desmond interrupted, waving the butler off. "You know more of what transpires at Colverton than I do. You're also in better favor." Sidestepping Bentley, Desmond strode toward the stairs. "In fact, you too will probably inherit a portion of what was originally mine."

Bentley stared speechlessly after Desmond, his head snapping around as the duke emerged, his stance and expression bleak.

"Can I do anything, Your Grace?"

Defeatedly, Kenton rubbed his eyes. "I love both my sons, Bentley. I always have."

"Yes, sir."

"Lord alone knows where I went wrong."

"Master Desmond lost his mother quite young, sir,"

Bentley suggested with the unprecedented familiarity afforded to him alone. "He doesn't truly remember her"—he tactfully cleared his throat—"or the fact that your marriage was an arranged one. He sees only the magnitude of feeling that exists between you and the present duchess. I believe that to be at the root of his resentments."

"Pamela has worn herself out for years, trying . . ."

"I agree, Your Grace. But self-doubt is often blinding—and destructive. Don't blame yourself, or the duchess. The problem lies with Master Desmond himself."

Kenton nodded bleakly. "Just the same, I cannot allow his jealousy and weakness to damage others."

"No, sir."

"Contact Hendrick," the duke instructed with sad resignation. "Summon him to Colverton posthaste. Advise him that my will is to be amended. Effective immediately."

"At once, Your Grace." Turning on his heel, Bentley moved off purposefully.

"Bentley?"

The butler paused halfway down the hall. "Sir?"

"Say nothing of this to anyone. Not even Pamela."

With an offended sniff, Bentley continued on his way. "That goes without saying, Your Grace."

Quiet male voices greeted Pamela as she entered Colverton the following evening—not a welcome reception given how exhausted she was. After two successive days of rigorous planting, the last thing she wanted was to entertain guests.

"Good evening, Your Grace." Bentley bowed, taking Pamela's wrap.

"Good evening, Bentley." She inclined her head quizzically. "Is that Kenton's voice I hear?"

"Yes, Madam. The duke and Mr. Hendrick are conducting a business meeting."

"I didn't know Ellard was visiting today. I'll stop in and say hello."

Bentley cleared his throat. "His Grace and Mr. Hendrick

have been closeted in the library for hours. It would seem their discussion is of significant import. Possibly you should postpone your greeting for later."

Pamela blinked. "Are you implying I wouldn't be welcome?"

"Thank you for coming on such short notice, Hendrick." The opening of the library door accompanied Kenton's voice.

"Not at all," Ellard Hendrick replied, strolling out beside Kenton. "When I read your missive yesterday, I saw immediately how urgent the situation was. Hence, I had my clerk clear my schedule so I could spend the entire day at Colverton. I'm relieved we were able to finalize the matter; now you can enjoy some peace of mind." Securing his portfolio, Hendrick headed down the hall. Halfway to his destination, he spied Pamela and hastily abandoned all talk of business. "Pamela, how wonderful to see you," he declared, striding over to kiss her hand. "And what a pleasant surprise; Kenton didn't mention you'd be returning this early."

"Nor did he mention your upcoming visit." Pamela cast a curious glance at her husband. "Had I known you were coming, I would have made certain to be home."

"Hendrick's visit came up rather suddenly," Kenton put in. "We had some complicated matters to address."

"So Bentley told me." Another speculative look, this time at the serene-faced butler. "In any case, won't you stay for supper, Ellard?"

"I wish I could." Hendrick ran a hand through his silver hair. "Unfortunately, I'm due back in London this evening. So I must be going." He smiled politely. "Another time?"

"Of course."

Turning to Kenton, he murmured, "I'll substitute these papers for their predecessors as soon as I reach my office."

Kenton's jaw set, his voice lowered to a fervent hush. "I, in the interim, will continue to delve into the matter. I want all the facts, Hendrick—every last one."

"I understand." The solicitor cleared his throat, his tone reverting back to normal. "Good night, Kenton, Pamela."

Pamela waited only until Bentley was outside showing Hendrick to his carriage. Then she drew Kenton aside, turning puzzled eyes to his. "What confidential and urgent business did you and Ellard have?"

"Why do you assume it was confidential?" Kenton straightened his waistcoat, looking as gray and tormented as if he'd just returned from battle.

"Because Bentley wouldn't allow me near the library." Tenderly, Pamela smoothed her palms over her husband's rigid shoulders, taking in every detail of his haggard state. "It's Desmond, isn't it?"

Wearily, Kenton nodded, the lines around his eyes stark with sleepless anguish.

"Won't you tell me what this is about?"

"It doesn't concern you, Pamela. This is between my son and myself." As if to counter the brusqueness of his retort, Kenton caught his wife's wrist, brought her palm to his lips. "'Tis something I must handle on my own," he added quietly.

"I understand." Pamela caressed her husband's jaw as if that act alone could ease his distress. "And I don't mean to intrude." She sighed, lowering her gaze. "Lord knows, I'm aware Desmond is *your* son and not mine; he's spent years reminding me of it. In truth, I've given up trying to change that which is unchangeable. But 'tis you I'm worried about—I cannot bear to see you suffer so. Whatever happened between you and Desmond yesterday is tearing you apart. Is there nothing I can do?"

"Now, no. Later, perhaps." He squeezed her hand. "Tomorrow, Garrety, my investigator, is due at Colverton, hopefully, to provide me with the missing pieces required in order to put this sordid matter to rest forever. Should he prove unsuccessful, I'll take the situation into my own hands."

Pamela paled. "Kenton, you're frightening me. This isn't dangerous, is it?"

"Dangerous?" Kenton shook his head. "I have no reason to believe so."

By the following afternoon, he believed otherwise.

Alone in his study, Kenton stared down at the terse message a footman had delivered to him not ten minutes past. He'd reread it a dozen times, and each time his skin crawled a bit more.

You're meddling where you don't belong. Should you continue, you'll die and Desmond will pay the price.

Kenton dropped his head in his hands and squeezed his eyes shut, wondering how to discover what he must while still protecting those he loved. For long minutes, he remained thus, contemplating the choices . . . and the risks.

At last he took up his quill.

"Darling? What is it?"

Pamela looked up from her dressing table to see her husband leaning in their connecting doorway, studying her pensively. "Kenton?" She rose, her nightrail swirling about her legs. "Is something wrong?"

"No." He smiled, crossing the bedchamber to enfold Pamela in his arms. "I was merely thinking how very much I love you."

She pressed her cheek against the silk of his dressing robe. *"That* you may contemplate as often as you wish."

"Pamela, I want you to do something for me."

Drawing back, she gazed anxiously up at him. "That sounds ominous."

"Not ominous. But very important." He withdrew a sealed envelope and a key from his robe pocket. "I want you to keep these for me. Conceal them in a place where no one—not even your lady's maid—need venture."

With a puzzled frown, Pamela examined the two objects her husband had given her. "The letter is for Quentin?" she asked, noting that their son's name was penned on the envelope.

"Yes, to read immediately upon his return. Until then, I want to be certain no one is privy to its contents."

"Very well." Pamela's brow furrowed. "But why don't you give it to him yourself? Our war with France is over; Quentin should be home any day now."

"Even if that's true, I might be—away—when he arrives at Colverton."

"Away? Away where?"

"Darling." Gently, Kenton raised Pamela's chin. "Please don't ask any more questions. Just promise me you'll make sure Quentin gets the note."

"I promise."

"And the key as well."

"The key." Pamela's gaze fell on the other object in her hand. "Why, 'tis the key to your strongbox; the chest that matches my own."

"Yes, I know. And I pray that, having read my message, Quentin will know precisely what I mean for him to do."

"This pertains to Desmond, doesn't it?"

"Yes."

"I heard Mr. Garrety arrive earlier this evening. Did he provide you with the information you needed?"

"No, not yet." Kenton rubbed his palms together, thinking that, given today's threatening note, he'd taken an enormous risk ordering his investigator to intensify their search. But the outcome of Desmond's forbidden scheme—albeit of his own making—could taint not only his own future but also the entire family's. So, disenchanted or not, it was Kenton's responsibility to protect his domain and all that went with it.

"Whatever Desmond is involved in—you're searching for details," Pamela murmured, as if reading Kenton's thoughts.

"Yes. I *must*—for all our sakes."

She nodded, her fingers closing around the note and the key. "I won't question you further—not about your quandary, nor the reasons for your unwillingness to share it with me. As for Quentin, you're right to trust him. Despite all

22

their differences, all the nonexistent rivalry Desmond perceives, Quentin loves his brother. He'll do the right thing."

The sadness in his beloved wife's voice tore at Kenton's heart. "Darling, this isn't about trust, for I'd trust you with my life. But should a conflict arise . . ." He searched for the least alarming choice of words. "I don't want you involved." *Or at risk,* he added silently to himself.

"All right, Kenton. As always, I'll respect your decision." She crossed the room, opening her bureau drawer to remove the custom-crafted strongbox that was an identical mate to Kenton's. "The key to your chest belongs nowhere but in mine," she informed him, groping along the box's rear panel for the notch in which she concealed her key. With a flourish, she extracted it, opening the chest and slipping both items Kenton had given her beneath a strand of diamonds and emeralds. "Moreover, 'tis an ideal hiding place. Since I only store my most valuable jewels here, no one touches the box but me. In fact, no one—other than Brandi—knows of the key's hiding place." Pamela gave a resigned sigh. "I offered Brandi complete access to my gems, hoping the prospect of donning them would entice her to attend a few more of the balls she so loathes. Unfortunately, my plan failed miserably." Lowering the strongbox lid, Pamela carefully locked it before slipping the key back into its home. "In any case, your articles for Quentin are safe." Meticulously, she replaced her chest in the bureau drawer, then turned to Kenton. "And now?"

"Now we wait."

A fortnight later, Kenton strode into his wife's sitting room, an air of purpose about him. "Pamela, I'm leaving for London."

Slowly, she put down her needlepoint, assessing her husband's intense expression. "You've learned something."

"Yes. And I've just dispatched a missive that will hopefully forestall any further damage. In the interim, I received a note from Garrety. I'm to meet with him this afternoon. Ardsley is accompanying me."

"Ardsley! Why?"

A brief hesitation. "Because I asked him to. This matter concerns him as well."

Pamela came to her feet. "Then why wasn't he present during your meeting with Ellard?"

"Because Ardsley didn't know of his own involvement. He still doesn't. In fact, he knows fewer details than you." Kenton's jaw set. "'Tis up to me to disclose them—for his own protection. After all, he is my oldest and closest friend."

"Enough." Pamela's chin lifted in an uncustomary display of willfulness. "I'm coming with you."

Even as she spoke, Kenton was shaking his head. "No."

"Please, Kenton, don't refuse me," she appealed quietly. "Whatever this is about, I'd be a fool not to realize it's serious. I have no intentions of prying. But I want to be with you, to offer whatever support I can."

"My meeting with Garrety must remain private—at least for now."

"Fine. I'll shop while you and Ardsley convene with Mr. Garrety. But at least I can be with you on the carriage ride to London and back. And, should your business run late, we can stay at an inn in Town."

Kenton's jaw unclenched a fraction. "Wouldn't you prefer spending the days at Emerald Manor with Brandi?"

"No." Pamela shook her head. "Brandi is relegating the entire week to assisting Herbert with the rock garden. She'll never notice my absence. Besides, I'd *prefer* to be with my husband."

A smile. "I'm flattered. I thought you cherished your garden above all else."

She returned his smile. "Almost all else."

Kenton could feel himself relenting. "How long would you need to collect your things?"

"A half hour at the most." She waited, a loving plea in her eyes.

"Very well." He sighed, pressing her palm to his lips. "You've convinced me." A new flicker of uncertainty flashed through his mind. "What about Brandi? Do you think she'll be all right alone?"

"She won't be alone; she'll have three sets of servants doting on her, at Townsbourne, at Emerald Manor, and here. Further . . ." A prophetic glint lit Pamela's eyes. "Brandi is going through a most significant awakening. I think the time alone will do her good."

Kenton's brows knit in question. "What is our Brandi awakening to?"

"Herself. Her future. What it will be like when Quentin returns."

"When Quentin returns?" Kenton looked blank.

"She misses him, darling. Surely you recall that the only time Brandi comes alive is with our son."

"They've always had a very special rapport," he conceded. "But I don't see what that has to do with . . ."

"Everything, Kenton. You must have noticed how her exuberance has dimmed during his absence—not to mention how she's loathed every aspect of her first three Seasons."

"And you think Quentin's homecoming would lift her spirits?"

"Don't you? If anyone can reach her, he can."

"They haven't seen each other for four years, Pamela. Brandi was a child when Quentin went to war."

"Was she?" Pamela mused aloud. "I wonder." Lovingly, she squeezed her husband's forearm. "I'd best pack."

Kenton glanced at his timepiece and nodded. "Ardsley should be here any minute."

"Have Bentley fix him a drink. I'll be ready straightaway."

An odd sense of trepidation pierced Kenton's consciousness. "Pamela . . ." He put out an instinctive hand as if to protect her—from what, he wasn't certain. "Maybe it would be best if you remained at Colverton."

"No." Pamela caught his hand between both of hers. "'Twould be best if I accompanied you. You see, darling, as I recently explained to Brandi, I love you. Our destinies are entwined. And whatever the future holds in store, we'll confront it together."

The trepidation vanished as quickly as it had come, annihilated by fate's iron will.

Forty minutes later, the imposing carriage bearing the Steel family crest rounded Colverton's winding drive and disappeared through the dense woods surrounding the estate.

Only the lone figure watching from a shadowed grove of trees by the roadside knew that the Duke and Duchess of Colverton and the Viscount Denerley would never arrive in London.

Chapter 2

Quentin paused at the grassy threshold of Colverton's peaceful, deserted burial site. Rain pelted him relentlessly, but he scarcely noticed. He was too consumed by the finality he would momentarily be forced to confront; a finality he hadn't yet accepted.

His parents were dead.

Slowly, he moved forward, his boots sinking into the soggy ground, guiding him, of their own accord, to his destination.

He saw the burnished head from fifty feet away, lowered as it had been the day he'd left her. Shoulders shaking, she knelt before Kenton and Pamela's gravesides, raindrops drenching her as she buried her face in her hands.

She must have heard him approach, for her back stiffened and her head whipped around to see who was intruding on her pain.

"Quentin . . ." She came to her feet, taking an instinctive step in his direction, then halting. Conflicting emotions warred on her beautiful, transparent face—joy at seeing him, anguish at the reason for his return, uncertainty as to how she should behave. Quentin could read her indecision clearly: After four years, did she greet him with the utmost propriety or with the impulsive abandon of the past?

Reaching out his hand, he took the decision away from her. "Hello, Sunbeam."

"Thank God you're home." She closed the remaining distance between them, seizing his hand and gazing up at him with a lost, haunted look in her dark eyes. "They're gone, Quentin."

Without a heartbeat of hesitation, Quentin enfolded Brandi against him, as comforted by the act as she. "I know, sweetheart." He felt her delicate body begin to shudder with long-suppressed sobs.

"Their carriage went off the road . . . that sharp turn near Oxford . . . the family who found them said they died instantly . . ." Brandi gasped fragmented details against Quentin's military coat.

"My message said only that it was a carriage accident," he replied, determinedly reserving his myriad questions for later. "And that there were no survivors."

"Papa's body was dashed on the rocks," Brandi was continuing, desperately trying to bring herself under control. "And Pamela and Kenton were crushed beneath the weight of the carriage. Desmond tried to keep the specifics from me. But I didn't want to be protected. I needed to understand. Yet I can't accept the fact that I'll never see them again. Oh, Quentin, I know it's a sin to think of myself, but I feel so utterly, totally alone."

"You're not alone." Jaw clenched, Quentin sought the strength to soothe her. "I'm here."

"Thank God," she whispered again, her voice muffled against his coat.

"When the news reached me, I caught the first ship leaving for England." He swallowed. "But I'm too late for the funerals."

Hearing the anguish in his voice, Brandi raised her head. "It doesn't matter. The church was so crowded, you wouldn't have been able to say a proper goodbye. Here you can." She gestured inanely behind her. "I just placed fresh flowers on their graves—geraniums; Pamela's favorite. I picked them yesterday at Emerald Manor. They're beautiful—so beautiful, in fact, that before I left Townsbourne this morning I placed a few on Papa's grave." Her lips trembled. "And Mama's, as well. Do you know what I was thinking?"

"No," Quentin answered gently. "What were you thinking?"

"That Papa can finally be happy now. That after twenty years he and Mama are together again."

Reflexively, Quentin smoothed damp wisps of hair from Brandi's forehead. "That's a lovely thought. Also an accurate one. Ardsley never cared for anyone after your mother died. Except you." His knuckles caressed her cheek. "I don't have to tell you how much your father adored you. He loathed seeing you unhappy." A small nostalgic smile played about Quentin's lips. "I can still recall how devastated he was the first time Poseidon threw you."

"He was terribly upset," Brandi agreed in a choked whisper.

"Upset? I was fortunate he didn't shoot my horse on the spot. And to think you weren't even injured."

"My pride was in shambles," Brandi returned, the haunted look fading a bit. "Papa knew how much I hated defeat."

"And how badly you took it, even at eight years old."

A half-smile curved her lips. "True."

"Sunbeam." Quentin sobered, tilting Brandi's face up to his. "Ardsley wouldn't want you grieving like this."

She nodded. "I know." Inhaling sharply, she studied Quentin's face as if truly seeing him for the first time since he'd appeared. "These lines weren't here before," she murmured, brushing her fingers over the corners of his compelling hazel eyes. "Nor was this." Her fingers glided upward, through the damp strands of his dark hair, pausing at those spots now tinged with gray.

An odd expression crossed his face before he gave her a rueful smile. "In case you've forgotten, four years have passed. My thirtieth birthday came and went."

"No." She shook her head. "Age has nothing to do with it. Experience does." She lowered her arms, twisting her hands in the folds of her cape. "How did you endure it? Facing death every day, watching others die? I can't even withstand three losses."

"You're being too hard on yourself, Sunbeam. These three losses were not mere acquaintances; they were your family."

"Yes." Her eyes welled up again. "They were."

"You've changed, too, you know," he added hastily, speaking his thoughts aloud, uncensored, in order to distract her.

His ploy was successful.

"Have I?" She looked more curious than pleased. "How?"

"You've grown up." Even as he spoke the words, he realized how very true they were. When he'd left, she'd been a vibrant, clever little imp, rife with the promise of beauty and allure, yet just shy of grasping it. In four years, she'd come into her own. The fine-boned features—no longer streaked with dirt—were accentuated by bottomless dark eyes and a luxuriant cloud of cinnamon hair. "You've become a beautiful young woman," he concluded aloud.

"Maybe." She sighed. "But I've hated every minute of it, just as I promised you I would."

An unexpected chuckle rumbled in Quentin's throat. "Oh, Sunbeam, I've missed you." He shook his head in amazement. "No one but you could make me smile at a time like this."

"I feel the same way." Her gaze fell to his coat, now thoroughly soaked by the rain. "You're drenched," she murmured, wiping droplets of water from his sleeve. "If you remain out here much longer, you'll become ill."

"As will you." Solemnly, he peered beyond Brandi's shoulder. "I need some time alone with them."

She nodded. "Shall I leave for Townsbourne?"

"No." Roughly, he cleared his throat. "That is . . ."

"I'll wait for you in the sitting room," she replied with gentle understanding. "We can have tea and talk. Besides, I'm sure Desmond is eager to see you."

"Is he all right?"

"Under the circumstances, he's remarkable. In fact, I don't think I could have survived this past week without him. He's been a pillar of strength, while I've hovered on the verge of collapse. I feel terribly guilty—not only about placing the entire emotional burden on him, but about taking so much of his time nursing my heartache. He has much to see to, and the details will only multiply after tomorrow."

"Tomorrow?"

"The wills are being read in Mr. Hendrick's office at two o'clock. I understand it's a mere formality, but once Desmond is officially declared the Duke of Colverton, I imagine his responsibilities will be staggering."

"Yes," Quentin concurred quietly, studying Brandi's face. "They will."

The rain intensified, fierce droplets transforming to a hard, steady stream.

"Go," Brandi advised, wrapping her cape around her. "Visit Pamela and Kenton. I'll tell Desmond you're home." She captured Quentin's hand in a hard, comforting squeeze. Then she gathered up her skirts and sprinted toward the manor.

With a reminiscent smile, Quentin watched her unladylike departure, strangely comforted that some things, at least, remained unchanged.

Then his smile faded and he turned to face the ordeal that awaited him.

"You look well, Quentin," Desmond pronounced from the sofa. He put down his coffee cup and leaned back, carefully assessing his half brother. "A bit thinner, but well."

31

"As do you." Quentin returned Desmond's scrutiny. His brother looked as young and fit at seven and thirty as he had at twenty—tall and well-muscled, his dark brown hair untinged by gray, his probing black eyes unmarred by lines. Time had indeed been kind to him.

Shifting his weight on the straight-backed chair, Quentin took a gulp of black coffee, wishing he didn't feel such a stranger in his own home.

A prolonged silence permeated the sitting room.

"Learning about Father and Pamela's deaths must have been a tremendous shock for you," Desmond commented at last.

"For all of us," Quentin amended. "And, yes, it was. In truth, I don't believe the full reality has yet sunk in."

"I awaken each day and expect to see Papa at breakfast," Brandi murmured from the armchair in which she was draped.

"But you're improving, little one," Desmond soothed instantly. He leaned forward, covered Brandi's hand with his. "Every day you come back to yourself a bit more."

"I suppose so. Still . . ." Her voice and gaze drifted off.

"Yesterday, we took that lovely carriage ride through the Cotswolds, and I distinctly recall your smiling at least twice."

"Hmm? Oh, the carriage ride. Yes, Desmond, it was splendid."

Desmond's teeth gleamed. "Indeed it was."

"Master Quentin, I just heard you'd returned to Colverton." Bentley awaited no invitation, striding through the sitting room to where Quentin sat. "Welcome home, sir—despite the tragic circumstances of your homecoming." A flicker of emotion crossed the butler's face, then dissipated as he regained his unfaltering dignity. Clearing his throat, he clasped his hands behind his back. "I've arranged for your bags to be unpacked."

"Thank you, Bentley." Quentin came to his feet, smiling fondly at the man who'd been at Colverton forever, and who was more family member than servant. "'Tis good to be back. I only wish . . ."

"As do I, sir."

"Quentin, you look exhausted," Brandi said softly. "Why don't you go to your chambers and rest? I've got to get back to Townsbourne, anyway."

That haunted look was back in her eyes.

"Why?" Quentin heard himself ask. "Why must you go back to Townsbourne?"

"I don't understand." She looked as lost as she had years ago, when he'd bid her goodbye at the gazebo.

"Are you overseeing the staff? The accounts? The property?"

"No." Bewilderedly, Brandi shook her head. "Desmond's handling the estate and the businesses for me. As for the staff, they need no supervision. They've all performed their jobs splendidly for years." Her lips trembled. "In truth, I think I'm more underfoot than useful. But they haven't the heart to shoo me away."

"Then, I repeat, why must you subject yourself to wandering about a manor that offers you naught but painful reminders?" As he spoke, it occurred to Quentin that his pointed insight applied not only to Brandi but to himself. "A manor you never truly had an affinity for anyway."

"Quentin is right, you know." Surprisingly—and for the first time in over a decade—Desmond enthusiastically agreed with his brother. "At a time like this, you should be among people who love you, people who can share your grief." He touched Brandi's cheek with infinite tenderness. "Why don't you stay here at Colverton?"

Quentin's eyes narrowed on his brother. "At Colverton?"

"Yes, where else?"

Brandi was shaking her head. "You're both generous and wonderful. Lord knows, I'm here often enough as it is. But I do need time by myself, time to think, to work through my own grief. Moreover, 'tis no secret that I have as little affinity for Colverton as I do for Townsbourne. My feelings are for the people who live here. And those who did." She swallowed. "So, though I deeply appreciate your offer . . ."

"I wasn't referring to Colverton," Quentin interrupted. "I was referring to Emerald Manor."

"Emerald Manor?" Desmond recoiled. "Whatever for?"

"Because Brandi's happiest hours have been spent there. Because she'll have the privacy she needs, the gardens she loves, and us nearby."

"Nearby? 'Tis a four-mile ride from Colverton to Pamela's cottage." Desmond's pointed description of Emerald Manor was not lost to Quentin. "Further, the cottage is deserted. There is no one there to care for Brandice."

"I don't need caring for, Desmond. I'm twenty years old," Brandi reminded him. "Besides, I would hardly describe Emerald Manor as deserted. Mrs. Collins runs the cottage as if it were an estate, with a staff—albeit small—that's as disciplined as an army. As for the grounds, Herbert is indispensable; he's a splendid gardener and one of my dearest friends. He loves Emerald Manor as if it were his own."

"Brandice, a housekeeper and a gardener are hardly enough to help you recover."

"But Emerald Manor is." Quentin met Brandi's troubled gaze. "I think you'll heal there, Sunbeam. You'll heal because you'll be home."

Once again, the sadness in Brandi's eyes seemed to recede. "Yes, I will." She inclined her head quizzically. "Do you think Kenton would mind?"

"He'd be honored. So would Mother." Quentin gave her an imperceptible nod. "We'll ride to Townsbourne and pack a few of your things. The rest can be delivered tomorrow. You'll be settled in by nightfall."

"But Mrs. Collins doesn't even expect me."

"Forgive me for interrupting, Miss Brandi," Bentley spoke up. "But I'd be delighted to ride ahead and advise Mrs. Collins of your imminent arrival. It will take the good part of two hours for you and Master Quentin to ride to Townsbourne, collect your bags, and reach the cottage. By that time, not only will Mrs. Collins have a room and a hot meal prepared for you, but—given her feelings for you—she'll probably have a string quartet performing on the lawn." Bentley's lips twitched ever so slightly.

Quentin chuckled. "I don't doubt it." His reassuring gaze returned to Brandi. "So, now that your concerns have been addressed and resolved, shall we head out?"

Briefly, Brandi glanced at Desmond. "Do you object?"

Desmond gritted his teeth. "Of course not. If it pleases you to stay at the cottage, then by all means, do so." His smile was brittle. "I'll come by tomorrow morning. We can have breakfast together before leaving for London."

"Yes—the wills." Brandi's lashes swept her cheeks. "That would be fine, Desmond. I'm sure I'll need the support."

His expression brightened. "And you shall have it."

"I'd forgotten just how beautiful Emerald Manor is," Quentin murmured, maneuvering the phaeton down the stone path leading to the cottage.

"'Tis a small piece of heaven," Brandi agreed, gazing about the manicured lawns. "Also my own little sanctuary. Thank you for suggesting I stay here."

"I'd prefer your smile to your thanks."

She turned to him and complied, her lips curving upward. "You have both."

Reining the horses to a deliberate halt, Quentin alit, lifting Brandi to the ground beside him. Then he turned, staring across the gardens to the lattice gazebo that signified all the joy of his past.

"Welcome home, Quentin," Brandi said softly.

A muscle worked in his jaw. "Home," he repeated in a hollow voice. "I wonder if that exists for me anymore."

"It exists for everyone. But I suppose each of us has to find our own." Soberly, Brandi watched Quentin rediscover Emerald Manor, his poignant gaze flickering over the familiar grounds. "One thing is certain," she added. "Colverton is no more home for you than Townsbourne is for me."

"My parents spent some of their happiest, most precious moments at this cottage."

"As did Pamela and I . . . and you and I, before you went away. Even Papa enjoyed his visits here. Emerald Manor is a joyful place."

Quentin nodded, turning to tug a lock of her hair. "Then perhaps being here will bring back your smile, Sunbeam."

"What about yours?"

He looked away and fell silent.

With acute insight, Brandi studied the hard line of his profile. "I was worried about you, you know. I've never gone so long without receiving a letter."

Everything inside Quentin tensed. "The last few months were . . . difficult."

She lay a hand on his forearm. "Toulouse must have been unbearable. From what I read, thousands of our soldiers died in that battle."

"Nearly five thousand," Quentin supplied. "And, yes, it was one of the cruelest and bloodiest battles of the war. My only consolation is that on its heels came Napoleon's abdication."

"Were you riding with General Wellington?"

"Yes. An hour after we rode into Toulouse, we received word of Bonaparte's flight. Had we but known his surrender was an accomplished fact, Wellington would never have issued the order to attack. He agonized over the needless deaths." A pause. "So did I."

Quentin's pain pierced Brandi's heart. "I'm so sorry," she whispered. "You were in the midst of a nightmare, and here I am asking why you didn't write more often. 'Tis only that your letters were my sole reassurance that you were well. When they stopped coming, I was terrified. Every day I prayed for your safety. I was so frightened we'd receive notification that . . ." Brandi broke off.

Reaching down, Quentin extracted an onyx-handled memory from his boot. "I was well-protected, day and night, thanks to your splendid gift." He placed the knife in her hands.

"You kept the blade!" Brandi's whole face lit up as she examined the token she'd given him a lifetime ago.

"Did you doubt that I would?"

"Not really, no."

"Good. Am I to assume, then, that you've been equally attentive to my pistol?"

Brandi grinned. "Indeed I have, my lord. To your pistol *and* your horse. Poseidon is twice as fit as when you left him. He's also decidedly happier with a woman on his back."

"Is he now?" Quentin cast her a sideways look. "And tell me, Sunbeam, is he also decidedly happier with a sidesaddle on his back?"

"I wouldn't know. He's never worn one."

Quentin threw back his head and laughed. "You're still my little hoyden, I see."

"Does that disappoint you?"

"It relieves me. I was half-afraid I'd come home to find you transformed into a proper lady."

"I? Proper?" Brandi's delicate brows shot up. "Did my letters convey that ludicrous concept to you?"

"Your letters consisted mostly of caustic comments about each Season's loathsome balls, and each ball's loathsome men."

Her eyes twinkled. "Then why would you think I'd changed?"

"Probably because I prayed you hadn't."

Quentin's words elicited a relapse of that faraway, anguished look he'd seen reflected earlier in Brandi's eyes. "I can well understand your prayer," she murmured, wrapping her arms about herself in a self-protective gesture. "So much has changed—so many irrevocable ties with the past have been severed. To recover even one precious, untouched memory is perhaps the greatest comfort of all."

"Then let us seize those untouched memories," Quentin suggested, his own melancholy receding beneath his worry over hers. "You yourself just reminded me what a joyous place Emerald Manor is. I propose we recapture that joy. Not today, for it's late and Mrs. Collins will be clucking over your food turning cold. Nor tomorrow," he said thoughtfully, "since our excursion to London will undoubtedly take the better part of the day. Therefore, our contest must be held the following morning."

"Quentin, what are you talking about?" Brandi asked dazedly. "What contest?"

"What contest?" Quentin echoed in mock offense. "Why, our marksmanship match, of course. Have you forgotten the challenge I issued the day I left England? I demanded the right to demonstrate my shooting prowess the instant I returned to Emerald Manor, in order that I might regain my pride—pride which a certain lucky hoyden completely annihilated."

"Lucky?" A competitive sparkle eclipsed the distant look from Brandi's eyes. *"Au contraire,* my lord. I remember the contest well, and it was won by sheer skill and unerring accuracy."

"Prove it."

"Gladly."

"Shall we say, ten A.M., the morning after next?"

"Consider the engagement confirmed, Captain Steel."

"Excellent." Gently, he brushed one stray cinnamon curl from her cheek. "Let's get you settled so you might rest up for the grueling competition ahead."

Abruptly, Brandi's mood altered, a myriad emotions reflected on her ever-expressive face. "Thank you," she whispered fervently, gazing up at him. "And thank God for bringing you safely home. Had anything happened to you . . ." She faltered, unable to continue, paralyzed by the very implication of her own statement.

"Brandi—" Quentin broke off, words suddenly inadequate. What more could he say? No false assurances would do—not when he was confronted with the bleak reality in her eyes. Further, how could he obliterate a fear that was so painfully valid?

EMERALD GARDEN

As if reading his thoughts, Brandi shook her head, tears glistening on the silken fringe of her lashes. "Don't," she entreated softly. "Don't say anything. Only please, never go away again." Her breath caught in her throat. "Never, ever again."

Gathering up her skirts, she sprinted toward the cottage.

Chapter 3

Quentin's mood was darkly pensive as he swung open the door to Hendrick's office the next afternoon. He'd slept not a wink, his heart heavy with the finality of his parents' deaths, his mind haunted by a picture of Brandi's broken expression as she'd run from him yesterday.

He could do naught to rectify either torment, for death was absolute, and his presence in England temporary.

Hell and damnation.

He felt so bloody helpless, like a leaf blowing in the wind—a man who, until this week, had impelled the lives of thousands, and now struggled helplessly in fate's unpredictable hands.

Inhaling sharply, Quentin slammed the door behind him, bracing himself for today's ordeal. In less than an hour, his parents' last wishes and provisions would be disclosed, and Pamela and Kenton Steel would truly be gone.

"Lord Quentin?" A wiry clerk hastened forward, his brows knit in concern. "Are you all right?"

Quentin blinked. "Hmm? Oh, Peters. Yes, I'm as well as can be expected."

Peters nodded sympathetically. "I understand, my lord.

I'm terribly sorry your homecoming was precipitated by such a tragedy. Please, have a seat. Mr. Hendrick will be with you shortly."

"Very well." Quentin turned toward the designated chair, starting as he saw Brandi sitting slumped in the seat beside him. "Brandi?"

She raised her head. "Hello, Quentin."

"Why are you here by yourself? I thought Desmond was joining you for breakfast, then escorting you to London."

"He did. But he needed a few minutes alone with Mr. Hendrick before the readings began. So I waited here."

Quentin frowned, wondering. "Today? Why on earth would he need . . . ?"

"Quentin." Ellard Hendrick strode out from his inner office, looking as solemn as the occasion warranted. "Welcome home—although, needless to say, I wish it were under different circumstances. Please accept my condolences on your tragic losses."

"Thank you, Ellard." Quentin nodded politely. "Have you and Desmond completed your business?"

"Indeed we have," Desmond acknowledged from within. Rising from the armchair beside Hendrick's desk, he strolled out to join the other two men. "Hendrick had prepared some documents Father requested, and needed my approval in order to finalize them. Fortunately, there were no unexpected complications, and everything can proceed as Father wished."

"Documents?" Quentin inclined his head. "Do they pertain to the wills?"

"Not in the least." Desmond's expression never altered. "They involve an agreement Father and I were on the verge of consummating. I wanted to be certain Ellard understood that he should continue just as Father originally outlined."

"Which I fully intend to do." With crisp efficiency, Hendrick dismissed the subject, glancing beyond Quentin to where Brandi sat. "Brandice? Are you certain you're up for this, my dear?"

"I'm certain." Brandi rose, looking so small and lost that

Quentin was accosted by a sudden and vivid memory of the precocious six-year-old who'd wept on his sleeve the day her first geranium died.

Quentin walked over, hooking a gentle forefinger beneath her chin. "Are you sure, Sunbeam? We can postpone this if need be."

"No." With more weariness than aversion, Brandi shook her head. "Waiting would be worse. Please, let's get on with it."

"Very well," Hendrick replied. "If you'll all have a seat in my office, we'll proceed."

"Come, Brandice." Desmond was beside her instantly, proffering his arm. "The ordeal is nearing an end. Once the wills have been dispensed with, we can put this nightmare behind us and concentrate on the future."

Reflexively, Brandi accepted his arm—and his strength. "Thank you, Desmond."

Soberly, Quentin followed them in, only half-listening to Hendrick's preliminary instructions. He was troubled, not only by Brandi's dazed state but also by an uneasiness spawned by her unexpected and obvious closeness with Desmond—a closeness Quentin could no longer ignore.

Frowning, he lowered himself into the chair on Brandi's right, glancing over the top of her shining head to Desmond's hard profile on her left. What precisely had developed between the two of them while he'd been away?

"The Last Will and Testament of Kenton James Steel," Hendrick was saying as he unfolded the first document. "'To my beloved wife, Pamela . . .'"

Two tears slid down Brandi's cheeks, and Quentin watched Desmond tenderly press his handkerchief into her hand.

"'. . . and all my assets to my son Desmond, who, in assuming his title as the Duke of Colverton, assumes all responsibilities herewith; including, but not limited to . . .'"

Quentin closed his eyes, suddenly inundated by the pain

of loss. Simultaneously, Brandi reached over and squeezed his fingers tightly in her small gloved hand.

"'. . . To my son Quentin, I leave the sum of one million pounds, and in return ask but one favor: take care of your mother for me. I fear my death will prove too much for her to withstand. Never before have I asked that you compromise your military career. But I'm asking now. Should Pamela need you, I beg you to stay by her side. You and Brandi are the only ones who might infuse her with the strength and the will to persevere. I know you won't disappoint me, Quentin, and for that I thank you.'"

Quentin bowed his head, unshed tears burning beneath his lids.

"'. . . In the event of Pamela's death, I also bequeath to my son Quentin that which means so very much to him, as it did to his mother and me—something I hope will keep us forever alive in his mind and his heart: Emerald Manor. It is Pamela's and my greatest hope that the cottage gardens will one day be alive with the laughter of our grandchildren.'"

A harsh sob escaped Brandi's lips, and Quentin tightened his fingers about hers.

"That concludes the Duke of Colverton's will." Hendrick cast a concerned look at Brandi. "Shall I pause between documents?"

"No." Brandi shook her head adamantly. "At least not for my sake. I'd prefer you finish."

Hendrick's gaze moved to Desmond, who gave him a concurring nod. Without further comment, the solicitor returned to his task, smoothing out the pages of Pamela's will. "Being that all the duchess's worldly possessions were legally bound to Kenton's, her will contains but one special provision. With your permission"—he glanced at Quentin—"I'll skip directly to that clause. You, of course, are free to peruse the entire document at the culmination of our meeting."

"You have my permission," Quentin consented.

"The paragraph reads as follows: 'To my precious

Brandice, I bequeath all that I would leave a daughter: my jewel case and all its gems, my silver, and, most of all, my love. While the possessions may be passed on to your children, the love is yours to keep. Shed no tears, Brandi, for in my heart I know you will never be alone.' "

Hendrick cleared his throat, lowering the document to his desk. "The rest is customary."

"You needn't read it, Ellard," Quentin interjected, acutely aware of Brandi's desperate battle for self-control. His thumb caressed her trembling fingers, feeling the tension that radiated from her hand to his. "Let's hasten this ordeal as best we can."

"I agree," Desmond said, shifting in his chair. "Read Ardsley's will and be done with it."

"Very well." Hendrick turned his attention to the final document. "I have before me The Last Will and Testament of Ardsley Edward Townsend."

The solicitor's voice droned on, pronouncing that all Ardsley's worldly possessions were to be left to Brandi and ultimately her children, and entrusting the administration of the Townsend businesses to Kenton and, upon his death, to Desmond.

" 'And finally,' " Hendrick concluded, " 'as to the well-being of my beloved daughter, Brandice, whose happiness means more to me than my own; in the event of my death, I hereby appoint Kenton Steel as her legal guardian, to oversee her future until the day she marries, at which point the privilege of caring for her shall become her husband's duty. In the event of Kenton's death, I hereby appoint his son Desmond as successor-guardian, to enact all the responsibilities described herein.' "

Unanticipated resentment surged to life inside Quentin as Ardsley's final stipulation struck home. Desmond— responsible for Brandi?

Quentin glanced over, gauging Brandi's reaction to the thought of being entrusted to a man she'd once called a relic. He could tell naught from her expression, which remained unchanged; her eyes vague, faraway. Had the reality yet to sink in, or had her relationship with Desmond altered so dramatically that Ardsley's provision was not only tenable but welcome?

"That concludes the will readings," Hendrick announced, coming to his feet. "Unless, of course, there are questions."

"I think it would be best if we postponed questions or discussion for another time," Desmond inserted at once, inclining his head meaningfully in Brandi's direction. Gently, he guided her from her chair. "Today has depleted the final vestige of our emotional reserves."

"I fully understand." Hendrick turned to Quentin. "Is that amenable to you as well?"

"Perfectly." Quentin rose. "Moreover, I have no need for clarification. The terms of the wills were quite clear."

"Brandice?" Hendrick asked gently.

"I'd like to go home now," Brandi whispered.

"Come, little one." Desmond cupped her elbow. "I'll accompany you back to Emerald Manor."

Brandi took two steps, then halted as Desmond's choice of words spawned a new concern.

Narrow shoulders tensed, she pivoted slowly to face Quentin. "Emerald Manor," she repeated, gazing at Quentin with a bleak, disoriented look that tore at his heart. "I don't know what your plans are, what you want me to do. Shall I pack my things and have them sent back to Townsbourne tonight?"

Quentin's brows drew together. "Why would you do that?"

"I . . ." She swallowed, her lips quivering. "The cottage is yours now. I'm sure Pamela and Kenton would want you, not I, living there."

Quentin stepped forward, framed her face between his palms. "You're wrong, Sunbeam. Nothing would make my parents happier than knowing you'd chosen their loving haven in which to heal. And nothing would insult me more than if you chose to leave." His forefinger traced a tender line down the bridge of her nose. "Moreover, who but you could help Herbert tend the gardens? Left in my inept hands, Emerald Manor's splendid gazebo would be surrounded by perishing flowers and unkempt ivy. Need I tell you how Mother would feel about that?"

A whisper of a smile. "No, you needn't."

"Good. Then that puts an end to your ludicrous suggestion. Unless, of course—" Quentin's eyes twinkled. "This wouldn't, perchance, be an attempt to back out of our shooting match, would it? If you recall, we did plan it for tomorrow morning."

This time, Brandi's smile appeared of its own accord. "I recall. And I assure you, my lord, I have no intentions of backing out."

"That's a relief. Then I suggest you stop spouting this nonsense about returning to Townsbourne and instead hasten off to Emerald Manor to prepare for battle."

"I'll do that." Brandi scrutinized Quentin's face, her disorientation temporarily held at bay. "Are you all right?" she asked softly.

"Yes. And so are you." Gently, he ruffled her hair, then urged her toward the door. "Now go with Desmond. I'll be by at ten tomorrow, pistol in hand."

"And—pistol in hand—you'll be defeated, just as you were four years past," Brandi managed to tease back. Complying with Quentin's request, she walked over to join Desmond in the doorway.

Quentin chuckled, vastly relieved by Brandi's attempt at humor, however small. His gaze slid from her to Desmond, and he started, taken aback by the sharp, disapproving look he saw reflected in his brother's eyes.

"Are you ready, Brandice?" The new duke's tone was curt.

Brandi seemed not to notice. "Yes." She paused to address Hendrick. "Thank you. You displayed patience and compassion—both of which I badly needed."

"Not at all, my dear," he replied. "Your grief is perfectly understandable, given the magnitude of your loss. I'll make arrangements to have Pamela's jewel case and silver delivered to Emerald Manor posthaste. In the interim, should you think of any questions once the shock has worn off . . ."

"I'll contact you with whatever questions Brandice might have," Desmond interrupted. "Good day, Ellard." He glanced coldly at Quentin. "You're going directly to Colverton?"

"Yes."

"Fine. I'll see you there." Without another word, Desmond ushered Brandi out.

Colverton was unusually chilly and dark when Quentin entered its doors that night—or perhaps it was only his mood which made it appear as such. The day had been understandably difficult, leaving him tired, drained, and vaguely unsettled in a way he had yet to examine.

Although it took little insight to discern that Brandi was at the heart of his unrest—Brandi and her nebulous relationship with his half brother. A half brother he recalled as small-minded and envious, a man far too self-centered to embrace someone's pain as his own, unless he had something to gain.

The same man Brandi had once loathed, yet now described as solid and supportive: "a pillar of strength," to be exact.

Obviously, Desmond had changed a great deal over the past four years.

Or had he?

"Good evening, Master Quentin." Bentley hastened over, his lips pinched into a tight line of worry. "Was the day as trying as you feared?"

"Yes, Bentley, it was." Quentin massaged his temples. "Would you mind pouring me a drink? I'm in sad need of fortification."

"You'll find a glass of brandy awaiting you in the sitting

room," Bentley instructed, relieving Quentin of his coat and gloves. One brow arched in response to his lordship's obvious surprise. "When I saw your approaching carriage, I took the liberty of fetching not only your brandy but a light snack. Undoubtedly, you've eaten nothing since breakfast."

A corner of Quentin's mouth lifted. "I'd forgotten how well you know me."

The butler sniffed. "Since the age of two, you've dealt with upset in the same manner—by neglecting your food."

"A vice you continually remedied."

"And one I will continue to remedy whenever I can." Bentley gestured toward the sitting room. "Your meal is ready whenever you are."

Quentin stared down the dimly lit hallway and hesitated.

"Do you know," Bentley remarked casually, "as luck would have it, I've just completed my evening duties and was about to indulge in a welcome respite. I don't suppose you'd like some company?"

Relief flowed through Quentin in a great wave. "Indeed I would, Bentley." He shot the butler a quick, knowing look. "You couldn't have arranged your respite at a better time— as luck would have it, of course."

"Of course." The barest glimmer of a smile. "After you, sir."

Warm and cheerily aglow, the sitting room was a splendid contrast to the dreariness of the entranceway. A delicious-smelling plate of cold roast lamb and mint sauce greeted Quentin, beside which sat a basket of sugar-iced buns and, of course, the requisite goblet of brandy.

Crossing over to the sideboard, Quentin surveyed the room, noting every one of Bentley's personal touches right down to the fire blazing cozily at the hearth. "Thank you, my friend," Quentin said simply, lifting his glass in tribute.

"You're quite welcome, sir." Bentley cleared his throat, hands clasped behind his back. "Will Master Desmond be returning tonight?"

Quentin tossed down his drink. "Not for another hour or so. He escorted Brandi to Emerald Manor."

"But he will continue residing at Colverton?"

Quentin halted, midswallow, lowering his drink to the sideboard. "That's an odd question. Of course he'll continue residing at Colverton. Where else would he live? After all, he is the newly appointed duke."

Surprise flashed briefly on Bentley's carefully schooled features. "Did you say the duke, sir?"

"I did." Quentin sighed. "I know it will take some getting used to, Bentley, but Father is gone. The sooner we come to terms with it, the better."

"Mr. Hendrick did read the wills today, did he not?"

"He did." Quentin nodded. "The documents yielded no surprises; Desmond will assume Father's title and businesses, both of which I'm sure he'll handle admirably." Turning to refill his glass, Quentin missed the startled look on Bentley's face. "He'll also oversee Ardsley's business and . . ." Quentin broke off. "I retract my statement, Bentley. There was one surprise. Not only will Desmond be responsible for Ardsley's business, he'll also be responsible for his daughter."

"Miss Brandi?"

"Yes. Father was designated her guardian, Desmond his successor. Hence, Desmond is now Brandi's overseer."

"I see." Bentley pursed his lips thoughtfully. "And how did Miss Brandi react to this news?"

"I'm not certain. She's taking all three deaths extremely hard and is still very much in shock. Frankly, I'm not even sure she comprehended what Hendrick was telling her."

"And Emerald Manor? Did the duke and duchess will their cottage to Miss Brandi?"

"No, they willed it to me. But, given the circumstances, I'd rather Brandi continued to stay there. You saw how precarious an emotional state she was in. Evicting her from Emerald Manor might be more than she can handle. Besides, where would she go—back to Townsbourne? That estate holds nothing for her but pain and emptiness."

"I agree, sir. But, where will you stay?"

"'Tis not as if I don't have a home here at Colverton,

Bentley. I'll stay here—for however long I remain in England."

"You plan to return to the continent?"

"When I'm needed, yes."

Silence.

"Sit down and eat, Master Quentin," Bentley said at last. "You need your strength."

Quentin complied, absently chewing his food, his thoughts troubled and faraway.

A prolonged interval elapsed.

"Bentley—" Quentin broke the silence at last, finishing his last bite and pushing aside the empty plate. "Has much changed since I've been away?"

"Changed?" A split second of hesitation, as telling as it was brief. "Are you referring to anything in particular, my lord?"

"No. Yes." Quentin's head came up, his probing gaze leveled at the butler. "I'm referring to Desmond. Has he, or any one of his relationships, undergone a transformation recently?"

Bentley's cough was uneasy. "I'm not certain how to answer that, Master Quentin," he responded, his composure slipping but a fraction.

A fraction was enough.

"It appears you know precisely how to answer that." Quentin was more determined than ever to get at the truth. "Bentley, I'm asking you to tell me what you know. How have Desmond's alliances altered while I've been—"

The sound of the front door opening interrupted Quentin's interrogation. With obvious relief, Bentley reacted, veering abruptly to return to his entranceway post. "Please excuse me, Master Quentin. We'll continue our talk later."

"Yes, Bentley, we most definitely shall."

Quentin had no time to ponder Bentley's uncustomary state of off-balance. An instant later, Desmond strode into the sitting room, his expression dark and brooding. He barely nodded in Quentin's direction, simultaneously tugging off his cravat and crossing over to the sideboard to pour himself a drink.

"Is Brandi all right?" Quentin demanded in response to his brother's obvious agitation.

The question seemed to intensify Desmond's annoyance. "Yes. Brandice is fine." He tossed off the contents of his glass. "However, you and I need to have a talk."

"Do we?" With a measured look, Quentin altered his tactics, sensing that some of his answers were about to find him. He leaned back in his chair, casually crossing one leg over the other, his posture deceptively relaxed. "I assume this talk pertains to whatever was plaguing you in Hendrick's office."

"Indeed it does."

"Does it concern the terms of Father's will?"

In the midst of refilling his glass, Desmond sloshed a bit of brandy onto the sideboard. "Father's will? Why would you suppose that?"

"Because it's a logical assumption. What else could possibly have upset you?" Quentin baited, convinced that the real cause for his brother's unsettled state had only to do with Brandi.

His suspicions were heightened by Desmond's terse response.

"I'm not distressed over Father's will." His hand now steadied, Desmond faced Quentin, shoulders squared with purpose. "I'm distressed over Brandice."

"Brandi?" Quentin's brows rose in apparent surprise. "Why? Has she done something to anger you?"

"Hardly. 'Tis her future that worries me."

"Her future?"

"Yes. 'Tis now my responsibility to shape it—as her legal guardian."

Quentin's eyes narrowed on Desmond's face. "Not to shape it, Desmond; to oversee it."

"I see little difference between the two." Desmond set

down his glass, slapping his palm on the tabletop and leaning forward to regard his brother. "But the point is a moot one."

"Is it?"

"Yes. The significant factor here is that, as a result of the accident, Brandice feels very much alone. Just as fate has robbed us of our father, so it has done to her."

"My mother died in that carriage as well," Quentin added icily. "Perhaps that detail is of negligible importance to you. But not to me. And not to Brandi, who adored Mother as if she were her own. So I think it's safe to assume that Brandi is also mourning that loss."

"I apologize for the oversight. Yes, Pamela's death is an equally devastating blow—for you and, perhaps even more so, for Brandice. Which only escalates my concern. The impact of this disaster has left Brandice vulnerable and in shock."

"I've noticed."

"I would hate for anything . . ." A pregnant pause. "Or *anyone* to intensify that shock and thwart her recovery."

That did it.

Like a lion prodded by a stick, Quentin lurched forward in his chair. "Are you implying that *I* would do anything to hinder Brandi's healing?"

"Not intentionally, no." Visibly startled by his brother's uncharacteristic outburst, Desmond softened his approach. "Quentin, you've been away for over four years."

"I'm well aware of that."

"Things have changed since you left."

"For example?"

"For example, Brandice has grown up. She's no longer the worshipful child you bid goodbye, nor is she the reckless young girl who galloped wildly through the woods by your side and raced barefoot through the stream at Emerald Manor. She's twenty years old now, very much a woman grown."

"I have eyes, Desmond. I can see precisely what Brandi is—and what she is not." Quentin's jaw set. "Can you?"

"Very clearly."

"I wonder."

"Would you like to know what I see?" Desmond demanded. "I see a frightened, abandoned young woman who needs someone to lean on, someone she's certain will remain by her side."

"And, if I view this brotherly chat in light of what I've witnessed these past few days, am I to presume that someone is you?"

Desmond's mouth tightened into a grim line. "I've never left her. As the duke of the manor, I'm committed to Colverton and will reside here for the rest of my life. I have no obligations which could take me away from England, perhaps permanently. Can you make the same claim?"

Quentin's gut twisted, his brother's intimation striking home.

"'Tis no secret that Brandice adores you, Quentin." Seizing the opportunity, Desmond pressed his advantage. "She always has. In all ways but blood, you're a revered older brother. But I cannot permit you to use that affection in a manner which could cause her pain."

"And how would I accomplish that?"

"By lulling her into a false sense of security. By encouraging her to depend upon you, leading her to believe you're home to stay, then deserting her the moment the military summons you: journeying to God knows where, putting your life in jeopardy, and perchance snatching away one of Brandice's final remaining constants."

"You make it sound as if I intend to willingly embrace death, arms open wide. I assure you, I don't."

"Embrace it, no. But the very nature of your career commands that you live, day by day, at the heart of battle. Can you honestly claim you aren't perpetually at risk? Can you guarantee your safe return?"

A muscle worked in Quentin's throat. "You know I can't. But, Desmond, after seeing the way our parents' lives were snuffed out, can you really claim that the life of a duke holds guarantees? Can you truly promise Brandi forever?"

"Perhaps not. But the odds of survival are far better as a landowner than as an army captain. And, even excluding the possibility of death, your career is abroad, Quentin, not in England. Your presence in the Cotswolds will always be temporary. How much security will that offer Brandice?"

Something inside Quentin snapped. "Is all this concern for Brandi stemming from the fact that you're her newly appointed guardian?"

"No, all this concern for Brandice is because I intend to become her husband."

Quentin had thought himself prepared for precisely this response.

He wasn't.

"Brandi's husband," he reiterated, the words burning like bile in his throat. "Interesting that she never mentioned your betrothal to me. Tell me, how does she feel about becoming your wife?"

"I can only surmise." Desmond's expression was the epitome of candor. "I hadn't the chance to offer for her before Ardsley's cruel and unexpected death. But if you're asking if Brandice cares for me, I believe the answer is yes. I also believe that had tragedy—and your homecoming—not intervened, Brandice's and my betrothal would be an imminent reality."

Quentin gripped the arms of his chair. "I can understand how the accident would deter your plans. But my homecoming? How does that interfere?"

"That's a particularly stupid question, Quentin." Desmond's tone was bitter. "As we just discussed, Brandice's affection for you is undeniable. Equally undeniable is your, shall we say, less than enthusiastic opinion of me. It stands to reason that Brandice would be negatively swayed by your sentiments."

"Not if her feelings for you are as strong as you've implied," Quentin refuted.

"You underestimate your influence over her. Nevertheless, that is not the point. The point is that I will not stand by, as Brandice's guardian, and allow you to build up her hopes, then dash them."

"How noble. So what do you suggest? That I have nothing to do with Brandi while I'm in England? That I wipe out a lifetime of friendship in order to deter any feelings of dependence?"

"Of course not. I'm merely asking that you emphasize the temporary nature of your stay. And the brotherly nature of your feelings."

A caustic smile. "And the pure, untainted nature of yours?"

Desmond inhaled sharply. "I don't need you to plead my case, Quentin. What exists between Brandice and me will flourish on its own—so long as no one interferes."

An icy chill blanketed Quentin's heart. "Do you even know Brandi? Have you any idea what she's about or what makes her happy?"

"The Brandice that existed four years ago? Maybe not. The Brandice of today? Yes, I believe I do. I suggest you ask yourself that same question."

The brothers' gazes locked.

"Pardon me, Master Desmond, Master Quentin." As was his way, Bentley knocked and entered simultaneously. "But a gentleman is here to see you."

"Send him away, Bentley. We're not receiving any visitors so soon after Father's death." Desmond turned, assessing the butler reprovingly. "Moreover, I think we should discuss your form of address. I realize you've known me since I was a tot. Yet I wonder if you comprehend that I am now the Duke of Colverton. Bearing in mind your many years of service, I'll permit your informality during private moments such as this, but I expect you to address me as 'Your Grace' in front of others."

"I'll try to remember that, sir." A muscle twitched briefly in Bentley's jaw. "As for your visitor, I wouldn't recommend sending him away. I believe he is with the authorities—if I comprehended his title correctly, that is."

"Did the gentleman wish to see us both?" Quentin's amusement at the butler's pointed sarcasm was eclipsed by his sudden sense of uneasiness.

"Yes, my lord, he did."

"Then you may show him into the library, Bentley," Desmond directed stiffly. "We'll join him there."

"Very good . . ." Bentley turned on his heel. "Your Grace," he added over his shoulder.

"Does that insolent man understand who works for whom?" Desmond muttered to Quentin.

"*He* does," Quentin responded dryly. "I'm not at all certain *we* do." Already on his feet, he headed for the door.

"Quentin." Desmond stayed him with his hand. "Before we go see what this man wants, do we understand each other? With respect to Brandice, that is."

A cold nod. "We do."

"Then you'll . . ."

"I'll do anything in my power to keep Brandi from being hurt," Quentin clarified. He shrugged off Desmond's restraining hand, his mind totally consumed with their awaiting guest and the unknown cause of his visit. "Let's go see what the authorities want."

The lanky man rose the instant Quentin and Desmond entered the library. "Gentlemen," he said without preamble. "Forgive me for intruding during this period of mourning. I wouldn't be here, were it not a matter of crucial import."

"We assumed as much," Desmond replied curtly. "What is this about?"

"You are the Duke of Colverton, I presume?"

"I am. And this is my brother, Lord Quentin."

A nod. "My name is Glovers, and I work with the Bow Street magistrate." He cleared his throat. "Your Grace, my lord, I'm afraid I have some very unpleasant news for you. It concerns the recent deaths of your father, his duchess, and the Viscount Denerley." Glovers opened his portfolio, rustling an official-looking page before him. "To be blunt, we've just determined that the late duke's carriage did not veer off the road by chance. It was tampered with; one of its axles severed partway through."

"What the hell are you suggesting?" Desmond demanded.

"'Tis no mere suggestion, Your Grace. The occupants of that carriage did not die by accident. They were murdered."

Chapter 4

*H*ow in God's name could he break this news to Brandi?

Quentin asked himself that question for the hundredth time as he alighted from his phaeton, making his way across the sun-drenched gardens of Emerald Manor to the cottage ahead.

It was just shy of ten A.M. He'd left Colverton a half hour ago, praying that the right words would materialize en route to his shooting match with Brandi.

They hadn't. In truth, even after yesterday's grueling session with Glovers and a painfully sleepless night, Quentin himself had yet to come to grips with the abhorrent reality that someone had actually murdered his parents and Brandi's father. So how could he expect Brandi to endure that knowledge? And what answers could he provide to her questions, when the authorities themselves were stymied?

For over an hour, Glovers had grilled him and Desmond, each minute of the arduous interrogation leading to the same unanswerable questions:

Who had tampered with the Colverton carriage?

Who was the intended victim: Kenton, Pamela, or Ardsley?

And the most heinous question of all: why?

Utterly baffled, Glovers had taken his leave, no closer to the truth than when he'd arrived. After which, Quentin and Desmond, both dazed and drained, had retired to their separate bedchambers, each needing to deal privately with his own shock and grief.

Dawn had found them both in the dining room, hunched over cups of black coffee, their thoughts consumed with what they'd learned.

"I'm riding to London to relay the authorities' findings to Hendrick," Desmond had announced. "You're due at Emerald Manor, are you not?"

"Yes. At ten."

Desmond had cleared his throat, and Quentin awaited the anticipated request. "Then would you do me the favor of breaking the news to Brandice? I'd go myself, but . . ."

"I'll tell her, Desmond." With renewed distaste, Quentin broke in, providing just the answer he knew his brother sought.

Sure enough, relief flashed clearly on Desmond's face. "Thank you." He rose, tossing his napkin to the table. "I'd best be off then. Please tell Brandice I'm thinking of her."

Thinking of her.

Quentin had watched Desmond go, reminded that, despite yesterday's fervent allegations of his commitment to Brandi, Desmond was the same shallow man he'd always been, avoiding emotional involvement at all costs. But then, how could someone totally lacking in compassion offer compassion to another?

In this case, it mattered not, for Quentin could envision no one but himself shouldering the responsibility of conveying this devastating news to his Sunbeam.

But, dear Lord, how would she take it? She was already teetering at the brink of emotional collapse. How could he tell her that Ardsley's death was not at fate's hands but at a murderer's?

Pausing, Quentin raised his head, staring numbly across

Emerald Manor's fragrant flower beds, for once oblivious to the cottage's unique tranquillity.

"Quentin." Brandi opened the front door herself and walked down the path to meet him. Clad in a simple muslin gown of Devonshire brown, her glorious hair tied back with a matching ribbon, Brandi looked very young and even more vulnerable.

Quentin felt a knife twist in his gut.

"You're right on time," she greeted, tilting her head back to gaze up at him. "Are you prepared to be defeated yet again?"

Unfooled by her lighthearted banter, Quentin scrutinized the tiny lines of sleeplessness about her eyes, the pale cast to her skin. Abruptly, he made a decision.

He'd inform Brandi of Glovers's revelation—*after* their shooting match. At least he could give her an hour of joy, a brief chance to forget, before he shattered whatever emotional reserves she had left.

"Is something wrong?" Brandi asked quizzically. She cast a self-conscious look at her gown. "Should I be wearing black? I thought—given Papa's aversion to mourning—that dark brown would be . . ."

"You look lovely," Quentin interrupted. "And you should most definitely *not* be wearing black. Your grief is worn where it matters—in your heart. Neither Ardsley nor my parents would want it any other way."

"Then you don't think our shooting match is disrespectful?"

He shook his head. "I think we should let Emerald Manor offer us the solace our parents wished for us."

Brandi smiled. "Very well, then." Visibly appeased, she reached beneath her hem, extracting the twin to Quentin's pistol. "I'm prepared to emerge victorious yet again."

A corner of Quentin's mouth lifted. "You've become unbearably cocky while I've been away. What makes you think you'll emerge victorious?"

"The fact that I'm a better marksman than you."

Unfeigned laughter rumbled in Quentin's chest. "Arrogant little hoyden. Very well, we've selected our weapons. What shall we choose as a prize?"

"The opportunity to gloat."

"Hmm." Quentin considered her suggestion. "Not a terribly impressive prize. What if we add a breakneck gallop through the woods, winner astride Poseidon?"

"Oh, yes!" Brandi breathed. "I can hardly wait to show you how expertly I handle Poseidon."

"*If* you win," Quentin reminded her. "If not, you'll have to demonstrate your prowess on Goddess's back." His eyes twinkled. "Astride, nonetheless."

"To be sure." Brandi shot him an impish grin. "And if *you* lose, *you'll* ride Goddess—astride, nonetheless."

"How gracious of you." Quentin chuckled.

"Shall we?" She gestured toward the trees behind the gazebo. "I've already chosen the perfect spot for our match."

"Lead the way, Sunbeam."

Guiding him through the trees, Brandi reached a small clearing, then halted. "Here."

With a nod of approval, Quentin surveyed the area. "An excellent choice. Now, where is our target and who shall begin?"

Brandi squinted, pointing ahead. "Right down that line of hawthorn is a Wych elm. Can you see it?"

"If you're referring to that sweeping tree dividing those two rows of shrubs, yes; I see it."

"I apologize." Brandi arched a saucy brow, looking anything but sorry. "I'd forgotten how little you know about perennial vegetation. Yes, that sweeping tree amid the rows of shrubs."

"Careful, Sunbeam. Such flagrant condescension might persuade me to reconsider my original intent to minimize my gloating."

"A moot point, my lord, since you're going to lose."

A glimmer of amusement. "You do realize that target is even farther away than our last—most likely ninety five feet or more?"

"I selected it for that very reason," she retaliated. "Our exact target will be the fourth limb from the bottom on the left side. As close to the trunk as possible. One bullet apiece. Agreed?"

"Agreed."

"Good. Now, take your best shot, Captain Steel."

"Very well." Quentin withdrew his weapon from inside his coat. "Let the contest commence."

Twenty minutes later, Quentin was still muttering as they trudged toward the stables. "I'm not sure how, but I'm certain you cheated."

Brandi laughed. "You're a terrible loser, my lord."

"And you're an insufferable winner, my lady."

"'Ello, Lord Quentin, Lady Brandi." Frederick, Emerald Manor's young stableboy, looked up in surprise. "Did ye plan to ride now?"

"Indeed we did," Brandi answered cheerily. "Would you mind saddling up Poseidon and Goddess for us, Frederick?"

"Poseidon is even more spirited than usual today, m'lord," Frederick cautioned, gazing at Quentin. "So take care."

"Lord Quentin will be on Goddess," Brandi corrected. "*I* shall be riding Poseidon." She rushed on before Frederick could convince Quentin otherwise. "And I promise to be extremely cautious. But as you well know, I've been exercising Poseidon daily. So he's quite accustomed to my being on his back."

Frederick glanced questioningly at Quentin.

"Do as Lady Brandi requested, Frederick. I'll make certain she is mindful of Poseidon's energetic state."

"Very good, m'lord." The stableboy hastened off.

"I need no overseeing, Quentin," Brandi muttered in protest. "I'm perfectly capable of taking care of myself."

"Tell that to Desmond." The words were out before Quentin could recall them.

Brandi gave him a puzzled look. "What do you mean?"

He averted his head, jaw set. "Only that my brother is taking his responsibility as your guardian very seriously."

"Is he?" Brandi shrugged. "That doesn't surprise me. You and I both know how rigidly traditional Desmond is. He probably assumes he owes it to Papa to properly manage my life."

"And do you intend to let him?"

A smile. "I never have in the past. Why would you think I'd begin now?"

"Brandi . . ." Quentin inhaled sharply. "A lot has changed while I've been away. You've matured, taken part in several London Seasons—met numerous gentlemen."

"I wrote you my opinion of those gentlemen."

"Yes, you did. But, tell me, has there ever been one in particular, someone who made you feel—differently?"

"You sound like Pamela," Brandi murmured, scraping the toe of her half boot through the dirt. "She was determined that I find my heartfelt mate."

"And did you?"

"No."

"Not even . . ."

"Here ye are, m'lord, m'lady," Frederick announced, leading Goddess and Poseidon to the stable door. "They're all saddled up and ready to go."

"Oh, thank you, Frederick." Brandi hurried forward, stroking both horses' muzzles. "Are you both prepared for a brisk gallop through the woods?"

Goddess blinked her huge dark eyes.

Poseidon jerked his gleaming black head up and down.

"I'll take that to mean two yeses." Brandi gathered up Poseidon's reins. "Are you ready, Quentin?"

"I am." He strode forward, his scrutinizing gaze sweeping Poseidon. "I visited the stables the other night after I'd settled you in," he told Brandi, his voice rich with pride. "But I was only here briefly. Therefore, I hadn't the chance to see what splendid condition you've kept Poseidon in. Thank you, Sunbeam. And you, too, Frederick."

"My pleasure, m'lord."

"And mine as well," Brandi added, glowing from his praise.

The two of them led their horses from the stables, into the late morning sunlight.

"To the stream?" Quentin asked instinctively.

Their eyes met.

"Oh, yes." Brandi's pleasure was a tangible entity. "It's been ages since I've ridden there." She swallowed, her long lashes sweeping her cheeks. "I do stroll the banks. I even wade and fish. But each and every time I consider steering Poseidon in the stream's direction, memories of you—and our glorious jaunts on horseback—intervene. And, with you away until Lord knew when, it hurt too much."

"Don't." Quentin stroked his knuckles over her cheek. "No sadness, Sunbeam. Not now." Valiantly, he squelched the painful reminder of what he had to impart. "Let's race through the woods to the southern tip of the property, then back to the stream. That should give you ample opportunity to flaunt your skills on Poseidon."

Eagerly, Brandi nodded. "Excellent."

"Shall I give you a leg up, or will that insult your independence?"

Brandi laughed aloud. "You could never insult me, Quentin. And I'd be very grateful for the assistance."

He helped her mount, grinning as she tucked her skirts unceremoniously between her legs to seat herself comfortably astride Poseidon.

"You begin the race, Sunbeam," he invited, hoisting himself onto Goddess's back.

"All right." Brandi grasped the reins, her cheeks flushed with excitement. "Go!"

They tore off, neck-and-neck, galloping wildly through the woods. Heads bent low, they raced along the familiar path, urging their horses faster as each sensed the other's nearby presence.

Brandi reached the clearing first, veering Poseidon into a

sharp turn toward the stream just as Quentin came up behind her. She didn't wait, but took off at a breakneck gallop, flying like the wind as she saw the stream approach.

Goddess's hooves thudded disturbingly close by, and Brandi caught a flash of gray as Quentin sailed by to her left.

"Come on, Poseidon," she urged, squeezing the stallion's sides with her heels. "We're almost there. Show me that spirit Frederick described."

Poseidon responded, lowering his head and increasing his speed until the trees were nothing but green blurs on the outskirts of Brandi's vision, and Goddess a gray streak that had long since been passed. The ground began to soften—a sure sign that the stream was drawing near—and Poseidon's gait became more labored as his hooves sank into the mud. Every one of Brandi's instincts told her they should be diminishing their pace so as not to lose control. But pride drove her onward, whispering that victory was in sight, vowing to slow down in just a few steps.

A few steps was too late.

Brandi heard Quentin's warning shout a split second before Poseidon slipped, whinnying angrily as he wrenched command of the race from Brandi's hands. With staunch determination, he fought to steady himself, the strong muscles of his back tightening beneath her, his powerful form striving for a firm foothold.

He found it the instant the stream found them.

Acting on instinct, Poseidon gathered his legs beneath him and jumped, soaring over the broad width of the stream to land gracefully on the other side.

Abruptly, he stopped.

Just as abruptly, he reared, tossing Brandi off his back and into the stream.

Mission accomplished, he began nibbling at the grass and flicking his tail to herald his utter vindication.

Quentin stopped and dismounted all at once. "Sunbeam?" He waded into the stream, reaching Brandi's side in seconds. "Are you all right?"

Submerged in icy water, Brandi struggled to her knees, alternately sputtering and laughing. "Other than my pride, yes," she gasped, shaking wet strands of hair from her eyes. "Actually, I'm lucky Poseidon's retaliation was minimal. With the foolish lack of judgment I just displayed, he could have enacted a far more vicious revenge. I believe I owe him my thanks."

Relief swept through Quentin, and he relaxed, helping Brandi to her feet, then assisting her to the bank of the stream. "You most certainly do. That was the most witless horsemanship you've ever demonstrated."

"You're right. I apologize, to you and to Poseidon." She shook her head in disgust. "I must learn to accept the possibility of defeat—at least upon occasion."

"Yes. You must." Quentin squeezed the water from her hair. "And to be more gracious a loser when defeat occurs."

Brandi's slender brows arched in amusement. "This coming from the man who accused me of cheating and sulked for a quarter hour after losing a shooting match?"

Quentin tossed her a disgruntled look, and she responded with a beatific smile.

"You made your point, Sunbeam. Let's get you home and out of this saturated gown."

Glancing down at herself, Brandi giggled. "I look like a drowned rat," she declared, hoisting her gown to her knees. With a sharp twist, she wrung out the fine material, thereby issuing a copious gush of water. Satisfied that she'd restored her morning dress to its original state, she released her skirts, groaning as the limp muslin tumbled unceremoniously to her ankles, wrinkled and beyond repair.

"Poseidon certainly managed to wreak havok with your dignity—*and* your gown," Quentin noted, biting back his laughter.

Brandi's expression clearly stated she wasn't a bit fooled by Quentin's feigned sobriety. "You're enjoying yourself most thoroughly, aren't you?" she accused, trying to keep her own face straight.

"Immensely." Brows drawn together, he tapped his forefinger to his lips. "Do you know, I believe that gown is a lost cause? I suggest you abandon all attempts at reviving it."

"I agree." With a last scornful glance at the offending garment, Brandi turned her attention to her hair. Purposefully, she tugged at the soaked ribbon, intending to shake out her tresses and coax them to dry. The ribbon caught on one tangled curl.

"Here, let me help you." Unable to stifle his grin, Quentin reached forward, carefully working the strands free of their velvet prison. "Mission accomplished." He feathered her hair about her shoulders in a shimmering cinnamon curtain. "The sun will help it dry."

Brandi tipped her head back, her mock reproachfulness supplanted by a radiant smile. "Thank you." With uninhibited exuberance, she stretched her arms overhead, laughing at the way the muslin sleeves adhered to her skin. "Muslin does not tolerate water well, does it?"

Quentin didn't answer. He couldn't.

Amusement vanished and time froze as in one lightning second the world shifted, and life as he'd known it was forever changed. Why here, why now, he hadn't a clue. All he knew was that the shutters shielding his eyes from reality abruptly lifted, jolting him into an inconceivable truth.

Brandi.

Of its own accord, Quentin's astonished gaze drifted down from her upswept arms, roving her petite form from head to toe. Transfixed, he absorbed all the evidence that, for some unfathomable reason, had eluded him, choosing this particular moment to permeate his consciousness: the flawless curves revealed by her wet, clinging gown, the golden skin exposed at her neck and throat, the high cheekbones and sculpted features crowned by the glorious mane of burnished hair. Blood pounded through his temples as the actuality struck him—hard, unexpected, staggeringly intense—along with a blaze of sensual awareness that exploded throughout him like gunfire.

Gone was his tousled hoyden, the child-woman he'd known since babyhood, his one and only Sunbeam. Before him was a beautiful, intoxicating woman whose laughter faded as she watched his expression change, felt the magnetic charges running between them.

"Quentin?" Brandi lowered her arms, her dark eyes wide with questioning wonder.

"What?" he heard himself vaguely reply. His fingers threaded through her damp hair, discovering its familiar texture for the first time, his entire frame of reference shattering and reshaping all at once. Nothing was as it had been, or perhaps it always had been and he'd just never seen it. "Brandi." He breathed her name in hushed amazement, still reeling from the impact of startling realization.

His gaze fell to her lips, the urge to kiss her suddenly so overpowering he couldn't breathe, much less speak.

"Quentin." This time it was an acknowledgment rather than a query. She stepped closer, her palms sliding up the front of his coat, gliding through the soft strands of hair at his nape.

His mouth found hers before he could think, before he could discern the madness and resist it. Warm, wet, agonizingly sweet, Brandi's lips yielded to his, melding in a kiss so poignantly significant it nearly brought Quentin to his knees.

As had the realization preceding it, desire erupted in a blaze of fireworks, thundering through his veins, shimmering along every nerve ending in his body. His hands clenched in her hair, drawing her closer, pressing her drenched body against his. Cold water saturated his clothing, but Quentin barely felt it, let alone gave a damn.

"Sunbeam . . ." His voice was hoarse, drugged with an incomprehensible yearning, and he slanted his mouth across hers again and again, drinking his fill before fate intervened to deem his sustenance be snatched away.

Brandi wouldn't recoil. Somehow he knew that. Still, he didn't expect the glorious, innocent ardor with which she met—and returned—his kisses. Her trembling mouth opened under his, and she welcomed his tongue with a bone-melting sigh, responding to his penetration by melding their tongues with an exhilarated, wholehearted joy that stunned and enthralled him all at once.

A hard shudder wracked Quentin's body, a warning that his control was about to snap. He battled his way to sanity, forcing himself to think about what was happening, to emerge from this staggering, mind-numbing inferno—before it was too late.

"No . . . don't." Feeling Quentin's withdrawal, Brandi's arms tightened, and she shook her head, refusing to release him. "Don't pull away. You can't." Her words were breathy, a reverent whisper against his lips. "I think I've waited for this all my life," she confessed, flushed and dreamy with discovery. "I never knew it until this instant, but I have. All my life."

"Ah, Sunbeam." Her confession pierced his heart—and resurrected his conscience. He wasn't sure what was happening between them, but he was damned sure he couldn't permit it to happen. Wasn't she vulnerable enough without his adding yet another facet of change to her life?

Deliberately, Quentin raised his head, creating a narrow but purposeful distance between them. Dazed as he was, he was nonetheless assailed by the knowledge of what lay ahead, the heinous news he had yet to impart—news that promised to rend Brandi's already fragmented life into bits.

And that wasn't his only deterrent.

In a rush, Desmond's warning resounded in his mind: *Your presence in the Cotswolds will always be temporary, Quentin. How much security will that offer Brandice? Don't let her rely upon you, then desert her . . . don't.*

Despite the self-serving nature of his brother's admonition, wasn't he correct? Wasn't Quentin's presence in England transient? Couldn't he—wouldn't he—rejoin the military whenever he was needed?

The answer was an unequivocal yes.

Armed with that knowledge, could he truly give in to this exquisite madness with Brandi? If their involvement—and their dependency—deepened with a new dimension, could he bear to walk away? More important, could he subject Brandi to his walking away?

A knife wrenched in his gut.

"What is it?" Brandi reached up with trembling fingers, stroked the hard line of Quentin's jaw. "Are you angry with me?"

"No, sweetheart, I could never be angry with you." Tenderly, he ruffled her hair. "I'm just sorry this happened."

"Why? I'm not."

"Brandi, you're still grieving. You've endured a devastating loss. The same is true of me. 'Tis only natural, given the special rapport you and I have always shared, for us to turn to each other for comfort."

Her dark eyes searched his face. "Is that all this was for you? Comfort? For me it was so much more."

"No, Sunbeam." It mattered not that his motivation was sound. He simply could not bring himself to belittle the enchantment that had just occurred between them, not for her sake, nor his own. "It felt like far more than mere comfort. But we cannot . . ."

"Shall I tell you what it felt like to me?" she interrupted softly. "Like nothing I've ever known or ever could know—with anyone but you." Her fingers brushed her lips as if to recapture the magic of his touch. "I should have guessed my first kiss could be shared with no one else."

Quentin sucked in his breath. Inherently, he'd known it was her first time in a man's arms; and yet, hearing her say the words made them all the more real—and all the more poignant. "Thank you, Sunbeam. That's the loveliest compliment I've ever received."

"I didn't mean it as a compliment. I meant it as a truth." Brandi paused, her fingers gripping the edge of Quentin's coat. "Did you enjoy kissing me?" she blurted at last.

"You must know I did."

"Then why did you pull away?"

This was the part he'd dreaded. "Brandi, I care so bloody much about you. I can't let you count on something that can never be."

"Why?" she whispered. "Why can it never be?"

"Sunbeam, do you remember what you said just before you ran from me the other night?"

"Yes." Her lashes drifted downward. "I asked you never to go away again."

"I can't give you that promise, Brandi. Not now. Maybe never. I could be recalled by the army at any time—to be sent anywhere. You're very precious—and very vulnerable. You need someone you can rely upon, someone who will never leave you. I'm not that man, Brandi."

Two tears slid down her cheeks, and Quentin felt as if he'd been punched.

"Please, sweetheart, don't cry." His thumbs absorbed her tears. "Nothing's changed. We'll go on as we always have." The vow sounded implausible even to his own ears, yet he had no choice but to enact it.

"Very well." Her voice was tiny, filled with bewilderment and sadness.

And the worst was yet to come.

"Brandi." He had forestalled the inevitable as long as he could. He had to tell her—now.

She was gazing at him quizzically, and Quentin framed her face between his palms, steeling himself for the heinous blow he was about to inflict. "There's something else. Something you don't know. Something I must tell you before I leave Emerald Manor today, and . . . damn it." He broke off, willing himself to absorb her pain. "I wish to God I could soften this. But I can't."

The gravity of his tone struck home, and she paled. "What is it?"

Gently, his forefingers caressed her cheeks. "A gentleman named Glovers visited Colverton last night. He's with Bow Street. He brought us new developments on the carriage disaster."

"Go on."

"The accident wasn't an accident at all, Brandi. One of the wheels was tampered with. The crash was intentional."

Brandi's pupils dilated as noncomprehension transformed into shock. "Intentional?" she whispered. "Are you saying someone murdered our parents?"

"Yes, Sunbeam. That's what I'm saying."

"Oh my God." She began to tremble violently, that vague, faraway look reinvading her eyes. "Oh my God."

He pulled her against him, pressing her head to his waistcoat and stroking her hair. "I have no further details, other than the fact that one of the axles was cut. Bow Street has no suspect, no motive, and no idea which of our parents was the intended victim."

"Maybe they're wrong." Brandi jerked away. "Maybe it's a mistake. Maybe the wheels broke free when the carriage struck the jutting rocks. Maybe . . ."

"Brandi—stop." Quentin gripped her shoulders, firmly shaking his head. "There are no maybes. The wheels didn't break free; their support was severed. Painful as it is, it's true. We must accept it."

"I can't," she said in a broken voice.

"You can." He held her gaze. "You're stronger than you realize, Sunbeam. And you're not alone. You have me—and you have Desmond. We'll see this through together."

"Desmond . . ." Compassion flashed across Brandi's face, temporarily eclipsing the shock. "He was so close to your father. He must be devastated."

"Desmond is holding up quite well." Quentin was stunned by the surge of jealousy that rushed through him. "He went to London to alert Hendrick to the situation." Abruptly, Brandi's statement registered. "Did you say Desmond and Father were close?"

"What?" Brandi massaged her temples, struggling to focus on Quentin's question. "Oh, Desmond and Kenton. Yes, Desmond was so proud of the new-found respect he'd established with his father. He'd worked hard to earn it. And Kenton, well, I don't have to tell you what a wonderful man your father is—was," she amended quickly. "He must have recognized how hard Desmond was trying. Toward the end, their relationship—business and personal—was apparently thriving."

"I see."

"Who would want to hurt Kenton, Pamela, or Papa?" Brandi whispered incredulously. "'Tis incomprehensible." She turned away, wrapped her arms about herself. "Quentin, this whole thing is like a heinous nightmare. Every time I think it's over, it begins anew."

"It *will* be over, Sunbeam," Quentin pledged quietly. "I'll make sure of it."

For a long moment, Brandi was silent. Then she pivoted slowly to face Quentin, a haunted look on her face. "As will I."

"What does that mean?"

"That means that if the authorities cannot uncover the truth, then you and I shall."

Chapter 5

Bentley rapped lightly on the study door as he entered.

Slamming his half-filled drink onto the sideboard, Desmond whirled about to glare at the butler.

"Bentley, would you kindly learn the art of knocking *prior* to entering a room?"

"I'll make every attempt to, sir." Bentley stood stiffly at attention. "In the interim, however, I do need to speak with you."

"I'm not in a conversational mood." Desmond turned his back and tossed off the remainder of his brandy in two gulps.

"Evidently not, Your Grace," Bentley returned dryly. "Which is comforting, since you will shortly be unable not only to converse but to utter an intelligible sound. In fact," he added, as Desmond swiftly refilled his glass, "should you continue at this rate, you will not only be unable to talk, you will need assistance to remain upright."

"Thank you for your unwanted assessment of my inebriated state," Desmond snapped. "Now if you'll excuse me . . ."

74

"I'd be happy to, Your Grace. But, as I said, I need a word with you first."

"Very well, what is it?" Desmond pivoted to face Bentley, weaving a bit in the process.

"I assume you'll wish to move from your current quarters to the master bedchamber?"

"Eventually, yes."

"With that in mind, I've taken the liberty of amassing your father's belongings and preparing them for storage."

Desmond's scowl softened. "That was very considerate of you, Bentley."

"I did it for the late duke, sir." A pregnant pause, during which Desmond downed the entire contents of his glass. "Nevertheless, in collecting His Grace's personal items, I noticed that his engraved strongbox is nowhere to be found."

"Engraved strongbox?"

"Yes, Your Grace. The one that was identical to his duchess's."

"Didn't Pamela bequeath it to Brandi?"

"I believe she did, yes. But that was the one belonging to Her Grace. 'Tis the duke's I cannot locate."

"Well, I can't help you, Bentley." Desmond blinked, trying ineffectually to focus. "I don't know what Father did with his strongbox. Nor, to be honest, do I care. I have far more pressing matters on my mind. Why don't you ask the other servants? Maybe one of them misplaced it." With a dismissive wave, Desmond turned back to his drink, frowning when he saw it was empty. "Close the door behind you, Bentley," he slurred, splashing another healthy portion of brandy into the goblet.

"Yes, sir. And, seeing how busy you are, I'll make certain you're not disturbed."

Totally oblivious to Bentley's pointed sarcasm, Desmond merely nodded. "Splendid," he muttered against the rim of his glass. "Just splendid."

With the barest glint of disgust, Bentley quit the study,

contemplating what the next sensible step should be in his search for the missing strongbox. Sanders, he deduced with a surge of insight. If anyone had knowledge of the box's whereabouts, it would be the late duke's valet.

The epitome of efficiency, Bentley turned in the direction of the servants' quarters.

"Bentley?"

Quentin entered the manor, spotting and summoning the butler simultaneously.

An immediate halt. "Yes, Master Quentin?"

"I must see you straightaway."

"Of course." Bentley retraced his steps, no questions asked.

"Let's adjourn to the library; this talk must remain confidential."

"Very good, sir."

Once the closed library door afforded them the privacy Quentin sought, he commenced without preliminaries. "Did Desmond inform you of Glovers's purpose last night?"

"Glovers? Oh, the gentleman from Bow Street. No, I assumed he merely had some final details to relay to you and Master Desmond before he could officially close the file on the carriage accident."

"I wish that were the case." Quentin massaged his temples. "Bentley, Glovers came to advise us that Father's carriage had been tampered with, that one of the axles had been cut."

All the color drained from Bentley's face. "No."

"I'm afraid it's true. Ardsley and my parents were murdered."

It took a full minute for Bentley to compose himself. "Have the authorities apprehended the culprit responsible for this despicable crime?"

"The authorities aren't even certain who the intended victim was. They have no suspects, no motives, and no clues."

"I see." A vein throbbed in Bentley's forehead. "I begin to understand your brother's unusual behavior."

"What unusual behavior?"

"Master Desmond—His Grace—has spent the past few hours alone in his study, drinking himself into oblivion."

"I can't really blame him." Quentin sighed deeply. "Everyone copes with shock in his own way. Desmond drinks. I brood. Brandi, on the other hand, wants to apprehend the culprits herself."

"That sounds like Miss Brandi."

"Bentley, I've been abroad for four years. I need you to relay things as if you'd been my eyes and ears."

"Sir?"

"Did anything transpire these past weeks or months to make you believe that either—or both—my parents' lives were in danger?"

Bentley shook his head, more in denial than refutation. "A bit of an upheaval took place, yes. You alluded to it the other day. But nothing of the magnitude you're describing now."

"Upheaval? What are you talking about? What did I allude to?"

An uncomfortable cough. "You questioned me about Master Desmond and any sudden changes I'd noticed in his alliances. Naturally, I assumed you were referring to . . ." A tactful cough, as Bentley searched for the most discreet words. "One relationship in particular."

"I was. I was referring to his relationship with Brandi."

Bentley's jaw dropped. "With Miss Brandi, sir?"

"Yes. Desmond led me to believe they were seriously involved. I merely wanted confirmation on that."

"Do you mean romantically, my lord?"

"That was Desmond's implication, yes." Quentin scrutinized Bentley's astonished expression. "Judging by your reaction, am I to assume you disagree with my brother's assessment?"

"Thoroughly, my lord. Oh, Master Desmond has been

most solicitous of Miss Brandi since the accident. In fact, he's rarely left her side. But, after all, she has no one else to turn to—at least not while you're away. But seriously involved?" A dubious sniff. "I hardly see them as a couple, do you, sir?"

"No, in truth I don't." Quentin shook his head, unable to ignore the surge of exquisite relief spawned by Bentley's appraisal. Temporarily, he suppressed it, nagged by a greater worry. "Bentley, you just expressed the belief that I was referring to a specific association of Desmond's and the transformation it has undergone. If not his relationship with Brandi, then with whom?"

Silence.

"Bentley, my parents are dead. I've just learned they were coldbloodedly murdered. While I normally applaud your loyalty and discretion, I must insist that, in this case, you forsake your principles. If not for my sake, for Father's."

"Of course, sir." Bentley cast a quick glance at the closed door. "I thought perhaps you had learned of Master Desmond's falling out with the late duke."

"Another one?" Quentin arched a sardonic brow. "I would hardly call that a change. Father and Desmond have been arguing all my life. Although," he added thoughtfully, "today Brandi mentioned they'd been getting along better these past months. Evidently, she was wrong."

"At the risk of sounding overly dramatic, Master Quentin, this was no customary spat."

Something in the butler's tone gave Quentin pause. "What made this falling out different than the dozens that have preceded it?"

Bentley clasped his hands tightly behind his back, readying himself to do what he must—no matter how painful. "The falling out was much as its predecessors, sir: loud, angry words, exchanged behind Master Desmond's closed bedchamber door. 'Twas what occurred immediately thereafter which alerted me to the seriousness of the dispute."

"Which was?"

"Your brother stormed from the room, obviously greatly upset. A moment later, the late duke emerged and demanded that I summon Mr. Hendrick to Colverton for the explicit purpose of altering his will."

Quentin's eyes narrowed. "Father used that exact phrase?"

"Yes, sir. Precisely that phrase. He was distraught and agitated."

"Clearly. Perhaps he calmed down and changed his mind."

"No. The missive was delivered as per your father's request; I myself sent it off. Mr. Hendrick arrived promptly the following day. He and your father were closeted in the library for long hours."

"What did they discuss?"

"I haven't a clue, sir. I wasn't privy to their conversation and His Grace confided nothing further in me."

"Damn it." Quentin raked his fingers through his hair. "It doesn't make sense. If Father revised his will, why wasn't it reflected in yesterday's reading? No mention was made of either a codicil or a recently amended clause to the existing will."

"Why indeed, sir."

"The only logical explanation is that between the time Ellard was summoned and the time he left Colverton, Father experienced a change of heart. But why? What—or who—convinced Father to alter his decision?"

A heavy silence settled over the room.

Roughly, Quentin cleared his throat. "From your description of the fierce argument between Desmond and Father, we can safely assume that whatever modifications Father intended were not in Desmond's favor. Nothing short of his own interests would enrage my brother so vehemently."

"I agree, sir. In fact, Master Desmond spouted something of the kind when he exploded from his bedchamber. I didn't place much credence in it at the time."

"Probably because he's raved the same nonsensical

doubts over Father's allegiance a hundred times in the past. Nevertheless, that preoccupation is all the more reason why our first logical assumption must be that it was Desmond who persuaded Father to leave his will intact."

"Only your brother can confirm or deny that premise. Will you probe the matter with him?"

"No." Quentin shook his head adamantly. "He'll only become defensive—just as he always has when faced with an issue concerning either of us and Father. He's bloody irrational, intent on believing Father favored me over him—even though both you and I know that was never the case. No, Bentley, talking to Desmond would yield naught but trouble.

Moreover," Quentin continued, exploring the situation aloud, "I'm certain Desmond never considered any ramifications other than those that would directly affect him. But you and I must. For example, we both know that Father and Desmond argued constantly over Desmond's irresponsible business practices. Suppose Father's contemplated will revision was triggered by something Desmond did—something that negatively impacted one or more of Father's business associates or their employees."

"I see where you're headed, my lord. You're supposing that a disgruntled—and unbalanced—colleague might have retaliated by tampering with the late duke's carriage."

"Indeed. After all, even if Desmond committed the indiscretion, it was Father who was the head of the Steel family, and thus the target." Quentin rubbed his neck wearily. "I'm groping; I realize that. But someone killed my parents. And until I know who, I have to delve into every possibility—no matter how obscure."

"Of course, sir. How, may I ask, do you plan to proceed? And in what manner can I be of assistance?"

"You can keep this discussion confidential—at least for the time being."

"That goes without saying, my lord."

"As for me, I think my ideal starting point would be to meet with Hendrick. He, better than anyone, will know what modifications Father contemplated making to his will, and whether, in fact, they were implemented. I'll ride to London at daybreak."

"A wise decision. Shall I have Wythe pack for you?"

"That won't be necessary. I'll only be staying the day." Quentin frowned, his own words prompting a new concern—one spawned by tomorrow's unanticipated trip to London.

Brandi.

He'd intended to travel to Emerald Manor at dawn to assure himself of her well-being. Between the horrifying news he'd dropped on her, and the raw confusion hovering in the wake of their unexpected kiss, her emotional state was bound to be precarious.

Doubtless, he was being overprotective. Brandi was a survivor. Nonetheless, he didn't want to leave her alone. And Desmond couldn't be counted on as a reliable substitute—not if he were as foxed as Bentley described.

So who could be trusted to call on her, to subtly, yet effectively, divert her thoughts until his return?

The answer was but three feet away.

"Bentley." Soberly, Quentin met his friend's gaze. "I have a favor to ask of you."

"Anything, sir. You needn't ask twice."

"I'll be away from the Cotswolds all day. This might sound foolish, but I'd like you to ride to Emerald Manor and check on Brandi. She didn't take the Bow Street revelation well. I'm worried about her. And Desmond, well . . ."

"I understand. Consider it done."

"Thank you, Bentley. You're an exceptional friend."

"'Tis no favor, my lord. I worry about Miss Brandi as much . . ." A delicate pause. *"Nearly* as much as you do."

Quentin blinked, trying to discern if there were any hidden message behind the butler's statement. But Bentley's expression was nondescript; his stance unchanged.

Whatever he suspected was concealed carefully beneath his dignified veneer.

And how could he suspect anything when Quentin himself didn't know exactly what had occurred during those precious moments when Brandi was in his arms?

"Will that be all, my lord?" he vaguely heard Bentley inquire. "Because, if so, I'll return to the search I was in the midst of when you summoned me."

"Hmm?" Quentin nodded absently, his mind four miles away on the grassy bank of a stream. "Of course, Bentley. Go on as you were."

"You didn't happen to see your father's strongbox, did you, sir?"

"Father's strongbox?" He had to forget the taste of her mouth, the perfect fit of her body curving into his. He had to—but how? How could he forget the breathless wonder he'd scarcely tasted, grazing his senses like a tantalizing shimmer of sensation, beckoning him back to drown in its exquisite flavor?

Brandi—his miraculous Sunbeam.

How had he been up so close, yet been so blind?

Abruptly, Quentin realized Bentley was regarding him with an expectant look on his face, presumably awaiting a reply—to what, he hadn't a clue. "I'm sorry, Bentley. What did you ask me?"

The barest flicker of amusement. "Your father's strongbox, sir. It appears to have been misplaced. I merely wondered if you'd spied it anywhere."

"No, I can't say that I have," Quentin responded, trying to think of some helpful advice to offer. "Possibly, since the strongbox was willed to Desmond, he's moved it to his chambers."

"You could very well be right, sir. When I questioned His Grace, he was too deep in his cups to recall what might or might not be in his possession. I'll approach him again tomorrow." With a purposeful nod, Bentley moved to the door and gripped its handle. "Good night, sir. I hope Mr. Hendrick provides you with the answers you're seeking."

The reminder of what lay ahead acted as a douse of cold water on Quentin's meandering senses. "As do I, Bentley," he concurred. "As do I."

"Peters, I'm here to see Mr. Hendrick. Is he available?"

The clerk bolted to his feet, staring at Quentin in dismay. He snatched up his calendar, nervously scanning its pages and shaking his head at the same time. "Forgive me, my lord; either Mr. Hendrick neglected to advise me of your appointment or I neglected to write it down."

"Neither. I have no appointment. But I'm confident Ellard will see me, given the urgency of the situation—a situation I believe Desmond advised him of yesterday. Suffice it to say, dire circumstances have ensued since our last meeting. I must see Ellard at once."

"Quentin, come in." Hendrick opened his office door and beckoned, simultaneously nodding to his clerk. "Thank you for your diligence, Peters. But Lord Quentin is quite right. Given the gravity of the situation, no appointment is necessary."

"Of course, sir." The wiry man whipped out a handkerchief and dabbed at his forehead, clearly weak with relief.

"Can I offer you anything, Quentin?" Ellard asked, closing the door behind them. "Or shall we get right to the appalling issue at hand."

"The latter." Quentin dropped into a seat. "Ellard, I know Desmond met with you yesterday. But he and I didn't cross paths last night, so I hadn't the opportunity to ask him what your reaction was to the authorities' discovery."

"My reaction?" Hendrick blinked. "I was horrified."

Quentin shook his head. "That wasn't what I meant. Of course you were horrified. What I meant was, did you—can you—think of anyone who would want to hurt either of my parents or Ardsley Townsend?"

Hendrick tapped his fingertips together thoughtfully. "No one," he said at length. "Pamela, Kenton, and Ardsley were three of the most well-liked and well-respected members of the *ton*. Who, in the name of heaven, would intentionally harm any one of them is beyond my comprehension."

"My sentiments exactly." Quentin frowned at an imaginary speck of dust on his trousers. "I've racked my brain trying to conjure up an answer. Thus far, I've been totally unsuccessful. It occurred to me that I should take your suggestion and glance over my parents' wills."

"Their wills?" Hendrick inclined his head. "Why would a Last Will and Testament provide any clues to the murderer's identity?"

"I don't know that they would." Quentin leaned forward. "Ellard, when were my parents' wills drawn up?"

"When? Why, about a decade ago, I believe. I'll have Peters fetch them so I can give you the exact dates. After which you can peruse them as thoroughly as you'd like."

"I'd appreciate that. And while Peters is collecting the wills, are any of my father's other papers on file—business documents, perchance?"

"Of course. I'll have Peters bring Kenton's entire file." He stood, exiting the office only to issue the brief instructions before returning. "Quentin, may I ask what it is you're searching for?"

"I have no answer for you, Ellard—not because I'm being vague, but because I simply don't know. All I'm certain of is that the authorities are stymied and I must do what I can to unearth the bastard who killed my mother and father."

"I understand." Hendrick glanced up as Peters entered, carrying a thick file.

"This is everything, sir," the clerk advised, setting the file on Hendrick's desk. "The papers are organized chronologically."

"Thank you, Peters. That will be all." Hendrick opened the file, removing the first document. "Your father's will," he pronounced, handing it to Quentin.

The instant the will was in his hands, Quentin sought and found the date. "Hendrick, this will is dated the twentieth of May, 1804."

"As I said, a decade ago."

"Are there any codicils? Any amended clauses whatsoever?"

"No, none."

"Then explain to me why Father summoned you to Colverton last week for the express purpose of revising his will."

Hendrick sighed, but didn't avert his gaze. "I was hoping you wouldn't learn of that meeting."

"Then it did occur?"

"Yes, it occurred. Kenton was determined to alter one particular paragraph of his will. Fortunately, I was able to dissuade him before it was an accomplished fact. And, since the change was never made, I saw no reason to broach the subject and risk upsetting you greatly."

"Why? What part of Father's will did he wish to modify, and why would the modification upset me?"

Hendrick drew a slow inward breath, rubbing a quill between his fingers. "Emerald Manor," he said at last. "Kenton wished to alter the provisions he'd made for its future."

"Emerald Manor?" Whatever Quentin had been expecting, it wasn't this.

An uncomfortable nod. "Yes. Your father cared very deeply for you, Quentin," Hendrick assured him—a prelude to the oncoming explanation.

"You needn't mollify me like a child, Ellard. I know my father's feelings for both Desmond and me. Get to the point."

"Very well." Hendrick folded his hands on his desk. "The original will—the one I read aloud two days past— bequeathed Emerald Manor to you. Kenton and Pamela both agreed that the cottage should be part of your legacy. However, as the years passed, Kenton's concern intensified. You'd shown no interest in choosing a wife, and no inclination of relinquishing your military career, or even of placing it second to marriage and a family. In other words, you were

a single man, without heirs, immersed in a life involving
daily confrontations with death. What would become of
Emerald Manor if you were to die with no heir apparent?"

"I assume that Desmond, as successor to my inheritance,
would then acquire Emerald Manor."

"Indeed." Hendrick cocked a brow. "And do you think
your brother would cherish that gift? Nurture it as Pamela
would wish him to?"

"I see your point," Quentin replied quietly. "So what
provisions did Father wish to make for the cottage?"

"He planned to will it directly to Brandice, thereby
keeping it from your brother's less-than-eager grasp."

"Had Father done that, I would have understood. Brandi
loves Emerald Manor as much as I do, and Mother could
rest easy that the estate was in the most caring of hands."

"True. But it would also be wrested from your family
forever. Suppose one day you *do* marry, have a family.
Wouldn't you want your children to revel in the beauty that
your parents and you held dear?"

"I hadn't thought about it, but, yes, I suppose I would."

"Therefore, what I recommended to Kenton accomplished both purposes: retained Emerald Manor as your
legacy and simultaneously ensured its future."

"How?"

"I convinced him to leave his will intact, in exchange for
my solemn promise to speak with you upon your return to
the Cotswolds—which I thoroughly intended to do, after
the trauma of the accident subsided."

"And what was it you intended to speak with me about?"
Quentin asked with a touch of dry humor. "The virtues of
matrimony? Or did you simply intend to drag me to the
altar, some unsuspecting young lady in tow?"

"Certainly not. I merely meant to explain the situation to
you—as I am now doing—and to suggest that you make
provisions for Emerald Manor in the event of your death."

"Father could have accomplished that directly by bequeathing the cottage to Brandi, should I die without an
heir apparent."

"Yes, that was Kenton's next suggestion, too. But, as I explained to him, that would be hasty and unfair to you. He and Pamela fervently wished for Emerald Manor to be yours; therefore, the arrangements for its future should, by all rights, belong to you as well. And, while I would strongly urge you to bequeath the cottage, first and foremost, to your heirs, I also believe it should be you who ultimately determines Emerald Manor's fate."

"And Father agreed?"

"Yes. In my opinion, Kenton never truly doubted you'd make the appropriate provisions. In truth, I think his worry over your safety temporarily eclipsed his reason, else he never would have considered altering his plans for the cottage. In any case, once he and I had spoken—at length—Kenton realized that, given the war was ended and you'd soon be home, it was both unjust and unnecessary to revise his will. He agreed to wait, trusting that you would faithfully see to the manor's future. All he asked is that you do so in writing, quickly and expediently, before the military has reason to recall you."

"I see." Quentin contemplated Hendrick's words. "In other words, I'm to resolve Emerald Manor's fate by deciding whether or not I intend to marry and ultimately sire children. And, in the event that I don't, by bequeathing the cottage to Brandi."

"That would be my recommendation, yes." Hendrick gave a self-conscious cough. "Of course, I reiterate, the decision is ultimately yours. And it goes without saying that, even if you agree, my drawing up the pertinent document should wait until this heinous crime is resolved."

"Definitely." Quentin came to his feet, placing Kenton's will atop the desk. "Moreover, until my parents' murderer is exposed, the problem is nonexistent. Because, until that time, I have no intention of returning to the army. So, there is no danger of my life being snuffed out by gunfire, and Emerald Manor is, thus, quite safely and legally mine."

"Of course." Hendrick pointed to the file. "Didn't you wish to peruse Kenton's remaining documents?"

"Yes, I did." Reseating himself, Quentin tugged the file toward him, flipping through the pages in the hopes of finding even the smallest of clues. But all he found were numerous business contracts, all straightforward and innocuous, with no foreboding overtones or detrimental terms for either party.

"Is that everything?" he asked, glancing down at the final document.

"It is. The agreement you're holding has yet to be executed. Kenton and I had just negotiated it when . . ." Hendrick's voice trailed off.

The solicitor's words triggered a memory, and Quentin lifted the draft for closer inspection. "Is this what you and Desmond were reviewing two days past when I arrived at your office?"

"Pardon me?"

"When I walked in that day, Desmond mentioned that you and he were finalizing a business contract. Is this that contract?"

"Actually, yes." Hendrick shifted forward in his chair. "'Tis the draft of a retainer agreement between your father and myself."

"So I see." Quentin skimmed the document, quickly assessing it as a standard retainer which provided that Hendrick continue as the Steel family solicitor for a period of five years, during which he would receive the sizable but not outlandish sum of ten thousand pounds per annum. "This seems in order," Quentin said, returning the document to Kenton's file. "Which clause was it that Desmond needed to review?"

"The clause pertaining to my wages." Sorrow clouded Hendrick's gaze. "If you'll notice, that unsigned agreement is the only contract between Kenton and myself in his entire file. The reason for that is because, in my opinion, the whole idea of requiring your father's signature on a written retainer was absurd and unnecessary. Kenton was a fine and ethical gentleman, and I'd represented his business interests for years. Also, to be blunt, he was already far too generous with my wages. So, every time he broached the subject of a contract, I dismissed it. But Kenton was not to be dissuaded. He insisted that, just as I protected his interests, I should protect my own. At last, I relented. Hence, the agreement. Evidently, Desmond—who was present in my office when Kenton outlined the terms—wanted to be certain your father's wishes were carried out as initially discussed. But, if you feel otherwise, I'd be happy to renegotiate the particulars or tear up the whole bloody retainer."

"Absolutely not." Quentin closed the file and placed it on Hendrick's desk. "As I said, the retainer seems in perfect order, and I concur with Desmond's resolution to execute it just as Father would have, had he been alive. With regard to your wages—you're right. Father was an inordinately generous man. He was also a superb businessman. Therefore, if he deemed your services deserving of that sum, then they are obviously worth no less." With that, Quentin rose. "Thank you for your patience, Ellard. I won't take up any more of your time."

"Nonsense." Hendrick stood, waving away Quentin's contention. "My time is inconsequential. What's crucial here is learning who murdered your parents. I only wish I could have been of greater help."

"As do I. But at least we've ruled out the majority of Father's business associates as potential culprits." Quentin paused, a thoughtful expression crossing his face.

"What is it? Have you perceived something we might have missed?"

"No, not really. It just occurred to me that we've only explored Father's file."

Hendrick's brows arched in surprise. "I kept no separate file for Pamela, if that's what you mean."

"I wasn't referring to Mother. I was referring to Ardsley." Quentin held up his hand, anticipating Hendrick's ethical dilemma. "Ellard, I'm aware I have no legal rights to view Ardsley's file. Nor am I asking to do so. But I'd deem it a great favor if you would examine the contents—

immediately, if possible—and advise Desmond, in his newly appointed role as administrator of the Townsend businesses, should you discover anything even remotely suspicious."

"Consider it done," Hendrick replied soberly. "I'll peruse Ardsley's papers at once and discuss my findings with Desmond. You have my word."

"And you have my gratitude," Quentin returned. "Good day, Ellard."

"Good day. And please, keep me apprised of any developments that occur—any at all."

"Of course."

Hendrick stared after Quentin's retreating figure, his thoughts consumed by the immediacy of the task ahead. Vaguely, he heard Peters bid their guest good day, after which the quiet click of the outer office door signified Quentin's departure.

Rousing himself from his reverie, Hendrick stood, crossing the room in five long strides and walking out to Peters's desk.

"Can I do something for you, sir?"

"Yes, Peters, you can. First, get me the entire file on Ardsley Townsend. Then send a missive off to the new Duke of Colverton. Tell him I need to meet with him posthaste. Tomorrow. At eleven o'clock. In my office."

"And if that's inconvenient for him, sir?"

Hendrick was already halfway back to his desk. "It won't be."

Chapter 6

Brandi trailed her forefinger through the stream, watching the gentle ripples her motion left behind.

Stretched out full-length on the damp bank where yesterday Poseidon had tossed her, Brandi propped her chin on her opposite hand, oblivious to the heat of the sun's late afternoon rays. She'd been here since noon, pelted by conflicting emotions, inundated and empty all at once, thoroughly, incomprehensibly overwhelmed.

Murder.

She couldn't fathom it. Some faceless, nameless assailant had brutally, premeditatedly taken the lives of three people she loved. The truth was beyond bearing; the part that remained unknown, worse.

Who in God's name had killed them? Why? Who was the intended target? Or was it targets?

Brandi squeezed her eyes shut, two tears seeping from beneath her lids, sliding down her cheeks. She hadn't slept a wink all night, each doleful chime of Emerald Manor's grandfather clock reminding her of the passing hours, each one as futile as the last. She'd arisen at dawn, hoping a morning of digging alongside Herbert would alleviate some of her anguish. But the noon hour had come and gone, and she'd abandoned her gardening, still as tormented and muddled as she'd been at first light.

And equally determined.

She'd meant every word she'd said to Quentin. She *would* find the animal who had killed their parents; she wouldn't rest until she did.

Quentin.

He'd laced through her nighttime reflections like a ribbon of warm honey, lingering through her morning hours in a sensual spell more potent than the gardens of Emerald Manor. Sweet, savory, the memory of being in his arms soothed her tortured senses in its healing balm.

And awakened something inside her she'd never known existed.

Quentin.

Like a summer storm, the enchantment had struck yesterday without warning, whirling her into its core, leaving her breathless and shivering. Why hadn't she seen it, when it had always been there—even when Quentin himself was away?

Pushing herself to a sitting position, Brandi absently brushed clinging grains of dirt from her gown, then wrapped her arms about her knees.

So this was what ladies whispered about behind closed doors; why Pamela had glowed whenever Kenton was near. She, too, must have felt this dizziness, this swooping sensation in the pit of her belly, this liquid warmth that turned her limbs to jelly. She must have known what Brandi had only just discovered.

And now?

Brandi stiffened, recalling the aftermath as clearly as she did the embrace. Quentin had pulled away, not only physically, but emotionally. How much of that had been spawned by the need to protect her, and how much by his own unaffected response to their kiss?

Oh, but he had responded. She'd felt his urgency, his

almost desperate need to absorb her into himself. Had it merely been comfort he sought? Dear God, it had felt like so much more.

Brandi slammed her fist down in frustration. For the first time, she found herself wishing she had more experience, that she'd encouraged the advances of all the foppish, arrogant men she'd met these three Seasons past. Maybe then she'd be able to distinguish passion from tenderness, desire from friendship. Perhaps then she'd better understand what had transpired between them.

Of one thing Brandi was certain. For her, there was no turning back. She cared not what Quentin claimed. To return to who she'd been before yesterday? To pretend the wondrous transition inside her had never occurred? To deem meaningless those breathless moments in Quentin's arms?

Impossible.

"Miss Brandi?"

Brandi started, her head whipping around in response to the tentative greeting.

"Hello, my lady." Bentley's smile was genuine, and he waited patiently as Brandi collected herself and scrambled awkwardly to her feet.

"Bentley." She brushed a lock of hair from her forehead, leaving a smudge of dirt in its wake. "I never heard you approach."

"You were lost in thought. I didn't mean to startle you." Hands clasped behind him, he studied her face intently. "Are you all right?"

"Quentin sent you." It was not a question, but a statement.

"Yes. His lordship rode to London at daybreak, and shan't return before nightfall. He was concerned about you and asked that I drop by for a visit. I hope you don't mind."

"You know I'm always delighted to see you." Brandi inclined her head. "Quentin never mentioned any plans to travel to London today."

"His decision was sudden."

"Why has he gone, Bentley?"

"I believe he intends to meet with Mr. Hendrick, my lady."

"You know, don't you." Again, a statement. "Quentin told you."

"About the carriage accident being intentional? Yes, Miss Brandi, he told me." Bentley made no attempt to disguise his compassion. "I'm so terribly sorry."

"Thank you." Brandi's lips trembled. "As am I." She swallowed, regaining her composure. "I promised Herbert I'd assist him in the rock garden later today, after he'd finished restoring the geraniums. I'm to meet him at the gazebo; doubtless, I'm late already. Why don't you join me there? I'll fetch a pitcher of something cool and we can talk."

"*I'll* collect the refreshments, my lady. I'm certain you've eaten nothing today. I'm equally certain, knowing Mrs. Collins, that she has prepared a full tray, laden with foods meant to revive you—if you are strong enough to carry the ponderous weight in one trip." Bentley's eyes twinkled. "I'll fetch the feast and bring it to the gazebo straightaway."

Emotion formed a tight knot in Brandi's throat. "You're a wonderful friend, Bentley," she whispered tremulously. "I'm so glad Quentin has you."

The slightest of smiles. "I believe he has both of us, has he not, my lady?"

"Yes." Brandi nodded, her eyes damp. "He has."

Bentley's perceptive gaze seemed to delve deep inside her. "Be patient with him, Miss Brandi," he counseled. "He has much to understand, and more to reconcile. As for you, be strong, be discerning. And most of all, be yourself. 'Tis the greatest gift you can offer Master Quentin."

Brandi blinked away her tears. "Sometimes I think you understand us better than we understand ourselves."

"Indeed. For example, I understand that Herbert is expecting you and will never forgive your failure to appear. I also understand that you'd best eat, else you'll never have the strength to assist him, much less solve a crime or win a heart. Hence, I'm off to fetch our sustenance."

Impulsively, Brandi leaned up and kissed Bentley's weathered cheek. "Thank you," she acknowledged softly. Then she turned, scooting off toward the gazebo.

Hearing her racing footsteps, Herbert looked up from where he knelt alongside the geraniums and tossed her a disgruntled look. "Well! It's about time you got here," he muttered. "I was beginnin' to think you'd fallen into the stream."

"I apologize for my tardiness," Brandi returned, undaunted by Herbert's intentionally—and misleadingly—brusque facade. "As for my falling into the stream, I swim like a fish—and you know it. Further, the water there is ankle-high, hardly a formidable depth." She paused, frowning as she peered over Herbert's shoulder. "Pamela's geraniums are wilting! Why?"

Herbert snorted, shaking his head at the crumpled flower he'd been tending to. "Damned if I know. I've tried everything I can think of. It's only these two rows closest to the gazebo. The rest of 'em look fine." He scowled, scratching his chin. "But not these."

"What could be causing them to—ouch!"

Brandi's question was interrupted by a sharp whack on the head. Her hand flew to her injury just as a hard acorn shell rolled to her feet. "Lancelot, that hurt!" Her chin jerked upward, but she knew precisely what she'd find.

Her scrutiny yielded no surprises.

The red squirrel stared serenely back at her from his comfortable perch in the oak tree. Nibbling on the succulent remains of his acorn, he paused only to scratch the white quizzing-glass patch about his left eye before returning to his midday snack.

"One day I'm going to empty every tree in Emerald Manor of its goodies," she warned him. "Acorns, berries—everything. Then you'll have nothing with which to attack."

"He'll find something, Miss Brandi," Bentley advised

calmly, climbing the gazebo steps and placing a heaping tray atop the table. "The last time I was here, your rodent friend pelted me with berries, tossed an annoyingly painful stone at my shoulder, and toppled a sharp branch to my brow. Not only was I injured, my uniform was torn in three places and hopelessly stained with berry juice. I considered finding a pistol and ending his wretched life then and there. I most likely would have, were it not for the fact that I know how fond you are of the scoundrel. Although heaven knows why." With a scathing look at the overhead branch, Bentley turned away from the oak. "Good day, Herbert," he greeted the gardener.

"Hello, Bentley." Herbert rose, mopping his face with a handkerchief. "And, by the way, I agree with every word you just said. That miserable troublemaker torments me all the time. Only in my case, he doesn't throw things, he steals 'em. So far this week I've lost a handkerchief, two shillings, and nearly half my food. I've half a mind to . . ."

"But you won't, will you, Herbert?" Brandi asked anxiously. "I know Lancelot is a bit of a mischief-maker, but he means no harm. Do you, Lancelot?" She gazed hopefully upward.

The squirrel continued eating.

"That was convincin'," Herbert grumbled. His eyes narrowed. "I wonder if that squirrel is doin' something to ruin my geraniums."

"Herbert, how could he do that?" Brandi reasoned. "He is, after all, only a squirrel."

"Humph."

"We've wasted enough time pondering the actions of your rodent friend, Miss Brandi," Bentley announced. "'Tis time for you to eat."

"Good thing you brought her a meal, Bentley," Herbert commended with an approving nod. "I can't get her to eat a thing. If she's not gardenin', she's worryin'. Pretty soon, she's gonna waste away." Roughly, he cleared his throat, averting a gaze filled with concern. "And then who'd help me with that blasted rock garden? No one else knows how to keep it up but Miss Brandi."

"I understand. And I quite agree." Bentley indicated the array of food with a grand sweep of his arm. "Sit, Miss Brandi. You and Herbert can discuss your afternoon project—*while you eat.*"

A trace of the old Brandi emerged as she erupted into spontaneous laughter. "And men claim women are the ones who nag." Dutifully, she sank down on the garden bench, her laughter fading into tenderness as she looked from Bentley to Herbert. "You're two of the most relentless and tyrannical men imaginable. And I don't know what I'd do without either of you."

"Then, how fortunate for you that we're going nowhere." Piling mounds of chicken, potatoes, asparagus, and biscuits on a plate, Bentley poured a glass of punch and gathered some utensils before descending the gazebo steps to place both glass and dish firmly before Brandi. "Isn't that right, Herbert?"

"Right indeed, Bentley."

Bentley's lips curved a fraction as he handed Brandi her fork. "Now, partake, my lady. As Herbert has just confirmed, he and I will remain to relentlessly tyrannize you. Therefore, you have one less dilemma to resolve."

Touched beyond words, Brandi studied her friends, silently vowing to ease their distress as they were so diligently trying to ease hers. Later, when she was alone, she'd plan her course of action—with regard to the murder *and* to Quentin. But for now, seeing Bentley's furrowed brow and Herbert's troubled frown, she resolved to conceal her anguish, even if it killed her.

"Do you know," she stated brightly, spearing a slice of chicken with great enthusiasm, "I hate to admit it, but you're quite right. I suddenly find myself ravenously hungry."

"Excellent, Miss Brandi," Bentley commended.

"It sure is," Herbert concurred.

Silently congratulating herself for a successful deception, Brandi proceeded to devour her meal.

Herbert resumed his digging.

Bentley returned to the gazebo to pour himself some punch.

Neither man was fooled.

"I've been awaiting your return, sir."

Bentley stood directly inside Colverton's entranceway doors, a regal bloodhound poised for the hunt.

The frustrating outcome of Quentin's unproductive meeting with Hendrick vanished in one lightning worry. "Is it Brandi?" he demanded. "Is something amiss?"

"No, my lord. I was merely eager to hear the results of your trip to London. Miss Brandi is fine. Pale, a bit more subdued than usual, but well." Scrutinizing Quentin's rigid stance, Bentley astutely elaborated. "Or, to be more precise, she is holding up, given the circumstances. She's upset and confused—by the murders, of course—and, if I'm to be honest, a tad disappointed that it was I who called upon her rather than you." Bentley cleared his throat. "In any case, I rode to Emerald Manor at three o'clock, where Miss Brandi and I spent the better part of an hour together. Herbert and I badgered her until she agreed to eat—a great relief to us both. She's lost a noticeable amount of weight over the past fortnight—for obvious reasons."

Tersely, Quentin nodded. "Did you explain to her where I'd gone? Why I wasn't able to visit?"

"I said only that you'd ridden to London to see Mr. Hendrick and would return by nightfall. She understood at once what that meant, just as I'd intended. Hopefully, it will keep her from racing off on her own impulsive quest to resolve the crime . . . at least until she hears from you."

Quentin blanched. "You don't believe she'd do something foolish, do you?"

A sigh. "You know, Miss Brandi, my lord. She will not remain passive while you rush about investigating the tragedy alone."

"Lord, I never even considered . . ." Quentin took an inadvertent step toward the door.

"I don't think you need worry tonight," Bentley assured him swiftly. "I made certain not to take my leave until Miss Brandi was immersed in helping Herbert arrange the rock garden. Herbert understands her quite well, sir, and knows just what he must do. He'll keep her occupied until dusk, when she's worn out and ready to retire. Mrs. Collins will take it from there. I spoke to her myself. She will oversee Miss Brandi until she is safely abed. So, rest assured, Miss Brandi is going nowhere tonight."

"Thank you, Bentley." Quentin's shoulders sagged with relief. "You've thought of everything."

"My pleasure, sir. However, might I suggest you plan an early morning visit to Emerald Manor?"

"I'll go there at dawn. Although I don't have one blasted thing to tell Brandi, reassuring or otherwise."

"Your visit with Mr. Hendrick yielded no results?"

Quentin hesitated, glancing toward the study.

"Master Desmond is abed, sir." Bentley gave a pointed cough. "He was a trifle out of sorts today. As I recall, he mentioned something about a pounding headache and a persistent bout of nausea. He skipped dinner and retired directly. But, to ensure our privacy, shall we talk in the library?"

"A wise idea." Quentin led the way, closing the heavy door firmly behind them. "Bentley, I looked through every bloody document in Father's file. There is nothing even remotely suspicious there."

"What about the late duke's will, sir? Did you learn anything about the existence of a codicil?"

"There is no codicil. Oh, Hendrick confirmed precisely what you'd already told me: that Father summoned him to Colverton for the express purpose of amending his will. But ultimately he convinced Father to reconsider, and the will was left intact."

"Did Mr. Hendrick mention the specific modification your father wished to make?"

"Yes. Evidently, the clause in question pertained to Emerald Manor."

"Emerald Manor, sir?" Surprise laced Bentley's tone.

"Yes. The whole issue is rather complex. To sum it up, Father was apparently distraught over the future of Emerald Manor, or, more specifically, over my inability to safeguard it—given that I'd made no overtures toward marrying and siring an heir. Therefore, while he truly wished for me to inherit the cottage, Father felt he had no choice but to consider willing it to Brandi, who, he knew, would not only cherish it but one day pass it on to her children."

"I recognize the late duke's reasoning, sir. What I fail to recognize is how his decision would affect Master Desmond. Certainly your brother didn't hope that *he* would be named the cottage's recipient, not with his resentment toward the duchess and the cottage your father built for her. The late duke would never consider bequeathing Emerald Manor to a man who . . ." Discreetly, Bentley broke off.

"Who coldly rejected my mother from the day she and Father wed," Quentin finished. "You're right; he wouldn't."

"Then there was no reason for Master Desmond to pressure your father about the clause in his will involving Emerald Manor."

"You're wrong, Bentley. There was every reason."

Bentley frowned. "I see only one other possible motivation and, if I'm to be frank, sir, I highly doubt its validity."

"And what is that?"

"That Master Desmond was arguing with your father on your behalf, that he rushed forward to convince the late duke *not* to bequeath Emerald Manor to Miss Brandi."

A harsh laugh erupted from Quentin's chest. "Not bloody likely. Not when Desmond resents me nearly as much as he did Mother." Quentin shook his head adamantly. "No, Bentley, I'm convinced that Desmond desperately wanted Father to alter that clause."

"But why? Simply for the smug sense of satisfaction he'd attain by depriving you of your heritage?"

"No," Quentin refuted. "For the smug sense of satisfaction he'd attain by acquiring Emerald Manor in my stead."

"I thought we just agreed, sir, that the late duke would never bequeath the cottage to your brother."

"We did. But if Desmond's personal plans came to fruition, Father's willing Emerald Manor to Brandi would be just as effective. It would become Desmond's the day he and Brandi wed."

Bentley stared. "Wed?"

A terse nod. "I told you Desmond claimed he and Brandi had grown close during my absence. What I didn't mention was that he informed me they were on the verge of becoming betrothed, that, had it not been for the accident, he'd have asked Ardsley for her hand—and received it."

"Forgive me, sir, but I suddenly need to sit down." Bentley sank into an armchair, drawing a slow inward breath. "Either I've been residing elsewhere these past years, or your brother is blatantly lying to you."

"Is he? I'm not altogether sure," was Quentin's quiet reply. "My instincts scream out that you're right, that the thought of Brandi and Desmond together is inconceivable. But Ardsley did entrust her into Desmond's care. And Brandi does seem far more tolerant of my brother's overbearing manner than she was in years gone by. Maybe there is a grain of truth to Desmond's claim."

Bentley gave an indignant sniff. "That is rubbish, sir. Tolerance and gratitude, perhaps, but nothing more."

"Ardsley might have thought otherwise. For whatever reason, he trusted Desmond. And trust, with what he doubtless perceived as a growing companionability between his daughter and Desmond . . . perhaps that was enough."

"Enough for the viscount, possibly, but what about for Miss Brandi?"

A muscle flexed in Quentin's jaw. "She accepts Desmond for who he is. And, to an extent, she relies upon him—hell, she should rely upon him." Quentin scowled. "He's always here for her."

"Is he?"

Quentin's eyes narrowed. "What does that mean?"

"It means, my lord, that trust can be earned, or it can be falsely elicited. Companionability, too, can be an illusion. And even when genuine, it does not in itself constitute devotion, any more than gratitude necessarily leads to love." Bentley held Quentin's gaze. "And love, Master Quentin, is still quite important—at least to those who seek it."

"When did you become a philosopher, Bentley?"

"Not a philosopher, sir—just a vigilant friend. A friend who, I'm told, ofttimes understands you better than you understand yourself."

"Really?"

"Indeed. I have it on the highest authority."

"Brandi?"

"Brandi, my lord."

A wistful smile curved Quentin's lips. "My insightful Sunbeam," he murmured, half to himself. "So you don't believe she'd be well off with Desmond? That his constancy would make her feel settled? Secure?"

"I believe you know the answer to that, my lord. Miss Brandi would be inundated with the wrong things and severely lacking the right ones."

"He'd crush her spirit," Quentin agreed in a low troubled tone. "He'd break her will in order to control her. And he'd strip all the simple joys from her life."

"I would say that's accurate, sir."

Again a flash of memory accosted Quentin: the pond, Brandi's lips parting sweetly under his . . .

"Bentley," he blurted out. "Would you deem me insane if I told you that since my return to the Cotswolds I've been feeling . . . wanting—" Abruptly, he broke off.

"Yes, sir?"

"Never mind." Wearily, Quentin rubbed his eyes. "Pay no attention to my rambling. I'm so tired I'm not even sure what I'm saying."

"Of course, sir." Bentley came to his feet. "You are tired.

You're also baffled and frustrated—which you doubtless will remain until you uncover the truth." A pregnant pause. *"All* of it."

Quentin's gaze narrowed. "Why do I get the feeling you're implying far more than you're actually stating?"

"I repeat, you're tired, my lord." Bentley opened the library door and gestured for Quentin to precede him. "Get some sleep. Perhaps the essential answers will find you."

Chapter 7

"All right, Hendrick, I'm here."

Desmond closed the door behind him, leaning back against its solid veneer. "What do you want?"

"Sit down, Desmond," Hendrick advised calmly, shuffling some papers around on his desk. "Or shall I say, 'Your Grace'?"

Paling, Desmond crossed the room and dropped into a chair. "I'm listening."

Hendrick closed the file he'd been perusing and folded his hands on his desk. "You're not looking at all well, Colverton. Have you, by chance, been drinking?"

"Don't toy with me, Ellard. I don't like it. Now, why did you send for me?"

"Your brother was here yesterday. He had numerous questions to ask."

Desmond went rigid. "Like what?"

"It seems he's taken it upon himself to investigate your father's death. In the process, he discovered the circumstances surrounding my final visit to Colverton, presumably from your attentive butler."

"We surmised that might happen."

"Indeed we did. Quentin's appearance in my office came as no surprise. Nevertheless, I thought you should know he asked to see your father's will—which he scrutinized, together with all the other documents in Kenton's file."

"Damn it!" Desmond slammed his fist on the desk. "I knew he'd ask questions, but I didn't think he'd actually examine Father's papers. Did he detect anything that aroused his suspicions?"

"He detected only that which I intended him to," Hendrick responded with a triumphant air. "As I said, I've been expecting Quentin's visit. Hence, I made certain to place the appropriate document in an equally appropriate—and visible—spot. Which reminds me, you have yet to execute my retainer. You do recall the terms we agreed upon, do you not?"

"Yes, of course I recall them. What the hell does your retainer have to do with Quentin?"

"Ah, Your Grace, you're not using your gift of perception. My retainer has everything to do with Quentin. After thoroughly examining the will, your brother was especially curious to scrutinize the contents of the document you and I were allegedly reviewing the afternoon of the will readings."

Desmond's pupils dilated. "You didn't show him . . ."

"Of course not. I'm not stupid. I told him we were finalizing my retainer—the one Kenton insisted I draw up to protect my own interests. Then I showed Quentin the agreement. He approved; in fact, he suggested that it be executed at once." Hendrick leaned back in his chair with a self-righteous smile. "Which eliminated his questions, and your dilemma."

"Don't look so damned smug," Desmond returned, vaulting to his feet. "'Tis not just my dilemma; 'tis yours as well—so long as you wish to continue receiving the lavish payments I'm currently providing. Moreover, this is only the first step. I know Quentin—and he doesn't give up that easily." Desmond's gaze swept the office. "Where the hell is your brandy?"

"It's not even noon."

"I'm thirsty," Desmond snapped.

"Open the sideboard. You'll find what you need there."

Desmond's hands shook as he tossed off two glasses in rapid succession. "What else?"

"Quentin asked me to go through Denerley's file as well. My instructions are to search for any possible clue and to alert you, as the appointed overseer of Denerley's businesses, to my findings."

"And have you searched Ardsley's file?"

"Yes. Ostensibly, nothing is amiss."

"Thank God." Desmond poured another brandy and leaned heavily against the sideboard. "The last thing I need is for Father's or Ardsley's business dealings to be connected with the murders. Still, we're far from safe. Quentin won't stop until he uncovers something. Heaven only knows what my wretched butler has divulged, and where his revelations will lead my brother."

"If Bentley offends you so, why not dismiss him?"

"Are you insane? I'm trying to elude suspicion, not arouse it. I might loathe the meddlesome pest, but Quentin sings his praises. So did Father. Further, Bentley has been with my family for ages. No, Hendrick, I have to keep Colverton running precisely as Father did, making absolutely no major changes that might give Quentin pause. Firing Bentley would be the most foolhardy step I could take."

"I suppose that's true." Hendrick frowned thoughtfully. "And I do see your point about Quentin; his prying is a bit disconcerting."

"His entire presence is a bit disconcerting," Desmond retorted, staring darkly into his drink. "I was making fine progress with Brandice before her bloody hero returned to the Cotswolds—damn him to hell." With a sharp snap of the wrist, Desmond tossed off half his brandy.

"Oh?" Hendrick's brows rose. "Is Quentin interfering in your betrothal plans?"

"You know bloody well how Brandice worships my brother. We could erect a blasted statue in his honor on the grounds of Emerald Manor." A bitter laugh. "So far as Brandice is concerned, when Quentin is home, no one else exists."

"Then maybe it's best for Quentin not to be home."

Desmond's head whipped around. "What does that mean?"

"You're the Duke of Colverton, my friend. Have you any idea how much power that position yields?"

"So?"

"So you know people in the highest of places; you have influence in areas others can't even approach—such as the War Department, for example."

A glint of understanding flickered in Desmond's eyes. "Go on."

"'Tis the simplest of plans. Merely use your ducal power to have Quentin recalled by the army. After all, General Wellington holds him in such high regard. Surely, he could utilize Quentin's brilliant tactical abilities in Paris? Let's say, to intercede in our very delicate controversy with King Louis over his slave trade? I needn't provide you with fabrications. You're quite good at inventing them yourself. The point is that if Quentin leaves England, he can neither pry into our business nor occupy Brandice's time and thoughts. Now am I making myself clear?"

"Clear as a bell." Desmond downed the remainder of his drink. With a flourish, he set his empty glass on the sideboard. "Now, if you'll excuse me, Hendrick, I have an unexpected meeting with the War Department."

"Of course." The solicitor took up his quill. "I wish you the best of luck in your endeavor. Oh, Desmond?" He held up his retainer. "Haven't you forgotten something?"

Desmond crossed the room in three strides, snatched the quill and document from Hendrick's hands, and dashed off his signature. "There."

"Excellent." Hendrick nodded his satisfaction. "I'm pleased we'll be continuing our association ... Your Grace." Methodically, he slipped the retainer back into the file. "By the way, when you return to Colverton tonight, tell

Quentin I summoned you for the express purpose of reporting that, after an exhaustive review, I discovered nothing amiss in Viscount Denerley's papers."

"I shall indeed." Halfway to the door, Desmond paused, giving Hendrick a mock salute. "Good day, Ellard. Soon this nagging complication will be eliminated."

Calmly, Hendrick resumed his paperwork. "I never doubted it for a minute."

"Hello, Sunbeam."

Quentin approached the quiet gazebo, unsurprised to find Brandi here at dawn, staring off into the dimly lit woods. "Are you all right?"

Slowly, Brandi turned, her wide dark eyes filled with painful questions. "I don't know."

Of their own accord, Quentin's feet climbed the stairs to reach her. "You look exhausted." His forefinger traced the circles beneath her eyes. "Have you slept at all?"

"A bit." She inclined her head, her unbound hair tumbling in a burnished waterfall down her back. "What did you learn from Mr. Hendrick?"

"Nothing."

"Quentin, please. I know you insist on viewing me as a child. But I'm not. And I need to know. What did you find out?"

Quentin's chest tightened. "First of all, I don't view you as a child. Second, I'm not keeping anything from you. I learned nothing. If you'll permit me, I'll elaborate."

"Very well." Brandi sank down on the bench, tucking the skirts of her midnight-blue gown beneath her. "I'm listening."

With a heavy sigh, Quentin lowered himself beside her, gripping his knees as he spoke. "After I left you two days past, it occurred to me that whoever murdered our parents might have been a business associate of Father's—one who, for reasons of his own, held a grudge. So I went to see Hendrick in order to scrutinize all Father's business documents."

"And did you?"

"Yes. I examined each and every paper in Father's file. Nothing even remotely suspicious caught my eye. Evidently, my theory was incorrect."

"Not necessarily, Quentin." Brandi sat up straighter, wrapping her shawl more tightly about her shoulders. "Perhaps your theory was correct, but your choice of victims wasn't. Perhaps it was *my* father who had the business enemy."

"The thought occurred to me." Quentin nodded, studying Brandi's tired, earnest face, marveling at the maturity he could both see and hear, but had never before discerned. Like her beauty, had it always been there, eluding only his clouded vision?

"Did you ask Mr. Hendrick to show you Father's papers?" Brandi was asking.

Quentin shook his head. "I have no legal right to search Ardsley's file, Sunbeam. But I did ask Ellard to do so for me and to advise Desmond, as overseer of your family businesses, of anything suspicious he might unearth."

"Father kept many of his documents at home." Brandi bolted to her feet. "I'll ride to Townsbourne at once and go through every paper . . ."

"Brandi." Quentin jumped up just as quickly, his hand automatically halting her departure. "I don't want you involved."

She stared at him as if he were insane. "You don't want me involved? Quentin, listen to yourself. My father was murdered, together with two people I loved as parents. I'm as involved as you are, maybe more so. You have the army, whereas I . . ." She drew a long, shaky breath. "Please don't do this to me. You, of all people, have never patronized me in the past. Please, Quentin, not you."

Quentin felt as if he'd been punched. "Sunbeam, I'd never patronize you. I only want to keep you safe. We're dealing with someone capable of snuffing out human lives without a second thought. Do you understand how dangerous that is?"

"Of course I do." Her gaze softened and she lay her palm against Quentin's jaw. "Thank you for trying to protect me. But there are some things from which one cannot be protected. This is one."

Soberly, Quentin brushed a cinnamon curl from her face. "You're right," he conceded quietly. "But I'm right as well. I can't spare you the anguish of this investigation, nor can you plunge headfirst into danger. Therefore, I propose a compromise."

A glint of humor warmed Brandi's eyes to a shimmering golden brown. "Ever the diplomat, my lord. Very well, what manner of compromise do you suggest?"

"Give Hendrick a day or two to examine Ardsley's files and contact Desmond. If his findings reveal nothing, then you and I shall ride to Townsbourne and thoroughly inspect each and every one of your father's papers—together. Is that acceptable?"

She nodded. "Yes. I'll agree to that."

"Good." Quentin wished he weren't so damned aware of her smooth palm against his skin. She'd touched him this way dozens of times in the past, but he'd never felt this surge of sensation, not only in his heart, but in his loins.

"Quentin?"

"Hmm?" His thumb traced the delicate bridge of her nose, and he cautioned himself to back away, promised himself that he would—in a minute.

"Would you kiss me again?"

His teetering resolve abruptly righted itself. "What?"

Nervously, she wet her lips with the tip of her tongue. "I've thought about this a great deal since our . . . since we . . . since our encounter at the stream," she concluded hastily. "And I understand the explanations you gave me— that we were reaching out to each other for comfort, that you can ultimately belong only to England. But, try though I will, I cannot accept your reasoning, nor can I dismiss our kiss as if it never transpired. It finally occurred to me that my inability to put our embrace in the proper perspective might stem from my total lack of experience from which to judge."

Inexplicable anger surged inside Quentin, escalating like an ominous, impending storm. "What exactly are you suggesting?" he demanded.

"I'm trying to explain that I've never been in another man's arms," Brandi continued in earnest. "That, unlike you, I haven't ever experienced kissing or being kissed and, thus, have no means of comparison."

"And just how do you intend to acquire this means of comparison?"

"From you."

Beneath Brandi's palm, Quentin's jaw muscles flexed. "From me," he repeated woodenly.

"Yes." She withdrew her hand to the less threatening curve of his shoulder, unconsciously gripping his lapel. "You've taught me all my most joyful pursuits: shooting, fishing, riding. Won't you teach me this as well?"

"You're asking me . . ." Quentin's mouth was so dry he could scarcely speak.

"To teach me to kiss," she finished with a small, hopeful smile. "Yes, that's precisely what I'm asking you. Without experiencing both a kiss of friendship and one of passion, how will I differentiate the two? And who can I trust to show me, if not you? Ponder it, Quentin. I know *I* have—during every sleepless hour not consumed with our parents' murders. I'm closer to you than I am to any other man on earth. Yet I read far more into our kiss than you intended. If *your* embrace confused me, imagine how befuddled I'll become when I'm kissed by others?"

He captured her chin. "Exactly how many men do you intend to kiss?"

"I don't know." Her brow furrowed. "How many women have you kissed?"

Quentin's jaw dropped, humor and amazement tempering anger. "I—" He cleared his throat. "Sunbeam, that's not at all the same thing."

"Why not?"

A long pause.

Then: "Brandi, didn't my mother ever talk to you about the differences between men and women—about what happens when men and women are . . . together?"

A slight flush stained her cheeks. "If you're asking if I know how babies are conceived, the answer is yes. But what has that to do with kissing?"

"Nothing. Everything." Quentin shifted, staring down into Brandi's beautiful, questioning face. Firmly, he reminded himself that she'd always come to him with her questions, that he'd always supplied the answers. It wasn't her fault that this time was different, that, rather than tender admiration at her candor and fond amusement at her naiveté, all he could feel was fury at the idea of another man touching her, and a raw, primitive need to crush her in his arms and teach her far more than kissing—far more than she had doubtless ever imagined.

With that thought in mind, Quentin fought back his new, unsettling hunger, struggling to think what the Quentin of four years past would have offered his Sunbeam in the way of an answer. "Brandi, kissing is not something I can teach you," he tried at last.

"Why not?"

"Because . . ." His gaze fell to her lips, which were parted sweetly in question, and his explanation died in his throat.

"Because?" she prompted. When he didn't reply, her hold on his coat loosened, her palm lightly caressing his collar—again, a gesture she'd made countless times in the past, only this time it burned through Quentin like fire. "Why not?" she repeated, searching his face.

Quentin had no idea what he would have said four summers ago. Nor, in truth, did he give a damn. One kiss, his conscience cried out. A chaste one. For her own good—to show her what she should allow, to prepare her for the legion of men who would undoubtedly be clamoring for her favors.

He wanted to choke each nameless suitor.

"Will you teach me?" Brandi murmured, shyly inching closer. "I promise not to behave as childishly as I did last time."

"You weren't childish." His fingers threaded through her hair. "You were beautiful."

"Then will you . . ."

"Put your arms around me."

Eagerly, Brandi complied, wrapping her arms tightly about his neck. "Like this?"

"Just like that." Quentin brushed his lips across her cheekbones—first one, then the other. "Now, what I'm about to demonstrate is the only kind of kiss you should permit a man. *Any* man. Do you understand?"

She nodded.

"Press your lips together."

"But . . ."

"Do as I say."

Brandi squeezed her lips tightly shut.

"Good." Quentin lowered his mouth to skim hers in a whisper of a caress: soft, swift, utterly proper.

He raised his head.

Brandi's lashes flew open and she blinked, surprise and disappointment clouding her gaze. "That wasn't a kiss."

"It most certainly was."

"It bore no resemblance to the one we shared at the stream."

"Nor should it. Never allow a man to embrace you so—so—intimately."

"But why not? It was wonderful." She smiled—a dreamy, faraway smile. "I can still remember that weak, trembling feeling in my legs, that swirling sensation in the pit of my stomach. Oh, Quentin, it was as if all the flowers in Emerald Garden were converging around me, intoxicating me with their perfume until my head was swimming with their scent. Or as if I were galloping astride Poseidon over an endless field, and we were racing so fast that I couldn't breathe, couldn't think, yet I'd never felt so vitally, totally alive." She sighed. "It was magic."

A rough sound emerged from Quentin's chest. "Sunbeam." He pulled her against him. "What am I going to do with you?"

It was a rhetorical question—one he didn't expect her to answer.

Brandi answered it anyway.

"What are you going to do with me?" she repeated softly, rising on tiptoe. "I can think of a wondrous solution." Her lips brushed his, first tentatively, then, feeling his inadvertent shudder, more boldly, her tongue tracing the warm curve of his mouth. "But then, it would involve kissing me in a way you've just cautioned me never to permit."

Restraint snapped.

With a harsh groan of capitulation, Quentin's mouth came down on Brandi's—not gentle and chaste, but hard, urgent, desperate. Displaying none of his silently vowed restraint, Quentin gave in to the need clawing inside him, this kiss every bit the wild, consuming, blazing inferno his entire being had clamored for from the start.

Brandi made a wordless sound of wonder, parting her lips with trembling excitement, drawing Quentin closer in a silent plea to continue.

"Brandi." He understood her unspoken invitation, and he penetrated her with his tongue, burying himself in her beauty. Twining his hands in her hair, he angled her head to better receive the blatant possession of his kiss, denying the madness even as it consumed him. "This can't happen," he rasped, making no move to release her.

"Don't stop," she beseeched, clutching him tightly, wanting never, never to be set free.

"Christ, Sunbeam, you're killing me." His lips left hers, blazing a trail of kisses down the slender column of her throat, then back up to the sweetness of her mouth.

"Just tell me you've thought about this," Brandi whispered breathlessly, shivering in response to each heated contact. "About what happened between us. At the stream."

"Yes, I've thought about it," he managed, raising his head

to gaze into the molten brown velvet of her eyes. "Too bloody much."

"Oh, Quentin, so have I." Brandi's fingers sifted through the silky hair at his nape, her voice unsteady. "Did you feel . . . that is, when we kissed, while we kissed . . ."

"Yes, yes, and yes." Quentin captured her mouth again, tenderness and hunger combined, as if to confirm that the dizzying excitement wasn't a temporary illusion.

It wasn't.

His arms locked around her like steel bands, dragging her closer still, pressing her soft, pliant body flush against his rigid one. Then he kissed her—again and again—until their initial embrace had dimmed beneath the scorching inferno of the here and now.

Brandi's legs buckled, and it was only the strength of Quentin's arms that kept her from collapsing to the gazebo floor. Alive, her every sense awakened, she returned his kisses with all the innocent ardor in her soul, melding her tongue with his, wondering if he could possibly be feeling even a fraction of the scalding physical sensations she was. "Please tell me . . ."

"Yes." He drank in her fervent appeal, giving her the answer she sought in the most poignant way possible. He deepened the kiss, possessing every tingling surface of her mouth, taking her tongue, her breath, and making them his. His arms shook as they loosened their grip—just enough for his hands to move. Restlessly, they shifted up and down her back, pausing at each hook of her gown, then forcibly abandoning it, battling the primal urge to bare more of her satiny skin to his touch, his view, his taste. Desire poured through him in widening torrents, and his entire soul throbbed with a feverish urgency that, despite the women who lined his past, was totally foreign to him.

It was that soul-shattering urgency which stopped him.

"Brandi—no." He literally tore his mouth from hers, an act as painful as a physical wound. He stared down at her, totally off-balance, seeing his own hunger and confusion mirrored in her eyes. "Sunbeam . . ." He had no idea what to say.

Brandi did.

"Why did you stop?" she whispered.

"Because I can't allow this to happen."

"Did you want it to?"

"That doesn't matter."

"Did you?"

"Even if I . . ."

"Did you?"

"Yes, damn it, I did!" He threw back his head, dragging air into his lungs, seeking help from the ubiquitous heavens that hovered silently about the semidarkened gazebo.

"If you wanted this to happen, then why did you pull away?" Brandi's breath grazed the column of his throat. "Did I do something wrong?"

"No, you did nothing wrong." Quentin lowered his chin to meet her gaze. "In fact, if you were any more right, I'd have—" His mouth snapped shut.

Brandi gave him a beatific smile. "Thank you, Quentin. That is truly all I needed to hear."

Gritting his teeth, Quentin forced out the words that needed to be said. "Sunbeam, I'm a captain in the army. My skills are needed and my loyalty is with my country. I could be recalled at any time."

"I understand." Brandi silenced him, pressing her fingers to his lips.

"Do you?" He caught her fingers in his. "Do you understand that regardless of what happens between us, despite any feelings I might have, my primary commitment is to England? Do you understand that I can't stay here with you? That I can't be here for you?"

A spasm of pain crossed Brandi's face. "I know," she managed in a small, choked voice. "But at least I know you want to be."

Reflexively, Quentin drew her to him, pressing her head to his chest. "Yes. I want to be."

Brandi swallowed past the lump in her throat. "Do you

know," she said, forcing a light note into her tone, "you've been home for nearly a week and you haven't taken me fishing?" Extricating herself from Quentin's arms, she inclined her head, gazing up at him with a bright smile. "Have you forgotten how, Captain Steel?"

Something profound flashed on Quentin's face, then vanished, as he, too, retreated to the safety of their long-standing companionability. "No, my lady, I assure you I have not forgotten how to fish. I just assumed that, after four years, you'd have either depleted or estranged the Cotswolds' entire supply of respectable bait."

"Or perchance you were concerned that, as was generally the case in the past, I would catch more fish than you, besting you in yet another sporting match?"

His hazel eyes twinkled. "Is that a challenge, little hoyden?"

"It is, my lord. Unless, of course, you have other plans for the morning?"

"Not a one." Quentin shook his head, gesturing toward the gazebo steps. "Shall we?"

Welcome laughter bubbled up inside Brandi, and gathering her skirts, she raced down to the garden. "I shall try to be a gracious winner, my lord," she called over her shoulder. "But I cannot make any promises."

Two hours later, disheveled and sodden, Brandi sat on the far bank of the stream—the only place where the water was deep enough to fish—engrossed in the task of assessing their contest results.

"You've caught two fewer fish than I," she announced, depositing the last trout on her pile. "Therefore, I win." Triumphantly, she faced him, tucking wet strands of hair behind her ears.

Propped up on his elbows, legs stretched out before him, Quentin turned his head, cocking a sardonic brow in Brandi's direction. "Yes, you win. You also cheat."

Her chin came up. "I didn't cheat. I merely sought a more comfortable position in which to fish."

"Three times?"

She stifled a grin. "I was getting cramped."

"I see. What a coincidence that each of the three times you resettled yourself you freed whatever bites I had on my line."

"Your concentration was not at its peak, my lord. Lack of practice, I presume."

"Evidently." From beneath hooded lids, Quentin watched her scramble to her feet and lean over the stream to purposefully wring out her soaked stockings. "And I suppose you've already selected your prize?"

"Of course." Brandi gave him a dazzling smile, raising the skirts of her waterlogged gown above her knees so that she might squeeze out the water. "I want you to buy me a pair of breeches."

"Breeches?" he repeated with a chuckle.

"Yes. Several pairs in fact." She eyed her gathered skirts mournfully, giving them another futile twist. "I'm tired of soggy gowns trailing at my ankles and bulky layers of muslin crammed between my body and my saddle."

Quentin's amusement vanished in a heartbeat, his mesmerized stare fixed on the exquisite limbs bared before him. His chest constricted anew, and with a mammoth effort, he dragged his gaze away, desperately trying not to imagine the feel of those silken legs wrapped around him. "I see your point," he managed. "Very well, Sunbeam. Breeches it shall be."

"Excellent." Brandi sank down beside him, her finger pressed conspiratorially to her lips. "But don't tell Desmond. He'll surely succumb to apoplexy."

Desmond.

"Brandi, what exactly is your relationship with my brother?" The question that had been plaguing Quentin for days burst out with a will of its own.

"My relationship with Desmond?" Brandi started at Quentin's unexpectedly harsh tone, her brows drawn together in puzzlement. "You know the answer to that as well as I do. As per Papa's instructions, Desmond is my guardian."

"What about prior to that?"

"I don't understand."

"Is he—special to you?"

Stunned realization dilated Brandi's pupils. "The other day in the stables, when you asked if any gentleman I'd met made me feel differently than the others—oh, Quentin, surely you weren't alluding to Desmond?"

"Wasn't I?"

"That's absurd!" she countered, shaking her head. "You, of all people, know how utterly different Desmond and I are."

"Yes, I do. But I also know how committed he is to you."

"And my gratitude for that commitment, as well as for his comfort and support, is boundless. I've made no secret of the fact that he's sustained me these past few weeks—I'll always be indebted to him for showing me such patience and compassion when I needed it most. But I have no romantic interest in him. Whatever made you think otherwise?"

"Desmond did."

Brandi's eyes widened. "What are you saying?"

Quentin sucked in his breath, determinedly squelching his momentary twinge of guilt. Maybe he was being unfair to his brother, severing any chance Desmond might have of swaying Brandi's feelings. But to hell with fate. All that mattered was Brandi—and her happiness.

"I'm saying that Desmond intends to wed you—soon."

"What?" All the color drained from Brandi's face. "Where on earth did you get an idea like that?"

"From Desmond. According to his pronouncement, he'd been on the verge of approaching Ardsley and offering for your hand when your father's death annihilated all his plans. Now, given the circumstances, he's allowing you time before he recommences his plan to escort you down the aisle."

"Quentin, this is madness. Father respected Desmond. _I_ respect Desmond. I even care for him—as a long-standing family friend. But I could never, would never . . ."

"It appears he believes otherwise." Relief flooded through Quentin in great waves, accompanied by a very powerful, very personal elation he wished weren't quite so pronounced.

"What shall I do?"

"I have no answer." Recalling Desmond's appraisal of Brandi's needs, Quentin forced himself to be frank, to give voice to what Desmond truly could offer her. "He does care for you, Sunbeam. And, despite all your differences, you know you can count on him to remain at Colverton, beside you, with no conflicting obligations to tear him away."

"So that's what this is about." Pain and hurt flickered in Brandi's dark eyes before her lashes descended, veiling her feelings from view. "The two of you are sitting about at Colverton, discussing poor, pathetic Brandi and how someone must remain in the Cotswolds to take care of her lest she fall to pieces. And, since your position in the army precludes you from assuming the bothersome responsibility, Desmond is the next best choice, right?"

"No, Sunbeam, not right." Leaning forward, Quentin grasped Brandi's chin, forcing her to meet his gaze. "My God," he breathed, seeing the humiliated anguish on her face. "How could you presume such a thing? Do you honestly, for one minute, believe I wish for you to be Desmond's bride? Why do you think I brought the subject up: because I applaud the thought of you and my shallow, self-centered, and—to quote your words of four years past—relic of a brother having a life together? Hardly. To be blunt, I believe you're all wrong for each other. I believe Desmond would crush your spirit and leave you empty. I believe he'd be oblivious to your beauty and resentful of your uniqueness. I believe you deserve far more from a husband than Desmond could ever offer, despite his ability to remain constant in your life."

Brandi blinked, temporarily distracted by Quentin's unprecedented verbal assault. "I've never before heard you speak so harshly of Desmond. All these years—and the countless times—I ranted and raved about Desmond's archaic views, you never spoke thus. Oh, to be sure, I always knew where you stood, that you sympathized, even—to a certain extent—shared my exasperation. But you never expressed such a vehement condemnation of your brother, at least not to me."

"Nor to anyone else," Quentin clarified.

"Not even Bentley?" Brandi's eyes grew wide as saucers, her genuine wonder causing Quentin's surge of protective anger to dissipate.

"Why are you so surprised?" A corner of his mouth lifted at the indisputable reality. "You always have had a baffling ability to elicit the raw truth from me."

"I believe, my lord, that some call that particular quality honesty."

A rich chuckle. "So they do. But for a man who's been trained to supplant candor with diplomacy, I find it a continual source of amazement that only you can reach behind the mask of discretion I show the world."

Desperately, Brandi tried to conceal the elation his admission invoked in her heart. "I'm glad," she stated simply. Another thought distracted her. "Quentin, if you feel so strongly about Desmond's and my incompatibility, why didn't you say so sooner?"

"Because, Sunbeam, as much as I take exception to your sharing a future with my brother, 'tis your opinion—and ultimately your wishes—that count, not mine. Thus, I vowed not to give voice to my sentiments until I was certain you had no interest in spending your life with Desmond."

Joy and gratitude illuminated Brandi's face. "Thank you for that." She covered Quentin's hand with her own. "Not only for understanding what is best for me, but—even more important—for allowing me a say in my own future." She stared at their joined hands, her mind consumed with the information Quentin had just imparted. "How could Desmond come to such a groundless conclusion?" she murmured, half to herself. "Dear Lord, I scarcely even speak to the man for fear of revealing how wrong is his belief that I've somehow radically changed. 'Tis easier to let him perceive me as the mature woman he envisions than to risk arousing his wrath by confessing that I'm the same hoyden I was in my teens, only older. In fact, to be perfectly candid—with the exception of the past fortnight—I avoided him as best I could. Not a difficult task since I was customarily with Pamela at Emerald Manor, while he was immersed in the task of becoming the fine businessman Kenton always wished him to be." Brandi shook her head incredulously. "Marriage . . ."

"I didn't mean to upset you, Sunbeam."

"To upset me?" Dawning awareness made Brandi's chin come up. "Is that why you didn't tell me of Desmond's intentions immediately—to avoid upsetting me?"

"I told you why I remained silent."

"To allow me the privilege of determining my own future."

"Yes."

"No."

Quentin's dark brows arched. "No?"

"No. That is only a reason to stifle your opinion, not to conceal the facts." Her small jaw set, Brandi rushed on before Quentin could reply. "This is my life, my future, we're discussing—not some tidbit of gossip you chose to squelch. And while I understand—and appreciate—your resolution to let me plot my own course, how could I do so when Desmond had already completed the task?"

"Touché, little hoyden." Quentin nodded, pride shining in his eyes. "You're quite right. I should have told you sooner."

"Exactly when did you intend to tell me, directly after Desmond's proposal—as you caught me in a dead swoon?"

Quentin grinned at her dramatic description. "I think I would have intruded a bit before that."

Brandi was on the verge of blurting out a defensive comeback when a sudden—and distinctly unpleasant—possibility struck her. "Quentin . . ." She frowned. "I've leaned heavily—perhaps *too* heavily—on Desmond since

Papa died. Could my actions have misled him? Could he have interpreted my behavior as romantically suggestive?"

"You are never suggestive, Brandi," Quentin countered. "You're forthright and direct. If you had any amorous feelings for Desmond, you'd never disguise them as dependency or friendship. So put that nonsensical notion from your head." He paused. "As for Desmond's perceptions, however—now that is another situation entirely. I've never understood the way my brother's mind works. He has a tendency to interpret things as he chooses to: my mother's fictitious dislike of him, my own supposed vying for Father's affection, even Father's alleged approval of his business practices."

For a fleeting instant, Quentin wondered if Brandi would take exception to the last, given her erroneous belief that Desmond excelled in business matters. But her preoccupation indicated that she was too absorbed in the issue at hand to grasp his pointed comment.

"Evidently, Sunbeam," he concluded, "Desmond's misconceptions extend to you—and the future he believes you wish to share with him."

Brandi snapped to action, gathering up her sodden skirts. "I must set him right. Immediately."

"Don't, sweetheart." Quentin stayed her progress with his hand. "According to Bentley, Desmond wasn't feeling well and took to his chambers early last night. He could, quite possibly, still be abed."

She paused. "Then I'll ride to Colverton and await his emergence," she determined, starting to come to her feet.

"Brandi." Quentin tugged her back to the bank. "I don't think that's the best solution."

Her expression was an enchanting combination of annoyance and amazement. "You don't think I should inform Desmond that I have no intentions—now or ever—of wedding him?"

"Oh, no. I definitely think you should tell him."

"Then why oughtn't I ride to Colverton?"

"First, because you're drenched and covered with mud—a sure indication you've been frolicking in the stream. I don't think Desmond would find that notion appealing."

Brandi's face fell. "I'd be lectured for a week."

"Um-hum." Quentin fought his grin. "Possibly two weeks, if Desmond is especially testy, given the fact that he's not feeling up to snuff. Second, as his indisposed state grants us time, why not use it to plan the best, most prudent approach? One that will achieve the desired results and yield the minimal bitterness? He is, after all, your guardian. Infuriating him would only serve to make your life hell."

Grudgingly, Brandi resettled herself. "I see England's most accomplished diplomat has returned," she muttered under her breath. "So much for my free-spirited fishing rival."

Quentin couldn't suppress a chuckle. "Fear not, Sunbeam. One trait does not preclude the other. I assure you, both aspects of me remain."

Brandi tossed him a skeptical look and tucked her legs beneath her. "If you say so."

Her dejected look and mournful tone were too much to withstand. "Did I say forthright and direct?" Quentin laughed. "I meant transparent." Impulsively, he tugged her to him. "I won't abandon my more spontaneous side. I promise." His hand slid beneath her damp burnished mane to stroke her nape.

An innocent caress, manifested countless times. But never before yielding such soul-shattering results.

Gasping softly, Brandi stared up at him, wide-eyed, stunned by the bone-melting sensations that surged instantly to life. It was just as it had been when they kissed: the tightness in her chest, the swooping feeling in her belly, and the liquid heat that coursed through her, sliding down to her feet in a scalding waterfall.

The universe vanished with the advent of his touch.

How can you not feel it, Quentin? she thought wonderingly, unconsciously moving her head from side to side, seeking more of the exquisite contact. *And, if you do feel it, how can you relegate it to nothingness?*

"Brandi." Quentin said her name—a harsh wisp of sound, a clash between longing and denial.

Refuting the denial, Brandi reached for the longing.

"Kiss me, Quentin." Her arms went around his neck even as she spoke, her lips softly brushing his. "Please."

"Sweetheart, we can't."

"Please." She knew she'd won, felt his fingers clench in her hair, and she reveled in the victory. "Please," she whispered again.

He groaned deep in his throat, taking her mouth with the same tender violence of a few hours past—an urgency Brandi found wildly exciting. She encouraged him, pressing closer, wishing she could show him, tell him, what his kisses did to her.

Maybe he knew.

His tongue stroked deep, withdrew, plunged again, his arms shaking as they crushed her to his chest. His mouth possessed hers, again and again, then moved recklessly to her neck, her throat, finding pleasure points she never knew existed and lavishing them with attention until wild jolts of excitement began to rush through her. Brandi shifted restlessly, drowning in a whirlpool of sensation, biting her lip to keep from crying out.

Quentin's palm left her nape, caressed her back, paused at the first hook—and relented. She held her breath as he unfastened it, slipping his fingers inside to caress the warm skin of her back. A shivering moan escaped her, and she clutched him tighter, wanting nothing but to soar higher, higher, to experience more of the exquisite sensations she knew she could only taste in Quentin's arms.

"Sunbeam," he rasped against her parted lips, "I'm going to . . ."

"I don't care."

"Brandi, you don't know what you're saying."

She could feel the cool ground beneath her back as he

eased her down. "Yes," she breathed, pushing his coat from his shoulders. "I do."

"Christ." He covered her with himself, devouring her mouth with a passion that stunned him more than it did her. The feel of her beneath him was the most intoxicatingly erotic sensation he'd every known. Damp, soft, undisguisedly impatient—God, how he wanted her. He wanted to take her here, now, to make her his in a way that would bind them forever. He wanted her just like this—beside the stream, amid the scented gardens of Emerald Manor, with nothing but the sky above them and the earth below.

He could never allow it.

Even as that warning reminder hammered in his head, Quentin was freeing his arms, casting his coat aside. "Brandi." He framed her face, kissed her again, losing himself in her beauty, her passion, the melting hunger in her fathomless dark eyes.

She whispered his name, arched closer to the promise offered by his powerful body. "Show me more," she managed. "Please."

"I want to show you the stars," he murmured, burying his face in the soft cloud of her hair. "But, Sunbeam . . ."

Vehemently, she shook her head, gripping him more tightly. "No. There are no *'but's.'*"

He smiled against her fragrant tresses. "Yes. There are."

"Damn that rigid control of yours, Captain Steel."

Her censure exploded like a bolt from the blue, as fervent as it was unexpected.

Laughter rumbled from Quentin's chest. He raised up, gazing into her flushed, furious face. "Sweetheart, you are the only person in the world who could make me laugh at a time like this."

"I don't find that to be a compliment."

An odd emotion darkened Quentin's hazel eyes. "I disagree. Too strongly, I'm afraid." Gently, he eased off her, brushing fresh clumps of dirt from her gown. "In fact, 'tis a compliment whose impact has the power to undo me."

Quentin broke off, not even trying to pretend the last few moments had never occurred. Brandi's ability to make him laugh had always been a miracle, one as rare and precious as her ability to permeate his veneer. But now, when melded with this newly discovered, bottomless passion that blazed between them, those qualities were acutely dangerous.

Rigid control, she'd said.

Hardly.

If she only knew how very little it would take to shatter that notoriously rigid control.

"How does a picnic lunch sound?" he proposed, an undisguised attempt to diffuse the sparks still shimmering between them. "I don't know about you, but our zealous fishing competition has left me ravenous. Why don't I ask Mrs. Collins to prepare a basket for us and we can eat in the garden?"

Brandi didn't answer immediately. Instead, she scrutinized Quentin's face, her insightful gaze probing beneath the facade they both knew was feigned. She'd always been able to see into his soul. Now was no exception. And her heart leaped at what she beheld.

He was as affected as she. But he was fighting it—for all the reasons he'd provided her earlier.

Prudent reasons.

Protective reasons.

Meaningless reasons.

So be it. Patience, Bentley had advised her. Very well then, she would try, after twenty years, to acquire some of that elusive quality.

It wasn't going to be easy.

But it was going to be worth it.

Smiling, she came gracefully to her feet. "A picnic sounds heavenly."

Chapter 8

"I'll never eat another morsel." With a sated moan, Brandi lay back on the blanket, arms overhead, eyes closed.

"Ah, but will you drink?" Quentin teased, capturing the empty glass from her hand.

One eye opened. "I'll consider it."

Quentin chuckled, refilling her goblet and waving it beneath her nose.

"Very well." The eye closed once more. "Maybe I will drink. But I *won't* eat. And I'll definitely never move."

Her final assertion made Quentin throw back his head in laughter. "Now why don't I believe that?" he asked wryly, nudging her until she opened her eyes and accepted the proffered goblet. "The idea of your remaining still is like envisioning the tide forever motionless on shore."

Brandi propped herself up on her elbows and gulped her wine with great enthusiasm. "That is, of course, unless the tide has eaten as much as I," she countered, her tongue capturing a few stray drops of the sweet inebriant from her lower lip. "In which case, I fear it is doomed to spend all its days on the sand." With a sigh, she resumed her reclining position. "I feel so content," she murmured, staring dreamily up at the sky. "Almost as if the horrors of the past fortnight were all some monstrous, fictional nightmare."

Sobering, Quentin nodded, gazing about the lush, euphoric gardens of Emerald Manor. He understood—and shared—Brandi's need to lose herself in this paradise of a sanctuary. The pain beyond it was too acute to bear. "We agreed to give Hendrick a day or two before we dashed off to Townsbourne to examine your father's papers," he commented aloud, as much a reminder to himself as it was to her. "In the interim, I think it would do us good to keep reality at bay—if only for today."

Brandi turned her head, giving Quentin a lost, heart-wrenching look. "The entire world has tilted askew," she whispered.

"Only temporarily, sweetheart." Quentin's knuckles grazed her cheek. "We'll soon set it right—I promise. But for now, let's just enjoy the beauty of Emerald Manor. Our parents would want no less."

A myriad emotions darkened Brandi's eyes: tenderness, loss, hope, gratitude, faith . . . and something far deeper, something that triggered an answering response in Quentin's chest.

His knuckles paused, lingered, then withdrew. "Suppose we talk about Desmond now," he suggested lightly.

"That's keeping reality at bay?" Brandi grimaced, sounding as enthused as if he'd proposed discussing next Season's ball gowns.

"I suppose not." With a surge of relief, Quentin welcomed her Brandi-like reply—a much-needed balm for his unsettled senses. "Nonetheless, we have yet to determine your best course of action with regard to my brother's intentions."

"I don't see any choice but the obvious." Sitting up, Brandi hugged her knees, a mutinous expression on her face. "I must tell Desmond the truth." She paused, accosted by a pang of guilt as she realized the harshness of her words. "'Tis not that I mean to be ungrateful," she explained. "Heaven only knows how I would have survived the past fortnight without Desmond's kindness. He's been by my side since Papa died, and I'll never forget that." Brandi's chin lifted a notch, renewed conviction swelling to life. "But my gratitude does not extend beyond friendship, nor does it grant Desmond an implicit right to my hand. Further, I cannot permit him to delude himself about my feelings— 'twould be crueler than telling him the truth." She gave an emphatic shake of her head. "No, Quentin, I see no alternative. I must ride to Colverton and inform Desmond in a gentle but straightforward manner that a marriage between us is a veritable impossibility."

A hint of amusement lurked in Quentin's eyes. "A most direct approach."

"One that, judging from your tone, you deem a mistake."

"Not a mistake, Sunbeam, only an extreme. An extreme that would doubtless yield unpleasant consequences."

"What consequences? Desmond's anger? I've aroused it more times in twenty years than I'd care to count. Once more will hardly matter." Brandi inclined her head, her brows drawn in puzzlement. "I won't be tactless, if that's what's concerning you. I'd never hurt Desmond—not after everything he's done for me. But, after all, it isn't as if the man is in love with—" Abruptly, she broke off, her eyes widening with startled disbelief. "Quentin, you're not implying that my rejection would devastate Desmond, are you? You don't truly believe his feelings for me run that deep?"

Quentin stared contemplatively at the ground, strangely moved, though unsurprised, by Brandi's concern for Desmond—a man totally incapable of recognizing or appreciating her radiance. "Frankly?" he answered, plucking a blade of grass from alongside their blanket. "No. I don't believe Desmond's feelings for *anyone* run that deep. But, I do believe he feels a tremendous sense of responsibility toward ensuring your future—the right future."

"The right future," Brandi repeated woodenly. "Pianoforte-playing and needlepoint."

Quentin's lips twitched. "I was thinking more of security and stability." Taking in Brandi's look of utter distaste, he couldn't resist teasing her. "Am I to assume then that four years have yielded no improvement in your pianoforte-playing and needlepoint skills?"

"Not even a glimmer." One slender brow arched. "Does that surprise you?"

"Not even a glimmer."

They dissolved into simultaneous laughter.

"I can't understand it, Quentin," Brandi pondered aloud, her amusement fading. "Responsibility notwithstanding, Desmond doesn't even *like* me. As a wife, I'd be more trouble to him than joy. Moreover, he's handsome, wealthy—a duke nonetheless—who could have his pick of brides. Why would he wish to wed me?"

"You're a beautiful woman, Sunbeam," Quentin replied, a husky note in his voice. "You're also vibrant, intelligent, and totally without artifice."

"All qualities Desmond loathes, with the exception of the first. And, in this case, even that is questionable since, based on what Desmond deems beautiful, I am severely lacking. I have no interest in jewels, nor do I understand why ladies covet and don them so lavishly. My hair is never dressed, for I can't sit still long enough to have it arranged. My gowns are *passé*, since I haven't the patience for Pamela's *modiste* to finish her fittings. Not to mention I loathe wearing rouge, retch at the sickeningly sweet scent of lotions, and feel a far greater revulsion at being confined indoors than I do at viewing the freckles I've acquired frolicking in the sun. Combine all that with my forthright manner, my dread for the London Season, and my unladylike pursuits, and I should think I'd send Desmond running in the opposite direction."

"My brother is a fool."

The proclamation was out before Quentin realized he'd spoken, its fervor slashing the air like a whip. He was livid—and he had no idea why. All he knew was that, rather than amusement, Brandi's enchantingly accurate self-assessment had aroused a fierce, almost irrational possessiveness inside him. "Desmond will never fathom your beauty. He's incapable of it."

Brandi blinked at the vehemence of Quentin's tone. "You're angry. Why?"

"Because I know Desmond. He would use your marriage as an opportunity to reform you, to convert you to the proper lady he believes you should be. And that would kill me."

"As it would me." Brandi's heart lurched with joy at Quentin's uncharacteristically emotional outburst. "Which is why I want to tell him the truth," she added, wisely keeping her observation to herself.

"Desmond does not take rejection well, Brandi. I worry at his reaction."

"'Tis impossible to reject a man you've never selected."

"In Desmond's case, a perceived rejection is the same as an actual one." Quentin scowled at the memories. "Believe me, I know that firsthand."

"You're not thinking of yourself. You're thinking of Pamela."

Quentin's head snapped up. "Did Mother discuss Desmond with you?" he asked in surprise.

"Not in the way you mean, no. She never complained about his refusal to acknowledge her as Kenton's wife. Quite the opposite, in fact. Pamela defended Desmond's loyalty to his own mother's memory. But I'd see the sadness in her eyes after each of her countless, unsuccessful attempts to reach him. On those days, she'd immerse herself in Emerald Manor, digging in the garden until long after the sun had set." Brandi's voice choked. "Pamela had the most extraordinary heart. She adored Kenton, and, needless to say, you—the son born of their union. Yet she had more than enough love left over for me and, most importantly, for Kenton's firstborn. She tried so desperately to love Desmond. But it just wasn't in his nature to let her."

Pain lanced through Quentin like a knife. "No. It wasn't."

"Pamela came to accept that reality." Instinctively, Brandi offered Quentin the solace he craved. "Thanks to you and Kenton, she always knew she was cherished. As a result, she felt truly blessed." An aching smile. "As she blessed us in return."

Slowly, Quentin shook his head, his expression filled with wonder. "You never fail to astound me, Sunbeam. Your insight is staggering."

Brandi's gaze was solemn. "I don't know why that stuns you so. I may be unsophisticated, even immature for my age. But I'm not stupid. Nor am I a child."

"You're neither childish, immature, nor stupid. Unsophisticated? Yes, and thank God for it. I don't think I could bear seeing you tainted by the world's ugliness. Never change, Sunbeam."

"You make me sound like a fragile doll that must be kept on a shelf, untouched and unscathed. I'm not a doll, Quentin. I'm a woman." She considered her description, then modified it a bit. "An unruly one, I admit, but a woman nonetheless. I understand pain and hurt and love. And I recognize them when I see them. Better, it would seem, than some."

"So I'm learning." Quentin swallowed past the odd constriction in his chest. "And your tender heart is all the more reason why I want you to tread very carefully during your chat with Desmond. I don't want him to retaliate."

"You keep using words like *retaliate* and *consequences*. What is it you fear Desmond might do?"

"Knowing my brother, he could decide to reverse your decision for you."

Brandi paled. "He'd force me to wed him?"

"If he were infuriated by your refusal and convinced that your decision was final, yes. Either that or marry you off to an equally unappealing substitute—all for your own good, of course."

"He can't order me down the aisle."

"Yes, sweetheart, he can. As your guardian, he has every right."

"Oh my God, I never thought of that." Brandi wet her lips anxiously. "Quentin, what shall I do?"

"Stall for time." Quentin had to fight the urge to reach for her, to enfold her in his arms and offer her himself, along with all the promises she deserved and which he could never keep. "Spend as little time in Desmond's company as you can, and avoid all mention of the future. He won't press you—at least not for a long while. He knows how deeply you're grieving. I'll make certain to emphasize that fact each time we speak. However, should he surprise us and broach the subject of marriage, tell him you can't think clearly—not until the murders are resolved and you've had time to mourn our parents."

"And then?"

"Then let time pass. By next Season, you'll be one and twenty. At which point, Desmond can no longer force you to marry against your will."

Relief swept through Brandi in great waves. "That's right. Quentin, you're a genius."

He dipped his head in a mock bow. "At your service, my lady." Straightening, he seized the bottle of wine, his lighthearted humor restored. "Shall we toast my superior intelligence?"

"Oh, indeed we shall." Brandi held out her glass, feeling reckless and giddy with pleasure. "Several times, in fact. And then we must eat Mrs. Collins's superb dessert."

"You've recovered your appetite, I presume?"

An impish grin. "'Tis necessary, if I intend to remain champion of our fishing matches. How else would I gain enough energy to jostle so many trout free of your line?"

Rich, incredulous laughter erupted from Quentin's chest, spanning Emerald Manor's renewing gardens.

Several hours later, having just finished her second slice of pie, Brandi blinked in the direction of the fiery western horizon. "What time is it anyway?" she asked, licking flaky crumbs from her fingertips.

"Judging from the position of the sun, I should say it's close to five o'clock," Quentin replied absently. He was absorbed in watching her, wondering when he'd ever seen anything as innocently erotic as Brandi's tongue gliding delicately over her fingertips. His loins tightened with each exquisite motion, and he had to physically restrain himself from dragging her into his arms.

His attraction was fast becoming a compulsion.

"Five o'clock?" Brandi's forefinger paused en route to her mouth, her tongue trailing the inside of her lower lip. "When did that happen?"

Quentin relented. Giving in to the need to touch her—however minimally—he smoothed her tousled hair from her brow . . . an infinitely safer gesture than the one he craved. "It happened while we were sprawled on this sun-drenched blanket, in this beautiful garden, unceremoniously gorging ourselves on cold chicken, warm scones, sliced fruit, strawberry pie, and a continuous flow of wine. Somewhere during that time, the sun reached its zenith and began its westward journey for a soon-to-arrive evening descent."

"Um." Brandi resumed her nibbling. "In that case, let's watch it set from our blanket. I'm far too sated to move."

"'Tis a shame you feel so lethargic." Quentin's mind was racing, acutely aware that to remain here much longer would tax his will beyond endurance. "I was about to suggest an afternoon ride. A *late* afternoon ride," he amended. "I was even feeling good-natured enough to offer Poseidon as your mount. But I suppose that's impossible, given your inability to move."

"Nothing is impossible." Brandi was on her feet before Quentin had completed his offer. "I'm ready."

A hearty chuckle rumbled from his chest. "That was the swiftest recovery I've ever seen." His gaze drifted downward. "'Tis a pity your gown cannot make the same claim. Despite the fact that it has dried, I fear it is beyond redemption."

Brandi glanced at herself, then rolled her eyes to the heavens. "Do you see why I need breeches?"

"I do. And you shall have them."

"After which you'll no longer have any hope of beating me when I'm astride Poseidon."

"A sobering thought. It appears, then, that I'd better make the most of today—my final opportunity to best you while you remain encumbered by layers of muslin. Horribly rumpled layers of muslin," he added, grinning. "But I won't be a complete cad. I'll wait while you change into a riding habit."

"Only to ruin it? No, thank you for your magnanimous offer, but I'll remain in this shredded garment. It couldn't deteriorate any further than it already has."

The next few hours proved her wrong.

Amid sharp-tongued banter, Quentin and Brandi toppled into the stables at half after six—filthy, wind-blown, and more than ready to return their mounts.

"Frederick?" Brandi called. "We're back."

The stableboy hurried out, then halted in his tracks, gaping. "M'lady, what happened? Are ye all right?"

"Oh, she's fine, Frederick," Quentin assured him dryly. "'Tis only her gown that's ailing. I, on the other hand, have been brutalized."

Frederick's stunned gaze shifted to the scratches on Quentin's face and brow. "Poseidon threw ye, m'lord?" he managed, assessing Quentin's torn coat and berry-stained breeches.

"Quentin didn't ride Poseidon," Brandi corrected, stifling a giggle. "I did."

Frederick leaned weakly against the stable door. "Goddess did that to ye, sir?"

"No, Goddess did not do this to me. Brandi's bloody aristocratic assassin of a cohort did this to me."

"I don't understand, m'lord."

"Lancelot is not an assassin," Brandi countered. "He's just loyal."

"Loyal? That furry, quizzing-glassed beast is as devious as any of Newgate's criminals. He specifically waited for me to pass under his tree, then blinded me with those damnable berries of his. And then, as if that weren't enough, he pounced upon me like a tiger, scratching my face and covering my eyes with his unwieldy tail until I smashed headlong into a branch and crashed to the ground."

Brandi's eyes danced. "He prefers that I win."

"Well, he certainly ensured that you did, didn't he? I couldn't very well cross the finish line lying facedown in the dirt."

"I don't know why you're so irritated. I'm as filthy as you are and spent nearly as much time in the dirt. In truth, I deserve your thanks, not your annoyance. After all, *you* had no choice with regard to your undignified disarray. While *I*, on the other hand, willingly embraced the dusty ground, nearly toppling off Poseidon in my haste to dismount and rush to your side. And why? For the purely selfless purpose of ensuring you were unharmed."

"How magnanimous of you." Quentin arched a sardonic brow. "But tell me. Why is it that you came to my rescue only *after* you'd completed the race—and won?"

An exasperated sigh. "Very well, would you feel better if I conceded my victory?"

"No." Quentin shot her a disgruntled look. "I would not. I'd feel better if that wretched creature found himself a new home."

"Are you admitting you were bested by a squirrel, Captain Steel?"

"Tread carefully, Sunbeam," he warned, wincing as he touched the gash on his jaw. "I'm not feeling at all congenial right now."

Frederick cleared his throat. "Pardon me, m'lord. Shall I relieve you of Goddess and Poseidon?"

"I'd prefer you relieve me of Brandi's pet," Quentin

retorted. "But, since he has long since fled into the oak's concealing branches, the odds of accomplishing that are nil. Therefore, very well, Frederick. Take the horses."

"Yes, sir." Frederick complied, looking suspiciously like he was smothering a chuckle.

"Come, Quentin." Brandi seized his arm. "I'll tend to those scratches." She leaned toward him, a conspiratorial forefinger pressed to her lips. "And fear not. Your secret is safe with me. No one will ever know you were undone by a rodent."

"That's it." He lunged for her.

Anticipating his response, Brandi was already in motion. Choking back laughter, she flung open the barn door and tore across the dusky lawn in a halfhearted attempt to escape.

Quentin caught up with her near the gazebo, grasping her waist and tumbling them both to the ground. He rolled Brandi to her back, looming over her like a vengeful god.

"Are you finished enjoying yourself at my expense, little hoyden?" he demanded.

"Never." She smiled up at him, undaunted by his mock fury. Abruptly, her smile faded as a thin stream of blood trickled down the side of his face. "You really are hurt," she murmured, gently touching his jaw. "I had no idea it was this bad."

"It isn't." His gaze fell to her lips. "But thank you for caring."

"I care," she whispered. "Oh, Quentin, I care so much."

Quentin's breath lodged in his throat, and helplessly he felt his defenses topple.

When they'd plummeted beyond his reach, he lowered his head.

Brandi raised hers.

Their lips met, parted, then met again in an exquisitely poignant, sensual caress—velvety soft, infinitely gentle. Possessing none of the urgency of their earlier encounters, this kiss was slow, deep, tender.

Terrifying.

Quentin gathered Brandi closer, sealing her mouth with his. He threaded his fingers through her glorious, disheveled hair, draping the burnished tresses about their shoulders, enfolding them in an intimate cocoon all their own. Twilight vanished, the gardens receded, and Quentin's heart thundered in his chest as his lips moved eloquently over Brandi's, conveying an emotion as vast and foreign as the impact of that which he could no longer deny.

With a whisper of a sigh, Brandi's arms stole around Quentin's neck, entwining tightly, wordlessly telling him that she felt as he did—yet with none of the apprehension, none of the clamoring reservations that gnawed at Quentin's soul.

His terror intensified.

"Sunbeam, I have to let you go," he breathed against her lips.

"No. You don't."

He raised his head. "Yes," he countered gravely, his hazel eyes darkening to a deep smoky gray. "I do."

Rolling away, Quentin gently eased Brandi to a sitting position. "The sun has set. I'd best get you back to the cottage."

"Quentin . . ."

"Don't, Sunbeam." He shook his head, lifting her hand to kiss its soft palm. "Some things are best left unsaid."

"I can't go back," she whispered, tears shimmering on her lashes.

"'Tis late. You must."

"I wasn't referring to the house. I was referring to us."

"I know you were." Slowly, Quentin came to his feet, feeling tired and drained and strangely empty. "Come, sweetheart. We don't want Mrs. Collins to worry."

Brandi rose, fighting back tears, wondering why she felt more bereft now than ever. She gazed at Quentin, her fingers reflexively going to his jaw. "At least let me treat your scrapes before you leave."

He nodded, aching at the raw pain he saw on her face—pain he could do nothing to alleviate.

Silently, they walked toward the cottage.

Halfway, Brandi came to an abrupt halt, two tears sliding down her cheeks.

"Why do I feel like I've lost you?" she asked in a tiny voice.

"You haven't." He pressed her head to his chest, feeling her arms steal around his waist, closing his eyes against the rightness of holding her. "You never will—not so long as it's in my power to decide."

"Oh, Quentin, I . . ."

"Well, here you are. Knowing the two of you, I should have searched the gardens before even visiting the cottage."

Over Brandi's head, Quentin met his brother's irritated gaze.

"Hello, Desmond. I had no idea you'd be looking for us."

"Clearly not." Desmond walked over, laying his hand on Brandi's shoulder and pivoting her around to face him. "Brandice?" He frowned at her soiled, tear-streaked face. "Are you all right?"

"Yes, I'm fine—just a bit overwrought." She dashed the tears from her cheeks, staring dazedly at Desmond as she attempted to right herself and, at the same time, to assess the extent of Desmond's anger.

"This was a difficult day for Brandi." Quentin's quiet voice penetrated her fog. "I didn't want her to be by herself."

Brandi understood Quentin's message as clearly as if he had spoken it aloud. He was reminding her that, based upon their long-standing friendship, it would appear to Desmond as if he had interrupted merely an act of comfort. Brandi had only to reinforce that assumption.

"I haven't yet adjusted to the fact that the carriage accident was, in fact, intentional," she heard herself say. "Quentin has been patiently trying to reconcile me to the monstrous truth."

Desmond nodded, frowning as he scrutinized her tousled

appearance. "What happened to your clothing?" He cast a sidelong look at his brother. "And yours as well?"

Brandi glanced uneasily at Quentin.

"We went riding," Quentin supplied smoothly. "Brandi's squirrel was frolicking about, causing us both to take a spill. It looks far worse than it is."

"I see." Desmond's frown didn't subside, and he looked but the slightest bit mollified. "Well, minor or not, the fall has rendered you both rather the worse for wear. Quentin, your face is bleeding. And Brandice, your gown . . ." He broke off, indicating by a harsh shake of his head that her disheveled state defied description.

"I was on the verge of treating Quentin's scrapes," she inserted swiftly. "After which, I fully intended to change my gown."

"'Tis a bit late in the day to go careening through the woods on horseback, is it not?" Desmond inquired with unconcealed disapproval. "The sun has already set."

"It was quite visible when we commenced," Brandi countered, feeling that all-too-familiar resentment kindle inside her. "Moreover, I didn't notice the time. I was too eager to take my mind off the unbearable reality that someone killed our parents."

Desmond's demeanor softened slightly. "Still, little one, you shouldn't be galloping about in the dark. You could get hurt. I'd prefer you limit your riding to those hours when the sun is high."

Brandi was on the verge of retorting when she felt Quentin's gentle nudge from behind.

Squeezing her lips tightly shut, she maintained her silence.

"Desmond, Bentley mentioned you weren't feeling well last night," Quentin interceded, both to change the subject and to determine if his brother were suffering from the aftermath of his drinking bout. "Are you better today?"

"Significantly better, thank you." Desmond stiffened, his expression guarded. "I feel very much myself."

"I'm glad to hear that." After careful assessment, Quentin concluded that not only was Desmond suffering no ill effects from the previous day, he was also, for the moment, quite sober. His speech was unslurred, his black eyes alert and clear. More than clear, Quentin mused. Positively glittering. In fact, for a man who'd just last night been drowning his anguish in liquor, Desmond appeared surprisingly lighthearted.

"Did you spend the day abed?" Quentin probed.

"No. I spent the day in London." Desmond paused. "With Hendrick."

"Hendrick?" Brandi leaped on the name, stepping forward to grip Desmond's forearms. "Has he pored through Papa's file? Did he find anything that could help us ferret out the murderer?"

Desmond's head snapped up and, over Brandi's head, his eyes narrowed questioningly on Quentin.

"I recounted the details of my meeting to Brandi," Quentin replied.

"How accommodating of you." Desmond's tone emanated pointed sarcasm.

"I presume Hendrick filled you in as well?"

"He did. But it would have been nice to have heard the specifics from my brother. Tell me, Quentin, did it occur to you to afford me the same consideration you did Brandice?"

Quentin made an exasperated sound. "Desmond, you were abed when I returned home last night and when I took my leave this morning. Had you been up and about, I assure you I would have discussed the situation with you first. Besides, what difference does it make who I spoke with first? We all need to know the status of the investigation. Now tell me, did Hendrick finish perusing Ardsley's file? Is that why he sent for you?"

"He did and it was."

"And?"

"And—nothing. Ardsley's papers are as devoid of clues as Father's were." Desmond folded his arms across his chest. "It appears this avenue has reached its end."

"Damn it." Quentin raked baffled fingers through his hair. "I truly hoped . . ."

"Hoped what? That Father's murderer had left explicit evidence of his crime in glaring view of our family solicitor? Honestly, Quentin, doesn't that seem somewhat unlikely? Further, with all due respect to your brilliant mind, I would hardly describe you as a qualified investigator. Why not leave the matter to the authorities?"

A spark of anger ignited Quentin's eyes. "Because my mother and father died in that carriage. And if I can do anything to hasten the exposure of their murderer, I intend to—with or without your support."

A whip-taut silence ensued.

"Quentin." This time it was Brandi who interceded, physically inserting herself between the brothers. "That cut on your jaw is bleeding badly. Let's go inside so I can treat it." She turned to Desmond. "I'll ask Mrs. Collins to make some tea. After I've tended to Quentin's bruises, I'll change my gown and we can discuss our next course of action."

"Our next course of action?" Desmond positively bristled, his lips thinning into a line of stunned censure. "Brandice, you're a delicate young woman. You have no place in resolving this ugly and dangerous matter. Quentin and I will address the issue later, back at Colverton."

Brandi sucked in her breath, reminded, yet again, that she and Desmond were worlds apart. To even attempt to span the unbridgeable gap between them would be utterly futile. "I don't want to argue," she demurred quietly. "We've already endured enough hardship. Let's not worsen it by bickering." Gathering up her soiled skirts, she headed toward the cottage.

With a flicker of pride, Quentin watched her retreating back. Then he gestured to his brother. "Come. Let's get Brandi settled before we head back to Colverton."

"Agreed."

The two men entered the cottage just as Brandi finished speaking with Mrs. Collins. The buxom housekeeper dropped a quick curtsy. "Your Grace. Lord Quentin." She frowned as she saw the blood on Quentin's face. "Are you badly hurt, my lord?"

"Only my pride, Mrs. Collins."

A motherly smile. "Your refreshments will be served directly. In the meantime, I'll fetch a basin of water and a clean cloth so Miss Brandi can tend to your wounds."

Quentin grinned at the housekeeper's choice of words. "There's no hurry, Mrs. Collins. My 'wounds' can hardly be described as such. They're mere cuts and scrapes."

"Nevertheless, they must be treated. I'll bring the necessary items to the sitting room." With a no-nonsense expression, she swept off.

"I could grow spoiled from such tender ministrations," Quentin teased Brandi a few minutes later, turning his face so she could apply the compress to his jaw. "First Mrs. Collins and now you." He settled himself comfortably on the plush Chippendale settee, watching Brandi from beneath hooded lids as she worked her magic.

Across the room, the sideboard banged open, and Quentin winced, recognizing the angry clinking of glassware as a sure indicator that Desmond was on the verge of another drinking bout. The question was, what had incited it? Was it the frustration and grief dredged up during his meeting with Hendrick, or was it simply fury at discovering Brandi in her current disheveled state?

Oblivious to both Quentin's reflections and Desmond's display of irritation, Brandi knelt on the Persian rug, brow furrowed in concentration. Gently, she washed the bloodstains from Quentin's face, frowning as she reached the most severe of his gashes. "A sharp branch must have slashed across your jaw to cause so deep a tear," she murmured, dabbing at the surrounding area. She paused, withdrawing the cloth just long enough to rinse it in the basin Mrs. Collins had supplied. "This will undoubtedly sting," she warned. "I'm sorry, Quentin. I'll be as brief as I can. Just try to endure it."

"I'll try."

"No matter how much it smarts, you must remain still if I'm to properly cleanse the injury."

Quentin had to bite back his smile. She sounded so bloody earnest and so worried about causing him pain. "I understand," he replied solemnly. "And I'll do my best not to move."

Brandi nodded, frowning anxiously. "Now, tell me if I hurt you." She leaned forward, the compress hovering over the ugly laceration.

"I'll call out—if I'm able." Quentin's lips twitched. "But what concerns me is, what if I should swoon before managing to gasp out my agony?"

Her patient's amusement finally registered, and Brandi sat back on her heels, lips pursed, as she met Quentin's playful gaze. "Are you mocking me, Captain Steel?"

"Never." He grinned. "I'm just unused to such compassionate treatment—and for so undeserving a wound."

Abruptly, Brandi realized how ludicrous Quentin must find her doting after the horrors he'd witnessed at war. "How dimwitted of me. You're right—'tis only a cut. I'm being foolish."

"No, Sunbeam, you're being you." He covered her hand with his and urged the cloth to his face. "Pray continue. I could grow accustomed to so delicate a touch."

Amusement curved Brandi's lips. "Does that mean I surpass the army in my healing skills?"

"Indeed. You are by far the most proficient and compassionate of physicians, not to mention the loveliest." He tugged a lock of her hair. "But I do think you can stop worrying. I promise to survive the ordeal."

"Without swooning, Captain?"

"Or thrashing about," he assured her.

"Pity." Brandi's eyes glinted with humor. "Now I'll have to amend the delicious tidbit of gossip I intended to submit to the *Morning Post*. And I so looked forward to seeing it posted in the dailies. Envision this . . ." She made a grand sweep with her arm. "'Lord Quentin Steel, hero of the

Napoleonic Wars, was overtaken by a ferocious red squirrel and sustained minor injuries which, when treated, reduced the Duke of Wellington's most prominent officer to a dead faint.' That would have done wonders for your reputation. Ah, well. The initial part will have to suffice."

A hearty chuckle vibrated in Quentin's chest. "That razor-sharp tongue of yours has become even more barbed, if that's possible, little hoyden."

"Only with you, my lord," she returned, her expression rife with mischief. "No one challenges me quite as you do. How unfortunate that you have yet to outwit me."

"One day I'm going to call your bluff, Sunbeam. Then we'll see who outwits whom."

"I await that day with bated breath, Captain Steel." Brandi resumed her task, cleaning the dirt from his wound. "In the interim, however, stay still. And try not to swoon. Else I shall gleefully submit my original story—in its entirety—to the newspaper, thus dashing any hopes you might have of preserving even a shred of your soon-to-be-ravaged dignity."

Their eyes met and together they dissolved into spontaneous laughter.

"I'm delighted you're both enjoying yourselves so heartily," Desmond snapped, slamming down his goblet.

Simultaneously, Brandi and Quentin started, having totally forgotten Desmond's presence.

"I think your levity is somewhat misplaced," he continued, refilling his glass. "Brandice, I suggest you cease fussing over Quentin's insignificant injuries and change your gown before our refreshments arrive. After which, Quentin and I will take our leave so you can retire for the night and regain your strength."

Holding Brandi's gaze, Quentin gave a nearly imperceptible nod.

"All right." She rose, making her way across the room. "I won't be a minute."

The door closed behind her.

With a dark look at Quentin, Desmond tossed off his second brandy, then replenished it.

"Don't you think you've had enough?" Quentin asked pointedly.

"No. I don't." Desmond downed half the contents before swerving to face his brother. "I was under the impression we'd discussed your relationship with Brandice and had arrived at an understanding. Do you recall?"

"I do." Quentin folded his arms behind his head, assessing Desmond warily. "I also recall informing you that I had no intention of terminating my friendship with Brandi."

"Friendship? Is that what that little exchange was an example of?"

"What would you call it?"

"A prelude."

Quentin's eyes narrowed. "A prelude? To what?"

"Oh, come now, Quentin." Desmond took two deep swallows of brandy, weaving briefly as he slurred out the words. "You had y'r first woman when you were fourteen. There have been Lord knows how many since then. Surely, by now you've mastered the art of discerning the overt signs of attraction?" He held up his hand, counting off on his fingers. "Let's see, flushed cheeks, radiant smile, adoring eyes—all indications of desire, not companionship. Wouldn't y'agree?"

Quentin had to fight to keep from striking his brother. "If you're implying I'm trying to seduce Brandi, you've lost your mind."

"You don't have t'*try,* brother." With a hollow laugh, Desmond drained his goblet. "In Brandice's eyes, the sun rises and sets on you. As I think about it, she probably fancies herself in love with you. After all, you were her childhood idol. The man who taught her to behave like an undisciplined boy, rather than a lady. The man who encouraged her recklessness, refined her outrageous pursuits, then plunged in and shared them all with her. And then went away, thus immortalizing himself in her mind." Desmond bowed deeply, mockingly. "Now you've returned—the conquering hero—resurrecting all her childhood adoration, melding her worshipful feelings with her newly awakening womanhood." A sneer. "How very convenient for you."

"You're drunk, Desmond."

"Without a doubt. And you're lying—to yourself, and to Brandice. Tell me, Quentin, can you honestly claim you haven't noticed that your little Sunbeam has changed? Physically, in case you're wondering what I mean. That she's no longer sixteen, but a very grown, very beautiful woman?"

Silence.

"I see you *have* noticed, reluctant though y'might be to admit it. I admire your taste, and your exalted principles. The very principles that, given your high regard for Brandice, will preclude you from acting upon your baser instincts, no matter how ardently they clamor. Right, Quentin?"

Again, silence—taut, charged with escalating ire.

"V'ry well then." Recklessly, Desmond pressed onward, leaning against the sideboard for balance. "Address this, if you will. Chaste though your relationship might be, Brandice's dependence upon you has obviously been rekindled. Have you considered how you're going t'handle it when you leave her? What will you say—now that she's come t'count on your presence—when you abruptly dash off to wherever the army next orders you to go?"

"Shut up, Desmond." Quentin bolted to his feet, turning to stare out the window.

"Ah, a raw nerve. Well, good. Because you'd best recall one crucial reality before you fuel Brandice's infatuation." Desmond blasted his decree like gunfire, all attempts at discretion abandoned. "You are a fleeting visitor, dear brother. Whereas I am the foundation of Brandice's future. And, even if you should unintentionally manage to break her fragile heart, 'tis I who will restore its pieces; just as it is I who will eventually share her bed, gladly and for many years to come. Bear that in mind. For, regardless of your impact on her life, I intend to make Brandice my duchess. And that's one certainty that not even you, with your damned almighty control, can alter. So don't even try."

Quentin's fist slammed against the wall, and he wrenched around, shaking with a rage as unfamiliar as it was powerful. "To hell with your insipid threats, *brother*. I've withstood all I intend to of your drunken blathering." He advanced on Desmond, his eyes ablaze, every iota of his prior control cast aside. "Our discussion of Brandi is at an end. She's not a piece of chattel to be bandied about, nor a horse to be auctioned off to the highest bidder. You're her guardian, not her ruler. As to the idea of your becoming her husband—"

The sitting room door swung open, severing the remains of Quentin's declaration.

Eyes wide with astonishment, Brandi hovered in the doorway. "I could hear your voices halfway up the stairs!" she exclaimed. "What on earth are you arguing about?"

"Nothing." Desmond slapped down his goblet, moving unsteadily across the room, nearly colliding with Mrs. Collins as she arrived with their tray.

"I'm no longer hungry," he informed the startled housekeeper. "M'reover, as my brother has so aptly noted, I've had too much to drink. So I'll save you all from further disturbance by climbing into my carriage and heading back to Colverton."

Swerving, he faced Quentin. "You and I *will* continue this conversation upon your return tonight—a return which should take place . . ." Desmond blinked at his timepiece. "In less than an hour. 'Tis nearly eight o'clock. Brandice needs her rest." Purposefully, he seized Brandi's hand, brought it to his lips. "Good night, little one," he murmured, his seething gaze fixed on Quentin. "Soon the tragedy of the preceding fortnight will be behind us, and the past can be laid to rest." His jaw clenched. "And then I'll see to your future."

Chapter 9

"*W*hat in the name of heaven was that all about?" Brandi breathed, staring after Desmond's retreating figure.

"My contemptible brother's drunken ravings," Quentin snapped. He averted his head, rage still pumping hotly through his veins—rage aimed, not so much at Desmond as at himself.

What the hell had come over him just now? Had Brandi not appeared when she did, he would have trounced his brother—not only with words but, quite possibly, with his fists. As it was, he'd managed to provoke Desmond in the very manner he'd cautioned Brandi *not* to, all but denouncing the prospect of her becoming his duchess.

Quentin drew a deep steadying breath, then another. So much for the consummate diplomat and the unbreachable control for which he was renowned.

What had he been thinking of?

The answer was as obvious as the question. He hadn't been thinking at all. He'd simply been feeling.

"Damn it," he swore softly, veering toward the open sideboard. The idea of drowning himself in strong spirits seemed suddenly appealing.

"Forgive me, my lord." Mrs. Collins cleared her throat, awkwardly shifting from one foot to the other. "Shall I take away your refreshment?"

Belatedly, Quentin recalled the housekeeper's presence. "No." He turned, goblet in hand. "Or rather, not unless Brandi is tired and wishes to retire for the night?" He cast a questioning look at Brandi, who stood rooted in the doorway, her astute gaze shifting from the now-deserted hall to Quentin.

"I'm not at all fatigued," she responded, appraising Quentin in an obvious attempt to discern his state of mind. "Besides"—her tentative smile burned away much of the residual tension permeating the room—"I've only just changed into an acceptable gown and washed away the dusty aftermath of our day's adventures. 'Tis a pity for my labors to be wasted."

"'Twould indeed be a pity," Quentin acknowledged, his jaw relaxing as he inspected her from the top of her burnished head to the hem of her sky-blue day dress, approval shining in his eyes. "Especially given that your labors yielded such lovely results."

"So, shall I leave the tray, my lord?" Mrs. Collins interjected.

"Hmm? Oh, Mrs. Collins." Quentin smiled ruefully, aware this was the second time in less than a minute that he'd forgotten the housekeeper's presence. "Yes. Leave it on the table so we can enjoy your incomparable cooking. Also, please accept my apologies on Desmond's behalf. He hasn't been himself since Father's death."

"Of course, sir." With a compassionate nod, Mrs. Collins placed the tray on a side table. "As to my incomparable cooking, I think you should know I brought only tea and scones. Normally, at this hour I would have provided you with a far more substantial meal. However," she said smiling, "after examining your empty picnic basket, it occurred to me you might not have recovered from your late afternoon repast."

"A wise judgment, Mrs. Collins," Brandi agreed, wincing

as she contemplated the notion of eating. "My sides still ache from that delicious, bounteous feast. 'Tis no wonder Poseidon and Goddess were so jubilant after ridding themselves of our cumbersome weight. Why, we must have been as ponderous as twin boulders." She wrinkled her nose. "Food? I doubt I'll be able to look at anything edible for days."

Mrs. Collins's face fell.

"Other than your sumptuous scones, of course," Brandi amended hastily. "No matter how I've gorged myself, I always have room for those. Accompanied by several cups of your splendid tea."

The housekeeper beamed. "Excellent. I've brought you a dozen scones—newly baked—and a large pot of tea. Should you require more, just ring and I'll fetch them."

"Wonderful." Brandi felt her insides lurch. "Thank you so much."

"Not at all, Miss Brandi. Now, will there be anything else?"

"Not for the moment, Mrs. Collins." It was Quentin who answered, coming to Brandi's rescue as he noted the greenish cast to her skin. "But, thank you—we promise to ring the instant we've depleted our supply of scones."

"Very good, sir." The housekeeper dropped a curtsy. "Then I'll return to my duties."

The door closed behind her.

Brandi inched far away from the side table, along with its wafting aroma of food.

Despite his lingering fragments of anger, Quentin couldn't resist teasing her. "I'll pour your tea," he offered gallantly, "and prepare a plate for you, as well. Would you like to begin with one mouth-watering scone or two?"

"That depends," she quipped back. "Would you like me to empty the contents of my stomach on one Hessian boot or two?"

A chuckle rumbled from Quentin's chest. "Not an attractive choice. Very well, Sunbeam, you needn't eat."

"And you needn't try to distract me." Gathering her skirts, Brandi marched across the room. "It won't work, Quentin—not this time. The situation is too disconcerting to ignore."

"What situation?" Again, that taut, uncharacteristic severity.

Brandi pushed past it. "In all my twenty years, I've never seen you like this—a veritable explosion straining to erupt. Further, I've never heard you berate anyone so vehemently as you just did Desmond. Why, Quentin? What instigated it?" She paused, steeling herself to address the worry that plagued her. "Was I the cause of your battle?"

Silence.

"That's what I was afraid of." Sighing, she tilted her head farther back until she could meet and hold Quentin's gaze. "'Tis not merely a guess. I heard my name spouted— several times. So I'll ask you bluntly, am I driving a wedge between you and Desmond?"

Brandi's ironic question elicited a harsh laugh from Quentin. "Hardly, Sunbeam. The particular wedge you're referring to was driven three decades ago."

"Perhaps." Brandi regarded him soberly. "But you've always allayed it to the best of your ability. Until now. Something's changed since your return to the Cotswolds."

"Many things have changed." An odd expression drifted across Quentin's handsome features. "I've been away four years. That's a long time, Brandi—as we're both finding out."

Her heart lurched at the poignant look in his eyes—a clear revelation of his underlying meaning. "Yes," she returned softly. "Four years *is* a long time—in many ways—for all of us." Staunchly, she squelched the emotion that surged to life inside her, determined to stick to the matter at hand. She *had* to get to the heart of Quentin's clash with his brother.

"Quentin." She snatched the drink from him, placing it on the sideboard so she could grip his forearms. "Talk to me—about Desmond. As far back as I can remember, you've always made allowances for him—his weaknesses, his jealousy, his detachment. You worked so hard to forge whatever minimal bond of brotherhood he'd allow. 'Twas I, not you, who constantly complained about his rigid narrow-mindedness. You tried to understand, even defend, him. And now suddenly, for the first time, you're displaying a hostility that's totally foreign to your nature."

"Desmond and I were arguing, Sunbeam. People lose their composure during arguments."

A vehement shake of her head. "Not you—you never lose your composure. Certainly not with Desmond. Besides, I'm referring to more than just the argument I interrupted—even more than your unprecedented rage. I'm referring to the disparaging way you've spoken about Desmond these past days, the bitterness I hear in your tone when I mention his name, the coiled resentment you emanate in his presence—none of which existed before you left for Europe. So, please, answer my question: What has transpired since your return to Colverton and how do I factor into it?"

"My differences with Desmond are very complex," Quentin hedged, frowning. "As for the argument you just overheard—yes, you were its subject. But that does not make you its cause."

"I'll decide that for myself—*after* you tell me what specific aspect of my behavior incited your altercation. Was it my riding? My fishing? My twilight gallivanting?"

"No, no, and no. The truth? It wasn't your behavior at all—'twas mine."

Brandi's brow furrowed. "Yours? I don't understand."

Quentin held her gaze. "Desmond claims I'm trying to seduce you."

"He claims you're . . . oh my God." All the color drained from Brandi's face. "He actually accused you of that?"

"Indeed he did. In no uncertain terms."

"How did you react?"

"Much as you overheard. I was furious."

"I could make out only your tone, not your words. You

denied his accusation—at least I assume you did, didn't you?"

"Of course." Quentin's mouth narrowed into a grim line. "But that didn't deter my brother, who believes what he chooses to believe. He's convinced that your future as his duchess was a certainty—until my arrival thwarted its realization. The violent way I reacted only made things worse. Hell, I not only lost my temper, I very nearly struck him. 'Twas an ugly scene." Unconsciously, Quentin's fingers entwined with Brandi's.

"I'm sorry," she whispered.

"Don't be." He relinquished her hands, seizing his drink and swallowing fervently. "The truth?" A pained smile. "Of course, the truth. When it comes to you, I've never been able to offer less. I'm not nearly as furious at Desmond as I am at myself. What he implied struck too damned close to home, gave voice to a reality I've been refusing to face since my return." Quentin stared broodingly into his goblet's half-filled contents. "You and I—there are strong feelings between us, Brandi. 'Tis insane to deny them. And just as insane to act upon them." A contemplative pause. "Ironic, isn't it? Desmond is finally correct in his perception—and 'tis the one time I most wish he were wrong." Quentin tossed off the rest of his drink.

"Why?" Brandi asked softly. "Why do you wish he were wrong?"

"You know why. Because, feelings or not, I can't promise you forever. And I won't let you settle for less."

"And if our feelings cannot be ignored or repressed?"

"They must be."

Brandi's dark lashes swept her cheeks, shadowing her aching frustration.

"In any case, Sunbeam, you—and our relationship—are but a portion of Desmond's antipathy. As you heard earlier, he's also livid about my decision to search for our parents' killer."

A small nod. "He turned three shades of red when he heard that you'd apprised me of your meeting with

Hendrick. And he very nearly erupted when I pronounced that I wished to take part in determining what your next step should be."

"He was only a tad less annoyed about my intentions to *take* a next step. He's convinced that only the authorities can uncover the truth."

"But you disagree."

"I do." One dark brow rose in question. "Don't you?"

"Yes," Brandi concurred. "Oh, I'm certain the Bow Street magistrate will cover every possible avenue. But 'tis up to us to explore the impossible."

Quentin's lips curved in a poignantly tender smile. "Your spirit alone is enough to sustain me."

Brandi's lashes lifted. "I'm glad."

Another exquisitely painful silence.

Roughly, Quentin cleared his throat. "Perhaps I should be getting back to Colverton."

"If you think it best." Brandi hesitated, then broached the very real, very immediate future. "Tell me, my lord, do you intend to honor your promise?"

He blinked. "Promise?"

"Yes. You said we had only to wait until Desmond received word from Mr. Hendrick before we rode to Townsbourne to peruse Father's papers. Well, we've received word and the results are nonexistent. Therefore, I'd like to go to Townsbourne tomorrow."

After a brief pause, Quentin nodded. "Very well, Sunbeam. Tomorrow it is. I'll collect you at nine o'clock, which will give us the better part of the day at your father's manor. All right?"

"All right." Brandi stood on tiptoe, brushed Quentin's chin with her lips. "Thank you, Quentin."

"For what?" His voice was husky.

"For not shutting me out. For not breaking a promise. For understanding me."

"Sunbeam . . ." He framed her face between his palms.

A sharp knock sounded at the sitting room door.

"Yes?" Quentin called.

"Master Quentin, Miss Brandi." Without preliminaries, Bentley entered the room, his lips drawn into a grim line. "Forgive me for intruding. But I need to see you right away, my lord."

"What's wrong, Bentley?" Quentin demanded, an unsettled feeling tightening his gut. "What's happened?"

Bentley scanned the room. "Is Master Desmond here?"

"He was. He just left for Colverton. You must have passed each other on the road."

"I see. Well, perhaps it's just as well. My reason for being here at this late hour is pressing and, most probably, confidential." The butler withdrew a folded envelope from his pocket. "This came for you, sir—it's from the War Department."

"The War Department?" Quentin's brows arched in surprise. Swiftly, he reached for the letter.

"Yes, my lord. 'Twas delivered by a messenger from Whitehall who stressed the immediacy of its contents. He was most distressed to learn you were not at home, and equally reluctant, at first, to turn the missive over to me. However, after I'd convinced him of my long-standing service to your family, he amended his decision—with the stipulation that I transmit the message to you as soon as possible."

Wordlessly, Quentin tore open the envelope, scanning the note's contents. "It seems I'm being recalled. Effective immediately."

"Recalled?" Brandi echoed, her pupils dilating with shock.

A terse nod. "Evidently, I'm needed in the colonies. Our troops are encountering unanticipated difficulty in deciphering enemy missives. I'm commanded to leave for America the morning after next, at the first light of day." He raked an unsteady hand through his hair. "Bloody hell."

"The day after tomorrow," Brandi reiterated, folding her hands in an attempt to still their shaking.

"I was afraid of that," Bentley murmured. "Little else could be so urgent."

"I can't go." Quentin stuffed the missive in his pocket and began to pace. "Not now."

"You must." Brandi wondered if those words really came from her. "You're an expert at deciphering coded messages, Quentin. Your skills are extraordinary—as is your allegiance. England needs you. You couldn't live with yourself if you let her down."

"You're right—I couldn't," Quentin agreed, halting in the center of the room. "Nor could I live with myself if I abandoned the search for my parents' murderer. No, Sunbeam, until that bastard is found and punished, I'm going nowhere."

"It would seem, sir," Bentley mused aloud, "knowing how highly the War Department regards you, that they aren't aware of the recent developments regarding the carriage accident. If the War Minister knew your parents were murdered, he would have conferred with you in an unofficial capacity before formally summoning you back to war."

Quentin's head came up. "That's true." His mind began racing. "I'll ride to London tomorrow and meet with the necessary officials. Surely they can delay my departure a week—a fortnight at most. By then, the killer will have been caught and punished, Ardsley and my parents can rest in peace, and I can resume my life."

"Quentin, you needn't delay your trip," Brandi interjected, firmly squelching her personal anguish at the thought of Quentin's departure. "I can continue the investigation on my own."

"No, you can't." Quentin moved forward, seizing Brandi's arms. "Or rather, you won't. Brandi, I told you, trying to unmask a murderer is not an exciting challenge. It's a serious and potentially dangerous business—not one I'll allow you to undertake alone." His eyes narrowed on her face. "I want your promise."

She blinked. "Promise?"

"Yes. Our trip to Townsbourne—the one we planned to make in the morning—promise me you won't go. Not tomorrow when you'll be unaccompanied. Give me your word that you'll wait." He frowned at the ensuing silence which, knowing Brandi as he did, could mean but one thing. "I'm only asking for a day, Sunbeam. That's all it will take for me to rectify things with the army. I'll return to the Cotswolds by nightfall. We'll ride to Townsbourne the following morning." He gave her a slight shake. "I want your vow that you won't pursue this alone."

"All right," she agreed. "You have my word—I won't go to Townsbourne alone. But, Quentin? Please make sure this is what you truly wish to do. I know how important your career is—not only to you, but to England. So please—be certain."

"I'm very certain." His forefinger traced the bridge of her nose. "Is this really the same young woman who begged me not to leave the Cotswolds? Who pleaded that I not abandon her to her first unbearable London Season?"

"That was four years ago, Quentin. I was little more than a child."

"Which, somewhere between then and now, you ceased to be."

"Until last week I would have refuted that statement. But now, since you've come home, I realize just how true it is."

Nonchalantly, Bentley made his way to the door. "Master Desmond will be pondering my whereabouts," he announced loudly. "So, having delivered my message, I'd best take my leave. Good night, Master Quentin, Miss Brandi."

Quentin's gaze flickered to the doorway. "Thank you, Bentley."

"Not at all, sir." The butler glanced down at his uniform, frowning in apparent annoyance. "Oh dear. It seems that in my haste to dismount I severed a button from my coat." He cast an inquiring look at Brandi. "'Twas a brass button— one I'd hate to lose. If it's acceptable, Miss Brandi, I'd like to return tomorrow morning to search for it. I'd do so now, but 'tis far too dark to locate so small an object. Further, as I've just stated, Master Desmond will be looking for me."

"Certainly, Bentley." A warm glow lit Brandi's eyes. "By

all means, return tomorrow to search for your button. In fact, come for breakfast. Mrs. Collins will be delighted. And Herbert will be thrilled to have another gentleman to listen to his complaints about the uncooperative geraniums beside the gazebo."

"Thank you." A half bow. "Then I'll be on my way."

He disappeared down the hallway.

"Bentley is a wonderful man," Brandi pronounced. She smiled up at Quentin. "And so are you."

"I?" Quentin was the picture of innocence.

"Yes, you," Brandi returned with great conviction, giving him a grateful, knowing look. "I don't expect—any more than you do—that Bentley will find his missing button in the cottage or anywhere on the grounds of Emerald Manor. In fact, I'd be willing to wager a thousand pounds that, if he chose to, Bentley could locate his button this very instant— right in his own pocket, of all places. Don't you agree?" Tenderly, she caressed Quentin's jaw. "I'm very lucky to have the two of you looking out for me. As Bentley obviously surmised, I wasn't feeling terribly enthusiastic about spending tomorrow alone. And, bless his heart, he came to my rescue. But then, neither his kindness nor his insight should surprise me. After all, he's enjoyed the same splendid companionship as I, provided by my wondrous instructor—the man who taught me to shoot, to fish . . . and to care." Brandi stood on tiptoe, skimming Quentin's lips in a whisper of a caress. "Thank you—for everything. Your devotion means the world to me."

Silently, Quentin threaded his fingers through her hair.

"What are you thinking, Captain Steel?"

"I'm thinking that you're as intelligent as you are beautiful." His thumbs moved lazily along the sides of her neck. "And I'm thinking that if I don't leave now, I'm going to cast all my noble intentions to the wind."

"I hope so," she whispered, her eyes deepening to a velvety brown.

"Brandi . . ."

"I know." Her forefinger silenced him, pressing gently

against his mouth. "Just kiss me good night." A teasing grin. "After all, since you also instructed me so diligently in the fine art of kissing, I'd like to practice what I learned."

His gaze darkened, falling to her lips. "Which type of kiss did you wish to practice—the type I told you to allow or the forbidden type?"

"The latter." Tenderly, she stroked his nape. "Just so I'm sure I understand what never to permit."

Quentin made a rough sound of surrender as he lowered his head, his mouth opening hungrily over hers. "God, Sunbeam, you shatter every damned resolution I make."

"I'm glad." Brandi leaned into him, deepening the kiss with all the skill he'd taught her. Her tongue traced his lips lightly, then glided into his mouth to meld with his.

A hard shudder racked Quentin's body, his arms tightening reflexively, molding her against him. He half-lifted her from the Oriental rug, fitting their bodies together in a way that made Brandi throb with the same unknown yearning that gnawed inside her each time they came together.

"Quentin . . . stay," she breathed as his lips left hers, hotly claiming her neck, her throat, the upper slope of her breasts that was unconcealed by her bodice. "Don't leave me—not now. I can't bear this ache."

His groan vibrated against her skin. "Sunbeam, if you only knew how badly I want to stay." His open mouth traced the curve of her shoulder. "But I can't—I can't."

"Why?" She cradled his head between her hands, reveling in the blazing heat that emanated from every inch of her he'd branded as his.

"Because with us . . ." Quentin raised his head, battling for sanity—finding none. "Brandi, with us, it could never be half-measure. It has to be all—or nothing."

"All," she whispered, her drugged gaze meeting his.

"No, sweetheart, not all." He kissed her again, slowly this time, tasting each corner of her mouth, nibbling first at her lower lip, then her upper, finally possessing her mouth with a consuming intensity that wrested her breath, captured her soul.

"Quentin . . ." She relinquished herself entirely, drowning in the bottomless hunger of his kiss, her entire body taut, straining, empty with a need only Quentin could fill.

Painfully aware that this was as far as things could progress—as far as he could ever allow them to progress—Quentin held nothing back, pouring his pain, his confusion, his desire into a kiss that took more, gave more, shared more than anything he'd ever experienced. He literally couldn't get enough of her: her taste, her scent, the incredibly erotic feel of her in his arms. Again and again, his mouth slanted across hers, until every shred of his control had dissipated and he knew that in mere seconds he was going to carry her to the sofa and make love to her.

He tore his mouth away, every nerve ending in his body screaming a protest, the ache in his loins so acute he groaned aloud.

"Quentin?" Brandi's breath emerged in short pants of uncertainty.

He pressed his forehead to hers. "We have to stop. Now."

"Are you in pain?"

A trace of humor glinted in the inferno of his gaze. "Excruciating pain. The kind I'd like to immerse myself in until hell freezes over."

She blinked, fathoming on some innate level that she was the cause—and the cure—for Quentin's pain: a pain much like her own, born of pleasure, not anguish. And she wanted nothing more than to assuage it. "Then why must we stop?"

"You know why."

"No—I don't." Brandi's protest was a tantalizing whisper against his overheated skin. "I want to give you everything. Oh, Quentin, don't you understand? I love you."

His head jerked up, wild emotions raging in his eyes. "Christ, Brandi, don't say that."

"Why not? 'Tis the truth. I do love you."

Sadness grazed the harsh lines of his face. "I know you do, Sunbeam. But not in the way you think." Slowly, he lowered her feet to the floor, reaching up to gently disengage her arms from around his neck.

162

"What do you mean, not in the way I think?"

"Friendship breeds a very special kind of love. And passion? Passion is one of the most powerful forces in life, compelling people to act in ways they would never otherwise have considered." Quentin's lips swept across her palms: first one, then the other. "'Tis only natural, when circumstances deem that two such profound emotions merge, for you to brand it as love."

Brandi's pupils dilated in stupefied amazement. "And you're telling me it's not love?"

"I'm telling you we can't allow it to be."

"You're a bloody fool."

Quentin's jaw dropped, her accusation a douse of cold water on his heated senses. "What?"

"You heard me." Brandi stepped away from him, running a shaking hand through her disheveled tresses. "You're so brilliant, yet so utterly blind. You have all the answers, yet the questions still evade you. Your reasoning is flawless, yet your conclusions can be naught but false, for they are founded in fact not feeling. In short, you're a bloody fool. And your obtuseness is not something I can remedy. That task, my lord, must be yours and yours alone." Her voice broke, tears glistening on her lashes. "No." She squelched Quentin's reply with a hard shake of her head. "Go back to Colverton. Ride to London and rectify things at Whitehall. But consider all I've said—not only about what's best for England, but about what's best for all you love. Good night, Captain Steel."

Chapter 10

"Good evening, Master Quentin."

At half after two A.M., Bentley's greeting was the last thing Quentin expected.

"Bentley?" He blinked, struggling to accustom his eyes to the glow of the entranceway lamps—lamps he'd assumed would be long since extinguished.

"Shall I take your coat?"

"My coat—oh, yes." Reflexively, Quentin removed his outer garment and handed it to the butler, feeling disoriented and out of sorts. Having just spent long hours driving aimlessly through the streets of the Cotswolds, he wanted nothing more than to lose himself to the blessed oblivion of a slumber he suspected was not forthcoming.

"Would you care for a drink, sir?" Bentley was asking, tying the sash of his robe. "Or perhaps a late supper?"

"Supper? At this hour?" Quentin appraised the butler's bedtime apparel and then, as if seeking further corroboration, groped for his timepiece. "It's nearly three A.M.," he announced. "Why on earth are you strolling about the manor?"

Bentley clasped his hands behind his back, looking as

proper as a dressing robe would permit. "Retiring at my usual hour was out of the question, sir." The briefest of pauses. "I had, after all, to prepare a suitable uniform for tomorrow, being that my current one is damaged."

"Ah, the missing button," Quentin acknowledged, a smile tugging at his lips. Despite his muddled state, he was warmed by Bentley's well-intentioned ploy. "I should have known you'd never consider receiving Colverton's visitors wearing a less-than-immaculate coat."

"Certainly not, sir." Bentley sniffed at the idea. "In any case, once I'd readied my uniform, I spent the duration of the night combing the servants' quarters for a matching button to replace its predecessor. 'Twould be a crime to discard a perfectly good uniform because of one lost button."

"I agree. And tell me, did you locate a matching button?"

"As luck would have it, yes." Bentley's expression remained unchanged.

"Now that comes as quite a surprise." The troubled lines about Quentin's mouth softened. "You're a fraud, Bentley." He waved away the butler's protest. "You're also the finest of friends—to Brandi, and to me. I apologize for keeping you awake worrying about my well-being. By all means, take your fictitious button and be off to bed."

"I'm not particularly tired, sir," Bentley replied, studying Quentin with quiet insight. "But you must be."

"No." Quentin shook his head. "I've too much on my mind to be tired. Although, Lord knows I've had ample time to reconcile my problems. I've been riding about the village for hours. And still I'm no closer to solutions now than I was then."

"It could be you need a willing ear."

Quentin gave a self-deprecating laugh. "I fear I need far more than that. This quandary extends beyond the realm of my experience—and my comprehension."

"Then I suggest we withdraw to the sitting room for a drink. It will help you relax and provide us with an opportunity to talk."

Instinctively, Quentin glanced toward the second floor landing, recalling only too well his brother's vow to continue their heated exchange later tonight. The prospect of another battle with Desmond was thoroughly distasteful—another reason why he'd delayed his return to Colverton. With Brandi's disturbing chastisement still fresh in his mind, the taste of her still warm on his mouth, he felt raw, uncertain—and the last person he wanted to contend with was his brother. "Is Desmond abed?" he asked Bentley.

"He is," the butler confirmed. A tactful cough. "Sanders and I placed him there ourselves some three hours past."

"In other words, Desmond was foxed and couldn't walk."

"Actually, he was out cold. But Sanders and I were very discreet; we made certain no one was about when we carted Master Desmond off to bed. I stayed only long enough to help maneuver the duke into his nightshirt—after all, 'twould be impossible for Sanders to manage nearly two hundred pounds of dead weight on his own."

Quentin made a disgusted sound. "Poor Sanders. When he worked for Father, he had only to act as a valet. Now, he must also be caretaker and wrestler. I wish Desmond would muster some inner strength and stop drowning his anguish in a bottle. It won't bring Father back."

Bentley diplomatically held his tongue, instead addressing Quentin's original concern. "In any case, you needn't worry about Master Desmond overhearing us. So, shall we adjourn to the sitting room for that brandy I suggested?"

"Lead the way, Bentley."

They walked down the hall, closing the sitting-room door in their wake.

Without delay, Bentley crossed over to the sideboard and poured two healthy portions of Madeira. "Here you are, sir."

"Thank you." Quentin paused only long enough to accept the proffered goblet before he began prowling the Axminster carpet, seized by the same restless tension he'd been unable to shake since leaving Brandi.

"It occurred to me, my lord," Bentley remarked, "that you might not be returning to Colverton at all tonight."

Quentin froze in his tracks. "Why? Where did you think I'd be spending the night?"

"At Emerald Manor."

"Damn it!" Quentin tossed off his drink and slammed the glass to a side table. "You, too?"

"Pardon me?"

"Desmond has already accused me of trying to seduce Brandi. Am I to assume you share his opinion?"

"Indeed not, my lord." Bentley drew himself up, the picture of righteous indignation. "I merely meant that, in light of the unexpected missive from the War Department, coupled with Miss Brandi's current emotional unrest, she might feel overwhelmed, in need of your strength and your comfort. Seduction never entered my mind."

"Really?" Quentin averted his head. "Then you're a better man than I. Because it most definitely entered mine."

"You're being too hard on yourself, sir."

"Am I?" Quentin snapped about to face his friend. "I've known Brandi her whole life, spent more time with her than all the residents of Colverton combined. I taught her to shoot, to fish, to ride. I reveled in her spirit, encouraged her independence—when it came to everyone but me. I told myself I did that for her sake, that she needed an understanding shoulder—mine. I never considered the possibility that one day I might . . . she might . . . we could . . ." He broke off, striding across the room to refill his goblet.

"I repeat, you're being too hard on yourself, my lord."

Slowly, Quentin lowered the bottle of Madeira, his gaze following it to the sideboard. "Bentley, I'd best be blunt. The feelings I've been experiencing for Brandi these past few days have been anything but brotherly."

"She has become a lovely young lady, hasn't she?" Bentley inquired pleasantly.

Startled, Quentin's head came up, his eyes fixed on Bentley's face. "You're not surprised?"

"By what? The fact that you're drawn to Miss Brandi as a woman? Hardly, sir. If you'll forgive the familiarity of my observations, Miss Brandi is beautiful, intelligent, and delightful company. Your feelings for her have always been powerful—even when she was no more than a slip of a girl. Why would the intensity of those feelings ebb now?"

"Bentley, I don't think you understand what I'm saying. It's not the intensity of my feelings at issue here; it's the direction they've taken. Desmond is right. I do want Brandi—and I don't mean as a friend, or a sister, or in any other platonic capacity. I want her. Period. Precisely the way Desmond accused. *Now* have I made myself clear?"

Bentley arched a brow. "I understood you the first time, my lord. And, might I add, your desire for Miss Brandi comes as no great revelation to me. But desire can be spawned by many things. It can also be displayed in many ways. And, despite anything Master Desmond might claim, seduction is an impossibility—at least in the case of you and Miss Brandi."

Quentin's jaw dropped in astonishment, and he shook his head slowly from side to side. "Your insight is astounding," he pronounced with undisguised admiration. "Is there nothing I can divulge that would surprise or shock you?"

"I think not." A corner of Bentley's mouth lifted. "It appears Miss Brandi's contention is proving to be true—I do know you both better than you know yourselves." He paused, modestly adding, "Although in this case, one needn't be a prophet to discern the obvious."

"And now that we've discerned the obvious, what do I do about it?"

"What do you want to do?"

"What I want and what I know to be right are two different things."

"If you say so, sir."

Quentin's eyes narrowed. "Is that supposed to be an answer of some kind?"

"Not at all, my lord. Only you can provide the answers you seek. And I don't believe you're prepared to do that."

"Seemingly not. Damn it—I'm so bloody confused." Quentin massaged his temples. "Brandi's in pain—pain I'm causing. And I don't know how to alleviate it— whatever path I choose will intensify her hurt."

"Remember that you care very deeply for her."

"I need no reminder of that."

"Clearly you do. Else why would you even ponder Master Desmond's ludicrous allegation? Seduction is shallow and selfish. Caring is neither—especially when it is mutual. And I don't think there's a question about whether Miss Brandi returns your feelings, is there?"

"No." Quentin's chest tightened. "There isn't." He stared off, seeing Brandi's flushed beauty as she'd gazed up at him, a rapturous look on her face.

Oh, Quentin, don't you understand? He could hear her declaration as clearly as if she spoke it now. *I want to give you everything. I love you.*

"Damn it." Fists clenched at his sides, Quentin shook his head, denying Brandi's avowal—and his own weakness. "I know what Brandi feels. I even know what she thinks she feels. But she's too young—and too innocent—to understand the consequences of what's happening between us. She's not thinking clearly. Christ, she's not thinking at all. So it's up to me to make decisions for both of us."

"And is your judgment unclouded?"

"'Tis unclouded enough to know what's best for Brandi." Quentin's jaw set. "I have no right to rob her of all she deserves—and I have no intention of doing so. As it is, she scarcely has the opportunity to recover from one emotional assault before she is catapulted into the next."

Bentley inclined his head, instantly perceiving a new and heightened tension in Quentin's tone. "Did something further transpire tonight?"

"Yes. Desmond and I were alone when he delivered his accusation. But it escalated into an ugly and heated argument—one that Brandi walked in on."

"She overheard Master Desmond's insinuation?"

"No, but she understood at once that she was the subject

of our battle. She wouldn't relent until I'd relayed the specifics to her."

"That shouldn't surprise you, sir. Miss Brandi is quite persistent when she chooses to be."

Quentin sighed. "I know. In any case, Desmond's slur upset her deeply. I suppose she expected more from him, given the compassion he's displayed this past fortnight."

"You're not still deluding yourself into thinking Master Desmond and Miss Brandi have a future together, are you?"

"No, that worry no longer plagues me. Not only am *I* convinced Desmond is all wrong for Brandi, she herself is convinced. No, with regard to Desmond's role in Brandi's life, I have but two concerns. The first is that he'll use his guardianship to bend her to his will—an endeavor I'm counting on you to subvert in my absence."

"I'll do my best, sir."

"My other concern—and the one that truly weighs on my mind—is that Desmond will prove far too weak to ensure Brandi's safety."

Bentley started. "Her safety, my lord?"

"Yes. Which is why I'm doubly glad you'll be riding to Emerald Manor tomorrow to unearth your nonexistent button." A dark scowl settled over Quentin's features. "I have no basis for my apprehension. Doubtless, I'm being overcautious—I always am where Brandi is concerned. It's one reason I haven't broached this particular possibility with her—that, and the fact that I refuse to compound her anxiety with a theory that is, most likely, groundless."

"I'm totally at sea, sir."

Pensively, Quentin set down his glass. "We still don't know who killed Ardsley and my parents, nor who the intended victim truly was. Suppose—for whatever reasons—that Ardsley was the killer's target. Wouldn't it follow that Brandi could now be in danger? Think about it, Bentley. Whatever motive the murderer had, whatever he wanted—be it money, family assets, property—isn't it probable that Ardsley willed it to Brandi and that it's now unknowingly in her possession?"

Bentley paled. "I never considered that possibility."

"'Tis my other reason for refusing to leave the Cotswolds until the murder is satisfactorily resolved. Not only to allow my parents to rest in peace, but to ensure that Brandi will be safe—permanently. And I refuse to entrust her well-being to Desmond, especially now. He's less than reliable under the best of circumstances. And, since Father's death, he's been drinking himself into a perpetual stupor. No, I simply cannot leave England at this particular time. I must convince the War Department to delay their orders." Wearily, Quentin rubbed his eyes. "Speaking of which, I'd best try to get a few hours' rest. 'Tis nearly dawn. I want to get an early start for London."

"Of course," Bentley agreed, noting the pale yellow cast to the eastern sky. "What time shall I have the carriage brought around?"

"At seven." Quentin crossed the room, pausing as he gripped the door handle. "Let's hope that my presence in the colonies is not imperative at this time and that, once I've explained Bow Street's findings, my superiors will reconsider and delay my departure."

"I'm certain they will, my lord. And, with regard to Miss Brandi's safety—at least for the next day or so while you're away—don't worry. I'll make sure she isn't alone."

"Thank you, Bentley." Quentin drew a slow inward breath. "You're indispensable. I only wish you were Brandi's guardian rather than Desmond."

Bentley gazed thoughtfully after Quentin's retreating form. "It matters not, sir," he murmured to himself. "My instincts tell me that Miss Brandi won't need a guardian for long."

Brandi needed something—but a guardian was the farthest thing from her mind.

Tossing onto her back, she stared up at the ceiling, wishing she'd paid more attention to Pamela's lyrical descriptions of love, her absolute knowledge of all the proper things to do.

Oh, Pamela, how I wish you were here to advise me, she thought, that all-too-familiar sense of loss constricting her chest.

Where did one go to find the answers? Where did poets gain their knowledge, courtesans their skill, mistresses their allure? They all had to begin as green as she—didn't they? Sometime in their lives, they had to have been ignorant and inexperienced—didn't they? Yet somewhere, somehow, they'd acquired all they needed to know of this mysterious emotion called love.

How could she?

Tossing aside the bedcovers, Brandi sat up, wrapping her arms about her knees and relinquishing all attempts at sleep.

From what she recalled of Pamela's talks and poets' sonnets, she was supposed to be feeling either breathtaking joy or heart-wrenching pain.

Instead, what she was feeling was total frustration and irrepressible fury.

Never had she dreamed Quentin could be such a dolt.

For twenty years she'd worshipped him, looked up to him as the most brilliant of men.

He'd been anything but brilliant tonight.

How could he explain away what was happening between them, refuse to acknowledge it as love? And how could he imagine that by ignoring it, it would vanish?

It *was* love. And damn him, Quentin knew it.

Brandi snatched her pillow, punching it soundly before depositing it on her lap and sinking her elbows into it.

She recognized Quentin's responses to women better than he imagined. She'd seen him with enough of them over the years: poised, beautiful women, their fingers twined about his arm like vines of manicured ivy. She'd never told him, of course. Like her father—and everyone else at Emerald Manor's quiet country house parties—Quentin had thought her asleep in this very room: the lovely green floral room Pamela reserved solely for her visits. But she wasn't. She'd wait until the strings had begun playing, then slip out her window, scooting down to the darkened ground. There, she'd hasten along until she reached and scaled the thick evergreen just outside the guest quarters—overlooking the cottage's most private section of woods. From her vantage point, she could easily conceal herself amid the tree's profuse branches and survey the entire grounds of Emerald Manor, undetected.

It had been quite a learning experience.

A half-dozen couples per night, gliding cautiously among the trees, evidently attempting to lose themselves in the darkness.

By the age of six, Brandi had been tall enough to reach the first branch of the fir and make the climb. By eight, she'd acquired a reasonable understanding of the significance behind what she was viewing: covert trysts of varying degrees, ranging from innocent moonlight strolls to passionate disrobing sessions. Although why two people would want to adhere to each other like two soggy peppermint sticks, she hadn't a clue.

But apparently these rendezvous were pleasurable because, more times than not, Quentin had taken part in them—he and any one of a host of different ladies, some of whom Brandi recognized, some of whom she did not.

She could vividly recall Lady Penelope Maller, her pale hair always arranged in the exact number of elegant curls, laughing softly and gazing up at Quentin as if he were a god sent to earth. Then there'd been that surly viscount's daughter—what was her name?—Edwina. Lady Edwina something-or-other. She'd been a tad older than eighteen-year-old Penelope—perhaps two and twenty. And her hair had been as black as the night. But the trail of laughter, the adoring looks—that had been the same.

And there'd been scads more.

Vaguely, Brandi could recall a breathtaking countess from Yorkshire, a Canadian official's daughter . . . and then there was that widow—the Marchioness of Elmswood. Brandi had been astounded that a once-wed matron at the advanced age of one and thirty would be interested in joining mouths with a young man of eighteen. Nevertheless, she'd seemed to revel in it, if those throaty sounds and teasing words were any indication.

Married women had pursued Quentin, too. That had shocked Brandi more than anything. But, as she'd expected, Quentin, with his customary moral decency, had spurned their advances, keeping to the unattached women who were free to promenade the woods without irate husbands appearing to challenge him to a duel.

Although there had been an irate father or two, Brandi recalled with a grin. Especially when Quentin's stroll with their daughters appeared to be transcending flirtatious chatter and chaste kisses. But Quentin was cautious with his choices, restricting his more intimate and heated embraces to older, more worldly women. Brandi always knew when he had something more scandalous in mind than kisses, for he'd lead the lady in question deeper into the woods where even Brandi, from her superb viewing station, could not discern their actions.

By the time she turned twelve, Brandi had lost count of Quentin's women. And that was only those he cavorted with at Emerald Manor. Lord alone knew how many there had been in total. After all, she'd no idea what forbidden encounters transpired at Almack's during the London Season, or throughout the long months Quentin was away at Oxford. Or most especially at the elaborate Colverton house parties—which Pamela and Kenton continually hosted and which Brandi continually begged off from attending, weeping until her father relented and spared her the ordeal of accompanying him. As a tot, Colverton had seemed aloof and endless.

An ironic smile tugged at Brandi's lips. As a woman, it still did.

In any case, she might have been young and somewhat uninformed, but her snooping had taught her to recognize the overt signs of Quentin's attraction to a woman—even from a distance of twenty feet: the husky note that crept into his voice; the subtle ways he'd touch his companion's face, her hair, even her shoulders; the purposeful way he'd seize her chin, lifting it to receive his kiss; and—ever so seldom—the slightest faltering in his ever-present control when he held the lady in his arms.

Back then, it had been merely girlish curiosity that compelled Brandi to watch and understand Quentin's actions.

Now it was more.

Sighing, she rubbed the fine muslin of her nightrail between her fingers, comparing what she'd witnessed over the years to what she'd experienced these first few exquisite times in Quentin's arms. Oh, he'd retained that damnable control of his, though just barely. But the tremor in his voice when he spoke her name, the harsh rasps of his breath, the unsteady urgency of his motions when he dragged her against him—all those were indicators of the emotional battle raging inside him. And they were also unprecedented, at least so far as Brandi's vivid memories could recall. Her intuition agreed, whispering that whatever magic eclipsed the world from view each time he and she came together was as new to Quentin as it was to her.

And perhaps twice as terrifying, given his older-brother role in their lifelong friendship and the resulting compulsion he had to protect her.

If he would only allow his feelings to supplant his reason—just this once. If he would only cast nobility and protectiveness aside, and listen to the dictates of his heart. Maybe then he would see the truth.

Lightly, Brandi's fingertips brushed her lips, savoring her recollection of the involuntary way Quentin had all but torn himself from her arms.

He thought her naive.

It was he who was the fool.

He believed her inexperience rendered her unable to discern love from passion.

He had never been more wrong.

He believed her a child—fragile, needing his shelter from pain.

Why couldn't he see that by denying her—by denying them both—he was causing more pain than his transience ever could? For, while Brandi realized he belonged first and foremost to England, she could bear savoring whatever fleeting moments life had to offer them, bear the anguish each time they parted, even bear the sleepless nights as she prayed for his safety, longed for his return.

What she couldn't bear was the thought of not having him at all.

Oh, Quentin, she lamented, gazing across the darkened room. *How can I open your foolish eyes? I'm not the rebellious sixteen-year-old you left weeping when you said goodbye. Oh, perhaps part of me is, perhaps part of me always will be. But I've evolved into so much more—more than even I realized until you came home. How do I convince you that I've changed? That we've changed? That what's between us now is beautiful and right? We can't go back anymore. And even if we could, I wouldn't want to. What's more, neither would you.*

She rose, gliding open her nightstand drawer and removing the pistol she'd kept close by since Quentin had gifted it to her four years past. Lovingly, she stroked its carved handle, remembering the instant Quentin had proclaimed it hers. He'd been going away then. 'Twas a reality she'd been too young, too childish to accept. And now? Now, if the War Department had its way, he'd be going away again.

It was the perfect opportunity to show him just how strong she'd become.

And show him she would—*after* she toppled that blasted control of his.

With renewed resolve, Brandi gripped the pistol more tightly, recalling the shooting match that had preceded Quentin's farewell—and yielded her victorious.

She'd never lost to Quentin yet.

Now was no time to begin.

Chapter 11

Quentin stalked the floors of his room at the London inn, feeling like a caged tiger who'd been prodded by a stick.

Something was amiss. He knew it.

His meeting with the War Department had been a bizarre series of unanswered questions and unaccounted-for demands.

After three hours of waiting in that bloody anteroom on Downing Street and four hours of moving from one petty official to the next, Quentin still had no idea what urgency required his immediate attention in the colonies or whose decision it had been to recall him.

But he sure as hell intended to find out—from Lord Bathurst himself, England's Minister of War.

Dropping to the bed, Quentin folded his arms beneath his head, livid at the incompetent and careless way he'd been treated. He'd finally lost his temper—something he rarely did—and stormed out, demanding a meeting with Bathurst first thing tomorrow.

His request had been granted posthaste by a red-faced, stammering subordinate, who'd assured him that the minister would receive his lordship at nine A.M. sharp tomorrow morning.

Which meant Quentin had to spend the night in London.

He'd dispatched a missive to Bentley straightaway, relaying the situation and asking Bentley to visit Emerald Manor—and Brandi—again tomorrow. He harbored no doubts that his request would be honored, simply by virtue of Bentley's loyalty to him and to Brandi. Not to mention that Desmond's addled state would provide the butler with ample opportunity to disappear for several hours. No, Quentin was certain Brandi would be cared for.

But damn it, he wanted to go home.

Home.

The thought made him smile, for it immediately conjured up an image, not of Colverton, or even the army, but of Emerald Manor—its gardens ablaze with summer's hues, its trees plush with greenery, and in the midst of it, her nose smudged with dirt, Brandi.

Quentin's smile faded.

What in God's name was he going to do with these interminable feelings of his?

Logic provided the answer.

The first thing he needed to do was face them.

He was falling in love with Brandi Townsend.

Brandi—his one and only Sunbeam: that irreverent little hoyden he'd pampered since birth, indulged beyond reason, teased and tutored and treasured.

And with whom he'd shared honesty, trust, and laughter—together with an openness and contentment he'd never shared with another.

Falling in love with her?

Hell, he was already in love with her.

The realization opened the flood gates of his awareness. Bolting upright, he stared—unseeing—across the barren room as the undisputed truth crashed through him in harsh waves of acceptance.

What a blind fool he'd been to deny the undeniable.

He'd cherished Brandi all her life: savoring the joys of her childhood, the wonders of her girlhood, even the aching transitions of her adolescence.

He'd left England with the tender memories of a rare and unspoiled young lady.

And returned to find her a woman.

Quentin's chest tightened as he recalled that odd, gripping feeling that had accompanied him to Europe—the sense that all he loved would be somehow changed.

It had.

His parents were gone.

So was his little hoyden.

Only in Brandi's case, she'd been replaced by a beautiful, desirable woman—a woman with whom he'd fallen in love the instant he spied her, kneeling at his parents' graves, the misty drizzle mingling with her tears of loss. She'd reached out to share his pain, giving him her warmth—representing all that was good and precious in his life.

What in the name of heaven was he going to do?

She loved him.

He knew that, just as surely as he knew she'd give him her soul, willingly and without question.

And just as surely as he knew he could never accept it.

Nor walk away from it.

With a muttered oath, Quentin squeezed his eyes shut. All that succeeded in doing was conjuring up an image of Brandi, her wet gown clinging to her like a second skin, her eyes soft as brown velvet, her smile illuminating the world with a glow all its own. And the way she felt in his arms. Like she belonged there, like he was incomplete when he released her, like he was going to explode if he didn't make her his.

Passion—stark, inescapable—pounded through his loins, and Quentin groaned aloud, wanting to scream his frustration to the skies. Damn, he wanted her. Wanted her with an intensity that nearly annihilated his reason.

She deserved so much more—a man who could make her the center of his world, offer her forever and all it entailed.

Whoever this fictitious man was, Quentin wanted to kill him.

Vehemently, Quentin swung his legs over the side of the bed, resuming his earlier pacing. One month ago, his life had been in order; he'd belonged to the army, and all those he loved had been safe and prevailing in the Cotswolds. Now his parents were dead, their murderer at large, the War Department behaving in a questionable manner, and he had no idea who he was or where he belonged.

And there was nowhere to turn, for the only person who understood him was the very one who was driving him crazy.

Brandi.

So much for the hope that facing his feelings would help provide an answer to his inner turmoil, Quentin mused. Instead, he felt more frustrated than ever, backed into an impossible corner from which there was no escape.

He had to rest. He couldn't afford another sleepless night, not with tomorrow morning's meeting looming ahead. He needed to be alert and ready to plead his case to the War Minister. Because, come hell or high water, he intended to convince the War Department to alter the timing of their orders—after he got to the root of their standoffish treatment.

Wearily, Quentin sank into a tufted chair, leaning his head back against the cushions. It seemed that all his problems—his feelings for Brandi, his concern for her safety, his future in the military—all hinged upon the resolution of his parents' murders.

Which made one decision an unalterable reality: He would not leave English soil until the killer was apprehended.

"Why, Bentley? Why won't Quentin be home today? What aren't you telling me?"

Reacting to Bentley's news, Brandi came to her feet, clutching the gazebo post with a combination of frustration and worry.

"I'm not keeping anything from you, Miss Brandi." Bentley stood dutifully in the garden below, having arrived at Emerald Manor not ten minutes past. He'd followed the identical procedure he had yesterday: circumventing the cottage and veering directly toward the gazebo, knowing he'd find Brandi in her customary position—staring out over the gardens, daydreaming within the soothing confines of her gazebo walls.

Patiently, he reiterated his message. "Master Quentin's note said only that he needed to speak with the War Minister himself and that he'd be doing so first thing this morning. He expects to return to the Cotswolds no later than tonight, or, at the very latest, tomorrow."

"The War Department is obviously not pleased by Quentin's request." Brandi frowned, crossing over and descending into the garden. "They're probably pressuring him to leave for the colonies as requested—posthaste." She inclined her head in Bentley's direction. "Am I the primary reason Quentin wants to delay his trip?"

A heartbeat of silence.

"Am I, Bentley?"

"Among other considerations, yes."

"I was afraid of that." Brandi's small chin set. "Well, I won't have it."

"Pardon me?" One brow rose in question.

"Bentley, sit with me for a minute." Brandi gestured toward the bench alongside the gazebo. "I believe 'tis time for us to have a candid chat."

"As you wish, Miss Brandi." Bentley waited until Brandi was settled before lowering himself beside her.

Brandi wasted not an instant, but plunged forth. "I'm in love with Quentin. You're aware of that fact, I presume?"

"You presume correctly." A corner of Bentley's mouth lifted. "Only a dolt could overlook your enchanting but transparent feelings for Master Quentin."

"Well, the dolt in question is currently at Whitehall."

Bentley coughed—a noise which sounded suspiciously like a chuckle. "I won't argue your depiction. However, in his defense, I do believe Master Quentin perceives your feelings. 'Tis only his own which elude him."

"Is that your subtle way of telling me that, in your opinion, Quentin returns my love?"

"Forgive my impertinence, my lady, but only another dolt would fail to notice so obvious a reality."

Brandi's eyes sparkled with laughter. "In this case, Bentley, I'm delighted to be the dolt of whom you speak." Her fingers interlaced in her lap. "Now that we've put our cards on the table, I'll be blunt."

"I wasn't aware you knew any other way to be."

"True." Brandi grinned. "Very well, then, I'll *continue* to be blunt. The only way to shake Quentin free of his absurd notion that I require solely his protection—and nothing more—is to demonstrate how very independent I truly am."

"Indeed, my lady," Bentley returned calmly. "And, knowing you, I assume you've already formulated a plan as to how this can be accomplished?"

"I have. In fact, if my plan is successful, it might not merely convince Quentin of my inner strength, but perhaps steer us closer to the discovery of our parents' murderer." Brandi leaned forward conspiratorially. "Are you willing to listen?"

"I'm all ears."

"While Quentin spends this extra day or two in London, I plan to do precisely what I promised myself I'd do upon learning that the accident was murder—take matters into my own hands. Directly after breakfast, I shall ride to Townsbourne and conduct a thorough search of Papa's study. He did keep some of his more important documents at home. 'Tis possible one of them will provide a clue as to the killer's motive. If such a clue exists at Townsbourne, I shall find it."

Bentley started. "I distinctly heard you assure Master Quentin that you would await his return before doing something impulsive—such as rushing headlong to Townsbourne and possibly endangering your safety."

"How would visiting Papa's—and my—home endanger my safety?" Brandi's delicate brows rose. "That's ridiculous, Bentley. Quentin is just being overprotective. After all, I hardly think the murderer is lurking about the grounds of Townsbourne, lying in wait for someone to arrive and discover his presence. And even if he were, Townsbourne is my home—I hardly think my presence there would arouse his suspicions, do you? Only you and I know the true purpose of my visit, just as only you and I will know if its outcome is successful and I unearth something incriminating. Moreover, Quentin's exact request was that I give him one day before I act. Well, I've given him that. 'Tis not my fault that he's been detained at Whitehall. In addition, what I assured him was that I would not travel to Townsbourne alone. Which I won't. *You'll* be with me." She caught her breath, gazing expectantly at Bentley.

"I, my lady?"

"Of course." She shot him a meaningful sidelong glance. "You'd planned to spend most of the day by my side anyway, didn't you? Just as you did yesterday—glued to me like a governess to her young charge? At Quentin's request, of course." She smiled. "I may be a dolt, Bentley, but I'm not a fool. I realize Quentin dispatched you to Emerald Manor in his stead, to ensure that I don't succumb to whatever emotional frailty he suspects I might succumb to. Well, I don't need a governess. But I do need a friend. A friend who believes in my ability to secure my own future." Brandi placed a beseeching hand on Bentley's sleeve. "Please help me. I won't be breaking any promises. Nor can Quentin be upset with my decision—not if you go with me."

"Very well, I'll accompany you to Townsbourne," Bentley announced, straightening his waistcoat. "But not because of the flimsy line of reasoning to which I was just subjected."

Brandi blinked. "Then why?"

With a flourish, Bentley rose. "Because you'll race off to Townsbourne whether or not I accompany you. Therefore, given the choice, I'd prefer—as you put it—to act the part of your governess and ensure your well-being, rather than permit you to dash off like a senseless twit."

"Oh, thank you, Bentley." Brandi flew to her feet and hugged him. "This senseless twit is more grateful than you can imagine."

Bentley's hands remained firmly clasped behind his back, but a flicker of a smile touched his lips. "I'm glad we arrived at this understanding, my lady. Especially given that, should you accomplish all you set out to do, Master Quentin will undoubtedly be making periodic trips abroad for the War Department, leaving behind the impossibly difficult woman he loves and, consequently, a splendid opening for a lifelong governess." Bentley gave an exaggerated sigh. "'Tis good to know my job is secure."

"For life, Bentley," Brandi vowed with a saucy grin. "Without question, for life."

"Bathurst, let's cease this game playing."

Leaning forward in his chair, Quentin regarded the War Minister over the piles of paper lining Bathurst's desk. "We've known each other a long time. I've deciphered more French codes than the rest of the British army combined. I've given you nothing but honesty. Now I'm asking the same in return."

"And I'm offering it to you." Bathurst frowned as he scanned the missive Quentin had thrust before him. "I issued these orders because, as my advisors agreed, you're needed in the colonies—more specifically, in the area surrounding Lake Erie. 'Tis the only location in which the Americans have a decided advantage over us. In order to subvert their attacks and regain control, we must first decipher their coded messages. And, frankly, no one is as skilled as you in doing so." Thoughtfully, Bathurst rubbed his chin. "Still, I've received no indication that an American invasion is imminent. Therefore, in light of what you've just told me—Bow Street's heinous discovery—I see no reason why our troops cannot survive another few weeks without you. Consider your request granted. Investigate your parents' untimely deaths. You'll leave for the colonies directly thereafter."

"I appreciate that, Bathurst." Quentin gripped his knees. "But that is not the honesty to which I referred. Why did all your subordinates act so bloody evasive yesterday?"

"Evasive?" The minister's frown deepened. "If you're asking why your request wasn't granted then and there, you already know the answer to that. 'Tis my signature on your orders, and no one but I am authorized to alter them. And, as I'm sure you were told, I was unavailable yesterday, as I spent most of the day with Parliament."

"So I was advised. And, no, I didn't expect anyone to subvert your authority. But I did expect my request to be heard by one of your aides-de-camp. Instead, I was deferred time and again, left waiting for meetings that never occurred. 'Twas as if no one wanted to address my predicament."

"I have no answer for you, Steel. I agree, that does sound odd." Bathurst came to his feet. "If you'll give me the names of all the aides with whom you spoke—or attempted to speak—I'll look into the matter."

The gnawing sense that something was amiss refused to be silenced. "That would ease my mind greatly," Quentin replied. He leaned over and took up a quill. "Allow me five minutes and you'll have that list."

Despite his expedient furnishing of the five names in question, the day passed without word from Bathurst. By six P.M., Quentin was back to pacing his room, angry and uninformed.

A quarter hour later, a messenger hurried into the inn, locating Quentin's room and delivering the official note from the War Department. Seeing the ill-humor of the note's recipient, the messenger pocketed Quentin's proffered coins, then beat a hasty retreat.

Impatiently, Quentin tore open the message, swearing under his breath as he read the annoying contents:

Numerous interruptions kept me from carrying out the task we discussed until late in the day. After speaking with all five aides, I've learned nothing of consequence. You're welcome to speak to each of the men yourself. I'll leave that decision to you. Bathurst

"Damn it!" Quentin crumpled the paper into a ball and tossed it across the room.

He'd just wasted an entire day for nothing. He should have gone directly home after his meeting with the War Minister; after all, he'd gotten what he came for—Bathurst's permission to delay his departure. So why hadn't he just dismissed yesterday's detainment as a mere inconvenience and gone back to the Cotswolds? It certainly wasn't pride which propelled him. His reputation was long established and hardly subject to evaluation, least of all by the civilians at Whitehall. Why, then, had it troubled him that they'd treated him in an unprecedented and peculiar fashion?

And why did it trouble him still?

Slowly, Quentin crossed the room, stooping to pick up the note.

Very well, he determined, smoothing the rumpled page. He'd already squandered a day. He'd squander one day more.

"Here it is, Bentley."

Brandi groped in the back of her father's desk drawer, feeling her way along until she found what she sought. "This should do it."

Bentley stared in astonishment as Brandi released the catch, revealing a hidden compartment. She leaned forward, peering inside before reaching in to extract a slim file.

"Papa always stored his more pressing papers in this spot," she explained triumphantly. "Knowing Papa, he probably did so to ensure that none of the staff had access to the file. As I'm sure you recall, Papa was very private about business affairs."

"Actually, I wasn't aware of that, Miss Brandi. The viscount always seemed quite straightforward when he visited with the late duke."

A reminiscent smile touched Brandi's lips. "That's because he was dealing with Kenton. I truly believe the only people Papa fully trusted were Kenton and his sons." She pursed her lips thoughtfully. "Actually, given that Papa named Desmond overseer of the businesses, it stands to reason that, at some point, he also apprised him of this drawer's existence. I'm surprised Desmond hasn't already removed the file." She shrugged. "Well, maybe with all his new responsibilities, he hasn't had the time to do so."

"Yes, Master Desmond has been finding it hard to maintain a clear head," Bentley commented dryly.

Brandi sighed, instantly comprehending Bentley's subtle message. "I noticed he's been drinking rather heavily. When he left Emerald Manor the other night, he was thoroughly foxed."

"So I discovered."

"Well, I hope he regains control of his life soon. For his own sake—and for Kenton's. After all, Kenton willed an entire dukedom to Desmond, along with a wealth of obligations—obligations he cannot fulfill without a keen—and lucid—mind." On the heels of her assessment, Brandi sank back into the desk chair and began flipping through her father's file.

"Forgive me for asking, Miss Brandi, but how did you know of that concealed drawer's existence?"

Brandi grinned. "Papa didn't tell me, if that's what you're asking. He'd never consider discussing business with a child—much less a female one." Her grin turned impish. "But I was most inquisitive and resourceful. Whenever I couldn't sleep, I'd toddle downstairs and peer through the study's keyhole, watching Papa work. I soon noted where he stored his papers."

"Indeed. It appears that, as a child, inquisitiveness was not your only affliction. Evidently, you also suffered from the consistent and annoying malady of insomnia."

Brandi's brows rose quizzically.

"Well, between your sleepless nights snooping about Townsbourne and your equally vigilant watches atop the trees at Emerald Manor, you rarely had time to close your eyes."

Color suffused Brandi's face. "You knew?"

"Someone had to keep an eye on you. Most times, you were so busy studying Master Quentin's antics, you nearly lost your balance. Who better than I to look out for your safety?"

"But you resided at Colverton . . ." Brandi protested weakly.

"Not when the duke's parties required my supervision. On those occasions, I traveled with him to Emerald Manor." A corner of Bentley's mouth lifted ever so slightly. "Don't worry, my lady. I guarded your secret well. No one knew of your adventures save I."

"You never told Quentin?"

"Of course not. Master Quentin would have been mortified. Besides—" A twinkle. "I'm certain you'll tell him yourself, when the right time presents itself."

Brandi lowered the file to the desk. "He is different with me than he was with those . . . other women, isn't he, Bentley? 'Tis not just my imagination?" Even as she asked, Brandi flushed. How could Bentley know what occurred when she was in Quentin's arms? For that matter, wouldn't he be shocked to learn that they were physically involved— even on the most casual level?

Soberly, Bentley met Brandi's gaze, ignoring the obvious embarrassment staining her cheeks. "Exceedingly different, Miss Brandi. Not only in actions, but in feelings. Trust me. The contrast is staggering."

Relief flooded her features. "Thank you. I think so, too."

Lowering her eyes, she returned to the task at hand, scooping up her father's file and flipping through its routine contents until she came upon a small ledger.

Curiously, she opened it, scanning the pages.

"These are records of Papa's recent business transactions," she murmured, assessing the figures. "Everything appears to be in order . . ." Abruptly, she broke off, her hand hovering over the page she'd been about to turn. "This is odd," she murmured. "Very odd," she added, leaning forward for closer inspection.

"What is, my lady?"

"I had no part in Papa's business dealings, 'tis true, but I do know—both from hearsay and from the size of my inheritance—that he was an exceptionally shrewd and successful businessman. Yet, from what I can discern of these figures, most of his recent investments were losing an exorbitant sum of money. In fact, the only ventures that show a profit—and a considerable one at that—are the ones he shared with Desmond." She raised stunned eyes to Bentley. "Clearly, Desmond wasn't exaggerating when he spoke of his business acumen. The way it looks, he was single-handedly responsible for Papa's sustained wealth, and that, without him, Papa would have been in dire straits. I never would have imagined . . ." Brandi's voice trailed off and her gaze returned to the ledger, seeking confirmation of the astonishing truth. An instant later, she leaned back, issuing a resigned sigh. "It appears I owe Desmond my thanks yet again."

During her entire explanation, Bentley had merely gaped, looking more astounded than she, as if he couldn't believe what he was hearing.

"Would you reiterate your findings for my benefit?" he managed, finding his voice. "Am I to understand the viscount's records indicate that Master Desmond made prosperous investments on his behalf?"

"Exactly." Brandi studied Bentley's stymied expression. "That shocks you. Why?"

Bentley cleared his throat, swiftly retreating behind his discreet veneer. "Like you, I find your discovery to be a startling revelation. So, yes—like you, I am shocked."

"But for a different reason." Brandi's chin came up, and

she met and held Bentley's gaze. "My shock is a reaction to my father's unexpected financial blunders. Yours is in response to Desmond's abilities as an investor." A vulnerable look drifted over her face. "I'm finding this whole discovery painful enough to handle," she admitted in a small voice. "So I'd appreciate your not making it more difficult by keeping things from me. I know you well, Bentley, and you never say anything without a reason. So would you please enlighten me?"

Perceiving her distress, Bentley hesitated, torn between protocol and allegiance. Then he pressed on. "My loyalties were and are with the late duke," he pronounced. "And his were with his family. However, his devotion did not blind him to certain truths—truths he would not want concealed at the risk of hurting you and Master Quentin. No, in this case, I feel certain that His Grace would want me to speak up. Therefore, Miss Brandi, to borrow your phrase, I shall be blunt. The Steel businesses thrived because of His Grace—and only His Grace. Delicately put, Master Desmond's business skills were, at best, dubious. He spent money recklessly and without thought. Despite numerous battles with his father, he showed no intention of altering that vice. 'Twas one of the late duke's major concerns."

Brandi's tension ebbed. "Thank you for your candor, Bentley. I realize I placed you in a very difficult position, and for that, I apologize. But I had to know the truth." Her brow furrowed. "Of course, now that I know the truth, I'm totally at sea. You claim Kenton deemed Desmond a poor businessman. A few days ago, Quentin implied Desmond was distorting the facts when he spoke to me of Kenton's pride in his accomplishments—both personal and professional. Perhaps the two of you are right that Desmond and his father clashed personally—Lord knows, I myself am not Desmond's most avid fan. But professionally? It doesn't make sense—not according to these figures. See for yourself; Desmond yielded tens of thousands of pounds for Papa—pounds that, according to these other losses, were desperately needed to keep Papa from drowning financially."

Bentley walked over to the desk, peering meditatively over Brandi's shoulder. "It does seem that way, doesn't it?" he murmured. "A rather odd discrepancy." Briskly, he straightened, putting a definitive end to their speculation. "I'll discuss it with Master Quentin when he returns." Smoothing his sleeves, he sought to change the subject and lighten the mood simultaneously. "Speaking of Master Quentin, we have quite a bit to disclose to him, haven't we? I'm eager to see his reaction when we tell him of our impulsive jaunt to Townsbourne."

The exasperated expression on Brandi's face proclaimed Bentley's diversion as successful.

"I haven't forgotten." She rolled her eyes to the heavens. "But I must tell you, not one of my childhood governesses was ever this strict."

"Which is why none of them ever knew when their young charge was frolicking about," Bentley returned with a wry grin. "Whereas I, on the other hand, did." Decorum reinstated, he gestured toward the door. "Shall we go? I believe we've exhausted every recess and alcove Townsbourne offers."

"I suppose so." Brandi chewed her lip. "Let's see—" She counted off on her fingers. "We searched Papa's chambers, the library, both studies, the anterooms, and every table and desk in sight. Other than this file, we've turned up only routine copies of documents, the originals of which— according to Papa's notes—are in Mr. Hendrick's office. Yes, 'twould seem our explorations here are at an end." Gathering up her father's file, she paused only to slide the ledger back within. "This is coming with me," she announced, closing the desk drawer and coming to her feet. "I want Quentin to see it." She tossed Bentley a saucy look. "After he berates us for our disobedience."

"Indeed, my lady. I've already begun quaking."

"Coward," Brandi teased, sailing by him.

The carriage ride home was quiet, both occupants pensive as they sought a plausible explanation for the discrepancies they'd encountered, contemplated what their next step should be.

Just as the carriage rounded the drive leading to Emerald Manor, Bentley made a decisive sound, his head snapping up to meet Brandi's hopeful gaze.

"You've thought of something?" she asked eagerly.

"Perhaps. Miss Brandi, would you object to my inspecting the viscount's ledgers once again?"

"Of course not." Brandi extracted the thin book and handed it to Bentley, waiting with bated breath as he examined it. "Well?" she demanded when she could bear it no longer. "Have you found something?"

"I don't know. 'Tis possible." Bentley raised his head. "Tell me, Miss Brandi—is Herbert tending the gardens today?"

Brandi blinked. Whatever she had expected, it hadn't been this. "Is Herbert . . . yes, why?"

"Because several of the gentlemen listed here as business colleagues of the late viscount—those who coinvested with him in seemingly futile ventures—make their homes in Berkshire."

"Is that significant?"

"I'm not certain. But it just so happens I have an old friend who resides in Berkshire."

Brandi grinned. "Is he as irreverent as you?"

"Nearly, my lady—but not quite." A glimmer of humor. "In any case, his name is Smithers, and he is the Duke of Allonshire's valet—an old and trusted friend of the duke and his family."

"Oh, I recall the Duke of Allonshire—I met him and his duchess, Alexandria, the first Season Papa brought me out. They make a lovely couple—so very much in love."

"Yes, well . . ." Bentley actually flushed. "Evidently, that's true, because they are currently on holiday—alone—in a most remote section of Scotland."

"Alone?" Brandi's lips curved. "In other words, even the duke's valet was not invited on this secluded respite?"

"Exactly. Smithers remained at Allonshire to enjoy some well-deserved time off. He has an entire fortnight to himself and has expressly asked that I visit. I'm thinking now that perchance I shall."

"Forgive me, Bentley, but what has all this to do with Papa's ledger?"

"As I said, several of the gentlemen listed in the viscount's ledger reside in Berkshire—a shire in which Smithers is both well-respected and established. I myself can vouch for his trustworthiness and his discretion. 'Tis no wonder so many servants in the nearby manors confide in him. Why, he's privy to as much gossip in Berkshire as I am in the Cotswolds."

Dawning comprehension ensued. "You're hoping that Smithers might have gleaned a tidbit of gossip from another servant—a servant who is employed by one of the Berkshire gentlemen on Papa's list?"

"Not just a tidbit, my lady. I'm hoping Smithers has gleaned news that one of his colleagues' employers has recently been boasting a prosperous outcome to a specific business investment—an investment we know from the viscount's ledger sustained a substantial loss."

Brandi nodded fervently as she followed Bentley's reasoning through to its obvious conclusion. "And, if such is the case, the gentleman in question is one of two things: a liar or a swindler."

"Precisely." Bentley cleared his throat. "Moreover, if the latter is true, there's one further possibility we must consider . . ." He hesitated.

"'Tis all right, Bentley," Brandi reassured him. "Whatever it is, I can withstand it. Tell me."

"Very well, my lady." His voice took on a soothing note. "So long as you realize this is all speculation."

"I do."

He nodded. "If my theory proves accurate and your

father were being cheated—and if he happened to stumble upon this fact, wouldn't that supply the gentleman in question with a reason to ensure the viscount's silence?"

"Oh my God." Brandi turned sheet white, instinctively clutching Bentley's hand.

For the first time, Bentley didn't withdraw into suitable butler-mode, instead leaving his right hand under Brandi's, covering her cold fingers with his left. "I didn't mean to upset you, my lady. I repeat, this is purely supposition and, very possibly, without a shred of merit."

"But your conclusion is logical," she managed. "I know in my heart Papa was too clever a businessman to invest as poorly as these ledgers imply. And if you're right—if one of the men on that list was swindling him—and if Papa learned the truth and refused to remain silent . . ." She drew a shaky breath. "Then it provides us with our first real motive since the murder."

"Those are numerous *if*s, Miss Brandi."

"Nevertheless, 'tis plausible and must be explored," she replied, the color slowly returning to her face as she called upon her emotional reserves. "By all means, go to Berkshire. Begin with your friend Smithers. And, if he cannot help us, then you and I will delve into the financial status of each and every man on Papa's list until we've either exhausted or confirmed your theory."

"What you're describing is a dangerous undertaking, Miss Brandi," Bentley warned, giving her hand a hard shake. "And I won't have you doing anything rash. So I repeat my original question: Is Herbert tending the garden at Emerald Manor today?"

"I've already answered: yes. But why is that important?"

"Because I won't leave you alone. And, being that today is my day off and Master Desmond is not expecting me to return to Colverton until late, 'tis the perfect opportunity for me to slip off to Berkshire. I'll be able to go and come without offering any explanations or igniting any tempers."

Brandi's eyes widened. "You want to go today, and you want Herbert to act as my governess during your absence?"

"I don't think Herbert would take kindly to being referred to as a governess—but, yes. 'Tis the only way I'll go."
Bentley frowned. "I'd prefer to await Master Quentin's arrival, so I'd know you'd be in the safest of hands. But I fear that isn't a viable choice, given Master Desmond's aversion to our investigation. So, if Herbert is willing, today it is."

The carriage came to a halt before Emerald Manor.

"We're home," Brandi announced, glancing out the window. "And, thanks to our early start, 'tis not even midday, giving you plenty of time to accomplish what you wish to." She took up her father's file, returning the ledger to its place. "Quickly. Deliver me to Herbert—as I know you better than to think you'd take me on my word. Then you can hasten to Allonshire with a clear conscience. As far as my being in safe hands, trust me, Herbert will be elated to stand guard over me—he'll have an able body to assist him in his rock garden, and a ready ear to listen to his complaints about the uncooperative geraniums."

Still Bentley hesitated. "And if Master Quentin returns before I?"

"Then I'll fill him in on everything." Seeing Bentley's dubious expression, Brandi couldn't help but smile. "Yes, Bentley, everything. I'll explain exactly how—and where—we found Papa's file. In fact, I'll confess to our Townsbourne excursion on bended knee. Would that be acceptable?"

"Perfectly. I do, however, recommend that you wait until I return to delve into the matter of Master Desmond's business skills—or lack thereof. He and Master Quentin are already on shaky ground. Perhaps I could broach the subject in a more subtle manner."

"And I'm anything but subtle," Brandi translated. "Very well, Bentley, I'll let you initiate the topic of Desmond. Quentin and I will have more than enough to discuss until your arrival tonight. Besides, this whole conversation could be moot. 'Tis possible Quentin won't return until morning." Impatiently, she flung open the carriage door, apologizing to the startled footman as she leaped down and landed solidly on his boots. "Forgive me, Gruthers, I'm in a dreadful hurry." She waited only until Bentley had alit before sprinting off toward the gazebo.

Bentley met the footman's gaping stare. "Hold the carriage, Gruthers. I'll be taking my leave momentarily."

"Yes, sir." Turning to stare after Brandi, Gruthers shook his head and resumed his post.

"Truly, you should be accustomed to it by now," Bentley commented as he strode off in Brandi's wake. He paused, scanning the oncoming path to determine her whereabouts. A minute later he spied her rounding the first bend, subsequently disappearing from view. "On second thought," he called over his shoulder to Gruthers, "perhaps one never grows accustomed to a recurring tempest."

By the time Bentley reached the gazebo garden, Brandi was talking excitedly to Herbert. The gardener was listening intently, wiping sweat from his brow and nodding.

"Hello, Bentley," he greeted. "Miss Brandi was just fillin' me in on your quandary." He chuckled. "I feel for you— needin' time off. I could use some myself—plan to take it later this week." He shot Bentley an understanding look. "It'll be a real pleasure havin' Miss Brandi help in the garden today. The work'll go twice as fast, and we'll be done before the sun sets. Yup, I could sure use the help." He wandered over to Bentley, ostensibly assessing the last few rows of geraniums. "Don't worry," he muttered for the butler's ears alone, "I figured out your real problem—and it's as good as solved. Until his lordship shows up at Emerald Manor, I'll keep an eye on Miss Brandi."

"I appreciate that," Bentley returned in an equally subdued tone. "Very well, my lady," he said in a normal voice. "Seeing you're in excellent hands, I'll be on my way."

Brandi regarded him soberly, gesturing with the file she clutched in her hands. "I hope your day is fruitful, Bentley."

"As do I," he agreed. With a half bow, he retraced his steps and was gone.

Gazing after him, Brandi shaded the sun from her eyes and said a silent prayer—although she was entirely unsure for what outcome she prayed. To discover her father was the murderer's target would be unbearable—but this vacuum of uncertainty was worse.

"These two damned rows still won't respond," Herbert muttered.

"What?" Brandi forced Bentley's mission from her mind, squatting beside Herbert.

"I said, these two damned rows of geraniums near the gazebo are still dyin'," he repeated. "I've tried everythin' I know, replanted them four times." He sighed. "Maybe I'm losin' my touch."

"You're doing no such thing," Brandi chastised. "Why, look at the rest of the garden. 'Tis doing splendidly. Perhaps the gazebo is blocking the sun, preventing it from reaching these flowers in particular."

"No, they're gettin' plenty of sun." Herbert scratched his head. "It makes no sense."

"I tell you what," Brandi suggested. "Why don't we consult my gardening books? I know you don't believe they have anything to offer"—she held up her hand to avert Herbert's protest—"but maybe one of them can provide an answer we haven't thought of. You must admit, 'tis worth a try."

He frowned. "If you say so."

An hour later, Brandi was leafing through the second of her gardening tomes and Herbert was snoring loudly under a neighboring oak.

Brandi smiled, lowering her book to the grass. 'Twas just as well Herbert was asleep. She wasn't able to summon up her usual empathy for his ongoing geranium plight—not today. Shifting restlessly, she wondered how Bentley would fare in Berkshire. Would his theory prove true? Could someone have swindled her father, then killed him for unearthing the truth? And if so, how had the culprit known her father would be traveling in the Steel carriage the morning of the accident? Was he someone her father confided in? Or was he a mere acquaintance to whom her father had casually mentioned his plans?

Muttering one of her rare profanities, Brandi opened the file and extracted the ledger, perusing, for the umpteenth time, the columns of numbers, as if by poring over them again and again she could discover something she'd previously missed.

She was losing her mind, tortured by unanswered questions, impeded by promises that rendered her helpless.

Quentin was at Whitehall. Bentley was en route to Berkshire. And she? She was sitting beside an oak tree staring vapidly at figures she could practically recite by memory.

She had to do something.

But what?

There had to be someone with the ability to resolve the baffling contrast between her father's customary success and his sudden, severe losses. Someone other than those who had perished in the carriage—and other than Desmond, who was an unthinkable source, given his lack of objectivity and unconfirmed business acumen. No, the someone she needed had to be impartial, familiar not only with her father's business ventures but also with the business ventures of those gentlemen whose names appeared in her father's ledger.

Someone like a solicitor.

Brandi was on her feet before the thought was complete.

Hendrick—that was it. Why hadn't she thought of it sooner?

Swiftly, she brushed the dirt and grass from her gown, careful to remain quiet so as not to awaken Herbert.

She'd promised Quentin and Bentley she wouldn't place herself in any danger; well, speaking to one's solicitor hardly qualified as perilous. And what better time to approach Hendrick than today, when both Quentin and Bentley were away and she wouldn't be missed? She could rush to London and back, returning, hopefully with some much-needed answers.

And what better person to supply them?

Triumph glistening in her eyes, Brandi considered the

obvious. Hendrick had handled the Townsend finances for years. Therefore, he doubtless possessed a thorough knowledge of all her father's investments and could possibly shed some light on the puzzling losses depicted in the ledger, as well as a plan to either prove or disprove Bentley's theory—somehow weeding out the innocent and, if necessary, converging on the guilty. Moreover, being that he was also the Steel solicitor, he might be able to clear up the perplexing discrepancy over Desmond's business acumen.

That he'd be willing to help was a certainty—hadn't he already offered her his assistance the day of the will readings? He'd be discreet, professional, and most of all, swift.

Her decision was made.

Ever so quietly, Brandi slipped away, hearing Herbert's snores echoing behind her. She dared not stop off at the cottage—Mrs. Collins was bound to intercede with a hearty meal or, at the very least, a nourishing snack. She'd go directly to the carriage house and, in mere minutes, be on her way to London.

'Twas a splendid plan, she congratulated herself—one that even Bentley would have to applaud. After all, it would expedite his search, provide them with answers . . .

And keep her far away from danger.

Chapter 12

"*P*lease, my dear, have a seat."

Easing back the tufted armchair, Ellard Hendrick waited politely until Brandi had complied.

"Thank you, Mr. Hendrick." She perched at the edge of the cushion, her father's ledger clutched tightly in her hands. "'Twas very kind of you to see me without an appointment."

"Nonsense." Glancing curiously, first at the slim volume Brandi held and then at the empty doorway, Hendrick asked, "You came unescorted?"

"Yes. I didn't plan this visit—it was totally impulsive."

"I see." Hendrick cleared his throat. "Pamela's jewelcase and silver—I presume they arrived without incident?"

"They did—the very day of the will readings." A heartfelt sigh. "To be honest, I placed them in my nightstand drawer and haven't touched them since. I'm simply not ready to confront such tangible memories. Especially the jewel case. It was a gift to Pamela from Kenton—and it meant the world to her." Brandi's voice faltered.

"I understand." Tactfully, Hendrick rearranged a few

papers, affording Brandi the opportunity to compose herself. "May I offer you some refreshment?"

"Thank you, no," she responded in her normal tone. "Only some advice—which is why I'm here."

"Very well." Ellard settled himself at the desk, an expectant look on his face. "How might I assist you?"

"First, I want to apologize for bursting in here unannounced. I sincerely hope I'm not keeping you from another appointment."

"Even if you were, I'd defer it. Whatever is troubling you must be serious if you didn't even take the time to ask Desmond to accompany you." A pause. "He does know you're here?"

"No. As I said, Mr. Hendrick, the decision to call on you was entirely spontaneous—and entirely my own. Once I've told you my reasons, you'll understand."

"Go on."

Brandi drew a deep, steadying breath. "I'm not certain where to begin."

"Does this relate in any way to your father's death? Have the authorities apprehended the murderer?"

"Unfortunately, no, they haven't. But, yes, it does relate to the carriage tampering—or, rather, it might." She fidgeted, staring at the ledger in her lap. "I know you searched through Papa's documents—at least those in your possession—and for that I'm grateful."

Hendrick waved away her thanks. "I only wish I'd unearthed something of import."

"Perhaps *I* have."

His brows drew together. "You?"

"Yes." Brandi leaned forward, offering Hendrick the ledger. "I had occasion to be in Papa's study today. I found this."

Frowning, Hendrick took the volume and began skimming the pages. "'Tis a ledger—an accounting of Ardsley's recent business ventures." Glancing up, he gave Brandi a puzzled look. "Why do you find this suspicious?"

"You don't find it odd for Papa to have concealed this book in his study rather than transferring it to your office?"

"Not in the least. Many of my clients maintain their own ledgers. It is, after all, their money. And while I provide them with interim statements of the profits and losses associated with their investments, some prefer to maintain personal records at home."

"I see. So you've seen these figures before?"

"Of course."

"And they didn't surprise you?"

"Why would they?"

Brandi chewed her lip. "Mr. Hendrick, I don't profess to be an accomplished business person. But Papa was."

"I agree." Hendrick toyed with his quill. "Forgive me, Brandice, but I'm not following your line of reasoning."

"Then I'll be blunt." Brandi almost smiled, recalling Bentley's dry observation about her inability to be anything else. "Given Papa's splendid business acumen, it seems peculiar to me that nearly all his recent ventures failed."

Hendrick gave her an indulgent look. "Skill is but one aspect of successful investing, my dear. An equally significant factor is luck. Unfortunately, during the past few months, Ardsley has been severely lacking in the latter."

"During the past few months." Instantly, Brandi jumped on Hendrick's words. "Are you saying that Papa didn't customarily suffer such losses?"

"No. He didn't." Hendrick paused. "If you're concerned about your inheritance, don't be. Your father's investments with Desmond more than made up for . . ."

"This has nothing to do with my inheritance," Brandi interrupted. She leaned forward intently. "Mr. Hendrick, suppose bad luck wasn't the underlying cause of Papa's losses. Suppose it was something else."

"Something else? Like what?"

"Before I answer that question, I have one of my own."

"Very well."

"Look at Papa's ledger once again." Brandi waited only until the solicitor had complied before continuing. "Are you familiar with any of the gentlemen whose names appear there?"

"Yes, of course."

"In your opinion, could any one of them be a swindler?"

"A swindler?" Hendrick's eyes widened, the ledger striking his desk with a thud.

"Yes. It occurred to me that since Papa's losses were clearly unprecedented, perhaps someone led him to believe their venture had failed, when in fact, that someone was reaping all the profits—profits that belonged to Papa."

"I hardly think . . ."

"But it is possible."

"I suppose so, but . . ."

"I have to be sure." Brandi hardly recognized that stern, purposeful voice as hers. "Because if one of those men was cheating my father and Papa learned the truth, that thief could just as easily have become a murderer."

For a long moment, Hendrick said nothing.

At last he spoke.

"That's quite a theory, Brandice. A bit far-fetched, wouldn't you say? Given the respectability of the gentlemen in question?"

"Perhaps. But, in all due respect, sir, 'twas my father who died in that carriage. And I intend to explore every avenue I can—probable or otherwise—to unearth the murderer."

Another pause. "Have you discussed your theory with Desmond? He is, after all, your legal guardian, and should be advised when you involve yourself with something as potentially dangerous as this. Not to mention the fact that he is responsible for Ardsley's businesses and should know if anything might be amiss."

"No. Desmond is—" Brandi hesitated, searching for what she could seldom find—tact. "Overcome with grief," she finished inanely. "I didn't think it was the best time to bother him."

A flash of comprehension crossed Hendrick's face. "I understand." He reexamined the list. "There are a dozen names here, Brandice. You can't ride to the estates of twelve prominent gentlemen and, based on obscure speculation, politely inquire of each of them if he is perchance a thief and a murderer." Hendrick shook his head in exasperation. "If it would ease your mind, I can peruse all their files, see if their profits contradict with your father's, but I don't see what else I can—"

"All their files?" Brandi nearly leaped from her chair. "Are you saying that every man on that list is a client of yours?"

"Why, as a matter of fact, yes."

"That's it!" Brandi leaned over Hendrick's desk, her eyes aglow. "We can establish the merit of my theory in one fell swoop." She thought for a minute. "Mr. Hendrick, I want you to organize a meeting for this week—or, at the very latest, next—in your office. Those in attendance will be you, myself, and every gentleman on that list. The Season is over—they should all be available. If not, they should make themselves available, which is precisely what they'll do if you stress the serious nature of our gathering—without being explicit, of course; we wouldn't want to inadvertently alert the murderer, should he be among them."

"A meeting," Hendrick repeated slowly. "And what, pray tell, have you in mind for this meeting?"

"By the time it takes place, you'll have scrutinized the files of all the gentlemen in question. I'll confront them as a group—explaining my plight and apologizing for any distress I might be causing them. I'll take full responsibility for arranging the meeting, therefore none of your business alliances will be hurt. In truth, I believe the gentlemen will understand my dilemma. The innocent will empathize, while the guilty one will, hopefully, give himself away. And no one can cast aspersion elsewhere, for they will all be in the same room at the same time, making lying a virtual impossibility. What a perfect solution!"

"And what about Desmond?" Hendrick asked in a tone of stern disapproval.

"Ah, Desmond." Brandi frowned. "I hadn't considered inviting him—although, of course, I planned to apprise him of the meeting," she added quickly, seeing Hendrick's censuring scowl. "My purpose is not to exclude him," she hastened to explain. "But he's excessively protective of me, and the last thing I want is to worry him, especially when he's still so . . . distraught." She rushed on, eager to finish before she ran out of euphemisms for the word *foxed*. "However, you're quite right; Desmond is my legal guardian as well as the overseer of Papa's businesses. Hence, sober or not, he should be in attendance."

She wanted to kick herself the moment her final words were out.

"Indeed he should." If Hendrick perceived her faux pas, he gave no sign.

Brandi didn't intend to tempt fate.

"I'll speak to Desmond myself," she vowed brightly. "Today, in fact. No, I won't reach the Cotswolds until Lord knows what hour. Tomorrow then. First thing in the morning. Unless, of course, he's still groggy from . . . that is, if he is unable to . . . if the effects of last night's . . ."

Her mouth snapped shut, presumably with her foot inside. *So much for my temporary brush with diplomacy,* she silently berated herself. *I'm hopeless.*

"There's no need for you to disrupt your sleep, my dear," Hendrick was saying. "As it happens, I'll be meeting with Desmond tomorrow. Once we've concluded our business, I'll fill him in on everything you and I discussed today."

Normally, such utter condescension would infuriate her. But in this case, Brandi was too elated by Hendrick's implication to pay attention to his placating tone.

"Then you'll see to the meeting?" she asked eagerly.

"I will."

"Immediately?"

A flicker of surprise crossed Hendrick's face, and Brandi bit her lip to silence her impatience. She must control her tongue, lest she insult Mr. Hendrick. After all, as the most respected solicitor in all of London—the expert who managed the funds of the *ton*'s most affluent noblemen—Mr.

Hendrick was clearly unused to tolerating pressure from anyone, least of all a woman.

"Forgive my appalling lack of manners, sir," she tried, attempting to explain her urgency. "But the monster who killed Kenton, Pamela, and Papa lurks somewhere about—free and unpunished. And I will not rest until he is apprehended and tossed into Newgate, where he belongs."

"I understand," Hendrick returned thoughtfully. "And there's no need for an apology." In a decisive gesture, he cleared a generous space on his desk. "I'll spend the next hour poring over the pertinent files. Immediately thereafter, I'll draft the first set of missives in order that we might explore the availability of the gentlemen in question. Those initial communications will be dispatched tonight."

Surprise and gratitude converged, sweeping over Brandi's face like a ray of sunshine. "Thank you, Mr. Hendrick," she acknowledged. "I can't tell you how much I appreciate your compassion—and how relieved I am that you'll be handling the matter."

"I'll do whatever I can. But remember, Brandice, don't get your hopes up. I'm well-acquainted with these gentlemen, and the probability that any one of them is guilty of duplicity—much less murder—is virtually nil."

"I recognize that." Brandi's mind had already taken another detour. "Sir, it just occurred to me that Quentin is due back from London any day now and that he, too, should be familiarized with the situation. If it's all right with you, I'd like to take the ledger with me, so I might show it to him and hear his thoughts. That doesn't present a problem, does it? You're free, of course, to copy down any figures you deem significant, although, as every gentleman Papa listed is your client, I'm certain your files are far more comprehensive than these pages."

"Undoubtedly." Hendrick jotted down a few notes, then rose, handing her the book. "By all means, take it. What's concerning me now is not the ledger but the lateness of the hour. The sun is already beginning to set. I'd feel much better if you were on your way back to the Cotswolds, particularly since you're traveling alone."

"You'll notify me should you discover something amiss in the files?"

"Of course. I'll also apprise you of the responses I receive to my missives, and advise you of the agreed-upon date and time for our meeting."

That prompted a thought. "You do know I'm continuing to reside at Emerald Manor?" Brandi asked.

"So I was surprised to learn. Tell me, Brandice, wouldn't you prefer being among those who love you at this painful time? I know for a fact that Desmond would be delighted to have you stay at Colverton with him—and Quentin, of course."

With gracious certainty, Brandi shook her head. "Emerald Manor is home. I'm not comfortable at Colverton; I never have been. Like Townsbourne—where I belonged only so long as Papa was alive—Colverton is too grand and impersonal to make one's own. No, Mr. Hendrick, I have no desire to stay at Colverton—despite my fondness for both Quentin and Desmond."

That possibility dismissed, Brandi toyed with the final nagging concern she'd yet to discuss with Mr. Hendrick—a concern that, if addressed with her customary lack of discretion, could be badly misconstrued.

Carefully, she chose her words, assuming the most nonchalant tone she could muster. "Mr. Hendrick, would you describe Desmond as a shrewd businessman?"

"Desmond?" Hendrick blinked, looking surprised and mildly curious. "Why, yes, I would say so."

"Did Kenton share that opinion?"

The solicitor rubbed his chin thoughtfully. "To be frank, Brandice, Kenton and I never discussed his personal views of his sons. But based on the intricacy of Desmond's involvement in the Steel businesses, I should say, yes, I believe Kenton concurred with my opinion. Why do you ask?"

"Just curious." Brandi gathered up her skirts, clutching the ledger to her side. "Well, I won't take up any more of your time. Thank you again, Mr. Hendrick. I look forward to hearing from you very soon."

By the time her carriage arrived at Cotswold Hills, Brandi was curled against the seat cushion, exhausted in the aftermath of her trying day. The sun had set, making the air dark and chilly, and she was grateful for the warmth offered by the closed carriage, equally grateful that it was her driver's responsibility—and not hers—to concentrate on the road, leaving her free to think and doze.

Her plan was in motion, and hopefully it would yield conclusive results—although the thought of confronting a murderer sent shivers up her spine. Still, she reminded herself, it was better than living in a state of perpetual uncertainty, with her life—and Quentin's—hanging in the balance.

Quentin.

Dreamily, Brandi wondered if he'd returned to Colverton yet. Had he resolved things with the War Department, or would he be sailing immediately for the colonies?

That prospect acted as a stinging blow to her senses.

Brandi sat bolt upright, all vestiges of sleep vanishing in a heartbeat.

Swiftly, she rolled down the carriage window. "Hamlin," she called to her driver. "I'd like to make a brief stop at Colverton before going on to Emerald Manor."

There was a slight pause, before Hamlin called back, "As you wish, my lady."

Judging from his startled tone, it must be very late, Brandi mused. Well, she didn't care. If Quentin were home, she wanted to see him. And if both he *and* Bentley were home, then she *needed* to see him; for Bentley would, by now, have informed Quentin of their day's adventures, and Quentin's foul words would, by now, be echoing through the elegant hallways of Colverton.

The image made her smile. Yes, 'twould definitely be in her best interests to see Quentin straightaway, to seize the opportunity to defend her actions while he still possessed a shred of reason.

Not to mention that she was itching to learn the outcome of Bentley's trip to Berkshire. Had he gleaned any information from Smithers or had his hectic dash to Allonshire been for naught?

Shifting restlessly, Brandi fixed her gaze out the window. Colverton suddenly couldn't appear fast enough.

A quarter hour later—although Brandi would have sworn it was a year—the carriage passed through the formidable iron gates and headed down the drive leading to the manor. Nearly hanging out the window, Brandi scrutinized the house to determine if any signs of activity were transpiring from within.

There were none.

The carriage rounded the drive and paused before the double entranceway doors.

"Will you be alighting, my lady?" Hamlin swung down to inquire.

Brandi counted windows until she found Quentin's bedchamber, noting that it was dark—a clear indication that the room's resident was either away or abed. Her disappointment intensified as she observed the rest of the manor: cast in shadows, unlit but for a few precautionary gas lamps in the entranceway.

"My lady?" Hamlin appeared beside the carriage door. "Shall I assist you?"

"Hmm? Oh, no." She shook her head. "I was going to visit, but it appears everyone has retired for the night."

"Well, it is half after ten, my lady."

"Is it?" Brandi blinked in surprise. "Then by all means, let's be on our way. Poor Bentley must be exhausted and, knowing him, he still intends to arise before dawn. As for Quentin . . ." Her voice drifted off and she scanned the second level one last time. Seeing no movement, she sighed. "Evidently, Quentin is either asleep or still in London. Hence, let's go on to Emerald Manor. I'll try again in the morning."

"Very good, my lady." Hamlin bowed and returned to his post. A moment later, the carriage resumed its motion, retracing its path through the iron gates and veering in the direction of Emerald Manor.

It was a little after eleven when Brandi dragged herself up the cottage steps, wanting nothing save a cup of warm milk and the comfort of her bed.

Her plans were quickly dashed by the sight that greeted her.

Like a sentry at his post, Herbert paced back and forth before the cottage door, alternately waving his arms and muttering agitated phrases under his breath.

"Herbert?" It took a full dazed minute for Brandi to focus on Herbert's obvious distress.

A minute was all she had.

"Miss Brandi . . ." He raced forward, grasping her elbows and searching her face. "Are you all right?"

"Well, of course. Why would you think . . . " Her hand flew to her mouth as realization struck, followed instantly by guilt. "Oh, Herbert, I'm so sorry. Were you worried about me?"

"Was I worried about you?" His brows shot up in disbelief. "You disappeared when I was supposed to be watching you—sneaked off like a thief while I was sleepin'. You didn't say a word about where you were goin'. You were gone for Lord knows how long. And you want to know if I was worried about you?"

Brandi's lashes swept her cheeks. "You're right."

"Where've you been?" he demanded.

"I rode to London." Her chin came up a notch, a puzzled expression on her face. "And I truly am sorry I worried you. But, Herbert, when did you become so protective? I've always come and gone as I pleased, and you never fretted over my whereabouts. Why now?"

"Because I . . ." Herbert shifted uneasily from one foot to the other. "Because Bentley said somethin' about you bein' in danger." Instantly, he pressed his lips together, clearly wishing he could recall his statement.

"I? In danger?" Brandi shook her head. "No, Herbert, you must have misunderstood. I realize Bentley asked you to look out for me today, but that was a mere formality— done out of respect for Quentin, who is convinced that I'm ever on the verge of doing something rash." She reached up, patted Herbert's weathered cheek. "But other than a few scrapes acquired fishing or, at worst, a bad fall from Poseidon, I assure you, I am in no danger." She chewed her lip. "Nevertheless, I feel terrible that I caused you such distress."

"Why'd you ride to London, anyway?" Herbert asked her.

"I had a bit of business to take care of."

"Business, huh? Like followin' after Lord Quentin?"

A flush stained Brandi's cheeks. Was there *anyone* who didn't suspect her feelings for Quentin?

"No, of course not," she denied. "In fact, I'm not even certain Quentin is still in London. He's due back in the Cotswolds anytime now."

"In that case, why didn't you wait for him before you went tearin' off to London? He could've gone with you. Was your business too important to put off for a day?"

Brandi's fingers tightened around the ledger, and she silently pondered how much she wanted to reveal.

Seemingly, her silence disturbed Herbert.

"Were you in London all this time?" he asked in a dubious tone.

"Yes—more or less."

"What does that mean, 'more or less'?"

Brandi blinked, unaccustomed to Herbert interrogating her. "It means that I stopped by Colverton on my way home. I'd hoped Quentin had already returned. Evidently, he hadn't. Neither, apparently, had Bentley." She paused. "Bentley didn't drop by Emerald Manor this evening by any chance, did he?"

"No." Herbert scowled. "Not that I would've noticed him anyway. I was too busy combin' the grounds for you." He cleared his throat. "I thought Bentley said he was goin' to Berkshire to visit a friend."

"Only for the day." Brandi sighed. "It doesn't matter. I'll speak with him tomorrow. I'll ride to Colverton at first light."

"Humph. Well, in that case, you'd better get some rest. If I know you, you'll be too excited to sleep. You'll be up before the first bird, and on your way to Colverton before the first glimmer of sunlight. Besides"—he yawned, turning to go—"I'm pretty spent myself. All that worryin' tired me out." Pausing, he offered, "If you want, I can stop by the carriage house now and tell Lakes to have the carriage ready at dawn."

"Hmm? Oh, no, thank you, Herbert. I think I'll take the phaeton and drive myself."

A nod. "Then I'll say good night."

Brandi reached out and squeezed his arm. "I really am sorry for dashing off without an explanation. It was thoughtless and stupid of me. Please don't be angry. Next time, I promise to tell you precisely where I'm going."

"Next time?" he grumbled.

Recognizing his softening tone, Brandi smiled. "Yes, my friend. With me, there's always a next time." She reached for the door handle. "Good night."

Herbert stared after her for a moment. Then he turned and made his way toward the woods.

A quarter hour later, Brandi slid between the sheets, plagued by a lingering sense of guilt. While it was wondrous to remain youthful, she admonished herself, in some aspects of life—aspects she had yet to master—it was very important to mature.

She'd let Herbert down tonight.

Obviously, he'd spent hours worrying over her safety. It wasn't important that his reasons were unfounded, nor his anxiety atypical. What mattered was that he'd felt responsible for her, and she'd overlooked his sense of duty, impulsively rushing off just as she willed. No, the fault was hers. She had to learn to think before she acted, to be more considerate of those she loved.

This metamorphosis to womanhood was even harder than she'd imagined.

Wearily, Brandi sank into the bed's softness. She'd make it up to Herbert somehow. The short-term solution was easy. After her morning visit to Colverton, she'd return to Emerald Manor and go straight to the garden, where she'd help Herbert replant his rows of geraniums.

'Twas the long-term that would prove tricky.

Brandi's lids grew heavy, an annoyance at best. Before she gave in to the relentless pull of slumber, she intended to finalize her plans for becoming an adult, mentally begin composing a list of questions for the gentlemen who'd be attending Mr. Hendrick's meeting, and think through tomorrow's chat with Quentin.

An instant later, she was asleep.

Bright sunlight danced across Brandi's face, teasing her into wakefulness. Her eyes opened, and she blinked, striving to clear away the final cobwebs of sleep.

Her first coherent thought was that it was late—very late. Her second was that Quentin would doubtless be home.

Bolting to a sitting position, Brandi sought out her bedchamber clock for confirmation—and received it.

It was ten A.M.

Ten A.M.?

With a muffled oath, she leaped from the bed, trying to run in three different directions at once. In her entire score of years, she'd never slept this late. And, while she recognized that it was because yesterday had obviously depleted her, she had no time to indulge herself.

She yanked on her clothes, her mind racing as it replanned her day in light of this annoying occurrence. She'd fetch the phaeton and ride posthaste to Colverton, praying all the while that no one had yet spoken with Quentin.

The odds were poor. Unlike her, Bentley never overslept. And Mr. Hendrick? Well, for all she knew the meeting he'd referred to—the one with Desmond today—was taking place right now, with her luck, at Colverton, not London.

She racked her brain, trying to recall if the solicitor had mentioned a location. He hadn't.

Damn. If Quentin and Mr. Hendrick were both at Colverton, then Quentin knew everything.

And she was in deep trouble.

Brandi paused in the process of dragging on her second stocking, the subject of Mr. Hendrick eliciting another thought.

Had the missives been sent? And, if so, how had the gentlemen in question reacted?

That anxiety supplanted all others. She simply had to know. So, no matter what manner of reception awaited, 'twas off to Colverton for her.

Twenty minutes later, her father's ledger safely tucked away in a pocket beneath her skirts, Brandi sprinted down the garden path toward the carriage house, a scone clutched in each hand. She veered off through the woods—the quickest route to her destination. The quickest and the most deserted. With a modicum of luck, she wouldn't run into anyone between here and there, and would, therefore, manage to spirit away the phaeton and tear off to Colverton in no time.

She didn't slow until both scones had been eaten, and she spied evidence that her goal was nearing—a flash of white glinting through a clearing in the trees. "I'm sorry, old friend," she called to her beloved gazebo, "but this is one time I cannot stop. We'll have to enjoy our customary morning visit in the evening—just this once."

Racing on, she wove her way through the stretch of trees that separated the gazebo from the carriage house.

Branches rustled overhead, followed by a whooshing sound and two loud thunks.

"Ouch!" Brandi came to a halt. Rubbing her head, she glanced from the shells at her feet to the culprit up above. "Those hurt," she chastised.

Without the slightest show of remorse, Lancelot finished off his snack, freeing up another nutshell. He stared down at her, shell poised to drop, his quizzing-glass gaze narrowed and somehow accusing.

"Don't even consider it," Brandi warned.

The squirrel blinked.

"I know you're angry with me for oversleeping," Brandi apologized. "But I can't make up for it now. I must see Quentin immediately. You shall just have to amuse yourself for a few hours. When I return—and after I assist Herbert—you and I can romp to your heart's content. How would that be?"

Another blink.

"Well, it will have to do." With an exasperated sigh, Brandi continued on her way.

A few minutes later, the rustling resumed from somewhere behind her.

"Lancelot, I'm warning you . . ." she began.

She never finished her sentence.

A high shrill cry echoed from behind—the shriek Lancelot used only when he was in distress. Frightened, Brandi whipped about, following the direction of the sound and scanning the woods for a sign of her squirrel.

Three things happened at once.

A flash of red dove from the sky, a roar of pain sliced through the trees, and a loud crack resounded, followed by a blinding pain in Brandi's temple.

With an agonized cry, Brandi crumpled, her hand rushing instinctively to her head.

Blood. Her hand was covered with blood.

Her stomach lurched, and a wave of dizziness accosted her, colors converging into a blinding, spinning kaleidoscope.

Somewhere in the distance, sounds of a struggle ensued: snapping twigs, muttered oaths, the distant thud of running footsteps.

And then . . . oblivion.

Chapter 13

"There, there, Miss Brandi. 'Twill be but a moment longer and your wound will be bandaged."

With a great effort, Brandi opened her eyes, blinking up at Mrs. Collins. "What . . . wound? Ooh." She moaned, a sharp pain piercing the side of her head.

"Lie still," Mrs. Collins soothed. "You're all right now. It feels much worse than it is."

Memory struck Brandi in a rush, and, instinctively, she started to come up off the sofa. "That loud crack. Lancelot . . . oh." For an instant, Brandi wondered if her skull had shattered. Shakily, she lay back, grateful for the soft pillows beneath her head.

"Your squirrel's fine, Miss Brandi." Herbert's voice drifted to her from across the sitting room. "I saw so for myself. I never thought the day would come when I'd be grateful to that bloody rodent. But I am."

"Herbert?" Brandi murmured weakly. "What happened?"

Herbert and Mrs. Collins exchanged glances.

"You were shot, Miss Brandi," Herbert answered quietly.

"Shot?" For some reason, Brandi's mind refused to comprehend. "How? By whom?"

"I'm not sure." The gardener made his way hesitantly to her side, his expression stricken. "A stupid accident, I'm guessin'. Someone huntin' here without permission, someone who didn't know anyone was livin' here but the servants. I was tendin' the flower bed around back of the cottage. I heard your squirrel friend screech—sounded like it was comin' from the woods. I took off in that direction. I'd barely gone a few paces when I heard someone bellow, then a gunshot, and then your scream. I got to you the same instant Bentley did. That squirrel of yours was sittin' next to you. He looked kinda funny—his fur was all messed up, like he'd been in a tussle. I could swear he understood you were hurt. He waited until Bentley and I got to you, then shimmied up a tree. That's how I know he was fine. *You*, on the other hand, were unconscious." A hard swallow. "And bleedin' badly. We were afraid we'd lost you."

"Bentley is here?" Brandi was desperately trying to think coherently.

"He was. He rode to the cottage this mornin' to check up on you. His carriage wasn't here ten minutes when he heard the commotion. He was as shook up as me."

"But, thank the Lord, 'tis only a flesh wound," Mrs. Collins inserted, sitting back with a flourish. "A well-bandaged one, if I must say so myself. Although I still wish you and Bentley had caught the scoundrel who did this, Herbert. I'd like to have given him a piece of my mind. Trespassing is bad enough, but hunting or target shooting without being certain the woods were deserted?" Vehemently, she shook her head. "Disgraceful."

"I heard Lancelot shriek," Brandi muttered unsteadily. "He leaped from the tree—I saw him. He must have attacked whoever the trespasser was. You said the man got away?"

"Yeah," Herbert confirmed. "After you were safe in the cottage, I went back out there, tore up every inch of those woods. But he was long gone. I wanted to get my hands on

218

him so bad. Humph—piece of my mind? What I wanted to give him was a piece of my fist."

Gritting her teeth, Brandi slowly turned her head in Herbert's direction. "You said Bentley *was* here. Where is he now?"

"He rode to Colverton a little while ago." An attempted smile. "He's fetchin' that hero of yours."

"Quentin's home?" That registered, dazed or not.

"Um-hum. And, accordin' to Bentley, he's not gonna be too pleased—not about this accident, or about your disappearance yesterday, or about a half-dozen other things."

As if on cue, the sound of horses' hooves raced up the drive, drawing closer, then ceasing. A door slammed, then another, followed by pounding footsteps echoing through the hallway.

The sitting-room door burst open.

"Brandi." Quentin crossed over in three long strides, waiting only until Mrs. Collins had stepped aside before perching himself on the edge of the sofa. "Sunbeam, are you all right?"

Despite her dizziness, Brandi recognized the stark fear in Quentin's voice, the panic on his face. She forced a weak smile. "Actually, I'm a bit under the weather, my lord," she murmured, reaching for his hand. "If you wish to best me in a competition, I should think now would be the perfect time."

"Reckless little fool." Quentin brought her palm to his lips. "I can't leave you alone for a minute. I swear I'd thrash you if I weren't so grateful you're safe."

"No, you wouldn't. Were you going to thrash me, you would have done so long ago. After twenty years, I've given you ample cause."

"More than ample cause," he amended. Frowning, he leaned forward, assessing the size of her bandage and the area surrounding it with an expert eye—an eye that had witnessed everything from flesh wounds to fatal ones. Ever so lightly, his fingers brushed the side of her face—the warmth of her skin a reaffirmation that she was alive. "How bad is it, Mrs. Collins?" he asked hoarsely. "Bentley said there was a great deal of blood."

"There was," Bentley confirmed, striding in. The tension on his face eased when he saw that Brandi was awake. "Miss Brandi. Thank heavens."

"'Tis true, my lord," Mrs. Collins was saying. "There was a lot of blood. But once I'd washed it away, I could see that Miss Brandi's wound wasn't serious; the bullet had only grazed her."

"We have her rascal of a squirrel to thank for that," Bentley put in. "From what Herbert and I could piece together, Lancelot assaulted the encroacher. In fact, judging from the scuffle we overheard and Lancelot's disheveled state, 'tis quite possible he saved Miss Brandi's life. Had he not acted so quickly, I shudder to think . . ." Bentley broke off, electing not to complete his thought.

Mrs. Collins's lips thinned into a grim line. "The man must have been drunk. Either that, or blind. How could he fail to notice Miss Brandi? Why, her hair color alone is bright enough to detect, no matter how thick the trees."

"Mrs. Collins." Quentin brought an end to the unsettling speculation. "Could you fetch Brandi some tea? And maybe a blanket or two?"

"Of course." The housekeeper hastened off.

The room fell silent.

Pointedly, Bentley cleared his throat. "My lord, I believe Herbert and I are both in need of fortification. Thus, if you can manage on your own for a while, he and I will retire to the dining room to enjoy a brandy."

"Go ahead."

"The dining room?" Herbert scratched his head. "But there's plenty of brandy right here in the sittin' room."

"Yes, but 'tis of questionable quality. Not a very good year for brandy, I suppose." Bentley's tone was clipped.

"Brandy is brandy. Besides, I want to stay with Miss . . ."

"Impossible. The entire sitting-room supply is being exchanged for a more suitable vintage." The butler's glare could fry an egg. "Therefore it must remain intact. Now, shall we?"

Bentley removed one hand from behind his back—only long enough to steer Herbert through the doorway. Glancing over his shoulder at Quentin, he raised his eyes to the heavens, then exited, shutting the door firmly in his wake.

Brandi bit her lip, stifling the laughter she knew would intensify the throbbing in her head. "I believe Bentley is picking up a bit of my tactlessness, my lord," she murmured. "That was done with a decided lack of finesse."

Unsmiling, Quentin leaned forward, brushing each corner of Brandi's mouth with his. "Is the pain bad?"

"It smarts." She reached up, wrapping her arms loosely about Quentin's neck. "I'm glad you're here." She sighed. "I didn't realize how much I missed you until now."

Emotion clouded Quentin's eyes. "I'm going to pour you a drink. I want you to finish every drop. Is that understood?"

"Very well."

Rising, he crossed over to the sideboard, pouring a healthy portion of brandy into a goblet.

Brandi watched him as he made his way back to her side. "Tell me, my lord, isn't that from the supply of questionable vintage?"

This time her jest had its desired effect.

A flicker of humor darted across Quentin's face. "The very one. But, for our purposes, it will do." He sank down beside her, anchoring her head with one hand, easing her into a half-sitting position. "It will alleviate the pain. Now sip slowly," he instructed, pressing the glass to her lips.

Brandi nodded, taking a tentative sip, then shuddering. "'Tis just as well to use this inferior bottle for my medicinal needs," she told him, making a face. "An exceptional vintage would be wasted. I loathe the taste."

"Pity. Because you're going to finish every last drop."

"Yes, sir, Captain Steel." With a martyred look, Brandi complied, grumbling her displeasure after every sip.

"Excellent." Quentin set down the empty glass. "You can

stop muttering. Your torment is over. Now just lie still and let the brandy do its job." He lowered her back to the sofa.

"You're an unfeeling tyrant, you know," she murmured, sinking into the cushions.

One dark brow rose. "This coming from the hoyden who brutally chastised me and accused me of being a bloody fool?"

A smile touched Brandi's lips, her lashes drifting to her cheeks. "You are a bloody fool." She yawned. "Did you hear what I said before? I missed you."

"I heard you." Quentin brushed tendrils of hair from her brow.

"And?"

Tenderly, he caressed her cheek. "And what?"

"And, aren't you going to answer me?"

"Are you certain you want me to? I should think you'd be reluctant to hear my reply after the shambles you made of my pride."

Brandi forced her lids open, all the vulnerability in the world reflected in her eyes. "I'm certain. Please, Quentin, answer me. Quickly. I need to know what you're thinking." She fought the warm languor already spreading through her limbs. "And what you're feeling."

"Still so impatient. And so frank. My honest, impulsive Sunbeam. No matter what turmoil the world inflicts, you're the one precious facet that remains untouched. Thank God."

Brandi's breath caught in her throat.

"I missed you every moment I was gone," Quentin breathed, giving her the answer they both sought. "But unlike you, I realized it. Constantly. Every second that ticked by I wanted nothing more than to race home to Emerald Manor and hold you in my arms." He twined a burnished strand around his finger. "You'll be pleased to learn that my obtuseness has vanished. I can now supply you not only with the correct answers but with the proper questions as well. Now, is that a satisfactory reply?"

"Most definitely, my lord." Tears shimmered on Brandi's lashes. "In fact, should this all be a dream—should it happen that I am badly hurt and presently unconscious—I'd prefer never to be awakened."

"I'll see if that can be arranged," Quentin replied soberly. "But, in my experience, pounding heads and bloody wounds are clear signs of consciousness."

"Good." Brandi reached up, lay her palm against his jaw. "Quentin?"

"Hmm?"

"Before we talk—which I know we must, before you begin shouting so fiercely that all but Bentley flee Emerald Manor . . ." She yawned again. "And before this brandy makes me so silly I won't be able to savor the memory—before all that, would you kiss me?" Her fingers stroked his nape. "After which, I won't mind your shouting nearly so much."

Ever so gently, Quentin's arms slipped beneath her, cradling her head to silence the pain. Then, he bent forward, taking her lips in a soft, beautiful, eloquent caress that Brandi felt to the tips of her toes.

"Not just one kiss," she protested, when he would have drawn back. "I want more."

A chuckle, part joy, part relief, rumbled from Quentin's chest. "Don't you always?" He kissed her again, molding the softness of her mouth to his, taking her tongue in a breathtaking whisper of a motion.

Brandi responded by sliding her hands beneath his coat, stroking the length of his back through the fine material of his shirt.

Her touch seemed to strike a chord of emotion deep inside him. "Christ, I was terrified," he murmured against her parted lips. "The thought of you being hurt—or worse . . ."

"I'm fine," Brandi assured him, her voice slurring a bit. "I wasn't even frightened. I didn't have time to be." Her lids fluttered. "I don't want to sleep," she protested, fighting the effects of the brandy. "I want to kiss." Her lashes swept her cheeks. "I love when you kiss me. It feels like heaven." Another yawn. "Besides, if we kiss forever, I never have to tell you about Townsbourne or about my plan." Her arms slid to her sides, her voice trailing off. "Or about my visit to Mr. Hendrick's office yesterday . . ."

She was asleep.

Quentin was not.

"Hendrick's office?" He jerked upright. "What visit to . . ." Seeing Brandi was asleep, he realized she couldn't provide him with answers.

But he intended to get them.

"Bentley." Quentin stalked into the dining room. "We need to talk. Herbert," he continued, still glaring at Bentley, "would you excuse us?"

"Is Miss Brandi all right?" Herbert demanded.

"She's fine. In fact, she's sleeping. Mrs. Collins is with her now. Feel free to peek into the sitting room on your way out."

"All right." Herbert placed his glass on the table, ill at ease but obviously determined to speak his mind. "Forgive me, my lord, but I was wonderin'—I'll be workin' at the gazebo. Would you mind sendin' for me when Miss Brandi wakes up? I'd like to see her—if she's feelin' well enough."

"I wouldn't mind at all. I'm sure Brandi will want to see you, too . . . *after* she and I have had a chance to talk."

"Of course, sir." Responding to Quentin's unmistakable cue, Herbert made a hasty retreat.

Bentley waited until they were alone. "What is upsetting you, my lord?" he calmly inquired.

"I think you should tell me. Before she drifted off, Brandi muttered something about visiting Hendrick's office yesterday. Would you care to enlighten me as to what visit she's referring to?"

"I haven't the slightest idea." Bentley frowned. "The only trip Miss Brandi made yesterday to which I can attest is the one I made with her to Townsbourne. And I've already relayed to you all the details and findings associated with that particular visit. As for Mr. Hendrick's office . . ." The butler pursed his lips. "'Tis possible that's where Miss Brandi went when she abandoned Herbert and stole off to London."

Quentin's fists clenched at his sides. "I cannot believe this. I've been away only a few bloody days. And in that amount of time, Brandi has persuaded my trusted butler to accompany her on a jaunt I expressly asked her not to make without me, discovered a hidden ledger that could possibly endanger her life, and eluded my sleeping gardener to sneak off for an afternoon in London, where she apparently met with my solicitor about Lord knows what."

"If you'll forgive me, sir, what you expressly forbade Miss Brandi to do was to travel to Townsbourne alone—which, in fact, she did not. You also requested that she wait one day before she acted—which she did. Therefore, neither she nor I disobeyed your instructions. As for her trip to Mr. Hendrick's office, I assume it concerned the allegedly life-threatening ledger to which you just referred—a ledger that, if my fruitless visit to Allonshire is any indication, is no more perilous than any other ordinary document. And last, Herbert is a fine, hard-working man. He just happens to require a fair amount of sleep. Not to sound immodest, my lord, but I believe I've spoiled you with my unique ability to perform splendidly on little or no rest. Most people do require an occasional respite."

Quentin shot him a look. "Are you quite finished proclaiming your virtues?"

"Quite, sir."

"Good. Then can we get back to the issue at hand?"

"I assume you mean Miss Brandi's trip to London?"

"Excellent assumption." Quentin began to pace.

"I assure you, sir, Miss Brandi made no mention of an intended excursion to Mr. Hendrick's office. I have no idea what prompted the immediacy of her trip. Frankly, when I left for Berkshire, she seemed perfectly willing to await my return before taking further steps."

"She seemed willing to await your return—you mean, much like she was willing to await mine?" Quentin cocked a derisive brow in Bentley's direction.

"I see your point, my lord."

"So do I—a bit too late." Quentin stalked the length of the dining room, his demeanor grim as he mentally assembled the pieces of the last few days' puzzle. "Hell, Bentley, we were both fools. You and I should know better than to believe Brandi could—*would*—stay put. She's as restless as a firefly and equally unable to remain still. Worse, she plunges headlong into a situation, giving no thought to the possible repercussions. My guess is that some brilliant notion entered her clever, reckless mind—one she deemed important enough to act upon. Now 'tis up to us to determine what that notion was and what were its consequences." He halted, meeting Bentley's anxious expression. "And if those consequences had anything to do with today's allegedly accidental shooting."

"Shall I prepare a missive for Mr. Hendrick, sir?"

"No." Quentin shook his head adamantly. "I don't want to meet with Ellard until I know precisely what he and Brandi discussed. Although, God help me, knowing Brandi as I do, I'm sure her intention was to get to as many of the men named in Ardsley's ledger as she could."

"At the risk of fueling your outrage, my lord, the idea is a sound one."

"For us to explore, yes. For Brandi, no." Quentin scowled. "You're sure Smithers knew absolutely nothing? He'd heard no gossip that could be construed as even remotely suspicious?"

"Quite sure, sir. He is on the friendliest of terms with the valets of all four Berkshire gentlemen listed in the viscount's ledger. Not one of their financial circumstances has altered in the past several months."

"That leaves eight men unaccounted for," Quentin reminded him. "Any one of whom could be our culprit. Damn it. I've got to get a look at Ardsley's ledger."

"I recalled nearly every name on that list for you, sir."

"That's not good enough. I need *all* the names. I also need to view them alongside their corresponding figures in order to come to any reasonable conclusion. In short, I need to examine the ledger itself."

"I see your point, sir. And inspecting the ledger should present no problem. Miss Brandi took it with her when we left Townsbourne. I assume she's secured it at Emerald Manor."

"Unless she gave it to Hendrick."

"I never thought of that." Bentley frowned. "What will you do if that proves to be the case?"

"I'll ride to London and speak with Ellard—which I'm certain I'll have to do anyway, given that Brandi has doubtless involved him in whatever scheme she's devised."

"I don't know whether or not this will affect your plans, sir, but Master Desmond received a late-night missive from Mr. Hendrick."

Quentin's eyes narrowed. "You wouldn't happen to know the contents of the missive, would you?"

"Not precisely, no. But, according to Sanders, Master Desmond read the note, then muttered something about meeting with Mr. Hendrick late this afternoon."

"At Colverton?"

"No. In London."

"Ah, so my brother is going to London. And we can both guess what Hendrick penned to prompt that excursion."

"You're suggesting that Mr. Hendrick notified Master Desmond of Miss Brandi's visit," Bentley supplied.

"Without a doubt. Poor Ellard must have been shocked speechless when Brandi appeared at his office without either a chaperon or her faithful guardian. I'm certain he finished composing that missive to Desmond before her carriage left his door." Comprehension glinted in Quentin's eyes. "Well, at least that explains why Desmond hasn't rushed to Brandi's side. He must be en route to London, in which case he doesn't even know of the accident."

"It's probable he doesn't know of the shooting," Bentley concurred. "But not because he's en route to Town. I don't expect that Master Desmond will be taking his leave for several hours now."

"Then where was he when you arrived at Colverton with the news?"

"Abed, my lord." Bentley gave an indignant sniff. "Sanders attempted to awaken him, but to no avail. With the precarious state of Miss Brandi's health, I was not about to waste time administering doses of reviving black coffee. Hence, I advised Sanders to relay the news to Master Desmond when he managed to lift his head from the pillow. Which, based upon the hour at which he staggered to his bedchamber last night"—Bentley extracted his timepiece, confirming that the noon hour had come and gone— "should be sometime around one o'clock."

"At which point he'll burst into Emerald Manor on his white steed," Quentin concluded icily. "I'm glad you told me, so I can prevent it from happening. The last thing I'll allow my deceptive lush of a brother to do is subject Brandi to the surly aftermath of one of his drunken stupors." Seeing the surprised lift of Bentley's brows, Quentin added, "If I sound uncharacteristically brutal, it's because my prolonged visit to the War Department yielded results that demolished my sympathy for Desmond."

"You've lost me, sir. You did say Lord Bathurst granted your request and deferred your orders, did you not?"

"I did. But not before I met with him personally—after a full day of his staff ignoring, stalling, and evading me."

Bentley looked puzzled. "That sounds like rather odd treatment, my lord."

"Odd and unprecedented. Which is what I told Bathurst. He was as perplexed as I. At his suggestion, I questioned each of his aides. It took forever, but I finally discovered the poor lad who was young and impressionable enough to succumb to aristocratic pressure. It seems he was 'urged'— should he wish to retain his position—to make it appear on paper that my presence in America was needed posthaste. And you'll never guess who did the 'urging'? None other than my loving brother."

Somehow Bentley found his voice. "Why would Master Desmond do such a thing?"

"Can't you guess?"

A heartbeat of silence. "Miss Brandi."

"Of course. Desmond doesn't want me near her—a goal which would be realized by my hasty departure for the colonies. However, his plan is doomed—and not only because I discovered it in time for Bathurst to defer my orders. But because even after the murderer is unveiled, even when I do leave England, I will never again denounce my role in Brandi's life, nor will I deny my feelings for her. And God help Desmond if he tries to stand in my way."

"Bravo, sir."

Quentin quirked a brow. "I'm glad I have your approval, Bentley," he acknowledged dryly. "And now that we've established that fact, can we return to the matter of today's mysterious shooting?"

"Pardon me, my lord." Mrs. Collins poked her head into the room. "But Miss Brandi is awake. And she's asking for you."

"Shall I wait here, sir?" Bentley inquired.

"No. Come with me."

Nodding, Bentley followed behind Quentin, remaining tactfully in the background as Quentin strode across the sitting room to where Brandi lay propped on the sofa, a blanket draped about her and voluminous pillows arranged beneath her head. Amid the copious bedcovers, she looked small and pale and very fragile.

"Did you have a nice nap, Sunbeam?" Quentin asked with offhanded ease, his casual tone belied by the intensity of his gaze.

"I suppose." Brandi touched her bandage tentatively.

"Is the pain better?"

"Yes, considerably." She searched his face. "The nap helped. But not as much as what I was doing beforehand." A pause. "I was doing what I think I was doing—wasn't I?"

A corner of Quentin's mouth lifted. "Um-hum." He sat

down beside her, pressed her palm to his lips. "We both were."

"Good." She looked relieved. Sensing Bentley's presence, she turned her head in his direction, not a shred of embarrassment tingeing her cheeks. "Thank you again for coming to my rescue."

"Your squirrel did that, my lady. All I did was assist him."

That made Brandi smile. "Then we shall have to prepare a special feast of nuts and berries in honor of Lancelot's heroic deed."

"Sweetheart," Quentin repeated soberly, "are you certain the pain has subsided?"

Brandi gave a deep, resigned sigh. "If you mean, am I up for your berating session, the answer, unfortunately, is yes. Just let me know how much Bentley has already told you, and I'll fill in the rest. Feel free to begin bellowing at any point along the way."

Bentley was assailed by a sudden attack of coughing.

Quentin scowled, first at Bentley, then at Brandi. "I know about your jaunt to Townsbourne," he informed her. "And about the ledger you found. Which reminds me, why didn't you ever mention the hidden compartment in your father's desk to me?"

"You never asked."

"Very amusing. In other words, you intended from the beginning to search the desk yourself."

"No, I intended from the beginning to search the desk with you. You were in London. So I searched it with Bentley." Again, she inclined her head in Bentley's direction. "Did Smithers provide us with any clues?"

"None, my lady. The four Berkshire gentlemen on the viscount's list are, evidently, not enjoying new and bounteous fortunes."

"Oh." Brandi's face fell. "Well, hopefully my plan with Mr. Hendrick will tell us if any one of the others is guilty."

"What plan with Mr. Hendrick?" Quentin ground out. "Damn it, Brandi, did you go to Ellard's office yesterday?"

"Yes. I asked him to arrange a meeting between all the gentlemen listed in Papa's ledger, and me." She frowned. "Oh, yes, and Desmond. Mr. Hendrick insisted he be there."

"I'm sure he did. Have you already spoken with Desmond about this?"

"No. Mr. Hendrick is meeting with him today. Actually, I rode by Colverton last night on my way home, although, in truth, it was you and Bentley I wanted to see, not Desmond. In any event, I saw no one. The manor was dark. You must all have been abed."

"I wasn't abed," Quentin countered. "I wasn't even there. I didn't arrive at Colverton until this morning."

"This morning? Early? Then why didn't you ride right out to see me?" she demanded.

Quentin shook his head in disbelief. "I don't believe this. No, not early. If you must know, little hoyden, my carriage arrived at Colverton just as Bentley was preparing to leave for Emerald Manor. He filled me in on the antics of the past several days, then went on ahead while I bathed and changed. After which, I fully intended to ride directly to the cottage, even before I knew you'd been hurt. Is that satisfactory?"

Brandi's eyes sparkled. "Yes."

"Good. Now let's try to recall who is grilling whom, shall we?"

"Whatever you say, my lord."

"Back to this meeting you're arranging." Quentin folded his arms across his chest. "What is its purpose?"

"Why, to determine if one of the gentlemen listed in Papa's ledger is guilty, of course," she said in an exasperated tone.

"Do you actually believe that if a murderous swindler is present in Hendrick's office, he will succumb to an attack of conscience and confess all? That the very sight of you will cause him to spring to his feet and proclaim his guilt?"

Brandi flinched. "There's no need to be sarcastic or insulting. Obviously, I know better than to believe that. But if one of those men did cheat my father, his records will conflict with Papa's ledger. And he won't be able to cast aspersion elsewhere—not with all his colleagues in the same room. Thus, his scheme will be exposed."

"Just like that." Quentin's scowl deepened. "Tell me, was this Hendrick's idea?"

"No. 'Twas mine."

"I don't even know why I bothered asking. The real question is, how does Hendrick factor into this grand plan of yours?"

"He represents the business interests of every man on that list. He promised to review their files and take the first step in arranging our meeting."

"First step?"

"He sent out missives in order to determine a mutually convenient time and day."

Quentin and Bentley exchanged glances. "When, Brandi? When did he send out those missives?"

"Last night."

"Hell and damnation." Quentin averted his head, a muscle working in his jaw.

"Why does that upset you?" Brandi asked, her brows drawn in question. "And why is your reaction so extreme? I expected you to be angry, but you're more than angry. You're downright cruel. Quentin, what is it? You've never treated me like this before."

A look of naked emotion crossed Quentin's face. "I've never cared like this before."

The admission—uttered as much to himself as to Brandi—settled softly about them, traversing an invisible span between past and present, melding the two into one.

Their gazes locked.

Unnoticed, Bentley slipped from the room.

Inhaling sharply, Quentin sifted his fingers through Brandi's hair. "Sunbeam . . ."

"Later." Tenderly, she pressed a silencing forefinger to his lips. "Not now. I want to savor the words the first time you speak them. Not hear them blurted hastily in the midst of a lecture, no matter how loving its intent." She leaned forward, brushed her lips to his. "Later," she repeated softly.

Quentin's hand slid beneath her burnished mane, caressed the warm skin at her nape. "My beautiful Sunbeam," he murmured. "Why is it that every cherished moment must be eclipsed by dark reality?"

"Because those moments are meant to stand alone, so that we might properly treasure them." With that, she sat back, inclining her head expectantly. "Now, tell me why you're so enraged about the missives Mr. Hendrick sent."

"Very well." Quentin weighed his explanation, seeking words powerful enough to inspire caution, gentle enough to preclude fear. "There's a possibility that, evidently, hasn't occurred to you. It's slim, I admit, but viable nonetheless. The reason I haven't mentioned it until now is because it's only speculation, and I didn't want to frighten you. Lord knows, you'd endured enough these past weeks. But maybe it's best that we discuss my theory now, if only to open those extraordinary, willful eyes of yours." He intertwined their fingers. "Not two hours ago, you missed being killed by mere inches and the grace of God. Did you ever think that perhaps the shooting was no accident? That someone might be trying to—" He struggled with the word *kill*, then abandoned it. *"Hurt* you?"

Brandi's pupils dilated. "Hurt me?"

"Think about it. Let's assume that your premise is correct—that, in fact, Ardsley was the intended victim of the carriage disaster. Take it one step further. Assume the killer wanted to silence your father from revealing not only the fact that he'd been deceived but the identity of the deceiver. And silence him he did, thus eliminating all threat of exposure.

"Then, without warning, Ardsley's bright, persistent daughter intervenes, delving until she finds a damning ledger. The culprit's anonymity is once again at risk. Brandi"—Quentin's tone gentled, his fingers tightening around hers as if to cushion the blow—"he's already murdered three people to protect himself. Do you honestly think he'd hesitate to do so again?"

Whatever color remained in Brandi's cheeks rapidly drained away. "Oh my God . . . I never even considered that."

"Listen to me, Sunbeam. This isn't a certainty. It isn't even a likelihood. It's simply a possibility. But even a possibility is too much when it comes to keeping you safe. Now do you understand why I became crazed at the thought of you dashing about London—or anywhere else—alone?"

Rather than answering, Brandi stared up at him, comprehension illuminating her eyes. "Now I see why you reacted so violently to the missives Mr. Hendrick sent," she murmured, half to herself. "You believe that one of the recipients is guilty, and that, upon reading Mr. Hendrick's note, he deduced what I had in mind. And that he then tried to . . ."

"I don't want you jumping to conclusions."

"I'm not. Nor do you believe I am, or you wouldn't even have considered this possibility, much less mentioned it. Moreover, your theory makes perfect sense." Brandi's chin quivered. "Herbert surmised that the man who shot me was probably a trespasser, someone who assumed no one was living at Emerald Manor but servants. I realize now how flimsy that explanation is—doubtless Herbert's attempt to shield me. The fact is, why would anyone believe Emerald Manor to be deserted? Pamela and I spent long hours in the gardens nearly every day, in full view of any and all passersby. And since her death, I've spent more time in the gazebo than I have in the cottage. No, Quentin. Whoever fired that pistol knew I'd be about." Terror filled her eyes. "He must have waited for me in the woods. He intended to kill me."

Tenderly cradling her injured head, Quentin gathered her to him. "Stop it, Sunbeam. This is pure speculation. We don't know if there's even a grain of truth to it." He brushed his lips across her forehead. "But until we're certain, no more stupid risks, all right?"

Dazed with shock, Brandi nodded. "I'm sorry," she managed. "What a fool I've been. None of this even entered my mind."

Quentin buried his lips in her hair, feeling the chill of her fear and hating himself for causing it. "You're not a fool," he countered, his voice rough with emotion. "You're a beautiful, courageous woman. And I don't want you to be afraid. Nothing is going to happen to you. I won't let it."

Brandi fought the panic, and lost. "When will you sail for the colonies?" she asked, dreading his response.

"Not until the murder is resolved. Lord Bathurst delayed my orders."

She drew back, relief flooding her face. "Thank God. Quentin . . ." That vulnerable look invaded her eyes, permeated his soul. "Stay with me. Don't go away."

It was the same plea she'd uttered to him a lifetime ago—on the day he'd returned to the Cotswolds.

The same plea, a different man.

"I won't," he heard himself say, offering the unfulfillable promise he'd vowed never to make. "I won't leave you—ever."

Brandi shook her head adamantly, negating the significance of his response. "That's not what I meant," she clarified in a fierce whisper. "I know it can't be forever. But it can be now. Here. At Emerald Manor. Until this nightmare is over. Please, Quentin. Stay with me."

Something painful and profound moved within Quentin's chest. "Brandi, I can't."

"Why?" Tears shimmered on her lashes. "Because it would shatter my reputation? I don't give a damn."

"No." He framed her face between his palms. "Because it would shatter my control."

"I don't give a damn about that either. In fact, I would welcome it."

With a half-laugh, half-groan, Quentin dragged Brandi back into his arms. "Ah, sweetheart, were it only that simple."

"It is."

"No. It's not. Damn it, Sunbeam, you can't possibly understand what's at stake."

"I know what's at stake." Brandi leaned back, searched his eyes. "Do you?"

"So well that I want to envelop you and free you all at once."

"What if I don't want to be freed?"

Silence.

"Quentin," Brandi murmured, easily interpreting the clashing emotions that warred across his face, understanding them with an intuition as old as time. "No matter what's changed between us, you're still my best friend. You always will be. I want you with me, if only for comfort." A mischievous smile darted across her lips. "And, should your never-failing control falter, mine shall take over. 'Twill be an interesting switch, wouldn't you say?"

Laughter rumbled in Quentin's chest. "Very interesting. And how, my impulsive hoyden, will you manage that?"

"I suppose you're too arrogant to believe I'm totally immune to your charms?"

The laughter faded as quickly as it had come. "To the contrary, Sunbeam, I'm humbled by what happens when you're in my arms. And I'm as helpless as you to prevent it."

Brandi lay her palm against his jaw. "Emerald Manor is yours. Need I remind you that the cottage includes your own bedchamber?"

He turned his lips into her palm. "Ah, but will I use it?"

"That's entirely up to you."

"You're tempting fate, you know."

"No, I'm tempting you."

Another chuckle. "You have no idea how much."

"I think I do. In fact, I'm counting on it." Brandi's eyes sparkled. "I'm also counting on the fact that you've never been able to say no to me."

Quentin raised his head. "Nor you to me," he reminded her.

"True." She gazed up at him, her heart in her eyes. "Stay with me," she repeated quietly. "Mrs. Collins will be here to silence any wagging tongues. Bring Bentley, as well. After all, once news of my accident becomes public, everyone will assume I'll need constant ministrations. Knowing how close our families are, the *ton* will simply presume that you and Bentley are helping Mrs. Collins take care of me."

"Which I intend to. In light of what's happened, I don't want you left alone for one bloody minute." Quentin frowned. "Damn. I've got to see Hendrick."

"He's probably at Colverton. He said he planned to meet with Desmond today."

"In London, not here. And speaking of my brother, I have a few unresolved issues to take up with him—when he gets his head out of a bottle long enough to listen."

"So do I. I want to show Desmond the ledger and ask him about Papa's unreasonable losses."

Quentin's eyes narrowed. "You didn't give the ledger to Ellard then?"

"Of course not. I told him to copy down the figures so I could show the ledger to you."

"Excellent. Where is this ledger?"

Pointing to her gown, Brandi grinned. "Under here. Would you care to fetch it?"

One dark brow rose. "You're playing with fire."

"I'm fully prepared to be burned." She nuzzled the bare warmth of Quentin's throat. "Go to London if you must."

"No." A tremor rippled through him, and his arms closed possessively around her. "I'll ride to Colverton, deal with Desmond. But I'm not returning to London. I'll instruct my brother to bring Hendrick back to the Cotswolds with him following their meeting. At which point, you and I will both have a chance to give voice to our questions. And our concerns."

"Fine. Then don't leave at all. You can simply send Desmond a missive, telling him to escort Mr. Hendrick directly to Emerald Manor."

"That won't work. Bentley left instructions with poor Sanders to apprise Desmond of your accident the instant he awakens. You and I both know that, once Desmond hears

the news, he'll insist on stopping here en route to London—
the dutiful guardian looking after his charge—especially
once he learns that I've returned. No, I'd rather deal with
Desmond now. Besides"—Quentin gave Brandi a melting
smile that singed her down to her toes—"I've got to go to
Colverton anyway. To pack."

Chapter 14

"Sanders, is my brother awake?" Quentin demanded, crossing the front hallway in long strides.

"Only just, my lord." The valet finished his descent from the second-floor landing, pausing now and again to glance uneasily over his shoulder. "How is Lady Brandi, sir?"

"Weak. Shaken. But fine. Have you told him?"

Sanders had no time to reply.

With a thud and a curse, Desmond staggered to the head of the steps, tightening the belt of his dressing robe and glaring at Sanders. "What the hell is going on here? I asked for a drink." From the corner of his eye, he spied Quentin. "Oh, I should have guessed. The incomparable Lord Quentin has returned to Colverton. Tell me Sanders, was that the crucial announcement you were hovering about me to make—the one that precluded your following orders and fetching me a fresh bottle of Madeira?"

"No, Desmond, it wasn't," Quentin said, his tone as stony as his stance. "Sanders was trying to tell you Brandi's been hurt."

Desmond's surliness vanished. "Hurt? How?"

"She was shot."

"Christ—when? Is she all right?"

"Several hours ago. And, yes, she'll recover. She's dazed and weak, both from blood loss and shock. She's also in a fair amount of pain. But, luckily, the bullet missed its mark and grazed her temple. Any closer would have killed her."

"Missed its mark? Are you saying someone tried to murder Brandice?"

"I believe so, yes."

Desmond swore, raking an unsteady hand through his hair. "Who the hell would want to . . ." He broke off, glowering at his valet. "Why didn't someone awaken me right away?"

"Sanders attempted to," Quentin returned, assessing his brother with utter distaste. "But you were even more uncooperative at that time than you are now. Difficult as that might be to believe."

"I didn't get to bed until dawn. I was exhausted. But for something like this"—Desmond shot another malevolent look at his valet—"you should have tried harder."

"Sanders is as splendid a manservant as they come," Quentin inserted, sparing Sanders the indignity of defending himself. "'Tis hardly his fault that you're too deep in your cups to know day from night."

"Thank you, my lord," Sanders acknowledged quietly.

Color suffused Desmond's face. "Evidently, my valet's been talking out of turn."

"He doesn't have to," Quentin refuted. "I have eyes. You've been perpetually drunk since Father's death."

Desmond's lips thinned. "We'll discuss my habits another time, Quentin. Alone," he added pointedly. "Right now, Brandice needs me. I'll get dressed and go to her." He turned and headed back toward his room.

"Don't," Quentin directed Sanders, staying the valet's progress with his hand.

"He'll need my assistance, Lord Quentin."

"I'll give him all the assistance he needs. I have a strong feeling he'd prefer to be alone for the conversation we're about to have."

"Oh, I see." Sanders mopped his brow uncertainly.

"In the interim, I'd appreciate your finding my valet and asking him to pack a bag for me. And one for Bentley. We'll be moving to the cottage."

Sanders blinked in surprise, but aloud all he said was, "Of course, my lord. I'll advise Wythe at once. I assume he'll be traveling with you as well?"

"No." Quentin gestured meaningfully toward the top of the stairs. "I think you'll require Wythe's services far more than I. Should it prove necessary, Bentley can act as my valet for however long we remain at Emerald Manor." A flicker of amusement. "It will help keep him humble."

Sanders's lips twitched. "For how many days shall I tell Wythe to pack?"

"I don't know. That depends on what we learn about Brandi's supposed accident, and on how quickly she heals. I won't leave her alone until I'm convinced she's fully recovered—and not in danger."

"I understand, my lord. I'll instruct Wythe to pack enough for an extended stay. We can always arrange for additional changes of clothes to be sent to the cottage as you need them."

Quentin nodded. "Thank you for your diligence, Sanders. I can understand why Father proclaimed you to be indispensable."

Unconcealed gratitude shone in Sanders's eyes. "Thank *you,* my lord," he said simply.

Ascending the first step, Quentin paused. "By the way, I'd suggest waiting about a half hour, then delivering that bottle of Madeira to Desmond's chambers. He's going to need it."

"As you wish, sir." Sanders bowed and hastened off.

Jaw clenched, Quentin took the stairs two at a time, never slowing until he reached Desmond's chambers.

He flung open the door.

Desmond whipped around in surprise, an empty bottle clutched in his hand.

"I thought you were dressing," Quentin noted with icy derision.

"I am. There's not even a bloody drop left." Desmond slammed the bottle onto his nightstand and looked past Quentin into the hallway. "Where the hell is Sanders?"

"Busy. I told him I'd assist you."

Desmond tensed. "Does that mean you know who shot Brandice—and why?"

"Not *who*." Quentin closed the door and leaned back against it. *"Why* should be obvious, even to a mind clouded by liquor."

"I'm perfectly sober," Desmond retorted, rubbing his red-rimmed eyes. "But if you're implying there's some correlation between the carriage accident and . . ."

"It wasn't an accident," Quentin interceded. "It was murder. Stop denying the truth by burying your head in a bottle. Glovers made the Bow Street findings quite clear. The carriage axle was severed."

"Even so, how does that relate to Brandice? Tell me the details of this shooting."

"She was in the woods at Emerald Manor. Evidently, so was her unseen assailant. He waited, then followed her and fired. She'd be dead had it not been for her squirrel, who attacked and clawed at the intruder until he fled. It's that simple."

"How do you know it wasn't a trespasser, hunting on the cottage grounds?"

"I don't. But, on the heels of our parents' murders, I suspect otherwise."

"I'm still at sea. What connection is there between the two incidents? Brandice wasn't anywhere near Father's carriage when it went off the road."

"No, but Ardsley was."

Silence.

"You think Ardsley was the target?" Desmond managed.

"'Tis certainly possible. And, if so, Brandi could now be in danger. She is, after all, Ardsley's daughter and has inherited all that was his."

"I need a drink." Desmond weaved toward the door.

Quentin seized his arm. "I'm not finished. In fact, I've

barely begun. We have another matter to clear up, which is why I asked Sanders to leave us alone."

"My Madeira . . ."

"Later." Quentin's grip tightened. "After I've said what I came to say."

A muscle flexed in Desmond's jaw. "What do you want, Quentin?"

"Answers. Explanations. Admissions."

A glimmer of uncertainty flashed in Desmond's eyes. "What are you talking about?"

"I'm talking about the War Department." Crossing the room, Quentin yanked open the drawers of Desmond's chest, tossing a shirt and cravat on the bed. "Start getting dressed. You have an appointment in town."

"How the hell do you know that?" Desmond snapped. Abruptly, he held up his palm. "Never mind. The ever-efficient Bentley." He ignored Quentin's command. "What about the War Department?"

"That's where I spent the last few days. You do recall that, don't you?"

"Of course. I'm not feeble. My memory is intact." Desmond casually fingered his shirt. "So, when will you be setting sail for the colonies?"

"Your memory is indeed splendid," Quentin commended with a mocking smile. "Considering I never mentioned the details of my meeting at Whitehall."

"Y-you told me you'd been summoned."

"Did I? Evidently, my memory is not nearly as reliable as yours. In either case, I am certain I never specified the reason for my summons. Nor where the War Minister intended for me to travel."

Silence.

"Tell me, Desmond." Quentin cocked an inquiring brow. "Does the name Lathrop mean anything to you? What a foolish question. Of course it does. You just told me your memory is intact. Therefore, how could you forget a discussion you had not one week past with one of Bathurst's aides?"

"Very well." Resentment flashed in Desmond's eyes. "Yes, I recall Lathrop. And, no, I've forgotten neither our discussion nor our arrangement."

"Excellent. Then tell me, are you so eager to have me gone that you'll resort to blackmail in order to ensure my departure?"

"I'd resort to worse if it would drive you away."

The vehement admission hung in the air.

Quentin drew a slow inward breath. "Ironic, isn't it? This is, I believe, the first honest conversation we've ever had. Bearing that in mind, and at the risk of endangering our new brotherly bond, might I ask why you're so eager to rid yourself of my presence? Is this all because of Brandi?"

"Yes. No. Damn." Desmond flung his shirt to the bed. "You're in favor of honesty? Fine. Here it is. I've wanted Brandice forever. But in her worshipful eyes, no one's ever existed but you. Finally, after putting myself through hell, risking things you couldn't possibly imagine, I'd very nearly won her over. Then you came home. And suddenly all my plans were for naught. She's bloody infatuated with you all over again. And what's worse is, now you want her, too, despite all your claims to the contrary. Do you think I'm blind? Damn you, Quentin, haven't you taken enough of what was mine?"

"Brandi was never yours, Desmond."

"She could be. If you'd stay the hell away from her."

"That's impossible."

"Why? Because of your supposed friendship?"

"No. Because I'm in love with her."

Somewhere in the back of his mind, Quentin wondered who was more stunned to hear the words spoken aloud, he or Desmond.

A timid knock sounded. "Your Grace?" Sanders opened the door a mere crack. "I have your Madeira, sir."

"It's about time." Desmond stalked across the room and yanked open the door, snatching the bottle from Sanders's hands. "Now get out."

"Yes, sir." Sanders backed away, glancing briefly in Quentin's direction. "Your bag is packed, Lord Quentin. As is Bentley's."

"Thank you, Sanders. I'll manage from here."

"Very good, sir." The valet nearly bolted down the hallway.

"So, you're leaving for the colonies after all," Desmond said with great satisfaction. "And how touching for Bentley to see you off." He poured a glass of Madeira, lifted it in tribute. "Farewell, dear brother. I trust a few months overseas will cure this ill-fated love you feel for Brandice." He downed half the contents of his goblet.

"I'm sorry to disappoint you, *dear brother,* but I shan't be going overseas—at least not as immediately as you'd planned. For the time being, I intend to stay very much on English soil."

The glass paused on its return trip to Desmond's lips. "Then where the hell are you packing to go?"

"To Emerald Manor."

The glass slammed to the table. "I beg your pardon?"

"You heard me. Brandi's life might well be in danger. I refuse to leave her alone."

"What a ridiculous pretense of an excuse. I'm her legal guardian. If she needs overseeing, I'll do it. I'll arrange for her to be brought to Colverton posthaste—which, if you recall, was where I initially suggested she stay. 'Twould be best for Brandice."

"You mean it would be best for *you.* Brandi hates it here," Quentin corrected. "Besides, the point is a moot one. She's too weak to be moved. She's staying at Emerald Manor. And so are Bentley and I."

"You've lost your mind. How can you consider such a thing?"

"Because Brandi asked me. And because I choose to."

"And, as Brandice's guardian, do you honestly think I'm going to permit it?"

"Try to stop me," Quentin said in a voice so low it was

barely audible. "Try to interfere with my feelings for Brandi. I'm warning you, Desmond. If you want a real reason to despise me—just try."

With a measured look, Desmond assessed the unprecedented rage emanating from his brother. Unsteadily, he refilled his glass and tossed off the contents. "The *ton* will talk."

"Let them."

"Brandice's reputation . . ."

"Is my problem."

"And when you rejoin the army?"

"That's between Brandi and me."

Caustically, Desmond delivered his final blow. "You're going to bed Ardsley's daughter under your precious mother's roof?"

An ominous silence.

"I could break your neck for that," Quentin ground out. "But, out of respect to Father, I won't. You're pathetic. You've wasted your whole life resenting my mother and me. And for what? Whatever it is you think we stole from you is all in your mind."

A bitter laugh. "You don't know what you're talking about, Quentin."

"Are we back to Brandi again? Let's stop pretending. You don't care for her; you never did. You just want to possess her, mold her into the perfect Duchess of Colverton. Well, hundreds of women would be thrilled to play that part. Think of the power that affords you." With an expression of utter contempt, Quentin watched Desmond gulp down another drink. "That knowledge alone should fill whatever void your liquor isn't potent enough to reach. In truth, Father inadvertently left you all you truly crave: his money, his estate, and his bloody dukedom."

"If he did, it wasn't by choice."

"Don't be a fool, Desmond. If Father didn't choose to bequeath his title to you, you wouldn't have it."

A bitter smile. "Get out, Quentin. Go to your precious

Sunbeam. As you announced earlier, I've got an appointment in town."

"Speaking of which, when you return to Colverton, bring Hendrick with you."

"Hendrick? For what purpose?"

"You'll understand once the two of you have concluded your meeting. I haven't the time, nor the inclination, to elaborate. Which is just as well, being that you've tossed off three glasses of Madeira in just as many minutes and are hardly clear-headed enough to absorb details of any great significance." Quentin grasped the door handle. "My suggestion is to put down that bloody bottle, get dressed, and leave for London. The sooner you meet with Ellard, the sooner you can bring him to the Cotswolds. And, Desmond." Quentin's tone, his stare, were as lethal as death. "Remember what I said. Forget any notion you have of controlling Brandi's life. Or of sharing it."

"I see you got my message. Good. We have a great deal to discuss." Hendrick leaned forward in his chair, watching Desmond make his way unsteadily into the office. "You've been drinking again."

"A brilliant observation. And I plan to continue drinking throughout our meeting." He poured himself a brandy and began to pace.

"Has something happened?"

"Yes. Brandice has been shot."

"What?" Hendrick's jaw dropped. "Is she hurt?"

"From what Quentin said, she'll be all right. Apparently, the bullet grazed her head. But my brother is convinced someone tried to kill her."

"Quentin was with Brandice when this occurred?"

"No. She was alone. In the woods at Emerald Manor. Quentin dashed to her side the instant he arrived from London—the legendary knight in shining armor." Desmond's eyes narrowed. "You don't seem particularly shocked by Quentin's suspicions."

"I'm not. Doubtless, Brandice told him what she and I discussed when she came to see me yesterday. That in itself would be cause for speculation."

"Brandice came to see you?" Desmond started. "Here?"

"Indeed." Hendrick gestured for Desmond to take a seat. "As I said, we have much to catch up on." He waited until Desmond had dropped heavily into the chair and placed his goblet at the edge of the desk.

"Brandice arrived at my office late yesterday afternoon," the solicitor continued. "She brought a most interesting file with her—a file she'd found at Townsbourne. In her father's desk," he added pointedly.

"I don't believe this." Desmond gulped down his drink. "Brandice actually went to Townsbourne and searched Ardsley's desk?"

"Apparently. Did you know of this file's existence?"

"I . . ." Desmond massaged his temples. "It seems to me I did. 'Tis a bit unclear in my mind."

"Damn it, Colverton, everything is unclear in your mind. Now think."

Desmond frowned. "Yes, upon reflection, I do recall Ardsley mentioning something about a drawer housing personal papers."

Hendrick slammed his fist on the desk. "Then why the hell didn't you remove them right after the will readings? How could you be so careless?"

"Why? What was in them?"

"A ledger, you fool. A line-by-line accounting of all the viscount's recent business transactions—as he perceived them—depicting the monumental losses he supposedly incurred."

"Christ." Desmond's pupils dilated. "And Brandice came straight to you with this ledger?"

"Her choices were nil." Hendrick's tone emanated undisguised censure. "You were, as she correctly assumed, drunk. Quentin was away. So, yes, she came directly to me."

"That was a stroke of luck." Desmond visibly relaxed.

"Well, Quentin's back now. So let's destroy the ledger at once."

"What good would that do? Brandice has already seen the damning evidence."

"Then let's modify the numbers to agree with the ones you have on file. Quentin will think Brandice read them incorrectly."

"You underestimate Brandice's intelligence."

"She's a woman, Hendrick. Exceptional or not, she doesn't possess the business aptitude of a man."

"Really? Well, she was clever enough to insist on taking the ledger with her."

Desmond stared. "And you let her?"

"What would you have had me do—wrest it from her hands?"

"You could have convinced her to leave it with you." Desmond leaped to his feet, circling the chair restlessly. "For Christ's sake, Hendrick, you are her solicitor."

"And Quentin is, as you put it, her knight in shining armor. If you can't combat his importance in Brandice's life, how the hell should I?"

"Quentin." Desmond seized his empty glass and sent it crashing to the wall. "Quentin. Quentin. Quentin. Every direction I turn, he thwarts me. I can't take a bloody step without tripping over my paragon of a brother Quentin."

"Have you finished having your tantrum?" Hendrick inquired icily. "Because, if so, we have a problem to address. And the ledger is only part of it. Brandice's plan is another."

"Plan?" Desmond veered to face him. "What plan?"

"The plan Quentin undoubtedly assumed I alluded to in the missive I sent you—the one that brought you charging to London." Frowning, Hendrick watched Desmond return to the sideboard, then glance bewilderedly about.

"Where the hell's my glass?"

"You smashed it just minutes ago," Hendrick reminded him in a frosty tone. "Against my wall. Which, incidentally,

I must instruct you never to do again. This is my place of business, not a London pub. Had today not been Peters's day off, we'd be forced to explain your childish outburst to him. As it is, I'll simply add the cost of the goblet to your bill."

"Very amusing."

"It was my intention to caution, not amuse, you. I suggest you take my advice to heart. Believe me, Desmond, the last thing you need is another drink. Now sit down."

Ignoring the admonishment, Desmond helped himself to another goblet, sloshing brandy nearly to its rim.

"I want to hear about this plan Brandice is devising," he reiterated, dropping back into the chair.

Hendrick cast a distasteful look at the brandy, but didn't comment on it further. "Brandice has deduced that Ardsley was far too shrewd a businessman to invest as ineffectually as the ledger implies. Which, as we know, is true."

Desmond's head shot up, his fingers tightening about his glass. "You didn't confirm that to Brandice?"

"I'm not an ass, Colverton," Hendrick retorted dryly. "Nor am I foxed." His gaze flickered pointedly to Desmond's drink. "I assured her that her father was indeed suffering a stretch of bad luck. She was dubious. Her suspicion is that one of Denerley's coinvestors swindled him. She intends to question each and every one of them, together, in a group meeting. Here. In my office. This week, if possible."

With a muffled curse, Desmond tossed down his drink. "When did she plan to mention this to me?"

"Probably when you took your head out of the bottle." Hendrick waved away Desmond's irritated look. "Did you believe Brandice hadn't noticed the frequency of your drinking? She was terribly concerned about you—and your perpetually inebriated state. However, I did manage to convince her that you should take part in this meeting of hers. I reminded her that, as her legal guardian and overseer of Denerley's businesses, you would be doubly concerned—first, for her safety in a potentially dangerous situation, and second, for ensuring the security of her inheritance as well as the future of Ardsley's investments."

"Splendid," Desmond muttered. "So I am now invited to my own undoing."

"Don't be a fool. I have no intentions of allowing that meeting to occur."

"And just how did you explain that to Brandice?"

"I didn't. I simply bought us some time. I promised her I would peruse the files of all the men listed in that ledger—all of whom, luckily, happen to be clients of mine—then send out preliminary missives alerting them to the seriousness of the matter at hand, and arranging the best date and time for our meeting."

"And you don't intend to do that?"

"To the contrary. I did both before leaving my office last night—in a modified manner, of course. My notes were far more benign in tone than I'd implied they would be. Not to mention I happen to know for a fact that at least three of the gentlemen in question are currently abroad, while two others are vacationing in Brighton. So we have several weeks to change Brandice's mind."

"And how are we going to do that? Brandice is not easy to maneuver, in case I haven't made that clear."

"You're not going to maneuver her. You're going to convince her."

"I?"

"*You*," Hendrick fired back. "At the same time *I* am going to speak with Quentin. If we both do our jobs right, the idea of this meeting will soon be abandoned."

"I suppose you have a way of accomplishing that?"

"Of course. Brandice is bound to have questions for you—questions pertaining to her father's ledger. After all, who worked more closely with Denerley than the man to whom he entrusted his businesses? All you have to do is admit to her—with the proper degree of reluctance—that the figures in Denerley's ledger are accurate. That, so as not to appear ineffective in his beloved daughter's eyes, he never told her how badly his investments were doing nor how necessary you were to his financial security. That will put a damper on her theory."

"I suppose I could manage." Desmond shook his head to clear it. "But how does Quentin factor into this?"

"Brandice obviously told Quentin, not only about our meeting yesterday, but about the missives I sent. Why else do you suppose he believes Brandice to be in danger?"

Desmond stared blankly.

"Think, Colverton," Hendrick commanded impatiently. "Your brother believes my missives alerted the killer to Brandice's intentions, that the culprit was threatened by the realization that she means to unmask his identity."

Abruptly, Desmond's cloudy mind made the connection. "He suspects one of the men in that ledger really did cheat and kill Ardsley—and is now after Brandice?"

"Very good" was the sardonic reply. "And it only took twice as long as it should have. Acceptable, I suppose, after—how many drinks today?"

"Not nearly enough." As if to prove his claim, Desmond started to rise; then, assailed by a wave of dizziness, he changed his mind, sinking back into the chair. "Now I know why Quentin wants you to return to the Cotswolds with me. He wants to question you on the prudence of this meeting."

"He's sent for me? Excellent." Hendrick slapped his palm on the desk. "Then I shan't need to fabricate a reason for summoning him. I'll ride to Colverton with you and express my extreme concern over Brandice's safety. That should dissuade him from pursuing the matter."

"You won't find Quentin at Colverton."

Hendrick's brows rose. "Oh? Was your visit to the War Department a success then? Is Quentin leaving England?"

"Hardly. He unraveled my entire plan, persuaded Bathurst to delay his orders. No, Hendrick, the only place my brother will be leaving is Colverton. He—and my nosy butler—are moving to Emerald Manor. To be with Brandice."

"I see." Hendrick grew thoughtful. "Your plan to prevent Quentin and Brandice from becoming involved is looking rather dim, I fear. Although, I must say, you're well rid of Quentin and Bentley. The less you see of them, the less likely you are to let something slip. As for your plans to wed Brandice, I'd suggest that, during your oncoming talk, you declare your deep and abiding devotion, as well as your concern for her safety and well-being—both of which you could ensure were she your duchess. Emphasize what would be hers: title, wealth, security. This might be your last chance."

"Very sensible, but futile." Desmond's lips thinned into a bitter, angry line. "Brandice cares not a whit for my title nor anything that accompanies it. And Quentin has all but threatened my life if I interfere in this budding love of theirs."

A flicker of surprise. "The alliance between Quentin and Brandice has plainly gone far beyond what I fathomed," Hendrick noted, his expression growing thoughtful. "The use of subtlety in your dealings with Brandice is more important now than ever. Even if you fail to win her hand, you cannot afford to lose her friendship—not when it's crucial that she heed your advice to abandon her plans for this meeting. Anything short of success in your upcoming chat could prove disastrous." He scowled. "I don't think I need to stress that fact."

"No. You don't."

"Good. Then you agree with me that, in order to be in full command of the situation, you must be in full command of your senses—in other words, totally and continuously sober. During our visit to Emerald Manor, you will not touch a drop of liquor."

"You're not my father, Ellard."

"Nor are you. Which is doubtless why Kenton chose to leave his entire legacy, including his title, to Quentin." A pregnant pause. "I wouldn't want to have to mention that fact during our jaunt to Pamela's cottage."

"You bastard," Desmond hissed. "I paid you a bloody fortune to destroy that amended will. I'm paying you even more to keep your mouth shut."

"I appreciate that. So let's not do anything to jeopardize things, shall we? Now, to sum things up," Hendrick continued, never missing a beat, "I told Brandice I'd be meeting with you today, which I have. You told Quentin you'd bring me back with you, which you will. Everything should then fall nicely into place."

"Except for one small unavoidable detail." Assailed by a sudden dark reality, Desmond dragged a shaking hand across his brow. "Who the hell took a shot at Brandice? You and I both know there's no link between your late-night missives and Brandice's episode in the woods. And while I loathe my brother, one thing he said was true. After this incident with Brandice, I can't hide from the Bow Street findings anymore. Father's carriage being tampered with, Brandice's near-fatal shooting—could they be related?"

"Why the sudden concern? Don't tell me you're actually feeling remorse?" Hendrick asked in surprise.

"Is that so hard to believe?" Desmond snapped. "I'm not proud of what I've done, even though I'm frank enough to admit I'd do it all again if I had to. But that doesn't mean I wished my father dead, nor Brandice harmed."

"Calm down, Colverton. I meant no insult." Hendrick shifted in his chair, absently rubbing his forearm. "However, you do have a point, although for pragmatic reasons, not emotional ones. The carriage disaster was an isolated incident of violence, and Bow Street has doubtless been investigating it as such. Now everything's changed. Should Quentin manage to convince them that Brandice's shooting was linked to her father's death, the authorities will be forced to view this whole messy business on a grander scale and will, consequently, intensify their search. And, if they probe long enough, they'll discover the very secrets we're striving to keep hidden. No, 'tis time for us to take matters into our hands."

"And how in the name of heaven do we do that?"

"You can't. *I,* however, can." Hendrick sat back, giving Desmond a measured look. "I know far more about the private circumstances of the members of the *ton* than

anyone at Bow Street ever could—their financial statuses, yes, but also their friends, their enemies, their liaisons. I'm sure I could accelerate the murder investigation—but in a more suitable manner. Discreetly. Covertly."

"Expensively."

"Indeed." Hendrick shrugged in an offhanded manner. "After all, it would take a great deal of my time—time I'd otherwise be devoting to other clients. Clients who pay handsomely for my services." He gave a dismissive wave of his hand. "Never mind. Disregard my offer entirely. I never would have made it had you not experienced a sudden jolt of sorrow and regret . . ."

"Cease your hypocritical show of concern." Desmond staggered to his feet. "You're as worried about discovery as I am. But fret not. I'll pay you. Hell, at this point, I'm paying you so much, what's another few hundred pounds a week?"

"An agreeable sum. Very well, I'll begin delving into the matter as soon as I return to London. Which brings this meeting to a close." Hendrick glanced down at the papers littering his desk. "Go to the coffee room at Limmer's—and I do mean for coffee, not port. I'll join you shortly. We'll be en route to the Cotswolds within an hour."

"All right." Desmond made his way to the door.

"Coffee, Desmond," Hendrick reiterated in a warning tone. "Not port."

"I heard you." The door slammed behind him.

Frowning, Hendrick leaned back in his chair, once again massaging his forearm. Desmond's drinking was fast becoming a problem, making him loose of tongue and careless of action. Judging from Brandice's diplomatic queries yesterday, the new duke's business acumen was also in question. Alerting him to that fact right now—when the drunken fool was too deep in his cups to react sanely—would have been a mistake. Hopefully, after a few sobering cups of coffee, he'd be rational enough to listen. After which, if the chat with Brandice were handled correctly, any concerns she harbored would be obliterated.

That left Quentin, whose besotted feelings for Brandice would make his own task easy and buy him a fair amount of time.

Still, he *had* to get out of the country.

But not yet. Not until Desmond found that cursed evidence Kenton had so carefully concealed—evidence more vast than the books that ensured Desmond's undoing, more damning than anyone but Kenton had known.

Coming to his feet, Hendrick withdrew his right hand from beneath the desk, where it had stayed throughout his meeting with Desmond. Touching the bandage, he flinched. Damn. He had to remove the dressing and don gloves to hide the bloody gashes that had yet to heal. He couldn't risk drawing attention to his wound, especially not while visiting Emerald Manor.

He crossed his office, carefully locking the door before he began the painful task of unraveling his bandage.

That blasted squirrel, he raged silently. *I should have wrung his bloody neck.*

Chapter 15

"*H*ow is she, Bentley?"

For the fourth time since midnight, Quentin flung open his bedchamber door and stepped into the hallway, waylaying Bentley the second he heard his footsteps.

"Quite well, sir." Bentley stood directly across from Quentin's room, having long since abandoned the notion of passing by without providing an update on their patient. "Better than you, in fact."

"I'm fine, Bentley."

"It's nearly one A.M., and you're still fully dressed. If you don't mind a gentle reminder, the whole point of my taking over sentry duty was for you to get some sleep. You haven't budged from Miss Brandi's side since late afternoon."

"I was watching for a delayed reaction, possibly even signs of a concussion."

"I think we can safely rule out anything dire, my lord. Miss Brandi just ate her second portion of supper—to make up for skipping her midday meal, she said—and is eyeing that oak tree outside her window in a manner I find most disconcerting."

"Oak tree?"

"Yes, sir. The one she's so adept at climbing."

"I didn't know she climbed . . ." Quentin broke off, his gaze narrowing suspiciously. "What do you mean by 'eyeing' it? How is she 'eyeing' it?"

"Longingly, my lord."

"She wouldn't dare."

Bentley cocked a brow. "What were your exact words this morning? You remember—after you called us both fools." He pursed his lips in apparent contemplation. "Ah, I recall. They were 'She's as restless as a firefly and equally unable to remain still. You and I should know better than to believe she could—*would*—stay put.'" Bentley gave a haughty sniff. "And you accuse me of underestimating Miss Brandi?"

"I'll throttle her." Quentin was already heading down the hall.

A corner of Bentley's mouth lifted. "Shall I have dessert sent up, sir?"

"No." Quentin slammed open Brandi's door.

"I quite agree," Bentley murmured under his breath. "It appears that, for once, dessert is not needed."

Turning on his heel, he headed toward the stairs.

"Quentin." Yanking the curtains closed, Brandi whirled about to face him. "What are you doing here?"

"My exact question." Quentin closed the door, folding his arms across his chest. "What were you just doing?"

"I, I . . ."

"Damn it, Sunbeam, didn't you hear a bloody word I said today?" Crossing over, Quentin pulled back the drapes, assessing the towering tree silhouetted against the darkness of night. "Where were you going?"

"I heard every word you said," she replied, fidgeting with the edges of her wrapper. "I was only trying to get some air. You've kept me locked up like an invalid all day."

"You're still weak. Have you forgotten you were shot this morning?"

"Of course not. But, other than a bit of tenderness—" Gingerly, she touched her bandage. "I feel wonderful.

Except for the fact that I'm being held prisoner," she said pointedly. "Stop worrying. I only wanted to stroll in the gardens. Not the far ones by the gazebo, but the ones directly beneath my window. Is that so dreadful?"

Quentin's gaze flickered from Brandi to the oak tree and back. "You've done this before, I take it?"

An impish grin. "Countless times."

"I'm almost afraid to ask . . ."

"Since I was six," she supplied. "Whenever Pamela and Kenton held a party here. I'd slip out this window via my dear old friend the oak, and scoot down to the ground."

"Why?"

Brandi caught her lip between her teeth, wondering how frank she should be, then accepting that degrees of candor were not her forte. "There's a fir tree just outside the guest quarters—overlooking that private section of woods in the rear. I'd inch my way along until I reached it. Fortunately, it had a sturdy low branch, perfect for a six-year-old's stretch, and a plush array of cushioned branches—perfect for sitting—amid the profusion of greenery. Best of all, it offered the finest of vantage points. I could hide there for hours, surveying the entire grounds of Emerald Manor— and all its occupants—undetected."

"But why?"

The very question she had dreaded.

With a sinking heart, Brandi raised her chin, meeting Quentin's curious gaze and wishing she could predict his reaction. Slowly, she began counting off on her fingers. "Lady Penelope, Lady Edwina, the Marchioness of Elmswood, that Yorkshire countess, the Canadian official's daughter . . ." She paused to suck in her breath and switch to her other hand. "Lady Elizabeth, whose father wanted to call you out . . ."

"Enough." Quentin held up his palm, staring at her in utter stupefaction. "You climbed that tree just to watch me?"

"No, my lord," she corrected. "I climbed that tree just to spy on you."

Without warning, laughter erupted from Quentin's chest. "Sunbeam, Sunbeam, what am I to do with you?"

"Are you angry?"

"That depends. What precisely did you see?"

"A great many unworthy women basking in the pleasure of being in your arms."

Quentin's laughter faded. "Is that all?"

"If you mean did I investigate what happened when you led a particular lady deeper into the woods, the answer is no." Brandi's lashes swept her cheeks. "Even then, I don't think I could have withstood it. For different reasons, of course. Then it was childhood possessiveness and repugnance that a man and woman would wish to touch in so intimate a manner. Now—" Her lashes lifted, a wealth of feeling in her eyes. "Now I couldn't bear your holding any woman but me."

Features taut with emotion, Quentin threaded his fingers through Brandi's hair. "God help me, I don't want any woman but you."

"I'm yours," she stated simply.

With a harsh groan, Quentin brought a burnished strand to his lips. "You're aging me, Sunbeam. Rapidly."

"Good. Then perhaps you'll realize I've aged as well."

Something shimmered in his eyes. "I've already realized that."

"I'm glad." Brandi reached up, smoothed her fingers over the exposed skin at his throat. "Thank you for staying," she said quietly. "Just knowing you're nearby, knowing you're here if I need you—that means everything."

Of its own accord, Quentin's gaze swept over her, taking in the soft lush curves concealed only by the diaphanous silk of her nightrail. His insides tightened, and the all-too-familiar battle commenced inside him, tearing at his soul, raging with all the fires of hell.

Brandi watched his face, then took a step backward, untying her wrapper and tossing it to the bed.

"What are you doing?" Quentin's voice sounded like gravel.

Her smile was seduction itself. "Precisely what I promised I'd do. Trying to tempt you, my lord."

"You tempt me without trying," Quentin returned, his hands defining the silky curves of her shoulders. "I'm fighting with all my strength, Sunbeam," he confessed quietly. "But I fear I'm losing."

"With this particular battle, I suspect defeat is far more wondrous than victory." She loosened his cravat, unbuttoned his shirt, tugging the edges away so her palms could discover the warm, hair-roughened surface of his chest. "You're so strong," she whispered, leaning forward to kiss the skin she'd bared.

"Brandi . . ." It was part protest, part plea, but Brandi hadn't the chance to address either. With an urgency as exciting as it was undeniable, Quentin tugged her head back and buried his mouth in hers. "Christ, I want you." He rasped the words against her parted lips, his arms tightening about her at the same time his tongue pressed deep into her mouth, taking her with deep hungry strokes. He gave her no time to breathe, devouring her with a hunger too long suppressed, a relentless determination that enveloped her and cherished her all at once.

With a whimper of joy, Brandi joined in the pagan beauty of the kiss. She met his tongue, melded it with her own, and pressed closer—until the silk of her nightrail was brushing the sensitive nakedness of his chest.

"Sunbeam, you're killing me." Even as he spoke, he rubbed his torso to hers, increasing the friction, intensifying the yearning. His hands slid around to cup her breasts, cradling them in his palms while his thumbs caressed her nipples into tight, hard points of need.

"Oh God." Instinctively, Brandi arched closer to the exquisite torture, her breasts aching, pleading for more. "Quentin . . ." Her fingers glided through his hair, urging him closer. "Please."

Rational thought eclipsed by need, Quentin lowered his head, closing his mouth around one hardened nipple, tugging at it through the confines of her nightrail. He drew the moist silk into his mouth, his tongue curling about the rigid peak, arousing it further with the wildly erotic friction of her damp nightrail as it rubbed against her sensitized breast.

Brandi was going to die.

Her legs gave out and her eyes closed, lulled by the elated sensation of Quentin scooping her into his arms, carrying her to the bed.

Her elation died a quick death when she realized he wasn't joining her.

Her eyes flew open, dazed, questioning as they sought him out.

"Quentin?"

He didn't answer immediately, his fists clenched at his sides, his lungs dragging in great calming gulps of air.

"Quentin?" she repeated, raising up on her elbows.

Slowly, he sank down beside her, keeping a careful distance between them as he took her hand in his. "I've been a fool, Sunbeam," he said solemnly. "Trying to deny the undeniable, to change what cannot be changed, to ignore something far too powerful to elude. The die has been cast. But you knew that all along, didn't you? As always, you recognized my feelings better than I."

"Say the words," Brandi put in softly. "Whether or not I know them to be true, I need to hear you say them. Please."

He kissed her fingertips. "I love you, Brandi. Hopelessly. Helplessly." He caught her as she flung herself into his arms, buried his face in her hair. "I'm so bloody in love with you. And I don't know what to do."

Brandi laughed softly, exuberance bubbling inside her like uncorked champagne. "Inexperienced though I might be, I'd say you were doing quite well until a moment ago."

He didn't smile. "So well that in approximately one more minute I was going to tear that nightrail from your body and bury myself so deep inside you that I'd bind you to me forever." An ironic laugh. "Do you hear me? Talking about forever? With one war just behind me and another just ahead, the bloody realist who swore never to offer you promises I couldn't keep. And here I am, proclaiming my undying love, wanting you more than I want my next breath, aching to make you mine in a way I have no right to do. God, Sunbeam, I tried so damned hard to stop this from happening. But it's no use. It's no bloody use."

"Quentin—don't." Leaning back, Brandi silenced him with a forefinger to his lips. "You're torturing yourself for an emotion that's as natural as the sunrise, and equally as impossible to repress. For days now, I've been listening to you spout nonsense about why we cannot allow our feelings to be termed *love*, why you're all wrong for me. Isn't it time you gave me a chance to speak?"

Uncertainly, he nodded.

"I love you, Quentin Steel." Brandi lay her palm over his heart. "I could never love anyone else. I have never loved anyone else. But just because I've loved you all my life doesn't mean that my love is the same now as it was then. It's changed, Quentin. Changed and reshaped and grown. When you left England four years ago, I was a child. Now I'm a woman. My love is stronger, deeper than anything a child could understand, much less feel. But it's also richer for having sprung from the closest and most wondrous of friendships." A reminiscent smile touched Brandi's lips. "I *know* you, Quentin. I shared your pride when you received your captain's commission—a commission that was earned, not bought. I reveled in your exhilaration when General Wellington himself requested your presence in Europe, affirming that you and you alone had the sophisticated skills needed to break French codes. I understood your fierce commitment to England. I understand it still. Do you truly believe I'd let you turn your back on all that just to spend forever by my side?" Her fingers drifted around to caress his nape. "I've grown up, Quentin—and I don't just mean physically. Yes, losing Papa, Pamela, and Kenton was devastating. Yes, I was drowning, seeking

---

something to cling to, something that would last forever. 'Tis only natural that I turned to you to fill that role. But don't confuse a temporary show of dependence bred by shock and grief with inherent emotional fragility. I'm strong. I survived. I shall continue to survive." Her voice quavered. "Now more than ever. Because now I know you love me."

"Brandi . . ." Quentin's hand shook as he pressed her head to his chest.

"You've opened your heart," she breathed. "Now open your eyes. Stop fighting. 'Tis time to concede." She smiled through her tears. "Do you know, you're still the very worst of losers? You refuse to yield, even when it's clear the contest has long since been lost. Whether 'tis a race or your heart at stake, you fight to the bitter end and then, when surrender is inevitable, you do so in a most grudging manner." Raising up, she brushed her lips across his. "A most unbecoming trait. One I suggest you rectify. Oh, I recognize only too well how you loathe relinquishing that impervious control of yours, but that's one of love's inevitable effects." A twinkle. "And if you must yield to someone, hadn't it best be me? I won't promise to leave your control intact, but I will vow to guard your heart with my life."

"My heart is yours, Sunbeam."

"As mine is yours. And, being that I could never pledge myself to a man I didn't love—and that the only man I'll ever love is you—your fate is sealed. All or nothing, you said." Brandi buried her face in his throat. "I want all."

"And when I leave England?" Quentin managed hoarsely, gathering handfuls of her hair.

"Then I'll ache for you. And pray for you. And await your return." She twined her arms about his neck. "But, above all, I'll love you."

With a rough sound, Quentin covered her mouth with his, crushing her against him and possessing her with a

264

naked urgency spawned by the budding hope that all he longed for could possibly be his.

"I can't walk away," he told her, his voice husky with the bittersweet joy of surrender. "I need you too damned much."

"Oh, Quentin . . ."

A sharp knock intruded.

"Miss Brandi?" Mrs. Collins's tentative voice reached their ears. "Herbert and I noticed your light was burning. I thought you might be hungry. So, I brought you some warm milk and a slice of pie."

Breaking apart, Quentin and Brandi stared dazedly at each other.

"Miss Brandi? Are you awake, dear?" The sound of a tray being shifted, presumably for balance, suggested that the housekeeper intended to enter the room and determine Brandi's condition firsthand.

In one quick motion, Quentin lifted Brandi from the bed, jerking the bedcovers out from under her and depositing her beneath. Then he bolted to his feet, simultaneously buttoning his shirt and tying his cravat. He bent forward, lightly touching Brandi's eyelids and gesturing for her to close them.

Brandi nodded her understanding and complied, listening to the sounds of Quentin's footsteps as he crossed over and opened the door. "She just dozed off," he whispered to Mrs. Collins. "I'm hoping she'll sleep through the night. I was about to extinguish the lamp and retire to my bedchamber."

"Oh, forgive me, my lord," the housekeeper replied anxiously. "I hope my knock didn't awaken her."

"I don't think so," Quentin assured her. "And no forgiveness is necessary. Your gesture was very thoughtful. Actually—" Quentin's natural charm took over, a palpable entity Brandi need not open her eyes to discern. "As Brandi is not awake to savor it, and as it so happens I'm famished, would you object to my enjoying your pie?"

"I'd be delighted, my lord." Brandi could actually hear Mrs. Collins beam. "I'll run down to the kitchen and bring you a larger portion."

"That won't be necessary," Quentin interceded hastily. "This slice is more than sufficient. What I would appreciate is if you would bring the tray to my chambers. I want to make certain Brandi is sleeping comfortably before I retire for the night."

"Certainly. I'll do it this instant."

Her solid footsteps disappeared down the hall.

Quentin closed the door. "You can open your eyes now, Sunbeam. Mrs. Collins and her pie are gone."

Brandi raised up on her elbows, met Quentin's gaze. "And had she not arrived in the first place?"

His eyes darkened to a deep smoky gray as the implicit meaning of Brandi's question sank in. Silently, he battled his conscience, a muscle working furiously in his jaw.

Brandi climbed out of bed and walked toward him, aching at the warring emotions she saw reflected on his face, yet unwilling to allow him to retreat. She stopped directly before him, raising her chin and holding his gaze, seeking nothing short of the honesty they'd always shared. "Quentin," she repeated softly. "Just before Mrs. Collins interrupted us, you said you needed me too much to walk away. Did you mean that in the vast poetic sense or in the immediate one?" She lay her palm against his jaw. "Please. I need to know."

"Both," he managed.

"Then, had she not knocked when she did . . ."

"I wouldn't have had the strength to leave you."

Joy sparkled in Brandi's eyes. "I'm glad."

"Are you?" Quentin framed her face between his palms, brushing kisses across her cheeks, the bridge of her nose, her lips. "We have a great deal to discuss, Sunbeam. But not tonight. Mrs. Collins has doubtless delivered my tray and is hovering about to gauge my reaction to her pie. I'd best not disappoint her." Quentin tugged Brandi to him, seizing her mouth in one last soul-wrenching kiss. "I'm going to my bedchamber now," he said in a rough whisper, the trembling of his body conveying volumes. "While I still can."

Brandi nodded unsteadily, reveling in the wondrous transformation tonight had wrought, knowing in her heart that an irreversible step had been taken.

She inhaled sharply, caressing the taut muscles at his nape. "Save me some pie," she breathed with a teasing sparkle in her eyes. "After all, it was originally intended for me."

For an instant, Quentin looked startled. Then laughter erupted from his chest. "My outrageous Sunbeam." He stepped away, kissing both her hands before releasing them. "Only you would think of eating pie at a time like this. Very well, I'll do better than save you a piece. I'll ask Mrs. Collins to bring me a second helping—that larger slice she referred to. When everyone is abed, I'll have Bentley sneak it into your room. How would that be?"

"Wonderful." Brandi gave him an impish grin. "Not as wonderful as if Bentley were sneaking you into my room. But I'll be patient." The look she gave Quentin was pure seduction. "That, too, will come. Mark my words, Captain Steel. That, too, will come."

"I believe the moment of reckoning has come," Bentley announced from the dining-room doorway. "I just spotted Master Desmond's carriage rounding the far end of the drive."

"My, my. Isn't he the bright and early one today." Quentin folded his copy of the *Times* and glanced at the mantel clock. "It's scarcely nine A.M. He and Hendrick must have left London before dawn."

"Or ridden back to Colverton last night," Bentley suggested.

"True." Quentin came to his feet. "In either case, dare we

hope that, due to the early hour, Desmond has yet to drink himself into an incoherent stupor?"

Bentley sniffed. "Indeed, sir. Dealing with Master Desmond is difficult enough when he's sober."

Quentin's lips twitched. "I couldn't agree more." Walking over to the window, he peered out across the sunlit gardens. "Where's Brandi? Have you advised her of my formidable brother's arrival?" An indulgent grin. "She's definitely up and about. In fact, she left the cottage before dawn. Either that or some other exuberant resident was bounding about the gardens beneath my window before the sun had risen."

"Oh, that was most assuredly Miss Brandi, sir. She and her squirrel were dashing through the trees when I took my five A.M. stroll."

One dark brow rose. "Since when do you take a five A.M. stroll?"

"Since I shouldered the task of overseeing a tireless young lady who means the world to me." Bentley cleared his throat. "In any case, sir, Miss Brandi has probably already spied Master Desmond's carriage. She's in the gazebo garden with Herbert, and has been since breakfast."

Quentin's smile faded. "She's not working, is she? 'Tis only a day since she was injured. I don't want her exerting herself, and that includes planting geraniums or digging in the rock garden."

"Actually, sir, she's awarding a small feast to her squirrel—a sort of tribute to him for his heroic rescue. To my knowledge, her banquet arrangements involve nothing more strenuous than preparing a small bowl of berries and nuts and showering Lancelot with well-deserved praise."

"Oh." Quentin visibly relaxed. "Well, I suppose I can't fault her for that. Even I'm feeling grateful to that trouble-maker of a rodent."

On cue, the front door slammed open. "Quentin?" Brandi raced breathlessly through the hallway and burst into the dining room, nearly knocking Bentley to the ground. "I'm sorry, Bentley. I didn't see you."

"No harm done, my lady." Bentley brushed a blade of grass from his uniform.

Brandi turned to Quentin. "Desmond is here."

"So Bentley tells me." Assessing her disheveled state—the tousled mass of cinnamon curls, the grass-stained gown, the dirt-smudged cheeks—Quentin grinned, wondering if this could truly be the same woman he'd burned to take to bed not eight hours past.

"Incidentally—" Brandi smiled and, abruptly, Quentin's wondering vanished. "As we haven't seen each other yet today—good morning." She walked toward him, her chin tilted up to meet his gaze.

"Good morning." Quentin tugged one shining curl. "How do you feel, or need I ask? 'Tis nine o'clock and already you've eaten breakfast, romped in the garden, and are now, I hear tell, holding a banquet in honor of your squirrel."

Her brow furrowed. "Did I disturb you when I took my stroll? It was rather early."

"Not at all. I'm delighted at the rate of your recovery. All I ask is that you don't overtax yourself." Quentin averted his head to the sound of horses' hooves, which rounded the drive, then stopped. "Are you up for this, Sunbeam?"

"Yes. I have dozens of questions to ask Desmond. I'm also anxious to learn if Mr. Hendrick has yet received any responses to the missives he sent."

"Don't expect miracles, Brandi," Quentin cautioned. "It's been less than two days."

"I know. And I won't."

"I'll see them to the sitting room, sir." Bentley pivoted and returned to his post.

Brandi reached the door in two racing steps. "Let's go to the sitting room," she urged Quentin.

He followed, pausing to take her arm once they'd reached their destination. "I mean it, Brandi. I don't intend to allow you to overtax yourself. Physically or emotionally."

Her lips curved. "I didn't think you would."

Not three minutes later, Bentley appeared in the doorway, accompanied by Desmond and Hendrick. "Master Desmond," he announced. "Oh, pardon me—His Grace—and Mr. Hendrick."

Desmond scowled, clearly piqued by the butler's intentional slip. Hendrick seemed not to notice, strolling past Desmond and into the room.

"Quentin," he acknowledged graciously. His anxious gaze flickered to Brandi. "Are you all right, my dear? Desmond told me of your horrible accident yesterday."

"I'm fine, thank you, Mr. Hendrick. Very much myself."

Brandi's words appeared to penetrate Desmond's silent, seething rage. "Brandice . . ." He hastened to her side, seizing her hands in his. "How are you?" His glance went to her bandaged temple. "How in God's name could such a thing have happened?"

"That's what we're here to discuss," Quentin inserted curtly. "Why don't you both have a seat. Mrs. Collins made enough breakfast for an army. Would either of you care for something to eat?" A pause, Quentin's censuring gaze flickering to Desmond. "Or to drink?"

"Neither, thank you," Hendrick forestalled Desmond by answering. "We had a large meal at Colverton not an hour ago."

"So you arrived in the Cotswolds last night?"

"Late last night, yes." Hendrick lowered himself into an armchair. "We went directly to bed in order to get an early start this morning." He inclined his head quizzically at Quentin. "It's not too early, is it? Desmond assured me you were early risers."

"We are." Quentin crossed over and sat down on the settee. "And I'm relieved you came as quickly as you did. I have a great deal of unresolved questions—and concerns. The sooner we address them, the better."

Desmond remained standing, his gaze on Brandi. Awkwardly, he cleared his throat. "Brandice, if you have no objections, I'd like to speak with you in private. I realize you're a woman grown, but your father did appoint me your legal guardian. And, as such, I'm dreadfully disturbed by what happened to you yesterday. I want to hear the precise details and explore ways in which we can ensure your safety. Would that be acceptable?"

Brandi's brows rose in surprise, unaccustomed as she was to Desmond actually seeking her approval or, for that matter, treating her in so reasonable a manner. Slowly, she nodded. "That would be fine, as I, too, have a matter I'd like to pursue with you."

"Good. Then, shall we adjourn to the library?"

"Fine." Brandi glanced at Quentin, giving him a reassuring nod. "We'll be back shortly, gentlemen." She smiled at Bentley as she passed through the doorway, fighting the urge to laugh aloud as Desmond sidestepped the butler, inching his way around him with a look of utter distaste.

"I'll be at my post, should you need me, my lord," Bentley apprised Quentin, his expression unchanged. "And fear not. The cottage entranceway is twice this width." He indicated the expanse that defined the sitting-room doorway. "Therefore, arriving guests run no risk of grazing my person as they enter. However, should I perceive that I've offended even one other visitor, I'll set aside my morning break for bathing purposes. Now, if you'll excuse me, sir . . ."

Stiff as a board, he exited the room, veered away from Desmond and Brandi, and headed toward the front door.

Quentin shook his head, his shoulders quaking with laughter.

Hendrick blinked in astonishment. "Your Bentley never ceases to amaze me," he noted diplomatically. "Although, I must say I don't recall his being so . . . forthright when your father was alive."

"He liked Father," Quentin responded with a shrug. "He doesn't like Desmond."

"So I see." Hendrick cleared his throat, aware that he was

entering volatile territory and, as such, ensuring that he trod carefully. "Desmond is an erratic and complex man. Further, his title is new, his responsibilities oppressive. I'm certain he'll settle down in time."

"Settle down, yes. Change, no."

Hendrick gave an uneasy cough. "Yes, well, as to Desmond's concern for Brandice, I do believe it is genuine. And, for that matter, justified. Why, even I was dreadfully unnerved by the news of yesterday's shooting."

"We all were." Quentin leaned forward, his fingers tightly gripping his knees. "I'll be blunt, Ellard. I want to establish if the shooting was really an accident, or a very real attempt on Brandi's life."

Hendrick nodded. "My worry exactly."

"Let's cut to the chase, shall we? Brandi told me everything: about her father's ledger, her visit to your office, the meeting you're helping her arrange."

"Of course. I assumed she would."

"The missives you dispatched—did you send them as promised? Directly after Brandi left?"

"Within an hour after her departure, yes. First I perused the files of all the gentlemen listed in Denerley's ledger."

"And did they reveal anything?"

"No. So far as my records revealed, all their losses were consistent with Ardsley's. However, you must recognize that my role in these business transactions is merely setting up the initial partnerships and providing periodic statements of profits and losses as they are reported to me."

"Meaning that if any one of the parties were dishonest in their business dealings, you would have no way of knowing it."

"Precisely."

"Did you explain that to Brandi?"

"To be blunt, Quentin, Brandice was determined to forge ahead with plans for that meeting. Nothing I said would have swayed her."

"That's my single-minded Brandi," Quentin concurred

with grim exasperation. "Very well. So you searched your files and found nothing incriminating. Then you sent out the missives?"

"I did. Based upon the whereabouts of the parties in question, the majority of missives reached their destinations that night."

"The majority of missives?"

"Three of the gentlemen are abroad and, as such, are probably first receiving their missives today."

"True." Quentin waved a dismissive hand. "And even if your timing was impeccable and a ship brought the messages to Europe yesterday, it wouldn't give any one of those men ample time to sail for England, ride to the Cotswolds, and take a shot at Brandi."

"Which eliminates three people as suspects," Hendrick declared thoughtfully. "Nevertheless, of the twelve men listed in Denerley's ledger, nine of them had opportunity to strike. And that's without even considering the dozens of businessmen funded by my clients."

"It sounds like you and I are thinking along the same lines."

"I believe we are. If any one of those men is a murderer, then Brandice is putting herself in grave danger by insisting upon this meeting."

"You think we should call it off." Quentin's assessment was a statement, not a question.

Hendrick answered it anyway. "Absolutely. If one of those men really did kill Ardsley—and your parents in the process—then it's very likely he was shooting to kill when his bullet grazed Brandice yesterday. In which case, I'd recommend keeping her as far from this investigation as possible."

Quentin's eyes narrowed pensively. "Maybe the best thing would be to go ahead with the meeting—only with me in attendance rather than Brandi."

"I'd say that was ill-advised, Quentin," Hendrick dissuaded. "Remember, this arranged meeting would only include the dozen gentlemen who are my clients, omitting the external parties involved and thereby alerting them to your suspicions. Trying to corner a dangerous criminal in this brazen and uncontrolled fashion is just as foolish a step for you to take as it would be for Brandice."

"Have you an alternative?"

"I hadn't considered this before, but I believe I have." Hendrick tapped his chin. "What if I were to conduct my own subtle but thorough investigation? I'm better connected—at least with regard to members of the *ton*— than Bow Street or its local magistrate. My clients' files are rife with family skeletons—more than you could possibly imagine. I'm well-received at White's, Brooks's, and at least three other St. James's Street clubs. In short, I could mingle, probe, and most likely glean and assemble a vast array of information without arousing the suspicions of either my clients or the scores of businessmen with whom they deal."

"That's very generous of you, Ellard. But I won't allow you to endanger yourself. Would you consider providing me access to your files so I could pursue the matter through your channels?"

Hendrick shook his head. "You know I can't do that, Quentin. It would be an unforgivable breach of ethics, even in dire circumstances such as these. Moreover, it's far less dangerous for me to conduct this investigation than it would be for you. Kenton and Pamela were your parents; thus, your intentions would be obvious with the advent of your first question. I, on the other hand, am an objective party, with no emotional connection to any of the murder victims. No one will suspect that my carefully worded inquiries are anything but innocent small talk. I'll be perfectly safe, I assure you."

"I don't know what to say," Quentin replied. "You have my deepest gratitude." He extended his hand. "It goes without saying that you'll be handsomely compensated."

Hendrick waved away the suggestion. "I'm doing this out of friendship—not only for you and Desmond, but for

Ardsley, Kenton, and Pamela, as well. If I succeed in helping to unearth the bastard who killed them, it will be compensation enough." He shook Quentin's hand—and winced.

"Is something wrong?" Quentin asked, frowning.

"Rheumatism," Hendrick said with a rueful smile. "I fear I'm growing old."

"Nonsense." Quentin came to his feet. "You're too vital to grow old." Pursing his lips, he glanced at the door.

"Let them talk, Quentin," Hendrick advised quietly. "Perhaps Desmond can find a way to convince Brandice that she must abandon the idea of this meeting."

"Perhaps," Quentin murmured without conviction. "But knowing how Brandi resents Desmond's tyranny, I rather doubt it. Although, believe me, Ellard, this is one time I hope I'm wrong."

Down the hall in the library, Desmond was hoping much the same thing.

He paced restlessly about the room, gazing longingly at the bottle of brandy that beckoned him from the side table.

"Don't, Desmond," Brandi said, rising from the settee. "You've been drinking far too much."

He pivoted to face her. "I had no idea you were concerned."

"Of course, I'm concerned. You're my friend, and you're in pain. But liquor won't bring Kenton back."

"No," he agreed. "It won't." Slowly, he crossed the room to stand before her. "Brandice, Hendrick told me about Ardsley's ledger. And about the meeting you're planning. I want you to call it off."

"I can't. I must know if one of those men killed Papa." Questioningly, she gazed up at him. "Desmond, did you know about the ledger? After all, you worked so closely with Papa—closely enough for him to appoint you overseer of all his businesses. He must have entrusted you with the knowledge of that ledger's existence."

Desmond lowered his eyes, more than prepared for this very question. "Brandice, I'm going to attempt some of the honesty you so extol. Yes, Ardsley told me of the ledger, as well as all the other papers he kept in that file. He even showed me the hidden drawer in his desk. But my mind hasn't been clear since Father's carriage went off the road. So, to be frank, I forgot all about both the drawer and the ledger."

Brandi's nod was sympathetic. "I appreciate your candor. Did Mr. Hendrick tell you what the ledger revealed?"

"He did."

"And that didn't surprise you?"

With an uncomfortable sigh, Desmond averted his head, seemingly grappling with his conscience. "No, Brandice, it didn't."

Brandi seized his arm. "If you know something, tell me. Please, Desmond, this is my father we're discussing."

"Very well." He turned back, soberly meeting her gaze. "This is very difficult for me. I vowed to Ardsley that I would honor his request to keep you from learning the truth. He was a proud man, adamant in his beliefs. He never wanted to give you cause for shame."

"Shame? I could never be ashamed of him."

"I was hoping you'd say that. Because, given the current circumstances, 'tis necessary for you to hear the truth." Desmond inhaled sharply, then exhaled in a rush. "To my knowledge, every deficit listed in that ledger was accurate." Seeing doubt veil Brandi's eyes, he pressed on with his rehearsed explanation. "As Hendrick told you, Ardsley's investments took a plunge downward these past months. 'Twas a matter of luck, not skill, as Hendrick also apprised you—and as I tried to convince Ardsley. I reminded him that every businessman encounters occasional periods where providence appears to shine down on everyone but him. Unfortunately, your father refused to accept that fact. He began poring over possible investments, determined to choose ones that would reap large profits.

"As fate would have it, Ardsley's losing streak coincided

with my own lucrative one. So, I approached him with the idea that he entrust a few of his investments to me. He agreed. I chose carefully. Our profits soared. In fact, they reaped more than enough to compensate for his other losses, as you doubtless saw reflected in his ledger. So you see, everything Hendrick surmised aloud to you was true— I'm confirming it, based upon firsthand discussions with your father. Accordingly, I'm certain all the figures listed in Ardsley's ledger were accurate, and you can thus safely dismiss the notion that one of his coinvestors is a murderer."

"Then your suggestion that I cancel the meeting is not incited by concern for my well-being?" Brandi queried, trying to discern the motivation behind Desmond's recounting.

"Oh, I'm concerned for your well-being, all right. You were shot, and I intend to find out by whom. But my worry on that score is unrelated to anything you discovered in your father's ledger. My suggestion to cancel the meeting is based, quite simply, on the fact that it would be a waste of time—yours, mine, and Ellard's." Desmond glanced about curiously. "Where is the ledger, by the way?"

"Hmm?" Brandi's mind was racing, nagged by the basis for Desmond's certainty. "Oh, it's safely hidden. Don't worry. No one will ever learn of Papa's difficulties but me." She frowned. "Forgive me, Desmond, but I still don't understand your unconditional belief that Papa's ledger is an accurate reflection of his losses, nor do I share your conviction that this meeting is naught but an unnecessary nuisance."

"Are you suggesting that I'm lying to you?"

"Of course not," Brandi asserted impatiently. "What I'm suggesting is that all you've really done is to reiterate what I already know: that Papa—and you, for that matter— believed his investments were losing money. But what if his perception was incorrect? What if someone were misleading him—or even worse, swindling him? Were that the case, neither Mr. Hendrick nor Papa would have any way of knowing. 'Twould never occur to Papa to demand proof. Being as honorable a businessman as he was, he'd never suspect anything less of his colleagues."

"Nor would he have had reason to," Desmond returned stiffly. "I'm acquainted with all those men, Brandice. Every one of them is as scrupulous as they come."

"With all due respect, I must discover that for myself." Brandi's jaw set stubbornly. "No, Desmond, the more I consider it, the more convinced I am that the only way to put these questions to rest is to hold that meeting. If the gentlemen with whom Papa invested are as principled as you suggest, then they'll understand my concern and no harm will be done."

"No harm will be done?" Desmond reiterated, angry lines forming about his mouth. "I beg to differ with you. You'll have needlessly embarrassed twelve highly influential, prominent noblemen."

"So that's the true cause of your unease. You're afraid that if I seek their help in unearthing Papa's killer, I'll be offending your peers? Forgive me, Desmond, but I can't agree. Nor, frankly, would I cancel the meeting if I did. There's far more at stake here than shame."

"In that case, I'm afraid I'll just have to forbid you from taking this course of action."

Twin spots of red stained Brandi's cheeks. "Forbid me? I'm not a child. And I won't be ordered away from a course of action I deem necessary. The decision of whether or not to pursue this meeting is mine and mine alone."

Desmond pressed his lips together, visibly striving to bring himself under control. "I apologize, Brandice," he managed at last. "I didn't mean to sound so harsh. My intention is not to dictate your actions, only to guide your way." With a forced smile, he grasped her hand. "'Tis you, not those noblemen, who are my primary concern. I want to protect you from public ridicule—something which, whether you comprehend it or not, can ruin your reputation and, consequently, your future. I plan to ensure that future, little one, to take care of you and to make you happy."

Coolly, Brandi eased her fingers from his. "Thank you, Desmond. I appreciate the fact that you have my best interests at heart."

His brow furrowed. "You appreciate it, but it doesn't please you?"

"It's not that it doesn't please me. It's only that . . ."

"You're angry with me, not only over my opinion of the meeting, but over the matter with the War Department," he guessed. "Brandice, I know you must deem my actions inexcusable. And I suppose they were. But you and I both know that Quentin is happier when he's in uniform. Since his return to the Cotswolds, he's done nothing but immerse himself in an investigation that could prove dangerous. I truly believe he'd be better off defending England in the colonies rather than submerging himself in peril right here in England. And, yes, I admit that I'm bothered by your obvious feelings for him. I have plans for your future, plans that include the protection of my name and my title. So I utilized my connections to accelerate Quentin's departure. Surely you can understand . . ."

"What are you saying?" Brandi gasped.

Too late, Desmond recognized his faux pas. "Didn't Quentin tell you?" he asked in a wooden tone.

She shook her head, staring at him for a long suspended moment of disbelief.

Then reality struck.

"You blackguard." Brandi backed away, shocked and trembling with rage. "You arranged for Quentin to be sent away? The missive, the visit to Whitehall—you devised all that?"

Desmond blanched. "I thought . . . that is, I assumed Quentin had mentioned . . ."

"Well he didn't. Knowing Quentin, he was probably protecting you."

"Protecting me? From what?"

"From my hatred," Brandi shot back. "No." She held out her hands, palms raised, warding off Desmond's advance. "Damn you, Desmond, I should have been blunt with you from the start. I've tried every subtle tactic I know to enlighten you. But I should recognize by now that subtlety is no more my forte than honesty is yours. You refuse to face the truth. Well, now you're going to hear it—loud and clear, whether or not you choose to.

"I'm in love with Quentin. I always have been; I always will be. And whether he is at home or abroad, beside me or away, my feelings will never alter."

"Brandice . . ."

"Listen to me," she commanded. "I don't love you, Desmond. There has never been anything between us other than friendship, except in your imagination. I have never even remotely entertained the prospect of wedding you. And not solely because of my feelings for Quentin, although that would be reason enough. But because you and I are as different as night and day. Just the fact that you can justify the unprincipled steps you took with the War Department is a perfect example of that. So is your relentless inclination to order me about. I don't understand you—not your archaic values nor your lack of ethics. And you understand me even less, or you'd realize that a title means nothing to me, and that what I truly crave—mutual admiration and respect— are things you are incapable of offering. I will not bow to your will, nor succumb to being molded into someone I'm not just to suit you: a man who's more concerned with proprieties than he is with feelings."

Splotches of color suffused Desmond's face. "As opposed to my brother, who is the essence of sensitivity and virtue. Well, if you think I'll stand by and allow you and Quentin . . ."

"Oh, I know you'll allow it. Because if you attempt to come between Quentin and me, I'll disappear from the Cotswolds in a heartbeat, hide somewhere you'll never find me. And I won't return until I'm one and twenty, at which point I'll be the official commander of my own fate." Her eyes blazed with anger. "Let it go, Desmond. I'll never become your duchess. Not if you drag me kicking and screaming down the aisle. What I will do is make a scene that will mark you the laughingstock of the *ton,* perpetuate rumors that will render you unable to show your face at Almack's, Carlton House, or any other playground where the fashionable world convenes. Don't push me. I'm warning you. Just graciously let me go, and maybe we can someday recapture a bit of our friendship."

Desmond's mouth opened, then closed, as he hovered between outrage and incredulity.

"I'll assume your silence means you accept my terms. A wise decision." Brandi gathered up her skirts. "Now if you'll excuse me, I have matters to attend to. Bentley will see you out. Should he choose to, that is."

Chapter 16

Crack!

The gunshot rang out, slicing the air like a knife, striking the elm's trunk dead center.

Without so much as a glance at the results of her impeccable marksmanship, Brandi reloaded, firing a second shot in the wake of the first, piercing the bark a scant inch from her previous target.

"That poor tree will be no more than a leafless, smoldering twig by nightfall," Quentin commented from twenty feet behind her. "What heinous act has it committed to incite such wrath?"

Shoulders taut, Brandi didn't even turn. "I'm pretending it's Desmond's head."

"Ah. Would this have any connection to why you bolted from the cottage directly after you and Desmond had your chat?"

Brandi stared down at the beloved pistol Quentin had given her, tracing the engraving on its handle. "Have they gone?"

"He and Hendrick left about an hour after you dashed

off. Needless to say, Desmond looked about as cheerful as the trunk of that elm tree. I believe he consumed a half bottle of Madeira before staggering off to his carriage, supported by Hendrick's arm."

"I hope he suffers the worst headache known to mankind."

Quentin chuckled. "You're supposed to keep me posted on your whereabouts," he reminded her, making his way to where she stood. "You've been out here for hours. Had Herbert not reported in every quarter hour or so, assuring me that you were indeed safe and continuing to splinter that poor tree, I would have worried myself sick."

Brandi pivoted to face him. "I'm sorry. I wasn't thinking. All I wanted was to get as far from Desmond as possible."

Gently, Quentin lifted her chin with his forefinger. "What happened?"

"Desmond did."

Quentin's lips twitched. "Could you be more specific? Did he order you not to arrange the meeting? Is that what this is all about?"

"That was but the tip of the iceberg."

"Sunbeam," Quentin framed her face between his palms, "I must be honest with you. Ellard wanted to cancel the meeting. I advised him to defer it." His thumbs forestalled her argument, lightly covering her lips. "Let me finish. 'Tis not that I want you to abandon your idea. To the contrary, I think your grounds for suspicion are well-justified. I scanned Ardsley's ledger yesterday afternoon while you were asleep. I agree the profits and losses make no sense, not only because your father was an exceptional businessman, but because my brother is not. But Hendrick and I came up with an alternative—one that is more subtle and less dramatic than a twelve-man confrontation, but—hopefully—equally as effective." With straightforward candor, Quentin explained Hendrick's plan. "Should Ellard turn up nothing," Quentin concluded, "we can still hold the meeting, as a last resort. Would that be agreeable?"

"And if I said no?"

"Then I'd ask if you were refusing because you truly believe the idea to be unsound or because you're testing the depth of my respect for your independence."

Brandi lowered her gaze.

"And," Quentin added huskily, brushing his lips across the top of her bowed head, "if the latter were true, I'd suggest that you and I are beyond that point in our relationship—if, in fact, we ever encountered it."

"You're right." Her lashes lifted. "You didn't deserve that. Of course I agree. Mr. Hendrick's plan sounds like a much better starting point." A spark of remembered anger lit her eyes. "Not to mention the fact that we won't run the risk of publicly embarrassing Papa's coinvestors."

Quentin's lips tightened. "Desmond's concern, I presume?"

"Of course." Brandi searched Quentin's eyes. "Why didn't you tell me Desmond was responsible for convincing the War Department to expedite your orders to sail for the colonies?"

"He told you about that?" Quentin asked in amazement.

"Not exactly. He assumed *you* had told me about it. So he plunged into a long-winded explanation defending the magnanimity of his actions in the hopes that I would forgive him for something that, in fact, I knew nothing about."

"No wonder you're so furious at him."

"Is that why you didn't tell me? Because you didn't want to turn me against him?"

Quentin's lips twisted into a cynical smile. "In this case, you credit me with a benevolent spirit far beyond my capabilities. Frankly, I feel nothing more flattering than pity for my brother, and even that pales in comparison to my contempt. Further, I harbor no qualms about conveying my distaste for Desmond to you, nor about your sharing it. No, Sunbeam, the reason I didn't tell you about Desmond's War Department machinations is that there simply wasn't time. I didn't discover his sordid blackmail scheme until I'd been in London for several days. I rectified the situation through Bathurst, then rode home to find you'd been shot. As soon as you felt stronger, I assure you I intended to regale you with the entire story."

"I'm glad," Brandi said simply. She drew a slow inward breath. "Quentin, I want to hear every unscrupulous detail. But first, I think you should know something."

"Hmm?"

"I told Desmond about us, about our feelings for each other."

"I'm sure he was thrilled. Especially in light of the fact that I also lambasted him with the truth—just before he left for London, in fact."

"You did?" Brandi's eyes lit up. "What did you tell him?"

"That I was in love with you." Quentin threaded his fingers through her hair. "That if he tried to stand in my way, I'd make him sorry he was born."

"Precisely what I said," Brandi concurred happily.

An indulgent grin. "Did you threaten him with bodily harm? Is that why you're practicing on that elm?"

"No. I threatened to make a public scene that would ruin him in the eyes of the *ton,* then run away from the Cotswolds until my twenty-first birthday, at which point I would return and oversee myself."

Quentin threw back his head and howled with laughter. "Oh, Sunbeam, I wish I'd been there to see his face. What did he say?"

"Not a word. He simply stared at me as if debating whether to choke me or take me at my word. Evidently, he opted for the latter." Brandi's brows knit as her mind focused on something Quentin had said earlier. "Quentin, you mentioned that you scanned Papa's ledger yesterday and that you, too, were puzzled by the severity of the losses—given what an exceptional businessman Papa was."

Instantly, Quentin sobered. "I was."

"You also mentioned being baffled by the enormity of Papa's profits on those ventures Desmond selected and controlled—implying, I presume, that in your opinion Desmond isn't proficient enough to make such shrewd and lucrative investments."

"That's exactly what I meant."

"This isn't the first time you've intimated that Desmond's business skills are questionable. As I recall, the last time the subject arose, you suggested that he incorrectly perceived your father's approval of his abilities in business matters."

Quentin's brows rose. "So you did absorb all that when I mentioned it. I thought perhaps it hadn't penetrated— given that, at the time, you were preoccupied with how to tactfully . . ." A twinge of amusement accompanied Quentin's particular choice of terms. "Instruct Desmond to relinquish any notion of wedding you, now or ever."

"I was. But I heard you nonetheless. 'Twas merely that the inconsistency didn't matter at the time. I assumed that, if Desmond had exaggerated his business aptitude, it was simply to impress me. But now I'm not so sure." Brandi's stomach clenched as she forced herself to continue. "When Bentley and I read Papa's ledger, his reaction to Desmond's apparent financial talents was much the same as yours. I pressured him until he explained why he was so astounded." Anxiously, Brandi searched Quentin's face. "Please don't be angry at Bentley. I backed him into a corner until he had no choice but to tell me the truth."

"I'm not angry," Quentin replied in a hollow tone.

Swallowing, Brandi continued. "In any case, after Bentley elaborated on how recklessly Desmond squandered funds and how apprehensive Kenton was about entrusting him with business matters, I felt totally confused. So I sought Mr. Hendrick's opinion of Desmond's business acumen."

"And?"

"Mr. Hendrick believed—based upon Desmond's total involvement in the family businesses—that Kenton applauded his investment skills."

"Which sustains Desmond's claim."

"Ostensibly, yes," Brandi acknowledged. "Now let's get to Papa. He, too, must have had faith in Desmond's abilities; why else would he have entrusted Desmond with his financial interests? More importantly, why would he have bequeathed the pivotal role of overseeing the entire Townsend business domain to Desmond?" Brandi chewed her lip pensively. "All that, combined with the iron-clad evidence of Papa's ledger, certainly leans favorably toward Desmond and suggests that you and Bentley are wrong. However, in here"—Brandi pointed to her heart—"I know you're right. So where does this disparity lead us?"

An odd expression came over Quentin's face. "Ever since you told me about the contents of your father's ledger, those very thoughts have been running through my head, plaguing me. Frankly, Sunbeam, I don't believe I've allowed myself to see them through to completion. Because if I do, they'll lead me to a conclusion I'm not certain I'm able to face."

Pain flashed in Brandi's eyes and, instinctively, she caressed Quentin's jaw. "I thought perhaps that was the case," she said quietly. "Quentin, I'm sorry. I loathed addressing this possibility, but . . ."

"It must be addressed."

"Then we'll do so together, just as together we'll face the outcome—if, in fact, our speculation has any merit."

Nodding tersely, Quentin gave voice to the unendurable prospect he longed to dismiss. "What we're both wondering is, could Desmond have 'persuaded' someone to tamper with Ardsley's profits and losses in order to show Desmond in a more favorable light? My answer—as his recent tactics with the War Department established—is a resounding yes. Oh, didn't I mention how he arranged the dispatch of that missive from Whitehall? He blackmailed one of Bathurst's aides—if the lad wished to retain his position—to report how urgently I was needed in the colonies. Now the question is, did he do the same with one or more of the businessmen in whose companies he invested on behalf of himself and Ardsley?"

"Did he?" Brandi murmured, digesting Quentin's explanation. "I don't know. Could he? Yes. Desmond would abandon ethics and pride to secure what he constantly sought to attain: Kenton's recognition and respect." She

Andrea Kane

shook her head sadly. "No one could convince him that his father loved both his sons equally."

"Lord knows we all tried." A muscle flexed in Quentin's jaw. "But in this case, it wouldn't be just Father's approval at stake, 'twould be Ardsley's as well. How else could Desmond hope to acquire both you and the Townsend businesses?"

"I hadn't considered that."

"Well, I had." A painful pause. "Now we've reached the part I can't abide. Was that the full extent of Desmond's crime, or is the truth far more heinous? Is it possible that Ardsley discovered Desmond's scheme? And if so, wouldn't he have threatened to sever all ties with Desmond, denying him the privilege of marrying you and of controlling the Townsend money? Worse, wouldn't he have proclaimed his intentions to go to my father with the truth?"

"Yes," Brandi admitted in a small voice. "At which point, Desmond would have become frantic."

"How frantic, Brandi?" Quentin demanded hoarsely. "Frantic enough to make certain Ardsley wasn't alive to carry out his threats? Frantic enough to murder him in cold blood?"

"No." Brandi tightly gripped the lapels of Quentin's coat. "Desmond is greedy and weak. But I don't believe he's inhuman enough to kill someone. And, Quentin, you're forgetting one crucial detail. Even if I'm wrong, even if Desmond is capable of all you surmised, he would never, ever arrange to harm Papa at a time when Kenton was present. Desmond worshipped your father. He'd never endanger his life. Never. No, if Desmond wanted Papa killed, he'd arrange it for when Papa was alone, not traveling to London in Kenton's carriage."

A flicker of hope lit Quentin's eyes. "That's true. And there's one other inconsistency. Desmond couldn't have been the culprit who shot you because he was at Colverton when the incident occurred. Had he attempted to sneak away, either Sanders or Wythe or one of the other servants would have spotted him." Quentin gave a hard, self-deprecating shake of his head. "Listen to me. I dislike and distrust my brother, yet I'm fervently hoping he's innocent."

"You're a wonderful, compassionate man," Brandi answered softly. "And, regardless of what else he may be, Desmond is your brother. You needn't explain—to me or yourself—why you feel as you do."

Bleakly, Quentin nodded. "Since you understand my misplaced loyalties, perchance you'll also understand why, although I realize it's necessary to determine the truth, Desmond's guilt or innocence is my responsibility to establish."

"Out of respect for Kenton."

A faint smile. "You know how fiercely Father protected his family. Were he alive, there's not a doubt in my mind how he'd handle this adversity. Even if he personally denounced Desmond and condemned his actions as despicable, he'd do his best to shield Desmond from exposure—simply because he's his son."

"I agree."

"Hence," Quentin concluded soberly, "I cannot discuss my suspicions with anyone, save you and Bentley, of course. Nor can I involve anyone else in this investigation. That includes Hendrick, although Lord knows how much easier my task would be if I could ask him to approach Desmond, to question the businessmen in whose companies Desmond invested, even to supply me with the names of those companies in order that I might investigate them on my own." Quentin sighed wearily. "But, Hendrick is not family. So it appears I'm on my own."

"Not entirely," Brandi reminded him, aching for the torment etched on his face. "You have Bentley and me." That precipitated a thought. "Why not begin by talking to Bentley?" she suggested. "Remember, he had the advantage of living at Colverton during the time all this was transpiring, while I was at Townsbourne and you were in Europe.

Perhaps, once you mention your theory, he'll have something to add."

"Good idea. I'll do that. Tonight." Quentin held Brandi's gaze. "And then tomorrow I'll confront Desmond."

"You seem especially preoccupied tonight, sir," Bentley commented from the center of the morning room.

Out on the terrace, Quentin gazed up at the night sky, grinning wryly. "You can surmise that from one glance?"

"I know what to look for."

"Such as?"

One brow arched. "Your dinner is sitting on the side table, uneaten, your tea is ice-cold, and you've been standing on the terrace overlooking the gardens for nearly an hour now." Strolling closer, Bentley inquired, "Is it Miss Brandi, sir? Are you still worried over her injury?"

"Yes and no. I'm no longer worried about the wound itself, but I am still concerned about who fired that shot and if he intends to try again. Not to mention that I'm mulling over my conversation with Hendrick, wondering where the common thread lies in this tangle of deception."

"Are you ready to discuss Master Desmond now, sir?"

Quentin's head snapped around. "What?"

Bentley shrugged. "I merely asked if you were ready to share your concerns with regard to your brother's involvement. If you'll forgive my intruding, sir, I believe it would do you a world of good to discuss it."

"Have you been chatting with Brandi?"

"Pardon me, sir?"

Quentin stepped into the room. "Did Brandi relay our discussion to you?"

"Actually, I haven't seen Miss Brandi all evening. She was exhausted from her hectic afternoon of splintering that elm tree. Mrs. Collins arranged an early dinner and a warm bath for her, after which, I presume, she fell asleep."

"Then how did you know of my concerns about Desmond?"

Bentley gave an exaggerated sigh. "Really, sir, this conversation is becoming tiresome. Need I repeat my innate knowledge of you yet again?"

"No." Quentin waved his hand. "You needn't. I'll do my best to remember that nothing I think or feel can remain a secret from you."

"Thank you, sir. Now, about Master Desmond . . ." Bentley inclined his head thoughtfully. "You and I both know how distraught the late duke was over Master Desmond's lack of principles. Frankly, everything your brother does is motivated by a desire for personal gain. So I do indeed fear—and have from the moment Miss Brandi showed me that ledger—that Master Desmond somehow arranged to have those figures altered. However, I find it inconceivable that he would harm his father, despite all that transpired just before the late duke's death."

"As do I." Quentin's eyes narrowed. "Bentley, think back to Desmond's behavior just before this chaos ensued. Is there anything—anything at all—that stands out in your mind? Anything that would shed light on this madness?"

"I've racked my brain, sir. Other than what I've told you—the heated battle between Master Desmond and your father, followed by the late duke's decision to change his will, a decision prompted by reasons Mr. Hendrick has already clarified—I can think of nothing out of the ordinary."

"Damn." Quentin clenched his fists. "What about Ardsley? Was he agitated during any of his final visits to Colverton?"

Bentley frowned. "Not in the least. Actually, I believe the viscount only dropped by once during that final fortnight—other than the day of the tragedy, that is."

"Was that unusual?"

"'Twas customary for Viscount Denerley and your father to spend several afternoons a week together, whether for business or sport. Their friendship, as you know, went back many years. However, the last weeks of his life, His Grace was deeply troubled—presumably as a result of his row with Master Desmond—and chose not to receive guests."

"Not even Ardsley?"

"The viscount was always welcome. But he evidently sensed your father needed time alone and diplomatically elected to stay away. He was, in fact, the only visitor His Grace received at all those final weeks. With the exception of . . ." Bentley broke off, stunned recall erupting on his face.

"Whom, Bentley?" Quentin demanded. "With the exception of whom?"

"Mr. Garrety." Bentley's brows knit in fierce concentration. "'Twas my day off, which is why I'd nearly forgotten. But he definitely visited your father some ten days before the accident. I remember seeing him climb into his carriage and ride off just as I returned to Colverton that evening."

"Garrety? The investigator?" Quentin's gaze grew dark, speculative. "As I recall, the only time Father employed his services was when there was a delicate business matter to delve into." He paused, features taut. "You don't suppose Father guessed what Desmond was about on his own?"

"'Tis possible, sir. As I said, your father was not himself that last fortnight."

"Nonetheless, that doesn't follow suit." Quentin shook his head. "We just concurred that Desmond would never harm Father. So how could Father's investigation—whatever it concerned—have been connected with a discovery that would threaten Desmond?"

"How indeed, my lord."

"We can't keep talking in circles," Quentin concluded with quiet resignation. "I have but one recourse—to confront Desmond. And to pray that all our suspicions are for naught."

"With so formidable a challenge looming ahead, you should get some rest, sir," Bentley suggested.

"That's out of the question. I couldn't possibly sleep."

"Apparently, you're not the only one."

"Hmm?" Quentin gave Bentley a quizzical look.

Bentley gestured beyond the terrace, where a lone figure was strolling among the gardens. "It seems you're not alone in your inability to sleep."

Quentin turned, following Bentley's gaze. "Brandi." He shook his head. "I thought you said she was abed."

"I stand corrected, sir."

A faint smile touched Quentin's lips. "As restless as a firefly," he murmured.

"But far easier to grasp."

Quentin felt his chest constrict.

"Your life is in a state of turmoil, my lord," Bentley observed quietly. "But in the midst of this chaos, your heart has found the peace it seeks. Is it not time to surrender the battle and win the war?"

Without turning, Quentin nodded.

"Have a fruitful evening, my lord."

The morning-room door clicked shut behind Bentley's retreating figure.

"The entire staff thinks you're abed."

Brandi whirled about in surprise; her hair, illuminated by moonlight, glinted with sparks of burnished fire. Seeing Quentin, she smiled. "Apparently, I didn't fool you."

"I was on the terrace. I saw you strolling through the gardens."

"Did you have a chance to talk with Bentley?"

"Yes. Nothing came of it." Quentin reached out, brushing his knuckles over her cheek. "And I didn't come out here to discuss Desmond."

Something in his voice made Brandi's breath catch. "Very well. Why did you come?"

"I was mulling over your childhood escapades—all those times you spied on me in the woods."

Brandi flushed. "I was hoping you'd forgotten."

"But I haven't. It grieves me that your education remained incomplete. What I'd like to do now is rectify that."

Puzzlement supplanted discomfort. "Rectify what?"

"Being that you never scrutinized beyond the initial section of woods, you witnessed naught but preliminaries. Your instruction is, thus, sadly lacking. I'd like to amend that."

Her eyes grew wide as saucers.

Quentin held out his hand. "Will you come with me?"

"Anywhere," Brandi whispered, placing her fingers in his.

They made their way through the woods, not slowing until they were enveloped by nature, invisible to all but the moon and the heavens. And even then Quentin led her farther, deeper into the concealing haven he sought.

Then he stopped.

Brandi drank in the natural splendor around them; her senses inundated by the grass's fragrance, the nightingale's soft trill, the dark cloak of trees that acted as a buffer between them and the world. "I hate all those women," she murmured.

"Don't hate them, Sunbeam." Quentin wrapped his arms around her from behind. "They meant nothing."

"I know." Brandi turned in his arms, twining her own about his neck. "But I'm selfish. I don't want to share this moment with anyone—not even a memory."

"You won't." He brushed her lips with his, a whisper of heated promise. "I never brought anyone here."

"But you said . . ."

"I lied." His eyes glittered devilishly. "The clearing we passed a hundred yards ago was the farthest I ever escorted anyone."

"But it's so much more beautiful here."

"That never mattered. Now it does."

Without another word, he lowered his head and kissed her, a deep, drugging, endless kiss that made everything inside Brandi go liquid with longing. She opened her mouth to him, taking and giving in a need as old as time.

"I love you," she whispered.

"Oh, Sunbeam, it's always been you." Quentin's arms tightened, bringing Brandi closer against him. "How could I not have known?"

He didn't wait for a reply.

The cool grass was a welcome contrast to her feverish skin. Brandi closed her eyes as Quentin lowered her to it, reaching for him even as she sank into the exquisite softness beneath her.

Quentin's breath rasped against her skin, his mouth urgently taking her everywhere—her neck, her shoulders, her throat. He gathered handfuls of her hair, dragging her mouth back to his, penetrating her with his tongue and devouring her with a naked urgency that neither of them questioned, both understood.

"Quentin."

Brandi sifted her fingers through his hair, moving restlessly beneath the onslaught of his kiss.

With a hunger that could no longer be ignored or contained, Quentin crushed her deeper into the grass, his hands hungrily exploring her body through the confines of her gown. He tangled his hands in her tresses, freeing the pins and scattering them randomly about. "God, Sunbeam, do you have any idea how long—how desperately—I've wanted this?"

"I've dreamed about you," Brandi confessed breathlessly, gliding her palms down his back, then under his coat, eliminating the first layer separating her from the warmth of his skin. "I've imagined us just like this: amid the trees, under the stars."

"I was a bloody fool to fight it." His hands shook as he unhooked the back of her gown, this time not allowing himself time to reconsider before he dragged it from her shoulders, down her arms.

"Don't fight it." Eyes closed, Brandi leaned back, gracefully offering him every exquisite inch of bare skin he exposed. "Quentin, it's so right."

His lips trailed along the edge of her chemise, inhaling her scent as he claimed the upper swell of her breasts. "The battle's over. I've lost, Sunbeam."

"No," she whispered, tugging impatiently at his waistcoat. "You've won. We've both won."

Andrea Kane

Gently, Quentin pushed her hands away. "Sweetheart, wait. I'm trying to go slowly. But if you touch me . . ."

"I don't care." She gazed up at him, her dark eyes filled with a bottomless wealth of emotion. "Quentin, I'm too afraid to go slowly."

"Afraid? Why?"

"Because," she admitted, a tiny wisp of sound, "if we go slowly, you might pull away."

"Never." Engulfed by tenderness, he covered her lips with his. "Never," he repeated, breathing the words into her open mouth, taking nipping tastes of her lower lip. "I could no sooner pull away than I could wrest the stars from the sky." Slowly, his tongue sank into her mouth, caressing every tingling surface before his hand tightened on her nape, urged her closer. "Brandi . . ." He melded their tongues, deepened the intimacy, then stopped, withdrawing until Brandi whimpered a protest. And still he held back—waiting, heightening the tension—refusing to comply with her unspoken plea.

A timeless moment passed before his tongue eased back inside, filling her mouth with his taste, his presence, beginning a rhythm of plunge and retreat in a blatant prelude of what was yet to be—an erotic imitation of what he wanted to do to her body.

Flames singed through her, inside and out.

With a rapturous moan, Brandi succumbed to Quentin's spell, her eyes drifting shut, her hands clutching at him, beckoning him closer. Willingly, wonderingly, she melted into the sensual haze that blazed hotter with every beat of her heart.

Her gown and chemise were at her waist. She had no idea how they got there, nor did she care. All she knew was Quentin's mouth, Quentin's hands, Quentin's breath on her skin as he whispered her name.

"Ah, Sunbeam, Sunbeam—where have I been?" He cupped her breasts, his tongue drawing each nipple into a damp, responsive peak. "You're more beautiful than any fantasy a man could dream."

296

"So long as I'm your fantasy."

His smoldering gaze met hers. "My fantasy and my reality." Without looking away, Quentin shrugged out of his coat and waistcoat, reaching up to yank his shirt buttons free.

"Let me." Without awaiting an answer, Brandi slid her hands under his, and together they fought each button free of its casing.

"Now—feel the fire," Quentin managed. He flung his shirt aside and purposefully lowered his upper torso to hers. "Feel me, Sunbeam."

"Oh . . . God." Brandi's breath refused to dislodge from her throat. Sinking deeper into the grass, she gloried in this initial joining of their bodies, painstakingly aware of every nuance—every filament of sensation in her being.

Her nipples contracted, the hair-roughened surface of Quentin's chest almost unbearably arousing as it seduced her with light, feathery strokes. His harsh exclamation of pleasure nearly undid her, and when she felt his body tremble against her, she thought for sure she'd died and gone to heaven.

"You . . . I can't . . . I've never . . ." Quentin shook his head wildly, unable to convey the intensity of physical pleasure that was coursing through his veins.

Brandi knew.

She wrapped her arms about his back, her hands exploring the powerful planes and contours, reveling as his muscles knotted beneath her caress. "Quentin." With feline grace, she arched upward, unconsciously crushing her breasts to his chest, her lower body to his.

"Christ . . ." Quentin's breath expelled in a hiss. With a will of their own, his hands moved down to grip her bottom, lifting her harder against his erection, which throbbed painfully beneath the confines of his breeches. Intentionally, he pushed deeper into her softness, circling his hips, letting her feel a sample of the searing magic that awaited them—and, in the process, driving himself closer to the edge.

He'd never intended to let it go this far. Tonight was to be but a turning point, the first step toward their future.

"Not like this," he rasped, forcing himself to still. "Not . . . yet."

"Don't." Brandi refuted Quentin's words, dizzy with passion, barely able to speak. "Please, Quentin. You've denied us too long already."

He raised up on his elbows, his heated gaze raking Brandi's half-naked beauty, warring emotions wrenching at his soul.

"Please . . ." she breathed, mimicking his earlier motion by circling her hips against his. "I can't bear the ache. Help me." Her dazed eyes searched his. "Quentin," she confessed in a heated whisper, "I don't know what to do."

A look of excruciating tenderness crossed Quentin's face, and all else was instantly eclipsed by the untainted beauty of Brandi's sensual awakening. "I know, sweetheart. I know." He kissed her with bone-melting thoroughness, suddenly very certain of where this must lead, what would forever designate this night as the bridge between past and future.

With shaking hands, Quentin reached for the hem of her gown, dragging it up over her calves, her knees, to the top of her thighs. His fingers slid beneath the fine muslin, stroking the silk of her stockings, the warm softness of her inner thighs, shifting higher and higher with each caress.

"Quentin, I'm going to die," Brandi vowed fiercely.

"Yes, I know, Sunbeam." He watched stark passion tighten her features, memorized every glorious detail of this never-to-be-equaled moment. "But not in the way you mean." Quentin kissed his way down to her breasts, his lips surrounding one taut nipple and tugging it between his lips. "The death I have in mind is caused by pleasure."

Brandi cried out, biting her lips to stifle the sound.

"Don't," Quentin ordered. "I want to hear every breathtaking little cry." His tongue swirled over her nipple's rosy peak, bathing it in fire.

"Which is worse." Brandi gasped. "Dying of emptiness or of a pleasure too acute to bear?"

Quentin smiled against her breast, ignoring the screaming hunger that clawed at his loins. "There's no contest, my little hoyden." He shifted to her other breast, lavishing it with the same attention as the first, his thumb following in the wake of his mouth, tracing teasing circles around first one breast, then its mate. "Let me show you. Let me give you this."

"I . . ." Brandi struggled for words, needing . . . needing, and not knowing how to ease the ache.

"Open for me." Quentin urged her legs farther apart. "Let me touch you."

"I'll die."

"You won't. Trust me." He kissed the frantic pulse at her neck, her flushed cheeks, her parted lips. "Open for me, Sunbeam," he murmured into her mouth. "Now. Give me all of you."

In a rush, Brandi complied, letting her legs go slack, quivers of anticipation making them quake uncontrollably.

"Yes—like that." Quentin himself was shaking so badly he could scarcely speak. "Brandi . . . Christ." His fingers opened her, claimed her, found her damp and soft and trembling in heated welcome.

A harsh sound ripped from his chest, and, at that moment, Quentin knew that passion as he had known it was forever changed. Vaguely, he heard Brandi's reckless sob, felt her nails score his back. But all he could think of, focus on, was the hot, wet, tight feel of her. His finger slipped inside her, testing her readiness, discovering the miracle of her response. Her inner muscles clung to him, luring him deeper, beckoning him to take more, to take all.

"I . . ." Brandi licked her lips, gone suddenly dry. "Quentin, I don't know what's happening . . . I . . ." Inadvertently, she moved against his hand.

"What's happening is heaven," he proclaimed, his thumb finding and caressing the tight bud that cried out for his touch. "More than heaven."

"Quentin . . ." Her body was responding on its own and, bewildered, she clung to him, frightened by her own utter helplessness. Reflexively, she undulated against him—once, twice—her eyes open and wide with shock.

"Don't be afraid," Quentin somehow managed to assure her. "Just give in to it, Sunbeam. This is the way it was meant to be with us." He slid another finger inside her, stretching her ever so gently, then withdrew a heartbeat at a time, only to push back inside her in one swift, inexorable motion, repeating the action again and again, stretching her a bit more each time, all the while his thumb circling, urging her deeper into the bottomless inferno of sexual oblivion.

It was too much.

"Oh . . . God." Brandi arched like a bowstring, and Quentin would never forget the look of consummate wonder on her face before she toppled over the edge, dissolving into exquisite spasms of release that clenched his fingers so erotically he would have plunged over the edge himself, were he not so immersed in her pleasure.

No climax—not even his own—had ever been this perfect.

"Quentin." Brandi breathed his name on a reverent, broken sigh, floating back to earth in shivering degrees, staring incredulously into his eyes.

"The only thing more exquisite than what just happened is you," he murmured. He kissed her again, claiming her even now, his fingers continuing to caress her even as they withdrew.

Abruptly, Brandi realized he intended to stop. "You said all or nothing," she whispered, reaching for him. "I want it all."

"So do I." He eased away from her, silencing her protests as he rearranged her disheveled clothing. "But only you can provide the answer as to whether or not we shall have it."

"I?" She pushed his restraining hands away, gripping the breadth of his bare shoulders. "But I've already given you my answer."

"That's impossible." Quentin averted his head, tenderly kissing her hand. "For I have yet to ask the question." He turned back to gaze into her eyes, framing her flushed face between his palms. "Brandice Townsend, will you marry me?"

"Will I . . ." She broke off, unable to speak the words lest they vanish.

Quentin smiled tenderly. "I love you, Sunbeam. I need to know that all I ever wished for you has come to pass—a husband who will rejoice in your spirit, awaken your passion, and take care of you for the rest of your life. So, if I'm blessed to be that lucky man, tell me. Because the only way we can have the 'all' we both crave is with a ring on your finger."

"Oh . . . Quentin." Her breath caught. "Am I dreaming?"

"Dreaming, yes—but awake. As am I." He caressed her face, savoring her expression of joyous wonder. "But I repeat, our future rests in your disarming hands. I want to join my heart, my soul, and my body with yours. Will you give me that gift—do me the honor of becoming my wife?"

Radiant fireworks erupted in Brandi's eyes. "I never thought this day would come. Quickly, tell me again that I'm awake."

"You're awake," he solemnly assured her.

"Thank God." She launched herself into Quentin's arms. "Yes." She kissed the warmth of his shoulder. "Yes, I'll marry you. Yes, I'll be your wife. Yes. Yes. Yes."

Quentin enfolded her against him, burying his face in her hair. "God, I love you, Sunbeam. How could I pretend otherwise—to either of us?" He grinned. "You were right. I am a bloody fool. No one but you could ever make me feel like this—so incomparably, unbearably happy."

Brandi drew back, giddy with exhilaration. "You're wrong on both counts, my lord. You're no longer a bloody fool, and I have yet to make you feel incomparably, unbearably happy—at least not to the extent that I soon shall. But consider yourself duly warned; I intend to rectify that, to make you happier than even you can imagine. And one thing more. Armed with my now-complete education—

thanks to the wonder I just discovered in your arms—I plan to decimate every iota of your iron control, Captain Steel."

Quentin grinned, a seductive smile Brandi felt to the tips of her toes. "I can hardly wait," he murmured huskily. "As for your education—trust me, Sunbeam, 'tis far from complete. But consider yourself duly warned." He traced the fluttering pulse at her neck, giving her back the very words she'd just uttered. "I intend to rectify that, to make you happier than even you can imagine." He brushed her lips in a slow heated caress. "And that, my love, is a promise."

Chapter 17

"*Y*ou look like hell."

Lounging in the doorway of Desmond's study, Quentin assessed his brother's disheveled state and red-rimmed eyes—eyes too glazed to focus on anything save the goblet in his hand.

Slowly, Desmond raised his head. "What d'you want, Quentin?"

"We need to talk."

Quentin strode into the room, closing the door in his wake.

"About what, your quest for th' truth or your Sunbeam?"

"Both." Quentin lowered himself into a chair. "Sanders is on his way in with a pot of strong black coffee. I'm going to wait patiently while you down cup after cup—as many as it takes to convince me you're capable of having a coherent discussion."

Desmond massaged his temples. "I'm not in the mood for coffee. I'm less in the mood for chatting. And I'm least in the mood to see you."

"Have I mentioned how impressed I am by this new show

of honesty you've been displaying lately?" Quentin stretched his legs in front of him, crossing them at the ankles. "I hope it continues when I get to the topics we need to confront after Sanders and I have sobered you up."

"Why the hell is Sanders delivering refreshment trays? He's my valet, not a bloody footman."

"He's also the only member of Father's staff who dares to cross your path these days. Given that fact, he was kind enough to offer his services."

Before Desmond could reply, a tentative knock sounded at the door.

"Come in, Sanders," Quentin called. "His Grace is awaiting his coffee with bated breath."

Sanders entered timidly, his eyes darting from Desmond to Quentin and back. Then he scurried across the room and deposited a tray of coffee and scones on Desmond's desk. "I wasn't sure if you'd had breakfast, my lord," he addressed Quentin, cringing beneath Desmond's black scowl. "So I took the liberty of providing an additional cup and saucer, should you wish some coffee, as well as a second plate, should you wish a bite to eat."

"That was very considerate. Thank you, Sanders." Quentin gave him a reassuring nod.

"You can get out now, Sanders," Desmond snapped, once the valet had filled two cups to the brim. "I assure you, I'm perfectly capable 'f swallowing my own coffee without assistance—foxed or not."

"Yes, Your Grace." Needing no second invitation, Sanders hastened from the room.

"Drink," Quentin commanded, when Desmond did no more than stare sullenly at the tray. "Or it will be I, not Sanders, who assists you. And the experience won't be a pleasant one."

Mumbling an oath, Desmond took a gulp, shuddering with distaste.

"Keep going. I'll let you know when to stop."

Four cups later—dispersed by several angry outbursts—

Desmond shoved the tray away. "Enough. I'm disgustingly sober. What do you want?"

Meticulously, Quentin sized up his brother's overall condition. Satisfied, he nodded. "Very well. This won't take long. After which, you're welcome to drown yourself in as many bottles of Madeira as your stomach can tolerate." His casual posture abandoned, Quentin sat up straight, leaning forward in the chair. "Let's begin with Brandi. This is the portion of our conversation in which I do the talking and you do the listening. Those roles will shortly be reversed."

"Save your breath with regard to Brandice." Desmond's hand sliced the air. "With her customary display of unladylike bluntness, she informed me of her feelings, both for you and for me. It appears that, once again, you emerge the victor, my oh-so-fortunate brother."

Quentin cocked a brow. "Think about what you just said, Desmond—the way you described Brandi. Would you really want to spend your entire life *attempting*"—his emphasis was intentional, a reminder of the improbable outcome of such a task—"to break her to your will and transform her into a demure and proper duchess?"

"What I want or do not want no longer matters, at least not to that stubborn hellion you've created. All that matters to Brandice, at the cost of all our reputations, is what— rather, whom—she wants. And whom she wants is you."

"As I want her—exactly as she is," Quentin said pointedly.

"How romantic."

"I wasn't seeking your opinion, nor your approval. In fact, let me stress that the following is not a request, but a statement of fact, proffered only because you are Brandi's legal guardian. The sole effect you can have is to determine, by way of your reaction, the avenue I take to enact my plan."

"What are you leading up to?"

Quentin held Desmond's gaze. "From Colverton, I'm traveling directly to London—for several reasons, the rest

305

of which I will address in a moment. But the main purpose of my trip is to obtain a special license. I intend to wed Brandi by week's end."

Desmond sucked in his breath.

"You have two choices, as I see it," Quentin continued, ignoring his brother's stunned expression. "You can be genteel and gracious, giving Brandi your consent and, thus, avoiding gossip and scandal among the *ton*—who, incidentally, never knew of your intentions to wed Brandi, so you'll remain untainted in their eyes. Or, you can oppose the marriage, at which point I will spirit Brandi out of England, return with her as my bride, and ensure that—what were my incomparable betrothed's words? Ah, yes. Ensure that you are rendered the laughingstock of the *ton.* And, trust me, Desmond, I have more than enough ammunition to do so, between your excessive drinking and the reckless squandering of Father's money I'm sure I'd uncover if I probed deeply enough. The choice, dear brother, is yours."

Desmond's eyes glinted with jealous enmity. "Our father—and *your* mother—are barely cold in their graves. We have a full year's mourning period to observe—a period that has scarcely begun. How can you consider . . ."

"Shut up, Desmond," Quentin interrupted in a lethal tone. "Don't even try using that particular tactic on me. The admiration and esteem I felt for my father and mother were immeasurable, rooted in something far more profound than protocol, and, therefore, impervious to public scrutiny. Recalling the love and respect they shared, I unequivocally know that nothing would grant them greater peace than the knowledge that Brandi and I are joining our hearts and our lives in the same manner as they did. As to the wedding itself, Brandi and I have decided to keep the ceremony quiet and private—not for the sake of appearances, but for the sakes of us and our parents—because we want only to be surrounded by those we love, and the spirits of those we love. Festivities will be deferred until the murderer has been unearthed and the year of mourning has passed." Quentin's eyes narrowed. "That should satisfy even you. Now, I'm waiting for your answer."

"You certainly have everything worked out, don't you?"

"All but the final detail, which your response will now determine."

Desmond gave a hollow laugh. "If this weren't so ironic, it might even be funny. Everything I risked . . ." He broke off, shaking his head. "Never mind. None of it matters anymore. In truth, I'm too bloody tired to give a damn. Fine, Quentin. Marry Brandice. Take her with you when you sail to the bloody colonies, for all I care. My life, my plans—they're all unraveling anyway." He slouched in his chair. "I've put myself through hell for nothing."

Put myself through hell. Everything I risked.

The words triggered a memory in Quentin's mind, and abruptly he recalled the last time Desmond had chosen those particular phrases to describe his attempts to win Brandi's hand.

Finally, after putting myself through hell, risking things you couldn't possibly imagine, I'd very nearly won her over.

An inner voice urged Quentin on. "What hell did you put yourself through? What is it you risked?"

"Nothing that affects you. You have my consent, and your revered Sunbeam. What else do you want?"

"Answers." Quentin's jaw tightened. "Which brings me to the second part of this discussion—my quest for the truth, as you put it. Desmond, I've seen Ardsley's ledger. And I found its contents strangely troubling."

A wary look crossed Desmond's face. "In what way?"

"Frankly, Ardsley was too good an investor to incur such drastic losses. But that alone wouldn't bother me. What bothers me is that you're too ineffective an investor to earn such overwhelming profits."

"Who the hell are you to . . ."

"There's no one here but us now, Desmond," Quentin interceded quietly. "There's no *ton* to impress, no fortunes to acquire, nor women to woo. So let's not insult each other by spouting nonsense. Your business skills are moderate to poor. So is your judgment. Couple those realities with the fact that your half-hearted attempts to reform were constantly subverted by reckless side ventures that cost Father a fortune. What I want to know is, did you tamper with the numbers listed in Ardsley's ledger?"

Desmond bolted to his feet. "I don't have to sit here and take this." His eyes blazed. "How dare you accuse me of stealing money?"

"I didn't accuse you of stealing it. I asked if you'd altered the distribution of it to make you appear the consummate businessman."

"And just how would I do that? I never even saw this notorious ledger, nor did I provide the figures designated in it."

"No, you didn't."

Desmond's lips thinned into a grim line. "Then your contemptuous suggestion is stupid as well as offensive."

"At least not directly, you didn't," Quentin qualified. "But did you goad someone into doing it for you?"

"Goad someone? As in, beat them into compliance?"

"No, as in blackmail them into compliance. You're extremely good at that—as we both know."

Desmond shot Quentin a poisonous look. "I'd hardly liken hastening your departure with blatantly falsifying records."

"I fail to see the difference. Nevertheless, your ethics, however dubious, are not at issue here. Your honesty is. So I ask again, did you arrange for someone to redistribute those numbers?"

A heartbeat of a pause. "No."

"Good. Then you wouldn't mind providing me with a list of all the companies in which you invested, both for Ardsley and for Father."

Dead silence.

"I've already asked Hendrick to gather that data for all the other investors listed in Ardsley's ledger, and then to investigate the companies funded by their ventures. During

the course of our exchange, I, of course, never mentioned
your name and it goes without saying that Hendrick would
never consider including you as a suspect—after all, you are
my brother and Kenton's son, right?" Quentin's eyes glittered. "Lest you wonder, Desmond, those are the sole
reasons I'm speaking to you directly rather than turning my
suspicions over to Hendrick or Bow Street: because of the
blood we share and out of respect for Father."

"You have me tried and convicted," Desmond muttered.
His agitated gaze darted about the study, settling on the
bottle of port that graced the side table.

"Suspicion and conviction are worlds apart," Quentin
amended. "Now, as for that list . . ."

"Let me understand this." Desmond licked his suddenly
parched lips. "You want a list of all the companies in which
I invested so you can verify if I hired someone to misrepre-
sent the profits and losses in order that I appear a hero?"

"Yes—and I want it before you take that drink."

"Go to hell, Quentin."

"I'm there right now." Quentin rose slowly, walking
toward his brother, anguish reflected in his eyes. "Tell me,
Desmond. Did Ardsley find out what you'd done? Did he
discover your deceit and threaten to tell Father, or to deny
you his money and his daughter? Is that what happened?"

"What are you babbling about?"

"Did he get to Father in time, or did you ensure he
didn't?"

Desmond's pupils dilated, and he recoiled as if he'd been
struck. "You think I killed Ardsley?"

"Did you?"

"You think *I'm* the one who arranged that carriage
accident?" Desmond stared at Quentin incredulously, all
the color draining from his face. *"You think I killed our
father?"*

"I pray to God you didn't."

"Well, pray somewhere else." Desmond's features hardened to stone, his body rigid with repressed emotion. "Get
out, Quentin. Get out of my home. You're no longer

welcome at Colverton. Go to your mother's house. Marry Ardsley's daughter. But don't ever show your face here again."

Snatching the bottle of port, Desmond stalked from the room, leaving naught but unanswered questions in his wake.

"Two missives were just delivered from London," Bentley announced, approaching the gazebo.

"For whom? From whom?" Brandi popped up, her nose smudged with dirt.

"Let's see." Bentley glanced thoughtfully at the envelopes in his hand. "The first is for Master Quentin from Mr. Hendrick. 'Tis a shame Mr. Hendrick didn't know his lordship was traveling to London. He could have met with him in person rather than communicated with him by message. Ah, well."

"And the other missive, Bentley?" Brandi pressed, wiping her sleeve across her forehead. "Who is it for?"

"Hey! Are you helpin' me dig up these dead geraniums or not?" Herbert demanded from his kneeling position. "I'm angry as a hornet, as it is. I've lost these two rows of flowers one time too many. I'm half tempted to put nothin' here but dirt."

"You wouldn't do that," Brandi retorted with a grin. "You care far too much about your garden. I told you; we'll figure out the problem. *After* Bentley tells me who the other missive is for." Hands on hips, she gazed pointedly at Bentley.

"Oh, didn't I mention that detail, Miss Brandi?" Bentley's brows rose in surprise. "How careless of me. 'Tis for you." He paused, fighting the twitching of his lips. "From Master Quentin."

With a squeal, Brandi snatched it from his hand. "Let me read it."

She tore the note open, scanning the few lines before letting out a yelp that made Lancelot pause, six trees away, in the midst of devouring a berry.

"He got it! Quentin got it!" She flung her arms about

310

Bentley's neck, hugging him so tightly the butler had to extricate himself in order to resume breathing. "I hardly dared let myself hope. But I should have known Quentin would find a way. Oh, I love you, Bentley . . . and you, too, Herbert." She whirled about, yanking at Herbert's work-worn hands until he stumbled to his feet, then, before he could stop gaping, she dragged him into a joyous little jig.

"What?" Herbert gasped, when at last they halted. "What is it his lordship got?" He looked bewilderedly at Bentley.

"I wouldn't know," the butler croaked, rubbing his throat before readjusting his slightly mussed collar. "Perhaps Miss Brandi can enlighten us."

"'Twould be my greatest happiness to enlighten you." Brandi's face glowed, emanating a pure, irrepressible joy. "Quentin and I decided to say nothing until we were certain he could acquire the necessary license—and the assurance that Desmond would do nothing to intervene. Both those obstacles have been overcome. Quentin will be home to-morrow. And the following day, I shall become Mrs. Quentin Steel." She gazed euphorically from Bentley to Herbert. "Isn't that wonderful?"

Herbert let out an exuberant whoop, enveloping Brandi in a most inappropriate bear hug. "More than wonderful!" he exclaimed. "I'm so happy, I could bust." Awkwardly, he drew back. "I've gotten you all dirty," he muttered, brushing grains of soil from her sleeves. "Don't know what I was thinkin'." He blinked, keeping his suspiciously bright gaze fixed on Brandi's gown.

She covered his hand with hers. "Thank you, Herbert," she managed, her voice rife with emotion. "Your approval means the world to me."

"Approval? I've been waitin' for this day for as long as I can remember. Finally, you're gonna be as happy as the duchess prayed you'd be." A nostalgic look crossed Herbert's face. "As happy as she and the duke were."

"I could wish for no greater blessing." Slowly, Brandi turned to Bentley. "Bentley?"

A broad never-before-seen smile split the butler's face. "I

must say, it was a challenging battle, Miss Brandi. But we won it, didn't we?"

"Yes, Bentley, at long last, we won." Brandi stood on tiptoe and kissed his cheek. "Thank you, my dear friend," she whispered.

Unclasping his hands from behind his back, Bentley tenderly patted her hair. "'Twas not my doing, but fate's," he murmured.

"Perhaps," Brandi replied solemnly. "But in this case fate had a bit of help." Dabbing at her cheeks, she stepped away. "You'll both be at the wedding, of course." An impish grin sparkled through her tears. "'Twill be a most unusual ceremony. The bride will be given away, not by one, but by two special gentlemen."

A rustle shook the leaves overhead.

"Squirrels are not allowed in church," Brandi called up to her red friend. "But we shall have a wedding picnic right here at Emerald Manor directly after the ceremony. And, to that feast, dear Lancelot, you are definitely invited. I believe you'll enjoy it ever so much more than you would the taking of the vows."

"Not I," Bentley asserted, his composure—and his clasped hands—restored. "These vows are most welcome, and long overdue."

"And now they're but two days away," Brandi stated, wonder lacing her words. Abruptly, her head snapped up. "Oh, Lord. What will I wear? I've been so busy fretting and praying that I completely neglected to plan."

"I believe Mrs. Collins has nearly completed your wedding dress," Bentley informed her offhandedly. "I'll verify that with her now, before I return to the garden to assist Herbert in gathering the appropriate flowers for your garland. As for your veil, Mrs. Collins has retrieved the one Her Grace wore on the day she became the Duchess of Colverton. I assumed that would please you."

Throughout Bentley's accounting, Brandi's gaping mouth grew wider. "Quentin and I told no one of our plans. How did Mrs. Collins know?"

One of Bentley's brows arched.

Smiling, Brandi waved away her question. "Never mind. I'm sure you knew of this wedding long before we did."

"Indeed. Although I must admit, his lordship did give me a moment or two of concern. His honor and virtue can, at times, be exasperating, can they not?"

"They certainly can," Brandi concurred. "As can his bloody self-control. In more situations than you can imagine. But fear not. I plan to burn all three of those assets to ashes." Oblivious to Herbert's flaming cheeks, she seized Bentley's arm. "May I go see the gown? I know you said you wanted first to verify its status with Mrs. Collins, but . . ."

"But patience is not one of your finer assets," Bentley supplied helpfully. "Nor, in this case, should it be. You are, after all, the bride. So, run along." He gestured toward the cottage. "Find Mrs. Collins. Revel in her creation. I shall remain here with Herbert and select a lovely arrangement of blossoms for your hair."

"Oh, thank you. Thank you both so much." Without pause, Brandi dashed off, nearly tripping over her skirts in her haste to reach the cottage.

"I hope she doesn't try that in the church," Herbert grumbled good-naturedly. "Or else she'll end up slidin' down the aisle on her bottom."

"I don't think Master Quentin would mind a bit," Bentley returned, a corner of his mouth lifting ever so slightly. "So long as she arrives at the proper destination and he is there to receive her."

With an answering chuckle, Herbert lowered himself to his knees amid the garden's rainbow hues. "Come on. We've got work to do."

With a final glance at Brandi's retreating form, Bentley nodded, glancing distastefully at the clumps of dirt already adhering to his polished shoes. "Ah, well," he conceded. "'Tis for Miss Brandi, after all." So saying, he rolled up his sleeves and gingerly squatted beside Herbert to amass the perfect blooms for Brandi's headpiece.

* * *

Exploding into the cottage, Brandi burst through to the kitchen—and smack into Mrs. Collins. "Oh, Mrs. Collins, you're wonderful!" She hugged the baffled housekeeper, who was struggling not to drop the hot pie in her hands.

"I didn't realize you were so hungry, Miss Brandi," she replied, pivoting to set down the pan. "I'll cut you a slice."

"I'm not hungry." Brandi dismissed the pie with a wave of her hand. "Nor is that why you're wonderful—although I'm sure the pie is splendid. But what I'm referring to surpasses its glory by far—my wedding gown."

Mrs. Collins gasped. "How did you learn about that?"

"Bentley told me."

Elation erupted on the housekeeper's face. "Bentley told you? Then that could mean but one thing. You and Master Quentin . . ."

"Yes. Oh, yes. Quentin and I are getting married. The day after tomorrow." Brandi seized the housekeeper's hand, dragging her away from the oven and toward the door. "Now, please, please, may I see my dress?"

"This instant." Mrs. Collins wiped her hands on her apron. "I'll fetch it from its hiding place in my room. You go to your bedchamber and—" A swift assessment of Brandi's smudged cheeks and grass-stained gown. "Clean up a bit."

"I'm on my way." Brandi sprinted up the steps like a filly.

A quarter hour later, fresh and glowing, Brandi twirled about before her bedchamber's looking glass, watching the silver lace sparkle atop the elegant white satin. She met her own exhilarated gaze in the mirror. "Is that really me?"

"No one else," the beaming housekeeper assured her. "And you are the most breathtaking of brides."

"'Tis the gown—it's what dreams are made of. How on earth did you sew it so quickly?"

"I was inspired." A twinkle. "I also didn't do it alone. Over the past fortnight, Bentley has supplied me with three competent seamstresses and a wealth of magnificent material."

"Here? At the cottage? Where was I?"

"When you weren't recuperating? Where you always are."

Mrs. Collins held up her fingers, counting off. "In the garden with Herbert, the woods with Lancelot, the stables with Poseidon, or the gazebo with your daydreams."

Brandi's expression turned sheepish. "I am dreadfully predictable, aren't I?"

"Never that, Miss Brandi." The housekeeper laughed. "Just too restless to remain inside, and therefore, easy to plan a splendid surprise for."

"How can I ever thank you? 'Tis the most exquisite gown I've ever seen." Brandi turned, clasping the housekeeper's hands.

"The joy on your face is thanks enough." Mrs. Collins squeezed Brandi's fingers. "Be happy, love."

"I'm marrying Quentin. How can I not be?"

"I agree. Which reminds me, when will his lordship be returning?"

"Tomorrow. Oh, Mrs. Collins, this is going to be the longest night of my life."

"I think not," the housekeeper amended wisely, smoothing the delicate lace that defined Brandi's bodice. "I think tomorrow night—the eve before your wedding—might even surpass it."

Brandi wondered if that were possible.

It seemed an eternity before the moon was eclipsed by the rising sun, longer still before the morning unfolded, bringing with it the sounds of Quentin's approaching carriage.

Nearly knocking Bentley to the ground, Brandi raced out the door, flinging herself into Quentin's arms before he'd finished alighting. "You're home!"

His bone-melting smile warmed her inside and out. "Yes, Sunbeam, I'm very much home." Drinking in her glowing features, he threaded his fingers through her hair and kissed her in full view of Bentley and the footmen. "Do you know, I could grow accustomed to greetings such as this?"

"Then you shall always have them," Brandi vowed breathlessly. "Whether you've spent days in London or months in the colonies, you have my word that you'll receive lengthy, loving—and shamelessly public—displays of affection upon your return."

"I shall hold you to that promise." Quentin's knuckles brushed her cheek, stroked a line down the delicate bridge of her nose. "I missed you."

"I've been going mad." She gripped his coat. "I did interpret your missive correctly, didn't I? You do have the license?"

Grinning, Quentin patted his pocket. "Safe and sound, and very, very legal."

"And Desmond?"

Quentin's smile faded.

"Was it terribly difficult? Did he make a scene?"

"Not about us, no. He was surprisingly acquiescent. But he also refused to give me the information I sought."

Brandi sighed. "That comes as no surprise. Whether Desmond is guilty or not, we both knew he wouldn't take kindly to being accused—especially by you."

"I quite agree, sir," Bentley murmured from behind.

"As do I." Quentin gave a weary sigh. "Confronting Desmond was one of the hardest things I've ever had to do."

"How did he react to the question you most dreaded asking?" Bentley queried. "Surely Master Desmond wasn't in any way involved in tampering with the carriage, was he?"

"In my opinion, no. As to his reaction, he was horrified. He ordered me from Colverton, never to return."

"Quentin, I'm sorry," Brandi murmured.

"Desmond and I never shared more than a flimsy bond of brotherly affection," Quentin stated grimly. "But whatever we did have has now been destroyed. Irreparably, I fear."

"Not if he's innocent," Brandi countered at once. "Your brother, better than anyone, knows your reason for delving into this whole sordid affair: to unearth our parents' murderer. Presumably, he wants the killer punished as much as you do. I'm certain he'll forgive you for exploring every conceivable avenue—even those pertaining to him." Soberly, Brandi met and held Quentin's gaze. *"If* he's innocent."

Gravely, Quentin nodded. "Yes—if."

"What about Papa's ledger? Did Desmond also deny that he'd tampered with that?"

"He did—but with a lesser level of conviction. When I suggested his connection with Father's death, he went wild with shock and outrage, while when I broached the subject of the ledger—more or less accusing him of blackmailing someone into altering it—he merely became sullen and evasive." Quentin scowled. "I can't shake the ominous feeling that Desmond is somehow implicated in all this—if not legally, then ethically. I spent much of my London trip trying to glean even an iota of information: visiting several companies with whom Father did business, asking a few casual questions—and walking away knowing as little as I had when I arrived. The truth is, I can accomplish nothing without Father's records—records that Desmond flatly refused to give me and to which I have no access now that I've been banned from Colverton. It appears my only remaining hope is to apprise Ellard of my suspicions and to ask for his help."

"Remember, sir, Mr. Hendrick is under no legal obligation to provide you with names," Bentley reminded him. "Officially, your father's title, estate, and businesses belong to Master Desmond. Hence, if your brother forbids Mr. Hendrick from supplying you with information, I fear Mr. Hendrick's hands are tied."

"I've considered that prospect. I'll just have to hope Desmond is either too incoherent or too ashamed to notify Hendrick of our falling out. And that, if neither is the case, Hendrick's loyalty to Father will outweigh his sense of obligation to Desmond."

"One would think so, sir. Oh, that reminds me—" Bentley reached into his pocket and extracted an envelope. "You received a missive from Mr. Hendrick yesterday."

"Good. Maybe he's learned something that will make my

whole ugly investigation unnecessary." Quentin tore open the note and scanned the contents.

"Well?" Brandi demanded.

"Nothing of importance." Quentin shrugged. "Ellard's plan is underway, but he's encountering the inevitable obstacles spawned by summer. Several of his clients and their colleagues are on holiday and choose not to be reached." Quentin refolded the note. "Unfortunately, this procedure is going to take some time."

"Why didn't you stop by Mr. Hendrick's office while you were in London?" Brandi asked curiously. "You could have spoken to him about Desmond then and there."

"Yes, I could have. But I chose not to."

"Why?"

Quentin's expression grew tender. "Because, little hoyden, I wanted to get home to you as soon as possible. These next few precious days belong to us. Our parents would want no less. The unanswered questions and suspicions are going nowhere, and can be addressed afterward. But for now—" He withdrew the license from his pocket. "I wanted to flourish this before your beautiful eyes, to see your face light up with joy, and—oh, to settle the score on a previous victory." So saying, Quentin reached into the carriage and extracted a large flat parcel, which he placed in Brandi's arms.

Brandi's brows drew together. "What is it?"

"An overdue prize." He grinned at her mystified look. "Open it and see."

Needing no further urging, Brandi tore open the package, squealing as she lifted out three delicately cut pairs of breeches: one black, one cocoa-brown, and one fawn-colored.

"I owed you those from our last fishing contest," Quentin informed her. "Now you no longer have to be impeded by—in your words—soggy gowns trailing at your ankles and bulky layers of muslin crammed between your body and your saddle." Watching Brandi's elated expression, he chuckled. "A most unconventional wedding gift for a most unconventional bride."

"A bride who can now ride astride as well as any man," Brandi said proudly. She stood on tiptoe and brushed her lips to his. "Thank you, Quentin. In light of the particular contest in question, 'tis a most generous prize."

"And why is that?"

"Because, my lord—" Brandi backed away, her eyes dancing with mischief, her breeches clutched in her hands. "Your suspicions were right. I cheated."

Laughter trailing behind her, she darted into the cottage.

"You'll never be bored, sir," Bentley commented.

"No, I don't suppose I shall," Quentin agreed. "Bentley—" Soberly, he turned to his friend. "Do you think I'm being remiss in deferring the investigation a day or two?"

"No, my lord. As you yourself just noted, nothing dramatic is going to transpire over the next few days. Mr. Hendrick will continue to probe and Master Desmond will continue to drink. This time, as you proclaimed to Miss Brandi, belongs to the two of you."

"This time," Quentin reiterated, shaking his head in bemused wonder. "Tell me, Bentley, how is it that, at what is in some ways the most painful point in my life, I'm able to feel such overwhelming joy?"

"That particular miracle, my lord, has a name." Bentley gestured for the footmen to unload Quentin's bags. "How fortunate for you that tomorrow you shall give her yours."

Chapter 18

*T*he morning room was quiet when Quentin stood on its terrace the next day, watching the sun rise. He'd drifted off to sleep at about two last night, only to awaken a few hours later, ready to embrace a future that had, despite his colossal stupidity, found him.

Sipping thoughtfully at his coffee, Quentin found himself wondering if Brandi had slept any better than he. He grinned, knowing the answer already. In all her twenty years, Brandi had never shut an eye on the eve preceding an exciting event. How many Christmas mornings had her sparkling eyes peeked at gifts from beneath heavy lids? How many birthdays had her spontaneous laughter been interrupted by sleepy yawns that escalated in frequency as the day wore on?

Quentin's smile grew tender, recollections flowing through him like warm honey. Brandi, his rare and beautiful Sunbeam—how miraculous were the extraordinary ways in which she hadn't changed.

Equally miraculous were the extraordinary ways in which she had.

Their evening together in the woods had been the most

excruciating combination of heaven and hell Quentin could imagine. Even now, his body burned as he recalled the unprecedented, unbearable ecstasy of her bare skin melding with his—her nipples contracting beneath the onslaught of his chest, his hands, his mouth. The wonder of her response had nearly been his undoing; her satiny wetness welcoming him with a desire that matched his own, her delicate inner muscles contracting around his fingers, the awed amazement in her eyes when she'd shivered in his arms.

It had been Brandi's first taste of passion, and while it was but the first glimmer of her awakening, it had driven him to the brink of insanity.

God, he wanted her. He'd never known wanting this fierce—primitive in its urgency, humbling in its basis.

So this was love.

Watching the steam curl slowly from his cup, Quentin marveled at the extent of this newly born emotion—an emotion that affected not only his heart but his thoughts, his plans, his future.

His life had been the army; home was where it took him. As for the Cotswolds—that had been the peaceful haven that awaited his visits, together with family, friends, and a tousle-haired hoyden who warmed his heart like a burnished ray of sunshine.

A burnished ray that had intensified, grown stronger, more ardent, until it permeated every fiber of his being.

And suddenly, his Sunbeam was his life.

That reality struck home, spawning a hunger Quentin had never anticipated, much less encountered.

Roots. He wanted roots. Not just a home, but a life that was his. A life, and a wife.

And children.

The thought of filling Brandi's body with his seed, watching her swell with his child, ignited a primal need for possession that pounded through Quentin's loins, surged through his soul. He wanted a houseful of little Brandis, their laughter echoing through the halls of Emerald Manor, their spirits as pure and exuberant as their mother's.

Gulping down the rest of his coffee, Quentin made peace with a decision he'd never thought to make.

It was time. When England was ready, so was he.

"Good mornin', my lord." Herbert paused near the small section of garden alongside the terrace. "I didn't know you were up." A wry grin. "Although I suppose I should've guessed. It is your weddin' day, after all. And your bride-to-be certainly didn't spend much time sleepin'. Her lamp's been burnin' for over an hour. I suspect she'll be visitin' the gazebo anytime now."

"I suspect you're right." Quentin grinned back. "And what is your excuse for strolling about at dawn? You'd best not be working—not on so important an occasion as today."

A chuckle. "I wouldn't dream of it, my lord. No, I just figured I'd head out to the gazebo—in case Miss Brandi wants to talk."

Quentin nodded, a spark of gratitude lighting his eyes. "You're a good friend, Herbert. You understand Brandi very well."

"Actually, sir, she's a lot like your late mother—at least in the way she loves and nourishes everything around her. Whether it was gardens or people, Her Grace was the one who could make them thrive. It's the same with Miss Brandi."

"I never thought about it in quite that way, but you're right." Emotion knotted Quentin's chest. "I remember Mother's claim that, other than herself, Brandi was the only one who truly appreciated the magic of Emerald Manor. I can see how accurate a statement that was every time I witness the unrestrained joy Brandi exudes when she's here. 'Tis the same elation Mother used to emanate." A reminiscent smile. "I can still remember—Lord, I couldn't have been older than eight or nine—the jubilation on Mother's face when we'd arrive at Emerald Manor for a visit, the way her eyes would begin to glow the instant the carriage rounded the bend and passed through these gates. She'd flourish like the gardens themselves."

"She sure did."

"This cottage was the most precious gift Father ever gave her. Nothing came close." Quentin gazed about nostalgically. "Tell me, Herbert, did things stay as I recall? Did my parents continue to spend as much time here as they did before I went away?"

"Yup." Herbert nodded. "When the duke was workin' at Colverton or travelin' to London, the duchess came by herself—with Miss Brandi in tow, of course. The two of them would putter in the garden for hours, talkin' and laughin'. Of course, Her Grace was happiest when the duke accompanied her, which he did as often as he could. I swear your mother's love for the cottage must have been catchin', because just this summer His Grace started visitin' a few times on his own. But mostly it was either the two of them together, or the duchess and Miss Brandi." Herbert scratched his head. "It's a happy house, my lord. And you and Miss Brandi are gonna keep it that way." A pause. "You are gonna live here, aren't you?"

Quentin looked momentarily taken aback. Then he chuckled. "Do you know, it never occurred to me that we'd live anywhere else?"

"I'm glad."

"So am I, Herbert." Quentin set down his empty cup. "And to that end, I'm off to get dressed for my wedding."

It was half after eight when Brandi made her way back to the cottage.

Ninety minutes more. After which, she would be Mrs. Quentin Steel.

The reality was staggering, and she'd already pinched herself a half-dozen times to ensure she wasn't dreaming. Then again, she couldn't possibly be dreaming, for she'd never gone to sleep.

How could she rest when her entire being was leaping with exhilaration?

She'd tried everything she could think of to relieve her excess energy, but to no avail. First, she'd romped with

Andrea Kane

Lancelot for an hour, then raced him to the gazebo where she'd chatted with Herbert for aeons—more for his sake than hers. In truth, she was far too excited to stay in one place today, even if that place was her most beloved sanctuary. Further, she had no idea why Herbert was suddenly stammering all over himself, spouting something about her new duties and how she shouldn't be afraid to perform them. She had no opportunity to ask for an explanation, because, abruptly, he switched subjects, brimming with sage advice for her future and how happy Quentin was going to make it, as well as assurances that he himself planned to remain at Emerald Manor for as long as she wanted, now that he knew for certain she'd be living here.

Well, where else would she be living? Emerald Manor belonged to Quentin and, in less than two hours, so would she.

Shaking her head in puzzlement, Brandi strolled up the cottage path, wondering what she might try next to pass the time. How was she going to survive the wait?

"Mrs. Collins is about to organize a search party for you, Miss Brandi," Bentley commented from the open doorway. "She and your bath water have been awaiting your arrival since seven."

"Oh Lord, I completely forgot." Brandi clapped a hand over her mouth. "I did ask Mrs. Collins to have my bath water brought up at seven, didn't I?"

"I believe so." Bentley cocked a brow. "However, on the bright side, you need a bath far more now than I suspect you did several hours ago."

Brandi glanced down at herself and giggled. "You're right; I'm filthy. Not appropriate for a bride, I suppose."

"I think not."

"Very well." Brandi gathered up her soiled skirts. "I'll run up and apologize to Mrs. Collins. Then I'll soak in the tub until I shrivel into a piece of dried fruit. By then it should be nearly time for the ceremony."

"A wise idea, my lady."

Pausing, Brandi chewed her lip. "No missives have arrived, have they, Bentley?"

"I'm afraid not, Miss Brandi."

"You did advise Desmond of the time and date of the wedding?"

"Two days past. In person. Just as two days past he refused the invitation. In person."

Brandi sighed. "Very well, then. If he chooses to behave like a petulant child, so be it. Today is the happiest day of my life. I shan't let him ruin it."

"Bravo, my lady," Bentley commended. "Now hasten to your bedchamber and emerge the radiant bride. I've rehearsed my role in the ceremony and have mastered the fine art of giving you away to perfection."

"Ah, but have you mastered the fine art of sharing that role?" Brandi teased back. "Or shall I expect you to sniff indignantly if Herbert takes an improper step during our procession to the altar?"

"I shall attempt to control myself, for the sake of propriety."

Lightheartedly, Brandi scooted up the stairs and hastened to her bedchamber, where she found Mrs. Collins pacing in circles.

"Mrs. Collins?" With a guilty expression, Brandi inched into the room, her contrition intensifying as she watched relief flood the housekeeper's face. "I'm here. And I'm sorry I worried you."

"Thank heavens!" the housekeeper exclaimed, wringing her hands.

"I meant to be back by seven," Brandi returned sheepishly. "But Lancelot was in a frisky mood, and Herbert in a loquacious one. Before I knew it . . ."

"Stop." Mrs. Collins held up her hand. "I ought to know by now never to expect the expected from you. 'Tis only that today is your wedding day. So naturally I assumed you'd be eager to bathe and—never mind." With an indulgent shake of her head, she indicated the tub of water in the center of the room. "In any case, I'll arrange to have this refilled. After one and a half hours, 'tis tepid at best."

"Are you angry?" Brandi asked in a small hopeful voice.

Mrs. Collins's lips twitched. "I should be. Since your accident, I fret every time you're dashing about the grounds alone. But how can I be angry with you on this all-important day? 'Tis far too special an occasion for that. So, no, I'm not angry. But next time I will be."

"There won't be a next time," Brandi vowed.

With a knowing chuckle, the housekeeper hurried out to make arrangements for more hot water. "Oh, yes there will be."

The bath felt wonderful.

For long minutes after she'd washed, Brandi just languished in the soapy water, leaning her head against the tub's surface and daydreaming about the future.

Her future as Quentin's wife.

The concept evoked all the wondrous little butterflies she'd always envisioned as part of the timeless love that led to marriage—a love she'd doubted ever to find. As she'd explained to Pamela, the man of her dreams couldn't possibly exist. Where could she hope to find a man who would revel in her spirit and rejoice in her unladylike diversions? A man whose passion for challenge matched hers, who loved her for who she was and not for the fictitious creature he yearned for her to become?

A man named Quentin Steel.

Dreamily, she smiled, sinking back into the water.

How could she not have fathomed that the man she'd described was the very man she'd worshipped all her life?

Pamela had fathomed it for her.

The sudden realization made Brandi sit bolt upright in he bath.

Brandi, she could hear Pamela's gentle voice as if she were right here in the bedchamber, *contrary to what you've concluded, I promise you are not destined to remain alone.*

The man of whom you dream does exist . . . I can see him as clearly as if he were standing before me. And he is someone special, someone rare. All that remains is for you to discover each other, which will happen in its own time—a time I suspect is not too far off.

"Oh, Pamela," Brandi whispered aloud. "You knew." Two tears slid down her cheeks. "All the time, you knew." Shakily, she climbed from the tub and wrapped a towel around herself. Acting on instinct, she walked over to her nightstand, opening the drawer she hadn't touched since the day of the will readings when she'd hidden Pamela's jewel case away, unable to bear the hollow pain evoked by its presence.

With trembling fingers, Brandi lifted out the exquisitely painted wooden box, running her palms over the surface.

For the first time since Mr. Hendrick had read the wills aloud, she permitted herself to contemplate the clause that had accompanied Pamela's gift:

To my precious Brandice, it had pronounced, *I bequeath all that I would leave a daughter: my jewel case and all its gems, my silver, and most of all, my love. While the possessions may be passed on to your children, the love is yours to keep. Shed no tears, Brandi . . .*

Smiling, Brandi obeyed Pamela's request, brushing the dampness from her cheeks.

. . . for in my heart I know you will never be alone.

Pamela's final phrase reverberated through Brandi's heart, offering her a peace she'd not known she needed, but had somehow been incomplete without.

Clutching the jewel case in her arms, Brandi tilted her head back. "Thank you, Pamela," she breathed to the ubiquitous heavens. "Thank you for giving Quentin and me your blessing."

"Miss Brandi?" Mrs. Collins sailed into the room, Brandi's wedding gown draped over her arm. Her gaze darted from the empty tub to the edge of the bed where Brandi sat. "Why didn't you summon me to help you from the tub? You might have slipped and hurt yourself."

"I'm fine, Mrs. Collins," Brandi answered, stroking the box before placing it on her nightstand. "Better than that, in fact. I'm wonderful."

The housekeeper glanced at the jewel case, her kindly face softening with compassion. "Do you know," she offered quietly, "it just occurred to me that the bodice of the gown leaves your throat utterly bare. To truly compliment the layer of silver lace I toiled over, you need the proper necklace—something in silver." She walked over, laying her hand on Brandi's shoulder. "Her Grace's necklace— you recall, the one the duke gave her last Christmas—would be ideal. It's delicate and refined, with just a spray of diamonds and emeralds amid the threads of silver."

Brandi swallowed past the lump in her throat, her lashes lowering as she stared at the jewel case.

"How proud and honored the duchess would be," Mrs. Collins added, "to see you carry a symbol of the love she shared with the duke into your new life with their son. Knowing the way she felt about you, I can't imagine anything that would mean more to her."

Slowly, Brandi lifted her gaze, meeting the housekeeper's. "I miss her so much."

"I know you do, love." Mrs. Collins patted her cheek. "But she's with you in spirit. Surely you feel it, especially today."

"Thankfully, I do," Brandi replied reverently. "More than I dared hope."

"Then consider my suggestion. In the interim, I'll have the water taken away, after which it will be time to dress."

Nodding, Brandi rested her palm atop the jewel case, waiting until she was alone to slip her hand around back. Other than Pamela, she was the only one who knew of the hidden notch in the box's rear panel. Pamela had emphasized that fact while demonstrating how to retrieve the key—on the evening of Brandi's coming-out. The jewels inside were valuable, she'd explained, and no one, not even her own lady's maid, had access to them.

A small smile touched Brandi's lips. It had been Pamela's fervent hope that, as a woman grown, Brandi would avail herself of the treasures within, for the Season's gala balls and the winter's endless stream of house parties.

It hadn't happened that way.

Brandi could still recall the disappointment in Pamela's eyes as she'd come to the realization that the young lady she loved as a daughter would always prefer pistols to jewels.

"Perhaps today I can make it up to you, Pamela," Brandi murmured. "Suddenly, for the first time, I have not only a longing but a reason to don your treasures. Perhaps that was really all it took, after all. Perhaps I can, at last, offer you the joy I never before could."

So saying, she extracted the key and unlocked the jewel case. Her hands shook as she lifted the lid, her eyes misting with tears as she gazed at the contents. Flashes of memory accosted her—memories of Pamela preparing for an evening at Almack's, laughing with Brandi as her maid fastened the clasps of her glittering bracelets or affixed the earrings that accentuated her dark cloud of upswept hair.

The necklace Brandi sought lay on the right-hand side of the box, and she carefully removed it from its velvet bed.

A patch of white caught her eye.

Frowning, Brandi reached for what appeared to be an out-of-place envelope.

A single word was penned upon it: *Quentin*.

Before she could ponder the envelope's significance, she spied a small object that had been hidden beneath it. A key.

Now totally at sea, Brandi lay the necklace on her lap and took up both items, studying them with a puzzled expression. The key appeared to be identical to the one she'd just used to open the jewel case—an extra, perchance, should the first one be lost?

But how odd to place a spare key in a spot that was unattainable without the original. And equally odd to store a letter addressed to your son in a jewel case.

"Miss Brandi?" Mrs. Collins poked her head into the

room, smiling when she saw the necklace on Brandi's lap. "The footmen are here to dispose of the water. Would you like to wait in your dressing room while they do so?"

"Oh." With a swift glance at herself—clad only in a towel—Brandi nodded. "Yes. Please just ask them to give me a minute."

"Certainly." Mrs. Collins disappeared.

Posthaste, Brandi returned the key and envelope to their original home, locking the jewel case and replacing the key in the back. Whatever the contents of the envelope, Pamela had meant them for Quentin.

She chewed her lip, wondering if she should act immediately, ask Mrs. Collins to go to Quentin's chambers and give the note to him posthaste.

These next few precious days belong to us, little hoyden. Quentin's assertion echoed in her head. *The unanswered questions and suspicions are going nowhere, and can be addressed afterward. Our parents would want no less.*

"He's right, Pamela," Brandi uttered aloud. "You would want no less." Lovingly, she carried the jewel case across the room to her dressing table, giving it the place of honor it deserved.

I won't wait beyond tonight, she determined silently. *Just in case the note can offer Quentin the solace my memories have just offered me. I'll show it to him tonight.*

Late tonight, she amended with a secret smile. *I have plans for the earlier part of this evening.*

Plans, Pamela, I have no doubt you'd applaud.

"You look breathtaking," Mrs. Collins declared, stepping away to survey her handiwork. "Oh, Miss Brandi, I've never seen a more beautiful bride."

Brandi stared at herself in the looking glass, tentatively touching one shining cinnamon curl. "Do you think Quentin will think so?"

"There's not even a doubt." Mrs. Collins bent to drape the satin skirts at Brandi's feet, nodding her approval as she stood. "You are perfection."

That elicited a smile. "That's not what you implied a while ago when I forgot about my bath."

"That was then. This is now," the housekeeper retorted, fussing at the bodice for an instant before checking the clasp of Pamela's necklace. "'Tis as if the duchess offered you this piece specifically for today. Why, it's just what the gown needed."

With a wealth of tenderness, Brandi touched the delicate strand of jewels at her throat. "You're right. 'Tis exactly right—for many reasons."

Mrs. Collins cleared her throat. "My lady, have you any questions you'd like to ask? I don't know how much you and the duchess discussed."

Brandi's brows drew together. "About what?"

"About what to expect. Tonight. When you and Master Quentin . . ." An uneasy pause. "That is, about performing your marital duties." Ever so slightly, she gestured toward the bed.

Awareness erupted on Brandi's face. "So those were the duties Herbert was babbling about this morning. I had no idea what he meant—in truth, I thought he was referring to some distasteful household chore I had to learn." She dissolved into laughter. "Forgive me, Mrs. Collins," she apologized, seeing the flush that spread across the housekeeper's cheeks. "I truly appreciate your attempts to prepare me. But I have a fairly good idea what to expect." *And 'tis far from a duty,* she wanted to add. Wisely, she said nothing, silently praising herself for that small semblance of tact.

"Are you certain?" Mrs. Collins asked, exuding relief.

"Quite certain. Pamela explained the procedure to me several years ago." *The procedure, yes, but not the pleasure,* she modified silently. *No one could explain pleasure as acute as what she'd experienced in Quentin's arms—and that was only a mere taste.*

The anticipation brought a glow of excitement to her cheeks. "In any case, we needn't pursue this further. I'm fully prepared."

"Excellent. Then I'll have Bentley summon the carriage and we can start for the church."

The next few hours passed in a golden haze of euphoria—a euphoria that was forever ingrained in Brandi's memory. The solemn reverence of the church, the security of Herbert and Bentley flanking her on either side as they escorted her to meet her future—but most of all, the love and pride reflected in Quentin's eyes as he watched her approach him, led her to the altar to become his wife.

The ceremony was simple—a few timeless words that would forever divide Brandi's life into before and after. The magnificent gold band, brandishing tiny diamonds Brandi recognized from Pamela's wedding band—an exquisite melding of two immeasurable loves. The warmth of Quentin's lips brushing hers, binding them together as husband and wife.

And then, the heartfelt congratulations of those who loved them—Bentley, Herbert, Mrs. Collins, the elderly Vicar Arbors who'd known them both since childhood—all wishing them well, sharing their happiness. Most important was the unseen but nonetheless tangible presence of their parents, joyously watching as their children were forever joined.

The picnic at Emerald Manor was a feast for the heart, as well as the body, stretching long into the afternoon hours.

The sun was beginning its descent toward the horizon, when Mrs. Collins spied the inevitable: Brandi depositing her punch on a nearby table, restlessly gathering up her exquisite satin skirts and—despite the profoundness of the day—preparing to initiate an all-too-familiar ritual. Swiftly, the housekeeper caught Quentin's eye.

She received the prearranged wink.

Her cue given, Mrs. Collins drifted over—and waited. "What are you doing?" she inquired, precisely as Brandi darted forward, whistling softly at an overhead branch.

Brandi froze, guilt etched onto every delicate feature.

"If you're planning to dash about with Lancelot, wouldn't

332

it be wise to change clothes first? Ruining a day dress is one thing, but your wedding gown?"

The admonishment had its desired effect.

With a sigh, Brandi released her skirts. "You're right, Mrs. Collins. What would I do without you?"

"What indeed." The housekeeper rolled her eyes. "Come. Those hooks are a bit tricky. I'll assist you."

"Very well." Brandi trotted over to her new husband, who was deep in conversation with Bentley. "Quentin?"

"Hmmm?"

"I'm going into the cottage to don a more suitable dress. Mrs. Collins is accompanying me. We'll be back before you miss us."

"Good idea." Quentin nodded his approval. "By all means, go ahead."

He resumed talking with Bentley.

"Do you know," Brandi muttered to Mrs. Collins as they entered the cottage, "Quentin didn't look the least bit sorry to see me go."

"Really? I hadn't noticed." Mrs. Collins escorted Brandi to her room, carefully unfastening the delicate clasps of the gown.

"Didn't you?" Brandi chewed her lip. "I suppose I'm being silly. Still, I wonder what he and Bentley were discussing that so captured his interest."

"I haven't a clue." Mrs. Collins helped Brandi step out of her gown and slippers. "I'll run down and store these in my wardrobe. Then we can select another gown—"

"Why not just store them in my wardrobe?" Brandi interrupted.

"Because, my lady, yours is overly crowded, while mine is half-empty. I don't want the lace I worked so hard on to catch and tear. Therefore, I'd prefer situating it in my room, at least temporarily."

"As you wish." Brandi strolled over to her wardrobe. "I'll pull out another gown."

Mrs. Collins headed toward the door, then paused, an

odd look on her face. "I'm so proud of you, Miss Brandi. You and Lord Quentin, be happy."

Brandi's brows drew together in puzzlement. "Thank you, we shall. But why are you talking as if . . ."

She hadn't a chance to finish her sentence. Mrs. Collins disappeared down the hallway.

With a shrug, Brandi resumed her search for an appropriate gown. Evidently, Mrs. Collins had just chosen that particular moment to become emotional. An odd moment, to be sure, but perhaps a memory had chosen that instant to flash through her mind.

In any case, Brandi would properly hug and thank her when she returned.

Frowning down at her chemise, Brandi admitted to herself that the last thing she wanted was to don another gown and resume the festivities. In truth, while she adored all those present, what she really wanted was to be alone with Quentin.

Who, judging from his rapt expression as he conversed with Bentley, didn't share her eagerness.

Utterly resigned, she reached for her lilac day dress, just as the bedchamber door clicked shut.

"I suppose this one is as good as any, Mrs. Collins," Brandi called over her shoulder. "I don't really have a preference."

"Ah, but I do."

Dropping the dress, Brandi whirled about, her eyes widening as she saw Quentin leaning against the wall, watching her.

"Leave the gown on the floor," he advised, his heated gaze absorbing every beautiful, bare inch of her. "You're breathtaking just as you are."

"Quentin?" Bewildered, Brandi glanced at the closed door. "Mrs. Collins will be back . . ."

"In three days, as per my instructions." Loosening his cravat, he crossed the room, his eyes blatantly disrobing his bride. "At the same time that Herbert, Bentley, and the entire staff will return." He paused, his heated gaze lingering on the dark shadows of Brandi's nipples, straining against her chemise, hardening beneath his scrutiny. "I believe I've changed my mind. I think perhaps you're still too overdressed."

"Three days?" Brandi managed, trembling beneath Quentin's openly carnal stare. "I don't understand."

"Don't you?" Quentin loomed over her, reaching out to sift his fingers through her glorious hair. "Then let me explain. I want my wife. Alone. For three days . . . and three nights. To that end, I relieved the servants of their duties. Now, does that alleviate your confusion?"

"You ordered the staff away?"

"Um-hum." Quentin's thumb trailed down the side of her neck, absorbing her tiny shiver. "Don't worry. They're well provided for, comfortably situated at a local inn, where they will remain for three days. They've been forbidden to approach this cottage for any reason whatsoever—and that command includes Lancelot." A slow smile. "Even your squirrel didn't dare challenge my authority—not this time."

Realization filtered through Brandi's deepening sensual haze. "You arranged this."

"From beginning to end."

"How did you know . . ."

"How did I know what? That you'd eventually be racing through the woods, wedding day or not?" Quentin lowered his head, his lips grazing the fluttering pulse at Brandi's throat. "Because I know you, little hoyden. Better, obviously, than you know me." He laughed, a heated wisp of sensation. "Did you honestly think I'd opted to spend my wedding night chatting with Bentley while you cavorted with Lancelot?" He brushed her hair aside, trailing damp kisses up her neck, drawing the soft lobe of her ear into his mouth.

"Quentin." Everything inside Brandi seemed to melt and slide down to her toes. Her knees gave way and reflexively she clutched the soft wool of Quentin's coat.

He caught her in his arms, carrying her the few steps to

the bed and lowering her to its waiting haven. "Have you any idea how beautiful you are?" he murmured, following her down. "Or how badly I want you?"

"How badly?" Brandi's fingers had already completed the task of unknotting his cravat, casting it aside and moving to the buttons of his waistcoat.

"So badly I'm shaking with it." Quentin covered her hands with his, letting her feel their unsteadiness.

"I want you, too." Tugging her hands free, Brandi unbuttoned his waistcoat and shirt. "Oh, Quentin, I've waited forever. I want you so much."

"Sweetheart . . . God." A hard shudder racked his body as her palms smoothed over his bare chest, gliding through the mat of dark hair, then lightly brushing his nipples. "What are you doing to me?"

"Discovering you."

Quentin's mouth crushed down on hers, kissing her with an unleashed urgency that told her more clearly than words that tonight there would be no limits, no restraints.

No stopping.

"Touch me," he commanded, seizing her wrist, pressing her palm to the hard ridge that pulsed through his breeches. "Everywhere. In every way. Christ, I need your hands on me."

With trembling fingers, Brandi explored Quentin's length, feeling the heat emanating through the barrier of his clothes. With her customary impulsiveness, unhindered by fear or reticence, she worked the buttons free, sighing with wonder as his rigid manhood sprang free, filled her hand.

Quentin went deadly still.

"Stop," he rasped, tearing himself away. He stared down at her, his eyes nearly black with desire, his forehead damp with sweat. "I don't believe . . ." He broke off, shaking his head, dragging air into his lungs.

For the first time, Brandi hesitated. "Did I do something wrong?"

"Wrong?" He could barely speak. "Sunbeam, I'm not going to last."

A brilliant smile illuminated Brandi's face. "I'm glad," she whispered, leaning up to kiss the straining tendons at his neck.

"You don't understand." He caught her arms, eased her away. "Christ, even *I* don't understand. If you touch me like that again, I'll never make it inside you."

Brandi looked puzzled. "Why not?"

With a half-laugh, half-groan, Quentin braced himself on his forearms. "Because, little hoyden, it appears you have the power to do precisely what you wanted. You completely undo me, splinter my control into a thousand irreparable fragments."

"Is that bad?" Brandi asked, searching his face with wide questioning eyes.

"It's a miracle." He caressed her face. "There will be times—many times, I'm beginning to realize—when I'll gladly surrender every iota of control I possess to you."

"But not this time?"

"No, not this time." He bent to brush her lips with his. "This time should be slow, soft, tender." He lowered one strap of her chemise, his tongue tracing her shoulder.

"Why?" Brandi managed.

"Because it's your first time—our first time. Because I want to savor you, cherish you, awaken every inch of you to the passion you're capable of feeling." His mouth teased the edge of her bodice. "Because I won't hurt you," he added fiercely.

"You could never hurt me."

"Sunbeam, the first time . . ."

"I don't care. I won't feel the pain. I'll only feel you." Brandi shivered as Quentin kissed the hollow between her breasts, the movement causing her chemise to slide down, baring one perfect breast to his gaze.

Abruptly, Quentin couldn't breathe or think or look away. His lips sought their goal, closing around her nipple, tugging it into the warm cavern of his mouth, bathing its rigid sweetness with his tongue.

Brandi cried out, tangling her fingers in the damp strands

of hair at Quentin's nape. "Yes," she gasped, all the remembered pleasures of the last time coursing through her body in a deluge of sensation. "Oh, Quentin, yes."

Her chemise gave beneath his hands, and Brandi sighed at the blessed relief of cool air against her feverish skin. Forcibly, she opened her eyes, watching Quentin drink in her nudity, his greedy gaze raking her from head to toe, lingering on the very core of her femininity that, days before, had blossomed to his touch. Harsh desire tightened his features, desire softened by a wonder so vastly beautiful it made her weak.

"My God, you're flawless," he said thickly, cupping her breasts, moving to trace the curve of her waist and hips. "Beyond flawless. Beyond description." He reached her thighs, caressing them from top to bottom and, at the same time, pushing her stockings down to her feet and off. "I want nothing on you when I make you mine," he breathed, his gaze returning to the burnished cloud between her legs. "Nothing but me." He stroked his way back up her legs, lifting them to kiss the inside of her calves, her knees, the sensitive softness of her inner thighs.

Brandi was drowning in sensation, hovering in a magical place where nothing existed but the anticipation of Quentin's touch.

His fingers found her, opened her, trembled as they encountered her velvety wetness. Brandi whimpered, undulated against him, and something inside Quentin snapped.

In one motion, he raised her legs over his shoulders, opening her fully to him, and lowered his head, burying his mouth in her sweetness. Brandi cried out, shock and ecstasy converging, melding into a pulse point of escalating sensation that threatened to submerge her with its intensity.

"Quentin . . . Oh God, Quentin . . ." She wasn't even aware she was urging him closer, begging him to continue. All she knew was the unbearable things he was doing to her—his tongue, his teeth, his lips—stoking a fire that was already out of control and threatening to burn her to ashes.

Recklessly, she struggled, needing in a way she'd never needed, so wild for fulfillment she would die if he denied her.

Denial was the last thing on Quentin's mind.

Caught in the grip of a clawing hunger, he was drunk on the taste, the scent, the very essence of his wife. Blindly, he slid his hands beneath her, lifting her harder, more fully against his seeking mouth, possessing her with deep hungry strokes that drove both of them to the very brink of madness.

He sensed her climax a split second before it crashed over her, and his lips surrounded her, his fingers sliding inside to intensify the wrenching pleasure—and to share it. Closing his eyes, he absorbed her convulsive spasms, listened to her wild cries of completion, reveled in the miracle of her response.

And fought for the control that Brandi's innocence couldn't fathom as necessary, but Quentin's experience warned him was, in order to minimize her pain.

Perhaps he'd have succeeded in capturing that elusive control if he hadn't raised up, watched Brandi's face, seen the look of wonder in her eyes as she whispered, "Oh, Quentin." Even then, he might have managed to temper his drive for possession long enough to take her slowly, reining in his hunger to lessen the pain he was helpless to prevent.

But when her warm searching fingers groped inside the opening of his breeches, finding and clasping his erection, exploring it with butterfly strokes, he was lost.

"Brandi." With that single word, he vaulted from the bed, shedding his clothing in a heartbeat, coming down over her with a primal need he'd never experienced and couldn't escape. "I've got to have you. Now."

"Yes." Brandi wrapped her arms about his neck, urging him down to her. "At last. The 'all' of which you spoke." For an instant, her gaze flickered over him, awed amazement reflected in her eyes as she worshipped the tangible evidence of his craving for her. "You're magnificent." One hand moved to stroke his rigid length, lingered at the tip to absorb the droplets of fluid he couldn't withhold. "So magnificent."

Quentin groaned, tremors of need shuddering through him. "Wrap your legs around me. I've got to bury myself inside you. Brandi, now." His hips were moving even as he spoke.

"Now," she echoed breathlessly, doing as he'd commanded, wrapping herself around him, body and soul.

In that last, feverish second, their eyes met and held.

"I love you," Brandi whispered.

"God, I love you, Sunbeam. Forgive me." In one uncurtailable thrust, he lunged forward, tearing her maidenhead and burying himself to the hilt inside her.

He felt her go rigid, heard her sharp intake of breath, and cursed himself for his weakness. "Brandi." He tried to raise up on his elbows, and failed, excruciating pleasure halting his progress as her virginal passage gripped him with fingers of fire, surrounded him with a liquid warmth that pushed him one step closer to climax. He gritted his teeth, swearing to himself to remain still until he was sure her pain was gone. "Sunbeam, are you all right?"

When his only answer was silence, he panicked, forcing his head up so he could see her face.

Brandi gazed back, her eyes bright with unshed tears.

"Brandi . . ." he began, despising himself.

"Why did you stop?"

"What?" Quentin blinked.

"I'm sorry I'm so . . . narrow. Am I hurting you?"

This time he was speechless.

"My pain only lasted a moment." She shifted, wrapping her legs higher around him, opening herself more completely to him. "Is that better?"

"It couldn't be better," Quentin rasped, giving in to his body's instinctive motions. "It's too damned perfect."

Covering her mouth with his, he made her his wife, lifting her into him, teaching her the age-old rhythm, and thereby discovering that he never truly knew it himself. Their bodies made magic together, arching closer, more wholly into one another, their senses lost in an all-encompassing pleasure that blazed hotter and higher with each thrust.

"Quentin . . ." Brandi began sobbing his name, clutching at his sweat-slick back, drowning in that spiraling pulse beat that permeated her very core, screamed for fulfillment.

Quentin was beyond words, beyond thought, beyond anything. The roaring in his head was deafening, the wildness in his loins unendurable, dwarfed only by the love in his heart.

"Brandi . . . now . . . come with me . . . Christ." Broken fragments, pleas and prayers, erupted a heartbeat before his seed, but Quentin never heard himself utter them.

Brandi did.

Arching up to meet him, she threw herself into the fire, screaming as Quentin stroked her inside and out, propelling her over the edge and into the blistering essence of completion.

Quentin met each contraction with a burst of wet heat, pouring himself into his wife again and again until he was drained, his hips still moving convulsively even as he collapsed on her shivering body.

How much time elapsed, he hadn't a clue. Gradually, he became aware of Brandi's fingers drifting, feather-light, over the muscles of his back, now blissfully relaxed.

"Is the pain gone?" she whispered, worry in her voice.

Once again, Brandi accomplished the impossible—Quentin's shoulders began to shake with laughter.

"Oh, Sunbeam, you are truly the greatest miracle of my life." He rolled to one side, taking her with him, enfolding her in his arms and reveling in the glorious feeling of being joined with her still.

"I didn't hurt you?" Brandi repeated anxiously.

"Only in the most spectacular of ways."

"I'm glad." She leaned back, inclining her head quizzically. "Why are you laughing?"

"Because I'm happy." He kissed the worried pucker from between her brows. "Because I'm the luckiest man alive.

Because you're my wife. Because I don't know what I did to deserve you, but I don't intend to question my extraordinary good fortune."

"Oh." Brandi digested that explanation. "Then I pleased you?"

"Pleased me?" Quentin framed her face between his palms. "Sweetheart, you humbled me."

"More than all those other women?"

Had he expected anything less? "Brandi," he replied solemnly, gazing deeply into her eyes, "Tonight was as much my first time as it was yours. Perhaps more so, now that I reflect on it. Trust me, Sunbeam. There were no other women. Only you."

Her smile warmed him, body and soul. "Now I really am your wife."

"In every way." He tucked her head beneath his chin, cradling her close, unwilling to relinquish the spectacular aftermath of their lovemaking.

Abruptly, the actuality of who had hurt whom struck home.

"Love," he began, praying his urgency hadn't made her pain more severe. "I meant to be gentle. I was anything but. Are you very sore?"

"Not very, no."

"Can you forgive me?"

He felt her smile against his chest. "That depends."

"On what?"

"On the reason why you weren't gentle."

Quentin relaxed into a grin, knowing precisely where this was leading. "I wasn't gentle, my smug little hoyden, because I lost every damned drop of control I possess. Happy?"

"Infinitely." Brandi nuzzled the damp column of his throat. "Will it hurt me next time?"

"No, Sunbeam. Never again."

"Prove it."

Quentin's head snapped down, and he stared at her in amazement. "What?"

"I asked you to prove it." Brandi's cheeks glowed as she shifted her hips—very intentionally—forward, enveloping him in her wet warmth, feeling his body leap to life. "I'm challenging you, my lord. In a way that, I'm stunned to discover, I find more exciting than fishing or riding."

"And marksmanship?" Quentin's hands slid down to grip her bottom, his touch wildly seductive. "Do you find this even more exciting than our shooting matches?" With tantalizing finesse, he urged her leg over his, hauling her against him with one fierce motion that melded their loins, elicited a sharp cry of pleasure from his bride. "Does that mean yes?" he asked, moving inside her in a way that made her moan his name. "Tell me, Sunbeam." He dragged her lips to his, penetrating her mouth at the same time that he penetrated her body.

"Quentin . . ." Brandi's eyes widened as she realized how close she was to climax.

"Let it happen," he commanded, feeling her tighten all around him, her inner muscles clutching him in what had to be the most exquisite torture he'd ever known. "Brandi." A harsh shudder. "I want to watch you." With one more deliberate thrust, he took her over the edge, battling his own completion in a primal need to know hers.

It was a fight not destined to be won.

With a groan of surrender, Quentin gave in to his own body's demands, exploding inside his wife with a force that defied the magnitude of his first climax, still simmering through his veins.

A radiant silence prevailed, broken only by the ticking of the clock and the harshness of their breathing.

At last Brandi stirred.

"I concede, my lord," she murmured, propping her chin on his chest. "You won that contest. However, I do demand another chance to best you."

Quentin threaded his fingers through her hair, regarding her from beneath hooded lids. "I never thought I'd hear you concede defeat. However, in all fairness, Mrs. Steel, I believe this victory belonged to us both. Still, I'd be delighted to offer you a second or even a third chance. When would you like to have it?"

"I'm not unreasonable, my lord. I'll wait until you've recovered." With an impish grin, Brandi rubbed her thigh across her husband's. "Despite my inexperience, I fully understand that you need to recoup your strength in order to excel in this particular competition. Therefore, I'm . . ."

Her placating words dissolved into laughter, and then into silence, as Quentin rolled her to her back and covered her mouth with his.

Chapter 19

"*I*'m afraid those breeches I bought you are going to be wasted," Quentin murmured, marveling at the burnished glow of early morning sunlight as it played on Brandi's hair. He sifted the silky strands through his fingers, letting them fall as they were, draped across his chest like a fiery waterfall.

"Why?" was the sleepy response. "I adore my new breeches. I plan to wear them whenever possible."

"Precisely. Which, given the amount of time I plan on keeping you in bed, is next to never."

Brandi smiled, rubbing her face over Quentin's taut abdomen like a contented kitten. "Whatever made me think I wanted breeches?"

"I haven't a clue."

Stretching, his bride blinked at the widening slivers of light peeking through the curtains. "Is it day?"

"Nearly."

"Must we get up?"

"Eventually. But only to collect the food Mrs. Collins left us to ward off starvation."

"Starvation? Impossible. Not when I feel so utterly sated." Brandi lifted her head, gazing at Quentin with loving fulfillment. "Thank you for the most wonderful night of my life."

"'Tis I who should be thanking you. And not only for the miracle of last night. But for so much more." Seeing the questioning pucker between his wife's brows, Quentin added softly, "You've made me whole in ways I never knew I was empty, perceived what I needed even when I didn't. You've given me joy and laughter and love. You've given me you."

Brandi's eyes misted. "I love you so much. I always have, even before I realized it."

A corner of Quentin's mouth lifted. "I think we were the last two to grasp the truth. Bentley, Mrs. Collins, Herbert—they were all lying in wait for us to behold the obvious."

"Don't forget Pamela."

"My mother?" It was Quentin's turn to look surprised.

"Yes. Had I listened to what she was saying more carefully, I would have understood." A wistful smile touched Brandi's lips. "She was trying to tell me you were my future."

"What did she say?"

"Ironically, it was during our last long talk. We were here, working in the garden and discussing my maturity—or lack thereof. Pamela listened to me ramble on about what I yearned for in an ideal husband."

One dark eyebrow rose. "Which was?"

"A passionate man who relished a challenge and, rather than trying to squelch my unconventional behavior, reveled in it."

"I see." Quentin traced the smooth skin of his bride's back. "And what did Mother say?"

"She told me that the man of whom I dreamed did exist, that he was rare and special, and that soon—very soon—we would discover each other. Not *meet*," Brandi stressed, "but discover. On the heels of that statement, she casually brought you into the conversation. I should have fathomed her meaning."

"Subtlety is not your forte, Sunbeam. Not employing it or distinguishing it."

Brandi gave a rueful sigh. "No, it isn't. And, in this case, it took me that much longer to distinguish because I haven't allowed myself to think about Pamela. It just hurt too much." A pause. "I miss her terribly."

"I know you do."

"My only consolation is knowing she's with Kenton." Brandi blinked, as another memory sparked to life. "That's something else she said during that last talk of ours. Something I'd forgotten until now. She said Kenton was her heart and soul. That, without him, she wouldn't want to live. I truly believe she meant that."

"As do I. My parents were like two halves of a whole, each incomplete without the other. Thank God they're together. In that way, at least, they're at peace."

Brandi's lashes swept her cheeks. "Perhaps this sounds foolish, but I believe our union grants them peace as well. I was recalling the clause in Pamela's will that was addressed to me. It ended with, 'in my heart I know you will never be alone.' I think she was giving us her blessing."

"That doesn't sound foolish," Quentin countered. "In fact, it makes a world of sense. Mother was bequeathing you her insight—something far more valuable than her jewel case."

Abruptly, Brandi's eyes widened. "The jewel case!" Climbing out of bed, she dashed, naked, to her dressing table, and groped behind the strongbox until she retrieved the key and unfastened the lid.

Taken aback by his bride's rapid flight, Quentin pushed himself to a sitting position. "The view is breathtaking," he teased. "But I am a bit perplexed. Why, after twenty years, have you suddenly acquired an affinity for gems?"

Brandi tossed him an exasperated look as she trotted back to the bed. "I haven't. I went to get these." She held out the mysterious items she'd unearthed just prior to the wedding ceremony.

Sobering, Quentin leaned over to turn up the lamp. "A key and an envelope."

"An envelope with your name on it and a key that was hidden beneath it," Brandi corrected.

"Hidden?" Quentin's glance darted to the dressing table. "In Mother's jewel case?"

"Yes. Yesterday was the first time I could bring myself to open it. But I so wanted to wear something of Pamela's the day I became your wife. For you, and for her. When I opened the case and lifted out the necklace I wanted, I found these. I don't understand the significance of the key, but the letter is obviously from your mother to you." Brandi's voice grew soft. "I thought perhaps whatever message she left might bring you a measure of peace."

Quentin frowned as he studied his name on the envelope. "This is written in my father's, not my mother's, hand."

"Your father's?" Brandi blinked. "I don't understand. Why would a letter from Kenton be concealed in Pamela's jewel case?"

"I don't know. But I intend to find out."

Tearing open the envelope, Quentin extracted two separately folded sheets. He smoothed out the first, noted that it was addressed to his father, and scanned the two lines written on it. "Christ."

"Quentin?" A frisson of fear quivered up Brandi's spine at the uncommon severity of his reaction. "What is it?"

"A warning. For Father, not from him. It says, 'You're meddling where you don't belong. Should you continue, you'll die and Desmond will pay the price.'"

"Oh my God." All the color drained from Brandi's face. "Someone threatened Kenton's life."

"Not only threatened it, Brandi. Took it."

Quentin's supposition pervaded the room like a sickly poison.

"This changes everything." Quentin's tone was hoarse,

his throat working convulsively. "We've been assuming Ardsley was the murderer's target. This note suggests it was Father." A painful pause. "You know how principled my father was. If he suspected someone of illegal or immoral doings, he would never have let the matter rest, threatening note or not. He'd pursue it until he discovered the truth. But what if the truth implicated the killer? That bastard would be forced to carry out his threat and silence Father."

Staring at the message, Brandi fought to think clearly. "The way this reads, Desmond is also the object of the threat. Which suggests he is somehow connected to whatever Kenton was investigating."

"Or the cause of it," Quentin proposed bitterly. "Remember, Desmond was presumably immersed in all Father's business dealings and is now privy to every aspect of Father's estate. Bearing that in mind, wouldn't he be aware if Father were engaged in a dangerous investigation?"

Brandi nodded. "One would think so, yes."

"Then why hasn't Desmond said a word, particularly since Bow Street confirmed the carriage accident as murder?"

"Oh, Quentin, we've exhausted, then dismissed, the idea that Desmond would physically harm Kenton."

"I know that. And, for whatever it's worth, Desmond didn't pen this note. The hand is not his. Consequently, unless he paid someone else to write and send it, the message originated from another source. Nevertheless, my instincts tell me my brother is somehow linked to all this—and I don't mean by mere chance."

Brandi rubbed the bedcovers between her fingers. "Clearly, Kenton knew he was in danger. He must have slipped that threatening missive into Pamela's jewel case as a precaution, so that, if anything happened to him, she would find it. Or perchance he gave it to her openly and asked her to hide it somewhere for safekeeping." Abruptly, Brandi indicated the other note. "Maybe the second message will clarify some of our questions. What does it say?"

Quentin's head snapped down, and he unfolded the second sheet. "This one is written in Father's hand," he apprised his wife, shifting so she could see over his shoulder.

Together, they read the following:

Dear Quentin:
   People, like gems, have many facets; some are visible, while others are cleverly concealed. The key to the truth is to learn to see beyond the surface. Then, no one can hurt you. My only prayer is that brotherhood and forgiveness, such significant facets of the man you've become, are implanted deeply enough in your heart to flourish over anger, however righteous. My faith in you is limitless.

Your father.

"I don't understand," Brandi murmured. "It doesn't even sound like Kenton; he never spoke in such obscure, flowery language."

"No, he didn't." Quentin scrutinized the page again. "But, in this case, he would."

"You've totally lost me."

"Father is relying upon me to interpret his hidden message."

"Are you saying it's in code?"

Quentin nodded. "Think about it, Sunbeam. You yourself just said Father realized his life was in jeopardy. My guess is that he didn't want to endanger his family or his findings by exposing the facts on paper. Thus, he concealed them in this message, anticipating that I'd be able to decipher it."

Frowning, Brandi reread the words. "Can you?"

"Yes and no. I understand Father's overall message, but there are subtleties I'm unable to perceive without one or two vital, but missing, pieces of the puzzle." Quentin turned brooding eyes to his wife. "I am certain of one thing. My brother is up to his unscrupulous neck in all this."

"How can you be certain?"

"Father's words. Look." Quentin pointed to the page. "He refers to brotherhood, immediately after which he urges me to supplant anger with forgiveness. Whatever ugly particulars he uncovered, he was protecting Desmond from them. And now he's asking me to do the same."

"Are the particulars themselves concealed in this note?"

"I think not." Quentin's brow furrowed in concentration. " 'People, like gems . . . gems—gems.' " Abruptly, his head came up. "What a cursed fool I've been. So bloody preoccupied with uncovering the truth that I missed the part that was staring me in the face. Gems—the strongbox."

"The strongbox?" Brandi's eyes widened. "Then 'the key to the truth' must be this." She held up the other object she'd found.

"Agreed. Let me see it." Quentin took the key, turning it over in his hands.

"Pamela's jewel case!" Brandi shot to her feet, crossing the room and snatching the ornate box from her dressing table. "Kenton must have hidden the evidence here."

"I doubt we'll find anything in Mother's box but jewels," Quentin countered. "But I'd like to inspect it nonetheless. As well as the key that opens it."

"You don't expect to find anything?" Brandi questioned, astonished. "Very well." With a dubious expression, she returned to the bed, removing the key from its hiding place and proffering both key and box to her husband. Pensively, she watched as Quentin rummaged through the jewel case.

"As I suspected, nothing," he pronounced. Moving the box aside, he seized its key and held it up against the one Kenton had concealed.

"They're identical," Brandi murmured.

"Not quite. Look closely; there's a slight difference in contour. If I'm correct . . ." He attempted to insert Kenton's key into the lock of the jewel case, without success.

"Then whose strongbox were you alluding to when you

said . . ." Brandi broke off, comprehension illuminating her face. "Kenton's." She met Quentin's assured nod. "I remember, 'twas an identical mate to Pamela's."

"Father commissioned them to be crafted that way—which is why the keys are so similar in design."

Brandi grasped Quentin's forearms. "Now we know what we must do. We'll wait until nightfall, then sneak into Colverton. No, wait." She scowled. "Nighttime won't work. Desmond is now occupying your father's chambers. Which, I presume, is where Kenton kept his strongbox. We'll have to wait until Desmond is either away from Colverton or passed out on his study desk in a drunken stupor. At which time we'll snatch the strongbox and—"

"'Tis a splendid idea," Quentin interrupted. "'Tis also pointless."

"Why?"

"Because Father's strongbox is missing."

Brandi gasped. "You know that for a fact?"

"I do. Bentley told me. More than a week ago."

"And it has yet to be found?"

"In truth, I think Bentley abandoned his search the instant we received the heinous news from Bow Street. Learning that our parents were murdered eclipsed all else—including the strongbox—from his mind. As it did mine, until this very minute. Nevertheless, I don't believe continuing the search would have yielded any results. Even if we'd ransacked Colverton, room by room, the strongbox wouldn't have surfaced."

"Kenton concealed it," Brandi deduced aloud. "Along with whatever evidence he wanted buried—to be found by you and you alone."

"I'm as sure of that as I am of the fact that the contents of the strongbox will lead us to whoever murdered our parents."

Soberly, Brandi regarded her husband. "But how do we find it?"

"Since Father's message centers around Desmond, we

begin by my returning to Colverton and, if necessary, beating the truth out of my brother."

"You can't be certain how much he knows."

"No, but I'm certain he knows something. And I don't intend to leave until he divulges what that something is."

"I'll go with you."

Quentin was shaking his head before her words were out. "Absolutely not. You were nearly killed once. I won't risk losing you again."

"Quentin." Brandi scrambled to her knees. "Emerald Manor is deserted, save you and me. I'll be in more danger here than I will if I accompany you to Colverton. Moreover, I don't believe Desmond murdered your father—and, despite your ire, neither do you. From the threat contained in that first note, it sounds as if your brother were as much a victim as he was a culprit. He's weak, Quentin. And severely lacking in confidence. But he's not a killer. He is, however, tortured by something—guilt, perhaps, or fear of discovery. That's why he's been drinking incessantly. As for Kenton, you and I both know what an ethical man he was. Do you honestly believe he'd appeal to you to protect a man he suspected was a potential murderer—even if that man were his own son? Absolutely not." Brandi paused, chewing her lip. "I agree that Desmond is involved. But, in my opinion, he didn't compose that threatening note nor did he sever the carriage axle. Moreover, we have yet to integrate all we've just learned with the mystery of Father's ledger and the discrepancies it contains. Perhaps both our fathers were delving into something that rendered them targets for the killer—have you ever considered that? There are still a gamut of loose ends. I don't profess to be able to tie them all together, but I do ask for the right to take part in the process of doing so. Please, Quentin, let me help you."

Quentin tilted her chin up. "And you call *me* a brilliant diplomat?" he teased with tender pride. "You may lack tact, Sunbeam, but your wisdom is staggering."

Relief swept over Brandi's face and she leaned up,

brushed her lips to his. "As I've stated in the past, my lord, I have the most splendid of instructors—proficient in more areas than even I realized."

"I don't want to shut you out, Sunbeam, only to keep you safe."

"You have no worries on that score, my lord." Brandi slipped out of bed, opening her nightstand drawer and extracting the pistol Quentin had given her four years past. "My instructor once directed me to protect myself at all times, even provided me with a weapon with which to do so. Since then I have carried this with me, a beloved safeguard from danger." She stroked the pistol's ornate handle. "How fortunate that now I have both my instructor's wondrous gift and his wondrous love to shield me."

"Indeed." Slowly, Quentin came to his feet. "What a coincidence. I am equally well-protected. As I shall demonstrate in thirty minutes."

"Thirty minutes?"

"Um-hum. That's how much time I'll need to get ready for our ride to Colverton. Twenty nine minutes to dress, eat, and fetch the phaeton . . ." A loving grin. "And one minute to slip my knife into my boot."

"What the hell are you doing here, Quentin? I told you never to show your face at Colverton again." Tightening the belt of his dressing robe, Desmond slammed into the manor's yellow salon, shoving unruly strands of hair from his face and blinking to accustom himself to the light. "Moreover, do you know what time it is?"

"Five-thirty," Quentin supplied from the settee, his hand tightening over Brandi's. "And I assure you, my business is urgent. Else I wouldn't have come, much less awakened you."

"I wasn't sleeping." Desmond's unsteady hands as he poured himself a drink—sloshing a third of it on the side table—left no doubt as to what he had been doing. "Speaking of bed, your bride must have been a colossal disappointment. You've been wed less than a day and already you've left her adoring arms to immerse yourself in investigative work?"

"Shut your mouth, Desmond," Quentin warned. "And open your eyes. Brandi is sitting here beside me."

Desmond pivoted toward the settee, noting Brandi's presence for the first time. "Well, well—so she is. The blushing bride. How touching. You accompanied Quentin on his visit to the lion's den. Couldn't you bear the hour's separation? I suggest you learn. Before long, there will be oceans and months separating you."

"Don't, Desmond," Brandi returned quietly. "I'm here because the matter Quentin has come to discuss concerns me, too."

"And because I won't leave Brandi alone at Emerald Manor," Quentin added, watching his brother's face. "It's too dangerous."

A derisive brow rose. "Dangerous? Nonsense. If another oncoming bullet dared pierce the cottage woods, why, Bentley and Mrs. Collins would simply throw themselves in its path just to protect their beloved Lady Brandice."

"You're right; they would. If they were there. But, you see, Emerald Manor is deserted save Brandi and me."

"You've alienated the staff and they've resigned?" Desmond inquired sardonically.

"No, I've simply ensured some time alone for my bride and me by giving the servants a few days off. Which I never would have done had I realized the danger."

Quentin's somber tone finally struck home. "What danger?" Desmond demanded, all traces of mockery abandoned. "Has something else occurred?"

"Not yet, no. But I believe we're on the verge of unmasking the murderer. So there's a strong possibility he'll retaliate."

Desmond rubbed his eyes as if to clarify what he'd just heard. "Father's murderer? You know who it is? Who?"

"I said, on the verge," Quentin repeated.

"Does that mean you no longer assume I did it?"

"We never assumed that, Desmond," Brandi put in.

"Perhaps *you* didn't, Brandice, but my brother openly accused me."

"I didn't accuse you—I asked some pertinent questions," Quentin corrected. "Questions you refused to answer."

"They didn't deserve answers."

"Well, you're going to supply them. Now. Like it or not." Quentin drew a calming breath. "Before we begin, how drunk are you?"

Desmond's laugh was hollow. "Enough to ease my mind, but not to dull it."

"Are you sober enough to read?"

"Shall I go to the library and extract a volume of poetry to recite aloud as proof?"

"No." Quentin vaulted to his feet. "Read these." He shoved both notes in Desmond's hand, deliberately positioning the one Kenton had penned on top. "They were written some weeks ago. One is to Father, one from him. They were accompanied by a key. I'm curious what your extraordinarily clever mind makes of all this."

Desmond opened Kenton's note, concentrating intently as he read. The lines about his mouth grew grimmer by the instant, until at last he lowered the page.

"How did you come upon this?" he asked hoarsely, his hands shaking—whether from alcohol or fear, Quentin wasn't certain.

"'Twas in an envelope with my name on it. Along with the other note you're clutching and, as I said, a key. I take it you know something about it?"

"A key you said?" Desmond asked, ignoring Quentin's query. "What kind of key? Where did you find these things?"

"All three items were in my mother's jewel case, which Brandi opened for the first time yesterday. As to the details of the key, I believe it's the one that fits Father's strongbox."

"Christ." Desmond sank down into a chair.

"Go to your chambers and collect the box, Desmond. I'd like to verify my theory."

Desmond's head came up, his eyes glazed. "I don't have it. In fact, I haven't seen it . . ." He broke off, beads of sweat dotting his forehead. "I just remembered. Bentley was searching for it. I can't recall what day it was, but he came to my study asking if I'd seen Father's strongbox. He must have it."

"He doesn't. It was never found. Nor do I think it will be—at least not in any conspicuous place."

"If you knew it was missing, why did you ask me to get it?" A guarded look crossed Desmond's face, supplanted immediately by rage. "You still think I had something to do with the carriage accident, don't you?"

"It was murder. And I don't know what to think." Quentin folded his arms across his chest. "It's time you and I talked. Seriously. And frankly. We both know you and Father had differences of opinion when it came to certain issues—most particularly, money. We also know how often—and how heatedly—you argued over those differences."

"How would you know? You were away for four years. As I told Brandice, a lot changed during that time."

"Nothing changed." Quentin dismissed Desmond's argument with a wave of his hand. "Stop lying. To me and to yourself. You remained the same weak, frivolous man you always were—trying to buy Father's respect rather than earn it. Just how low did you stoop, Desmond? What machinations did you effect?"

Something inside Desmond seemed to snap. "It's that bastard Bentley, isn't it?" he shouted, bolting to his feet like a bullet. "I knew that bloody butler would ultimately relay everything to you. I was just waiting to see when. Damn him, he never did learn his place. He eavesdropped on that whole last argument, didn't he? Listened to every word of Father's threats? And he couldn't wait to convey it all to you the moment you returned to the Cotswolds. Well, the hell with him. The hell with all of you. You'll never find what you're looking for—I've taken steps to ensure that there is no amended will. And without it, you have no evidence, regardless of what Bentley overheard Father say. It's your word against mine and, taking my title and influence into account, you haven't a prayer in the world. So don't even consider trying to wrest Father's legacy from me, Quentin. Because, damn you, I've earned it. All of it. The title. The money. The estate. The business. I've paid for them in sweat and in guilt. Besides, you're not suited to be the Duke of Colverton. You'd never stay home long enough to oversee the endless responsibilities. That's what I kept trying to make Father see. I never succeeded. Regardless of your transience, he was hellbent on changing that bloody will. I couldn't allow that to happen. So I took matters into my own hands." Abruptly, all Desmond's anger drained away. "Ironic that now it's all I have left."

Both Quentin and Brandi had gaped silently throughout Desmond's diatribe.

Quentin reacted first.

"You filthy son of a bitch." He lunged forward, grasping the edges of Desmond's robe and shaking him. "That's what you meant the day you told me that if Father left you his legacy, it wasn't by choice. He planned to change his will . . . and you prevented it by killing him?"

"I didn't kill him!" Desmond gasped, shaking his head. "I'd never . . ."

"You're lying."

"Quentin, stop," Brandi interrupted, coming to her feet. "I don't think he's lying." She inclined her head solemnly at Desmond. "What did you mean when you said you 'took matters into your own hands.' How did you stop Kenton from amending his will?"

A wary look crossed Desmond's face and he shrugged free of Quentin's grasp. "I convinced him to leave his original will intact."

"How?"

Silence.

"Desmond, did Kenton truly leave that will intact, or did he actually have a new one drawn up? Is that what we'd find hidden in his strongbox?"

"No." Desmond raked a shaking hand through his hair. "I mean, I don't know what's in the strongbox, but it's not an amended will. Father's sole will is the one Hendrick read aloud."

"Then what is frightening you so?"

"Brandice, I don't answer to you. Go back to Pamela's precious cottage with your bridegroom. Learn how to please him in bed—maybe that way you'll keep him on English soil a month or two longer."

Quentin's fist shot out, striking Desmond squarely in the jaw.

Reeling backward, Desmond clutched the chair to right himself. Eyes ablaze, he rubbed his throbbing jaw. "Get out, Quentin. Both of you, get out."

"Give us your business records and we'll go," Brandi offered, her chin raised defiantly.

"What?"

"If you're innocent, if all you did was argue with Kenton and ultimately win a verbal battle, then you should have no objection if Quentin and I peruse your ledgers. Unless, of course, you were involved in unscrupulous business practices—practices that would have distressed your father. And that you're unwilling to furnish your ledgers because your dishonesty is clearly documented in them. Or is it that you're not unwilling, but unable, to furnish the ledgers? Are they the mysterious items Kenton secreted in his strongbox?"

Desmond's pupils dilated. "Were you mine, I'd have silenced that audacious, brazen tongue of yours. As it is, Quentin is welcome to you." Abruptly, he veered toward the door. "Sanders!" he bellowed. Turning his head, he shot Brandi and Quentin a withering look. "Sanders will fetch the books. Scrutinize them to your hearts' content. But at Emerald Manor, not here. Don't set foot in my home until you're ready to beg my forgiveness. At which time I suggest you approach me on bended knee. And then maybe, just maybe, I'll consider hearing your apologies."

"You summoned me, Your Grace?" Sanders appeared in the doorway.

"Yes. Collect all my business records. And Father's as well. Give them to my brother."

"Yes, sir." The valet darted off.

"Read the other letter, Desmond," Quentin put in ominously.

"What?"

"The other message." Quentin pointed to the forgotten page which was clutched, unopened, in Desmond's tightly clenched fist. "Read it."

Desmond unfolded the sheet. Scanning and rescanning the two lines, he turned a sickly shade of green. "Dear Lord . . ." His entire body sagged. "Do you realize what this means?" he muttered, half to himself.

"I do. Do you?" Quentin fired back.

With a trapped expression, Desmond backed away. "I need to think. I need a drink. I . . ." He broke off, fear glittering in his eyes. "That threat—it was also meant for me." He licked his lips. "I'm going to my chambers. When Sanders brings you the ledgers, tell him to send a bottle of brandy to my room. Immediately."

"Desmond . . ." Quentin stalked toward him.

"Let him go, Quentin," Brandi said quietly. "He has nothing else to offer us." She came to stand beside her husband, watching as Desmond bolted—from the room, yes, but from Lord knew what else.

"Don't tell me you think he's innocent?" Quentin demanded.

"Of course not. But neither do I think his crime was murder. Someone else is involved—someone whose objectives were far more sinister than Desmond's. And that someone killed our parents." Brandi drew an unsteady breath. "The question is, does Desmond suspect who that murderer might be?" She shook her head as Quentin made a move to go after his brother. "You'll gain nothing by pursuing him right now. He's paralyzed with fear. To continue grilling him would be a waste of time—time we could be using to scrutinize the ledgers."

"If Desmond is blithely handing the ledgers over to us, there can be nothing incriminating in them."

"True. But maybe they'll provide us with a clue that even Desmond, in his frozen state, hasn't discerned. Let's take them home and examine them. My guess is that Desmond's fear will render him drunk and ineffective for days."

"Damn it, I want answers," Quentin ground out.

"I know. So do I." Brandi laced her fingers through his, strangely moved by the fact that, at last, *Quentin* was turning to *her* for sanity and strength. "And we shall find them. Soon." She brought his hand to her lips. "In the interim, let's stop at the burial site and visit your parents before we leave Colverton. My heart tells me that feeling close to them and their love will rekindle our spirit and reinforce our faith. And that the peace with which they infuse us will provide the strength we need to ensure theirs."

Quentin's eyes darkened with emotion. "Your knowledge of me is uncanny," he said huskily. "God, I love you, Sunbeam." He enfolded Brandi against him, burying his face in her hair. "And I need you. Forever. Always."

"I'm glad, Captain Steel," she replied in a broken whisper, very aware that this was the first time Quentin had allowed himself to speak of forever. "Because you have me—always."

Chapter 20

$\mathcal{D}$amn. The cursed walls were closing in on him.

Unlocking his private office safe, Hendrick withdrew the missive that had tormented him for a fortnight, scrutinizing it for the umpteenth time. His hand balled into a fist of impotent fury, and he began to pace, clutching the single sheet and racking his brain for a solution. Damn Kenton Steel to hell. Why couldn't the principled bastard have dispatched his shattering proclamation one day sooner? Just one bloody day, giving him time to beat the truth out of Kenton before eliminating him—and the threat he posed.

Rubbing his throbbing temples, Hendrick stared at the words yet again, their significance burning through him like a deadly poison:

> *Hendrick:*
>   *Consider this letter to be written notice that you are hereby discharged as my family solicitor. Needless to say, the contemptible results of my investigation make any association between us an impossibility. Further-more, be advised that I plan to notify the authorities of my findings and, with the proof now in my possession, to*

have you stripped of your credentials and thrown into prison.

Hendrick scowled, regarding the final paragraph of the missive—the one that had been the true thorn in his side since Kenton's death:

As for your odious threat, I've taken precautions to carefully conceal the evidence and, should any harm befall me, it will find its way into the right hands, thus implicating you, not only of fraud and theft, but of murder as well. Rest assured, your crimes will not go unpunished.

Kenton Steel, the Duke of Colverton

Muttering a foul oath, Hendrick stalked across the room, shoved the note back into his safe, and slammed it shut.

If only he'd known that Kenton had not only assembled evidence but secreted it somewhere—right along with Desmond's ledgers. But he hadn't known . . . not until it was too late. Not until he'd killed the only man who knew where the damning proof was, thus sealing his own fate and condemning himself to Newgate.

Unless Desmond managed to find the evidence before Quentin or the authorities did.

That had been his only hope, and he'd pursued it with a vengeance, using every ounce of cunning he possessed. Of course, Desmond hadn't a clue that Kenton's findings went far beyond the paltry doctoring of Desmond's ledgers.

And that was precisely the way Hendrick wanted to keep it.

Should Desmond perceive even a glimmer of his true crimes, the far-reaching nature of his guilt, it might just penetrate the fool's drunken haze and trigger the realization that Hendrick had killed his meddlesome father.

"Hendrick! Open the door!"

A violent pounding nearly brought him out of his seat.

"I know you're in there. Let me in or I'll tear off the damned lock."

Gritting his teeth, Hendrick rose, wishing Peters were back from lunch to toss Desmond out on his ear. This was the annoying pest's third visit in as many days. And all because he'd lost his precious Brandice and Quentin was grilling him about Kenton.

Still, he couldn't dismiss Desmond entirely. After all, if Quentin were beginning to suspect him, those suspicions might eventually lead to the family solicitor.

Another round of thunderous hammering.

"Hendrick, open this blasted door or I'll break it down. I swear it."

"I'm coming, Colverton. Calm down." Crossing the room, Hendrick unlocked the door and flung it wide. "What in the name of heaven are you bellowing about?"

Wild-eyed, Desmond shoved his way into the office. "Where's Peters?"

"At his midday meal, I presume." Hendrick cocked a brow, assessing Desmond's frazzled state. "Are you drunk?"

"Not this time." Desmond slammed the door behind him. "You son of a bitch." He advanced on the solicitor. "How could you do this?"

The depth of Desmond's fury gave Hendrick pause. "I don't know," he answered cautiously, making no move to retreat. "That depends on what you're referring to."

"I saw it, you bastard," Desmond bit out. "I saw that ominous note."

Hendrick went very still. "What note?"

"Both. But I'm talking about yours. The one where you threatened to kill Father and ruin me. Does that sound familiar?"

"Desmond, you're not making any sense." Smoothly, Hendrick crossed over to the sideboard, pouring a tall glass of Madeira. "Here. Drink this. It will help soothe you."

Savagely, Desmond knocked the goblet from Hendrick's

grasp, wine spraying everywhere, the glass splintering against the wall, shattering to bits.

Hendrick winced, clutching his hand, his eyes blazing as dark stains of Madeira drenched the rug. "Have you lost your mind?"

"Definitely. I've also opened my eyes. You killed my father. You threatened his life and then you took it."

"You are insane." Hendrick flexed his fingers, trying to ease the sting without calling attention to his still-inflamed wound. Damn, he wished he'd worn his glove. "I don't know what note you're ranting about. And why in hell's name would you think I killed . . ."

"What's wrong with your hand?"

Instantly, Hendrick thrust it behind his back, cursing Desmond for choosing this visit to arrive sober. "You just struck it, you fool."

"Not that hard." Desmond frowned. "What were those gashes I saw?"

"Gashes? Those were drops of the Madeira you just showered about my office. I think your excessive drinking has begun to affect your vision, Colverton."

"You're lying." Desmond lunged forward, grasping Hendrick's arm and yanking it forward before the solicitor had time to react. Staring at the deep cuts, Desmond felt his stomach lurch.

And another heinous piece fell into place.

"Christ." Raising his head, Desmond met Hendrick's icy stare. "You're the one who shot Brandice. My God, Hendrick, you planned to kill her, too?"

"Unhand me, you sniveling fool." In one harsh motion, Hendrick shook himself free. "I've had enough of your childish blathering. You want the truth? Fine, I'll give it to you. Yes, I killed your father. How? It was easy as hell, thanks to you. You apprised me of every move Kenton made, from the instant he confronted you about the ledgers. Daily, you raced to my office like a terrified child seeking protection, reporting the steps Kenton planned to take in the hopes of saving your own cowardly neck. Once I knew he'd engaged Garrety's investigative services, 'twas elementary for me to forge an urgent note in Garrety's hand, summoning Kenton to London at precisely the right time. And just as easy, in the dead of night, for me to slip into Colverton's carriage house and tamper with the coach. So, yes, I killed Kenton. And, yes, I tried to do the same to your tenacious, cherished Brandice. Does that satisfy you?"

Shock and rage converged on Desmond's face. "Satisfy me? You murdered my father and you want to know if that satisfies me?"

"Oh, save your righteous anger. You got what you wanted. You're the Duke of Colverton, remember? You have all those precious assets Kenton wanted to wrest away."

"I don't give a damn . . ."

"No? Shall I flourish Kenton's amended will then? Send for Quentin and tell him the whole estate is his?"

A strangled laugh emerged from Desmond's throat. "Go ahead. At least it will end this nightmare." He shook his head in agonized disbelief. "I can no longer remember what I wanted or why."

"Then let me refresh your memory. You paid me to doctor Denerley's books so you'd look like a financial genius in order to win Brandice's hand and Kenton's respect. Does that sound familiar?"

"Unfortunately, yes. And, ironically, I won neither."

"Is that what's bothering you? Well, look at it this way. Brandice is too much of a handful for you, anyway. Find yourself a nice docile chit. As for Kenton's respect, you no longer need it. You have his legacy, which is far more valuable in the long run."

"I'm going to the authorities." Desmond veered about, headed toward the door. "'Tis worth forfeiting the bloody title to see you hang. Which, between your note and Father's, I'm certain you will."

"I wouldn't recommend doing that." The click of a pistol being cocked halted Desmond in his tracks. "I've killed three people, Colverton. Nearly four—had Brandice's blasted squirrel not intervened. I've not the slightest compunction about making it five. 'Tis very noble of you to sacrifice your title. But are you willing to sacrifice your life?"

Silence.

"I thought not." Hendrick strolled around until he reached the closed door, leaning back against it to block off escape. Calmly, he met Desmond's white-faced stare, leveling the pistol at his heart. "My suggestion? Don't get any ideas about becoming a hero. Not at this late date. Besides, it doesn't become you. You're a much better drunk than you are a savior. Leave that role to Quentin. He does it proud." Hendrick's mouth thinned menacingly. "You mentioned another note—written by your father. Tell me about it."

"I scarcely read it. I don't remember the specifics."

"I don't think you understand how serious this is, Colverton," Hendrick ground out, his forefinger easing toward the trigger. "So answer my question."

Desmond wet his lips. "The note was stilted, its message concealed. I understood its meaning solely because I knew what to look for, and Father's motives for penning it."

"Which were?"

"To tell Quentin of the ledgers and their hiding place— but warily, since he obviously feared for his life. Under the circumstances, Quentin missed a good deal of the note's significance."

"Do you think I'm dimwitted?" Hendrick snarled. "Your brother is an expert at deciphering code. If he saw this note, he interpreted it. And, obviously, he saw it. Is he the one who discovered it?"

Desmond averted his gaze.

Hendrick's forefinger found its mark, hovering just atop the trigger. "Did Quentin unearth this note and, if so, where and when?"

Paralyzed with fear, Desmond stared at the pistol, loathing himself for his cowardice. "Brandice found it. Early this morning. It was in Pamela's jewel case, along with the note you sent Father." He swallowed, hard. "And a key."

"A key?"

"Quentin believes it fits Father's strongbox."

"Of course." Hendrick's eyes gleamed. "Whatever Kenton concealed, he hid in his strongbox."

"What do you mean, whatever Father hid? You know what he hid—my records—the real ones." A pause. "Unless there's something more."

"That needn't concern you. Just tell me what the note said. In detail."

"I didn't commit it to memory."

"Where is the strongbox hidden? Tell me, and I'll allow you to live. Refuse, and I'll shoot you where you stand."

The briefest of hesitations. Then: "It's at Emerald Manor."

"How can you be sure?"

"Because Father used terms like 'gems' and 'facets'—all jewel-related words, alluding to both the strongbox and its location."

"Emerald Manor. Of course." Abruptly, Hendrick's eyes narrowed. "By now, Quentin has undoubtedly torn the cottage apart and discovered the box."

"To the contrary. I'm sure he hasn't." Desmond's denial erupted with a will all its own.

"How can you be so certain?"

"That's what I meant by my earlier statement that, given the circumstances, Quentin missed a good deal of the note's significance." Desmond pushed on, painfully aware that, were he unable to convince Hendrick of Quentin's ignorance, the unthinkable would happen. Hendrick would explode into Emerald Manor, possibly killing both Quentin and Brandice—a reality Desmond could not abide. Not with the shocked guilt of his father's death pounding at his skull.

"Explain yourself," Hendrick commanded.

"You're right about Quentin's interpretive skills," Desmond expounded, forcing his gaze away from the pistol. "However, in this case he only deduced that Father's carefully chosen phrases relating to gems alluded to the strongbox, overlooking the double meaning entirely. Which, considering the facts, makes perfect sense. Quentin knows nothing of Father's amended will. Not of its existence nor of its terms. If he did, he'd realize Father meant for him to be living at Colverton, rendering Emerald Manor relatively uninhabited, save Quentin's visits—the ideal spot to conceal something for his eyes alone. As things stand, Quentin believes Father intended the cottage to be his home—the very definition of which suggests a host of residents, including not a meager staff of servants but a thriving one. Hardly the deserted spot Father would choose to conceal his strongbox. Thus, it would never occur to Quentin to ransack Emerald Manor—nor even to deem it a possibility."

"Excellent." Hendrick's evil gleam told Desmond he'd been lucid enough to be convincing, rendering him weak with relief. "I'm impressed, Colverton. Perhaps there's hope for you after all. *If* you behave yourself and keep your mouth shut."

"What are you going to do?"

"What I should have done from the first. Relieve you of this unwanted task and shoulder it myself." Hendrick lowered the pistol. "I'm going to take a little jaunt to Emerald Manor and tear it apart, bit by bit, until I find Kenton's strongbox."

The very thing Desmond had feared.

"And Brandice and Quentin?" he asked hoarsely.

"What about them?"

"Are you going to harm them?"

"Would you care?"

Irony coupled with bleak resignation. "Would I care? Yes. I resent the hell out of my brother. I've wished him away from Father, from Colverton, and from England. But I've never wished him dead. And Brandice—I still don't understand why you're so threatened by her. Is the prospect of her stumbling upon your involvement in altering Ardsley's ledgers daunting enough to shoot her?"

"Ardsley's ledgers?" A crack of sardonic laughter. "That's

the least of my concerns. Your Brandice is determined to unearth her father's killer. And, should she succeed, I'd be convicted of murder."

"But how could she succeed? The only step she's taken is to try to arrange a meeting with a dozen investors. How would that lead her to conclude you're a murderer?" Desmond broke off. "The dozen investors. They're all your clients." Comprehension struck, hard. "There's more to your monetary bleeding than just me, isn't there? Just like there's more in Father's strongbox than my records, which in themselves would never incite you to murder."

"Again, I'm impressed." Hendrick slipped the pistol into his coat pocket. "However, for your own sake, stop your speculations where they are. Suffice it to say, I prefer not to have all my clients congregate in one room. As to your father's strongbox, I intend to recover it posthaste. Your brother and Brandice are expendable. If they interfere, they'll be dealt with, as will the servants."

"The servants are away," Desmond blurted, his mind racing as he attempted to protect Quentin's and Brandice's lives without sacrificing his own.

"Pardon me?"

"Quentin sent them to an inn for several days so he and Brandice could be alone. But now, with the emergence of these notes, the two of them are probably dashing off in search of the strongbox, either to Father's Somerset estate or to his equally modest manor in Essex. Both are unoccupied save a handful of servants and are, hence, well-suited for concealment. Moreover, even if Brandice and Quentin remained at Emerald Manor, they'll doubtless be devising the best course of action while gallivanting in their favorite place: the woods. Why not survey the cottage until you see them leave? Then, you can slip in while the house is deserted and accomplish what you intend without any more bloodshed."

"And what will you be doing during all this?" Hendrick asked suspiciously.

"What I've been doing for a fortnight," Desmond replied

with self-deprecating bitterness. "Drinking. And drowning in guilt. Because the truth is, I'm not acting out of decency—much as I might tell myself otherwise. I'm acting out of cowardice. I don't want to die, so I won't interfere. Nor do I want to go to prison, so I'll do all I can to keep us both from being discovered."

"At least you're honest." Hendrick took out his timepiece and glanced at it. "I'll head for the cottage at once."

"I beg you, don't kill anyone else, Hendrick." Desmond executed his final—and most potent—ploy. "Bow Street is already heatedly investigating the carriage disaster. If other members of Ardsley's or Father's families should be murdered, the authorities will delve into every person associated with them—business and personal. In which case, you'll be found out and hanged."

"As will you," Hendrick reminded him. "You had as much motive as I to kill Kenton. And if I'm apprehended, you can be sure I'll produce the amended will and all the altered records, declaring you the murderer and myself no more than an accomplice in your twisted scheme."

"I expected as much," Desmond returned somberly. "So let's make certain that none of this comes to pass. Find the strongbox. Ransack Emerald Manor to your heart's content. But ensure that its occupants stay alive."

Chapter 21

"Thus far, every one of these investment figures match up."

Brandi shut both her father's and Kenton's ledgers, shoving them aside and leaning her head against the chair cushion. "I feel like I've pored over these figures for hours, yielding nothing more than a throbbing headache."

Quentin rose from the sitting-room settee and walked over to his wife. "I feel much the same." He caressed her cheek, frowning at how pale she looked. "Sunbeam, we've been examining these books all morning. The sun is shining; the woods are beckoning—let's saddle the horses and go for a ride."

Instantly, Brandi's head came up. "Really?"

"Really."

"I'll don my new breeches."

"By all means." Quentin gestured toward the door. "So long as your pistol is tucked in your boot."

"Fear not. I'll be back in five minutes." Brandi dashed from the room, the sound of her racing footsteps echoing behind.

With an indulgent smile, Quentin chastised himself for not having insisted upon a diversion before now. The answers hovered just beyond their reach—and they would find them. But they'd also only just found each other. And, investigation or not, he intended to take time with his bride.

Four and a half minutes later, Brandi burst into the sitting room, tying back her burnished tresses as she ran. "How do I look?"

Quentin's gaze drank her in, lingering on the soft curves of her waist and hips, clearly defined by the breeches. "Seductive as hell."

"Seductive?" Stunned, Brandi glanced down at herself. "I look like a boy."

"Hardly." Quentin reached around to tie the hair ribbon Brandi was struggling with. "In fact, given that your attire offers you a distracting advantage, I'm officially conceding our race before we begin. I'd prefer to ride behind you and watch."

Brandi's eyes sparkled. "How terribly improper of you, my lord."

"If you wish to see terribly improper behavior, wait until after the race."

"That sounds most intriguing. I can scarcely wait." Brandi's gaze fell on the ledgers, and a shadow crossed her face. "What about the records? We haven't finished perusing them."

"They'll wait."

She hesitated, chewing her lip.

"I have an idea," Quentin proposed spontaneously. "Why don't we bring them to the gazebo? That way, later— much later—we can continue scrutinizing them, but in the garden rather than the sitting room."

"Wonderful." The shadow vanished. "Let's go."

The ride never took place.

Ten minutes of walking through the woods, withstanding the exquisite agony of watching Brandi move, her breeches clinging to her hips and bottom, was all Quentin could bear.

His own breeches stretched to the breaking point, he came to an abrupt halt. "I don't think riding is feasible any more," he got out through gritted teeth.

Brandi blinked in surprise. "Why not?"

"Because of your breeches. And the way they affect mine."

Slowly, her gaze slid down her husband's torso. "Oh," she whispered, focusing on the rigid evidence of his claim.

Quentin bent, his lips finding the pulse point in her neck. "I have an alternative. Unless, of course, you object."

"No." Brandi shivered, her breath lodging in her throat. "Since you've conceded the race, there's no point in holding it."

Her words ended on a moan, as Quentin dragged her against him. "I've conceded, yes," he said raggedly. "But I demand my prize nonetheless." Anchoring her head, he covered her mouth with his. "Now."

With a tiny whimper, Brandi flung herself headlong into the kiss, twining her arms about her husband's neck and parting her lips to his tongue. "Oh . . . Quentin." She shivered, pressing closer to his fiercely aroused body.

"Make love with me," he commanded. "In our woods. Here. Now." His fingers were already dispensing with her shirt buttons. "Christ, I want you, Sunbeam." He groaned as her breasts spilled into his hands, budding beneath his urgent caresses.

"Yes. Quentin." Brandi's voice was urgent now, too, her body arching up to him of its own accord.

He tore himself away, stripping off his coat and stretching it out on the ground. Then he undressed in quick, unsteady motions, flinging his clothes haphazardly about and turning his attention to his wife.

Brandi was naked in a heartbeat.

Drawing her down to the soft wool, Quentin blanketed her with his body, kissing and caressing her with a wild, feverish urgency that pounded through them both like great crashing waves.

"Are you ready for me?" he rasped, moving between her thighs, opening her to his touch. "I've got to be inside you." A harsh sound ripped from his chest, as his fingers found and stroked the satiny wetness that was his answer.

374

He entered her in one hard inexorable thrust, burying himself deep, deeper still, until she sobbed his name, wrapped her arms and legs about him as if to bind them together forever.

Forever.

Quentin would accept nothing less.

"Brandi . . ."

It was both passion and prayer, a harsh rasp of sound that penetrated Brandi's soul as profoundly as her husband penetrated her body.

Enveloping him, sharing his frenzy, Brandi met Quentin thrust for thrust. Her body coiled tighter with each powerful drive of his hips, her own body trembling with the need for release. She sobbed his name, her nails digging into his shoulders, feeling his muscles go rigid as he increased his rhythm.

Quentin knew nothing, felt nothing, but Brandi. He threw back his head, gripping his wife's bottom and lifting her into his thrusts, possessing her totally, inside and out. Wildly, he hoisted himself higher, stroking on her and in her, propelling them over the edge and hurtling them into completion.

Brandi screamed, shuddering in his arms as her body reached its peak and toppled over the other side. Her contractions clasped at Quentin's throbbing length, clenching spasms that hurled him into a climax so shattering he wasn't sure he'd survive.

Survival, he decided, delicious moments later, was severely overrated.

"Do you know," Brandi murmured, snuggling against her husband's chest, "I believe I finally have grown up."

Quentin's lips twitched, the irony of Brandi's announcement, given the past minutes' sensual abandon, too humorous to ignore. "Really?" He cradled her to him, threading his fingers through her tangled tresses. "What makes you say that?"

"The fact that I've abruptly lost interest in all my

unladylike diversions. Riding, fishing, even shooting—not one of them seems nearly as exciting as it once did."

"A fascinating observation." Quentin kissed the bridge of her nose. "And does that upset you?"

"No." Brandi's eyes sparkled. "As Pamela promised, maturity brings other diversions to take their place—diversions, I'm finding, that are even more exhilarating than their predecessors."

"I agree." With a wicked grin, Quentin glanced about the deserted woods. "But, in the opinion of most, your scandalous approach to these diversions render them even more unladylike than those that preceded them."

"Is that so?" Brandi arched one delicate brow, looking distinctly unimpressed. "Who invented these absurd rules, anyway?"

All teasing vanished. "Unfortunate souls who will never know the magnificent beauty we just shared," Quentin answered solemnly. "A beauty I intend to last forever."

"Quentin . . ." Doubt clouded Brandi's face. "Don't promise . . ."

"Forever, Sunbeam," he repeated fervently. "'Tis a vow to myself as well as to you—one we'll discuss the instant this investigation is behind us. But, in the interim, you have my word." Tenderly, he brushed her lips with his. "Forever, my beautiful wife."

A sharp object dropped from above, shattering the poignancy of the moment as it struck Quentin atop his head.

"What the . . ." He jerked to a sitting position, rubbing the stinging pain and glaring at the tree overhead.

Lancelot blinked solemnly down at him.

"I believe our romantic interlude is at an end," Brandi determined, casting a disdainful look at the branches. "Apparently, Lancelot is more possessive than I realized."

"If he hadn't saved your life, I'd end his," Quentin muttered, coming to his feet and pulling on his clothes in brusque, angry motions. "Blasted squirrel."

"In a way, Lancelot's interference is a reminder that we have work awaiting us at the gazebo." Brandi rose as well, slipping into her shirt and breeches. "Besides, husband," she whispered, handing Quentin his blade as she tilted back her head to gaze up at him. "We have forever."

A look of profound emotion crossed Quentin's face. "You're right, Sunbeam." He slid the blade into his Hessian, then bent to scoop up her pistol and tuck it into her boot. "We do."

Straightening, he surveyed the magical glow on Brandi's cheeks, and a pang of guilt accosted him. "Sweetheart, are you sure you want to continue reading the ledgers now?"

"I'm sure." Brandi reached up to finish buttoning her husband's shirt. "Along with the pleasures of maturity come the responsibilities." She lay her palm against his jaw. "Let's make our way to the gazebo."

Ten minutes later, they settled themselves on the white lattice bench, the records spread out around them.

"Where do we begin this time?" Brandi questioned. "We've covered every investment Papa and Kenton shared during the last six months of their lives. And there's not a single discrepancy."

Peering down at the array of ledgers, Quentin frowned. "As I said earlier, I didn't expect there would be. Remember, Desmond has handled Father's books since the murder. For all I know, he had access to them even before that. Either way, he knows what's in them. And, rest assured, were there a single inconsistency, he never would have offered them to us."

"Then what are we looking for?" Brandi asked in utter frustration.

"Something subtle. Too subtle for Desmond to notice. I haven't a clue what that might be. Nor will I until I see it." Quentin's brows knit. "In the meantime, there's another detail plaguing me. Something Desmond babbled during this morning's confrontation."

"About Kenton's death?"

"No, about Father's decision to amend his will."

"According to Desmond, that change never occurred. He convinced Kenton to abandon the entire notion."

"That was the explanation Desmond gave us *after* he'd regained control and had enough presence of mind to modify his response. During his tirade, however, he phrased it a bit differently."

"I remember." Brandi nodded. "His assertion—that he'd taken steps to ensure there was no amended will— disturbed me, too. That's why I asked him to clarify what he meant."

"Given that more truths are revealed in anger than devised in contemplation, let's assume Desmond's outburst betrayed his true actions. What 'steps' could he have taken to ensure that no amended will existed?" Quentin held up his fingers, counting off. "The way I view it, there are three avenues Desmond could have taken: silencing Father, persuading Father, or subverting Father."

"Silencing? I thought you and I were in agreement that Desmond didn't kill Kenton. Are you changing your mind?"

"No. I still believe my brother is incapable of anything so violent as murder—especially when it came to Father. Which eliminates silencing. Let's explore persuasion. Do you honestly think, knowing all we do about Desmond's lack of ethics and competence, that he could influence Father about something as important as his legacy?"

"Not influence him, no. But that doesn't mean Kenton wouldn't agree, out of that fierce sense of familial loyalty he had, to defer his decision in the hopes that Desmond would change."

"Change—Desmond? After seven and thirty years? Father might have been unduly loyal, but he wasn't stupid or unrealistic. If his belief in Desmond were as shattered as Bentley described, and if his intended will revisions were spawned by their last angry quarrel, why would he reverse his decision and compromise his estate simply to placate Desmond?"

"You've lost me," Brandi inserted, inclining her head quizzically. "What quarrel? What did Bentley tell you?

Does this pertain to whatever it was Desmond was raving about this morning?"

A terse nod. "Evidently, Father and Desmond had a falling out—a bad one—some days before the accident. Bentley couldn't help but overhear their shouting, nor could he fail to comprehend the quarrel's severity. Especially in light of the fact that, immediately thereafter, Father instructed him to summon Hendrick to Colverton for the express purpose of revising his will."

Brandi's eyes widened in surprise. "Kenton voiced that intention to Bentley?"

"He did. And Hendrick arrived the next day."

"Have you asked Mr. Hendrick what transpired during his meeting with Kenton?"

"Yes. According to Ellard, the change Father was contemplating had only to do with Emerald Manor—a change Ellard convinced him not to make. That's when I pored over Father's entire file. There wasn't a single mention of an amended will, nor was there any draft or unexecuted document to be found—other than a standard retainer agreement with Ellard."

"Then I don't understand."

"Nor do I. But if Desmond didn't persuade or silence Father, he must have subverted him. The question is, how? Whatever he did must have been extreme for Father to opt against proceeding as planned with his will changes. Yet that's precisely what happened, if Father and Ellard's discussion the following day pertained only to Emerald Manor." Quentin slammed his fist to his leg. "I feel as if we have all the pieces, but are lacking the central one to which all the others connect. The ledgers, the will, the note from Father. Damn it. What's missing?"

Brandi gazed down at her father's ledger. "I've exhausted every figure in this book, every investment Papa made and every payment he issued for . . ." She broke off, leaning forward to reassess something. "That's odd."

"What is?"

"I just noticed this." She pointed to an entry:

For services rendered on Parsons Shipbuilding investment; Ellard Hendrick, 300 pounds.

Quentin scanned the words. "Why is that odd? Parsons is a legitimate shipbuilder. Father and Ardsley were equal partners in that investment."

"Yes, I know. I recall seeing an identical entry in your father's books. Only Kenton's draft was for five hundred, not three hundred pounds."

Nodding, Quentin replied, "I noticed that right away. But, if you compare all the sums Father paid Hendrick with those Ardsley paid Hendrick, you'll note that the same disparity exists."

"But why?"

"As I just mentioned, Father had not yet executed his retainer agreement with Ellard. Evidently, Ardsley had. Therefore, his individual payments were substantially less than Father's simply because he was drafting quarterly sums to Hendrick as per the terms of their retainer. It makes perfect sense."

"Except for one thing. Father had no retainer agreement. Not with Mr. Hendrick or anyone else. 'Tis one of the few business philosophies he deemed important enough to spout in my presence—again and again. 'People should be paid their worth,' he would say. 'Retainers inhibit the ambitious and encourage the lazy.'"

Quentin's mind had begun racing at the onset of Brandi's explanation. "Then why are Father's payments so much higher than Ardsley's?" he wondered aloud. Decisively, he seized Kenton's ledger, flipping through it and studying each entry to Hendrick.

Abruptly, fireworks ignited in his eyes. "Of course. How could I be so stupid?" A mirthless laugh. "When will I learn that, to some, greed eclipses all else—loyalty and ethics included?"

"What have you found?"

"Look." Quentin pointed to the various entries. "All the drafts to Hendrick are entered in Desmond's hand."

"Is that significant?" Brandi squinted in puzzlement. "You yourself said Desmond probably had access to the records. After all, Kenton was trying to groom him to run the family businesses."

"Yes, but think about it, Brandi. Even though Hendrick managed Father's and Ardsley's mutual investments, they would have no reason to discuss what he billed each of them individually. Therefore, how would Father know if he were being overcharged? He wouldn't. He'd simply accept whatever sum Desmond wrote as appropriate for the services rendered. Even if that fee, in fact, were for services over and above those indicated in the ledger entry."

"What services?"

"Unscrupulous ones." Quentin gritted his teeth as another, more heinous reality, stuck. "Rheumatism, the lying bastard said."

Brandi was still fixed on Quentin's initial statement. "Unscrupulous? Are you saying Mr. Hendrick is involved?"

"Up to his wretched neck."

"What could Desmond have been compensating him for other than soliciting services?" She sucked in her breath, a portion of the answer exploding in her mind. "Papa's ledgers."

"That's the least of it, but yes. It would be simple for Hendrick to doctor those figures in order that Desmond might appear a masterful businessman. After which, he'd report the same altered figures to Ardsley, so the records would coincide. As long as the total profits and losses were the same in both ledgers, no one would suspect."

"Kenton would be devastated if he found out," Brandi put in. "Not only because Desmond was behaving unethically, but because the person he was deceiving was Papa."

"Indeed. Devastated enough to change his will."

Shock was supplanted by icy realization. "Then Hendrick was lying. Kenton did revise his will—or rather, attempt to. And Hendrick found a way not to comply in order to keep

Desmond, and his generous payments, at the helm—heir to Kenton's dukedom."

"Correction. Doubtless, the amended will was drawn. And executed." A muscle worked convulsively in Quentin's jaw. "And stashed Lord knows where."

"What makes you so certain?"

"The amounts of Desmond's payments to Hendrick." He tugged Ardsley's ledger over until it lay alongside his father's, flipping both books back a month and comparing entries from then on. "The gap between Ardsley's and Father's drafts to Hendrick grew wider during the final weeks of their lives—at about the same time Desmond and Father had their falling out."

Bleakly, Brandi stared at the figures. "And at about the same time Kenton summoned Mr. Hendrick to alter Kenton's will."

"Precisely. So, in my opinion, Father definitely did amend his will. After which, Desmond began paying Hendrick to disregard its existence. And, when the time came, to read its predecessor."

"Do you think Kenton deduced Hendrick and Desmond's scheme? Could the terms of his amended will be what he concealed for you in his strongbox?"

"No. That would leave his legacy to chance—something Father would never do. If he suspected Desmond and Hendrick's arrangement, he'd have engaged another solicitor and redrafted the will before taking any punitive steps. That way, his estate would be protected even if he weren't."

"Then what *is* in the strongbox? Just evidence of Desmond and Hendrick's wrongdoings? I can't imagine that alone would incite either of them to murder three people."

"Nearly four," Quentin amended with barely suppressed fury. "And, if I'm right, Hendrick's swindling extends far beyond Desmond, beyond even Father and Ardsley. It extends to at least a dozen clients, a fact that might readily surface if all those men were to convene in a single meeting—a meeting you were hellbent on arranging."

All the color drained from Brandi's face. "Nearly four," she repeated slowly. "The intended fourth victim . . . was I?"

Quentin's palm covered hers. "Yes. In my opinion you unknowingly backed Hendrick into a corner from which there was no escape. He couldn't manage to dissuade you from scheduling that meeting. Nor could he risk holding it and possibly having his illegal dealings exposed. So, the only choice left was for him to eliminate you and the upcoming meeting before his clients discerned the truth." Quentin's grip tightened as he spoke. "Remember when Hendrick and Desmond came to Emerald Manor the morning following your shooting? Well, when Hendrick clasped my hand, he winced, claiming he was suffering from rheumatism. Oh, he was suffering, all right, but not from rheumatism."

"Lancelot's claws," Brandi breathed. "He attacked Hendrick, didn't he?"

"Yes. I didn't see the damage firsthand because Hendrick wore gloves when he visited the next day. So I have only gut instinct to go on. But that gut instinct is screaming that my loyal family solicitor is guilty as sin. Now all we need is evidence." Quentin fell silent, then abruptly bolted to his feet. "I'm going to the cottage to fetch Father's note."

"You've thought of something," Brandi submitted. "Is it about the strongbox?"

"Yes."

"You needn't go to the cottage. I tucked both notes Kenton left you in Papa's ledger." Reaching over, she withdrew them.

"Excellent." Quentin unfolded Kenton's stilted message, pacing as he pored over the words. "Here." He came to a dead halt. "The answer is staring us in the face. We just didn't know where to look, not without all the facts. Tell me, if Father did discover Desmond's ugly deeds and, as a result, amended his will, what changes do you suppose it would reflect?"

"I assume Kenton would strip Desmond of any portion of

the estate he feared he'd destroy: the title, the businesses—everything but the family name."

"Making me heir to the dukedom."

Brandi frowned. "Even though you'd loathe the idea, yes."

"And making Colverton my home. Leaving Emerald Manor virtually unoccupied—a perfect hiding place for Father's strongbox."

Swiftly, Brandi rose, walking around to stand beside Quentin and read Kenton's letter. "Yes. It fits perfectly. 'Flourish' and 'implant'—allusions to Emerald Manor's garden."

"And the references to gems that we assumed meant only the strongbox—those point to Emerald Manor as well." Quentin's palm sliced the air. "Damn it, now it all comes together. The day of our wedding, Herbert said something to me about Father making solitary visits to the cottage. Just a few times, and just prior to his death."

"He must have been seeking a place to conceal his strongbox." Brandi gripped her husband's arm. "Quentin, I know Emerald Manor better than anyone. If Kenton hid the box here, I have the best chance of determining where. Tell me what else Herbert said."

"Only that Mother's love for the cottage must have been catching, thus inspiring Father's visits."

"I'm right. I know I am." Brandi scanned the plush flower beds surrounding them. "The gardens. Kenton's references to Emerald Manor all pertain to them. Pamela spent every moment puttering in them. And Herbert virtually lived in them. If he observed Kenton's visits, it was here, not in the cottage itself. He rarely set foot inside, other than for meals. Not to mention the fact that Mrs. Collins and the rest of the staff, though modest in number, dart from one room to another all day long. 'Twould be impossible for Kenton to find an opportunity or a location to secrete the strongbox."

"Then when Father says 'seeing beyond the surface'—"

"He means that he buried the strongbox in the garden." Restlessly, Quentin surveyed the manicured lawns. "But where do we begin? We have acres to search. For the first time I wish I hadn't sent the staff away. If Herbert were here he would remember precisely where he saw Father. I'll have to ride to the inn and question him."

"I'm trying to think," Brandi murmured. "Where did Herbert spend most of his time? The hedges near the north end of the cottage are a possibility, although lately they've been thriving and thus required very little of his efforts. The rock garden." She pointed in its direction. "That would be a good guess. Herbert and I spent a week supplying and arranging new stones after I drenched the old ones with stream water."

"We'll search there before I go. Where else, Sunbeam? Where else did you and Herbert work, beside the rock garden?"

"Everywhere." Brandi made an exasperated sound. "Herbert took great pride in keeping the gardens flourishing. To accomplish that, he seldom confined himself to one area unless there was a particular problem. Which there rarely was. Except for those geraniums." She gestured toward the box of wilting flowers beside the gazebo. "They've been causing Herbert such aggravation. Pamela and I planted them just before she died. They've never thrived, no matter how hard Herbert tried to . . ." Brandi broke off, her eyes widening with realization. "Quentin . . ."

Quentin was already in motion, swinging off the gazebo to look closely at the drooping blossoms. "I can't tell anything from a glance. Other than the fact that the area's been recently spaded. But, since Herbert's obviously been replanting, that in itself divulges nothing."

"He only digs directly around and beneath the flower bed," Brandi murmured, darting down the steps and squatting beside her husband. "But what about the area surrounding it?" Her trained eye searched carefully. "There." She poked Quentin, indicating a tiny, irregular patch of earth five feet away. "'Tis barely noticeable. But someone has definitely spaded here. Not too recently." She raised her head, her gaze locking with Quentin's. "But not too long ago either. Quentin, it would explain everything. Kenton's strongbox was elaborately painted. If he buried it here and the paint leached into the ground, it would doubtless contaminate the soil and kill the geraniums. No matter how often they were replanted, they would come into contact with the poisonous soil and die."

"That's all I need." Quentin stood. "Where are your garden tools?"

"In the shed near the cottage. I'll get them." She was on her feet and running all in one motion. "There's a shovel behind the gazebo," she instructed over her shoulder. "You can start."

"Good." Staring after her, Quentin frowned, accosted by that same sense of foreboding he'd experienced four years ago in this very spot. He'd been right then. Was he right now?

Fear—stark, irrational—clawed at his gut.

"Brandi!" he shouted after her.

"I'll be back in a minute," she called, disappearing from view.

Trying to shake his ominous feeling, Quentin walked around and fetched the shovel. Swiftly, he began to dig.

The area had, without question, been recently disturbed. Quentin's pounding heart accelerated. What had his father buried? What was the proof that had pushed Hendrick over the edge?

A branch snapped behind him, and Quentin jerked about.

"By all means, keep digging," Hendrick directed affably, his pistol cocked and aimed at Quentin's head. "'Tis a pleasure to let someone else complete my task. I must admit, I was becoming, not only tired, but despondent. After an hour of ransacking your cottage, I'd found nary a clue to the location of Kenton's strongbox. I should have guessed your brilliant mind would do my thinking for me."

"So." Quentin lowered his shovel. "It was you."

"Who murdered your parents? Indeed it was. But, in my

own defense, I must tell you I meant only for Kenton to die. The others . . ." He shrugged. "A tragedy, to be sure. Actually, if I'm to be completely candid, I never intended to kill anyone. Your father, however, is the most tenacious man I've ever met. Had he only left well enough alone, he'd be alive today." Hendrick's eyes narrowed. "Dig."

Dutifully, Quentin complied, calling upon every ounce of self-control he possessed. To go berserk right now would only result in immediate death. That would leave Brandi—and the strongbox—at Hendrick's mercy. No. He had to keep the bastard talking long enough to devise a plan. "What did Father do to so enrage you?" Quentin scrambled for a starting point. "Was it the fact that he hired an investigator?"

Hendrick gave a harsh laugh. "Garrety? Hardly. The dolt was as transparent as glass. The instant he arrived at my office requesting a list of contacts at the companies in which Kenton was investing, I easily hurled one obstacle after another in his path—ranging from businessmen's fictitious trips abroad to company records being updated.

"No, Quentin, the problem wasn't Garrety. It was Kenton himself. While I entertained his dimwitted investigator, he delved into other avenues. Dangerous ones. How many tête-à-têtes with colleagues and friends do you think it took for him to deduce that the discrepancies were not only in his records but in the records of over a dozen men? Discrepancies that, though I was careful to keep minimal on an individual basis, totaled a sizable sum?" Hendrick's lips thinned into a grim line. "Not one of those filthy rich noblemen would miss several thousand pounds. Nor would any of them have suspected a thing. After all, they trust their solicitor. Except Kenton. Once he figured out I was the one aiding Desmond, he delved deeper and deeper. Not even the threatening note I sent frightened him off. I thought for sure, if only to protect Desmond, that he'd comply with my command and abandon his investigation. But he didn't. Instead, he'd pressed on, his suspicions of me escalating by the day. The thought of spending the rest of my life in Newgate was distinctly unappealing. So, you see, I had no choice but to silence him."

Pausing to wipe his sleeve across his brow, Quentin bit back his violent reply. "Why didn't you wrest the evidence from Father before you killed him? Dead men aren't terribly adept at supplying information."

Impotent rage flashed across Hendrick's face. "Don't you think I would have if I knew it existed, you fool? I didn't get your Father's menacing note until it was too late. Kenton was dead, and I had no idea where his proof was hidden. Damn him to hell. If his missive had only reached my office *before* I sped off to Colverton, everything would have been perfect. I would have beaten the location of that dooming evidence out of him. *Then* I would have killed him on the spot, disposed of the body, and your mother and Denerley could have been spared. A most unfortunate twist of fate."

"What was in this threatening note Father wrote you?"

Hendrick's finger tightened on the trigger. "I'm not stupid. You're stalling for time." He glanced about the gardens. "Where is your lovely bride, by the way? I hope you're not expecting *her* to rescue you?"

All Quentin's restraint snapped.

"What have you done with Brandi, you son of a bitch?" Furiously, he tossed down the shovel. "You nearly killed her once. If you've so much as harmed one hair on her head . . ."

"Stop right there, Steel." Hendrick's eyes flashed. "I haven't even seen your Brandice. Although I must say I find it amusing that you believe her capable of saving your life. Quentin Steel, famed war hero, awaits a twenty-year-old chit to wrench him from the hands of death. Well, nothing is going to prevent me from shooting you dead, despite all your brother's sniveling attempts to the contrary. However, I suggest you dig quickly and effectively. In that way, I might be gone before Brandice comes looking for you, thus sparing her the same unhappy fate I intend for you. The choice is yours. But bear in mind that, this time, I won't miss."

"You bastard." Quentin snatched up the shovel, the muscles in his arms standing out as he plunged it into the earth in hard, uncompromising strokes.

The sound of metal striking metal signified the attainment of his goal.

"Splendid," Hendrick praised icily. "I'll take over from here. Which means you've suddenly become expendable." His finger closed on the trigger.

The shot rang out, slicing the air and finding its mark.

Hendrick's scream echoed through the trees, and he dropped his gun, clutching his shoulder as blood spurted from between his fingers. He spun about, his wild stare finding Brandi where she stood, fifty feet away, her pistol still smoking. "You contemptible little hell cat!" Ignoring the pain in his shoulder, he snatched up his weapon and raised it, simultaneously moving in Brandi's direction. "I should have killed you the first time. I'll teach you to . . ."

He never finished the sentence.

The onyx-handled knife slashed the skies, striking Hendrick dead-on, embedding itself in the center of his back.

He was dead before he hit the ground.

Quickly, Quentin strode over, seizing Hendrick's pistol and leveling it at him as he verified that the solicitor was, in fact, dead.

Raising his head, Quentin found Brandi's gaze.

He nodded.

She raced across the grass and flung herself into his arms. "Oh, Quentin, are you all right?"

For the second unlikely time, Quentin wanted to throw back his head in laughter.

"Yes, Sunbeam." He enfolded her against him. "I'm fine. And so are you."

Brandi drew back, white-faced, and stared incredulously into her husband's eyes. "You nearly died. Why on earth are you grinning?"

"Because I love you. Because you're incomparably, exquisitely beautiful. And because every time you ask if I'm all right, I feel suspiciously like you've stolen my line." He kissed her, deeply. "It's over, Sunbeam. At last, it's over."

So saying, he released her, walking over to the hole he'd dug and bending to lift the strongbox from its hiding place.

"I abandoned my gardening tools when I saw what Mr. Hendrick was about to do." Brandi cast a shuddering glance at Hendrick's body as she dug in her pocket. "But I do have the key."

An instant later, they raised the strongbox lid, revealing a ledger and a stack of papers.

"I suspect all the proof we need is right here, Sunbeam. The records, I'm certain, contain Father's accurate profits and losses. And the papers would have relegated Hendrick to Newgate for the rest of his days."

"It certainly looks that way," Brandi murmured, inspecting the pages. "From what I can make out, Kenton also documented the details of Hendrick's spending habits. Based upon the blackguard's lavish mode of living, he did more stealing than soliciting."

Glancing at his father's detailed notes, Quentin nodded. "The contents of this strongbox provide us with more than enough for Bow Street."

"All that's missing are these."

Hearing Desmond's voice, both Quentin and Brandi pivoted, staring.

Desmond sidestepped Hendrick's body with but a flicker of revulsion, then walked toward them, proffering what appeared to be a legal document and a missive. "Father's amended will and the message he sent Hendrick. The latter, I'm sure, will explain why Father feared for his life. It certainly clarified a few things in my mind—things of which I was stupidly unaware. In any case, I was with Hendrick when he decided to tear off to Emerald Manor to find Father's strongbox. So I put myself to some use, staying in London and searching Hendrick's desk until I located the key to his safe. Both these papers were inside."

"Why?" Quentin asked hoarsely. "After paying Hendrick

to conceal that will, why did you work so hard to unearth it?"

"I found myself severely lacking in options," Desmond returned with a candid shrug. "You see, as we both know, I'm too much of a coward to ride to your rescue. And, as things turned out, I wouldn't have been needed." His admiring glance darted to Brandi. "Your life was evidently in the finest of hands, your rescuer far more competent than I." Assessing her unconventional attire, a faint smile touched Desmond's lips. "You were right, Quentin," he declared, his gaze returning to his brother. "I fear your Sunbeam was born to please you, not the *ton*. She would . . ." A breath of a pause. *"Will* make a most irreverent duchess."

Brandi bit her lip, determined to stay silent while the miracle hovering before her unfolded.

"Go ahead," Desmond urged Quentin. "Take the papers." A corner of his mouth lifted, more with sadness than amusement. "You're effectively the Duke of Colverton. And, I suppose, rightfully so. You may be transient, but you're intelligent, responsible, and honest. Perhaps that's what Father realized all along."

"Father realized a great deal more than that," Quentin returned, an odd expression on his face. "Like the fact that, beneath your flaws, you do have a conscience. A conscience *and* a heart." Awkwardly, he cleared his throat. "Let me ask you something. Before he died, Hendrick implied that you'd attempted to save our lives. What did he mean?"

"Nothing too heroic. Only that I tried to discourage him from harming you. I was hoping to divert his efforts long enough for me to get to Emerald Manor and warn you. But it didn't work that way. So I chose this avenue instead, since I knew damned well Father's amended will was undestroyed. If there's one thing I never questioned, it was Hendrick's greed. He was making too much money in blackmail payments to shred his winning ticket." With an ironic shake of his head, Desmond added, "It's funny, the way things turn out. When Father first executed that amended will, I would have given all I had to tear it to bits. Now? The truth is, I'm rather glad it still exists. Effecting it won't erase what's happened, but at least I'll feel slightly less guilty knowing Father's wishes have, ultimately, been met." Desmond pressed the papers into Quentin's palm. "And, lest you suspect otherwise, I assure you, I am sober. I'm also ready to go whenever you are."

"Go? Go where?"

"To Bow Street, naturally."

Quentin swallowed, seeing his father's words in his mind's eye and understanding at last what Kenton wanted him to do.

More surprisingly, what *he* wanted to do.

Forgiveness . . . brotherhood . . .

"Desmond, I can't pretend to condone your illegal dealings, nor the motives that provoked them," Quentin said quietly, staring down at the documents he now held. "But I think these last few weeks have taught you something. Lord knows, they have me. They've taught me what's important, what's replaceable and what's not. And while I'm certain you and I will never be much alike, you are my brother."

"What are you saying?"

"First, stop destroying yourself with guilt. You didn't kill Father. Hendrick did. As to what I'm saying, it's simple. Judging from Father's note, I believe he forgave you your wrongs. In light of that, I intend to try to do the same. To that end, I shall furnish the authorities with the papers that incriminate Hendrick, and bury the past where it belongs."

"And me?"

"What about you?"

"My wrongs, as you called them. They're crimes, Quentin, not insignificant blunders. I paid Hendrick to doctor Ardsley's records. And Father's records. I also paid him to conceal the amended will."

"The will is no longer concealed—it's in my hands. As for the records, you altered the distribution of profits and losses, but not the totals yielded. Both Ardsley and Father received their proper sums, so no actual theft was committed. What's more, neither Brandi's father nor ours would want your indiscretions made public—not only for your sake, but for the preservation of our family names. As for retribution, no punishment inflicted by a magistrate could be worse than the one you've already rendered upon yourself."

"How true," Desmond replied in a hollow tone.

"Lastly," Quentin raised his head, his jaw set with purpose, "your motivation was rooted in a resentment I recommend we put to rest, along with the past."

Desmond didn't pretend to misunderstand Quentin's meaning nor the generosity of his offer. "There's still the matter of Father's evidence," he prompted, pointing to the book Quentin held. "The actual records showing the discrepancies I requested."

Glancing down at the ledger, Quentin realized with a start that his brother was actually giving him one last chance to change his mind—a self-sacrifice the Desmond he knew would never have made.

Quentin's final qualms vanished in a heartbeat.

"What records?" He slipped the ledger under his arm.

"Why are you doing this?" Desmond's voice was unsteady.

"I told you. We've changed—both of us. If I doubted it before, I don't any longer. And we're brothers. After all we've lost, 'tis time for us to recognize that." Quentin cleared his throat. "We can begin by reading Father's will together, and deciding how to best implement his wishes. We'll also send for the authorities, so they can collect the data on Hendrick and dispose of his body."

"Thank you," Desmond said stiffly. "I won't claim to deserve such leniency. But I'm not foolish enough to refuse it." So saying, he climbed the gazebo steps and lowered himself to the bench, awaiting his brother.

Quentin turned to Brandi, smiling when he saw the delight in her eyes. "I take it you approve?"

"Absolutely." She stood on tiptoe, brushing her lips to

his. "I'll ride into the village and have a message sent to Bow Street. You and Desmond need some time alone."

Wrapping his arm about her waist, Quentin drew his wife to his side. "Have I thanked you for saving my life?" he murmured for her ears alone.

"No." Brandi dimpled. "But I'd much prefer you do so later. Proper thanks are best offered in private, don't you agree?"

"Unquestionably." Quentin's grin was the essence of seduction. "But I must caution you, there's nothing proper about the thanks I have in mind."

"I should hope not."

A husky chuckle. "You're a superb marksman, my lady."

"As I said in the past, I've had the finest of instructors. He also happened to provide me with the finest of pistols. It remains ever by my side, ready to protect me."

"What a coincidence. So does your instructor." Tenderly, Quentin framed her face between his palms. "Forever, Sunbeam."

"Oh, longer than that. I insist." Brandi's eyes sparkled with anticipation. "After all, forever has been done. 'Tis up to us to surpass it."

"A challenge, my lady?"

"But of course, my lord."

"Very well then." Quentin kissed her, savoring the miracle that was his. "In that case, I accept."

Epilogue

*L*eaning her head against the gazebo post, Brandi stared dreamily across the cottage grounds, reveling in the news Quentin's letter had conveyed.

The Hundred Days were over. Napoleon had been defeated at Waterloo and was en route to St. Helena, banished into exile for the rest of his life. His reign, at last, was at an end.

Which meant Quentin was coming home.

Brandi gazed down at the missive in her hand, smiling as she reread it for the hundredth time:

> *Sunbeam,*
>   *I'm sailing for England to resume our ongoing challenge. Be forewarned: With the contest I have in mind, there are no losers. So ready yourself for the sweetest of victories.*
>
>   *All my love,*
>   *Quentin*

"Do you require anything before I leave, Miss Brandi?"

Brandi turned, gazing fondly at Bentley. "I'm sorry, I didn't hear you. I was daydreaming."

"Obviously." Of its own accord, a corner of Bentley's mouth lifted. "And I needn't ask about what. Or, rather, whom."

"No, you needn't." A grin. "Did you say you were leaving?"

"Yes, I'm en route to Colverton. Master Desmond has summoned the entire staff for a meeting. Which reminds me, would you object if Herbert, Mrs. Collins, and the remainder of the cottage staff were to accompany me? The duke specifically requested we all be there."

Brandi's brow furrowed. "Of course not. But why? Has something in particular prompted this?"

"I wouldn't know, my lady," Bentley responded in a tone that told Brandi just the opposite. "But I'll furnish you with full details upon my return."

"When will that be?" she asked suspiciously.

"Oh, several days." He turned, hands clasped behind his back as he headed off. "Enjoy yourself, Miss Brandi. You most assuredly deserve it."

"Enjoy myself?" she muttered under her breath. "All alone here?"

A berry fell at her feet.

"All right, I'm sorry—*nearly* alone," she amended, gazing apologetically up at Lancelot.

Evidently, he forgave her, for he scurried up the tree and disappeared.

Sighing, Brandi stared off toward the woods, wondering what Desmond's meeting was all about. Maybe he was planning a large welcome-home party for Quentin—a possibility she never would have contemplated a year ago. But the transformation that had taken place since then was extraordinary.

Desmond had discovered something he'd never known: contentment. Once he and Quentin reviewed the terms of Kenton's amended will and decided how to best enact them, he'd readily done so, learning to share control of the family assets, giving ultimate say to Quentin—as their father had requested—while keeping his title, home, and pride intact, as Quentin had insisted.

Most wondrous of all, Desmond and Quentin had become brothers.

Raising her eyes to the heavens, Brandi gave silent thanks for all the blessings that were theirs.

Far above, she felt certain Quentin's parents and hers were smiling down on them.

"I thought I'd find you here."

Brandi whipped around, her whole face lighting up at the sight of her husband lounging at the foot of the gazebo, purposely repeating the words he'd spoken five years before when he'd left for war.

Back then, she'd been a child.

Now, she was a wife.

"Quentin!" Brandi's feet never touched the steps. She launched herself straight into her husband's open arms.

"Ah, Sunbeam." Quentin's voice was hoarse, his hands shaking as he clasped her to him, enveloping her in his embrace. "God, I missed you."

"You're home," Brandi whispered, needing to confirm the truth aloud in order to believe it.

"Yes. I'm home. For good."

Brandi drew back, searching his face, touching every beloved line and contour. "You're thin. And you look so tired. But in no time . . ." She broke off, her eyes widening as Quentin's pronouncement registered. "For good?"

"Um-hum. And forever. Correction: beyond forever."

"But . . ."

"No *buts*." Quentin smoothed her hair from her face, bending to taste her mouth—once, twice—lifting his head with the greatest reluctance. "I've given England my all," he answered simply, seeing the question in her eyes. "Now, it's time for us."

"But Wellington . . ."

"I have his blessing. Hell, even his approval." Quentin grinned. "Do I have yours?"

Brandi didn't smile. "Quentin, are you sure?"

"Surer than I've ever been of anything. I'm at peace, Sunbeam. And so is England. My skills have been passed on to others equally capable; I made sure of that these past few months. Napoleon is gone. The Treaty of Ghent with America was signed months ago. The War Department will now have more than ample time to complete the training I began. I won't be needed—except, of course, by my beautiful wife."

"Are you doing this because of Desmond? If so, 'tis unnecessary. Even with you away, he's done a wonderful job at Colverton, and . . ."

Quentin pressed his fingers to her lips. "No, it's not because of Desmond. And I know what a splendid job he's doing. I've just come from Colverton."

She blinked. "You stopped there?"

"Of course. How else could I summon the servants away?"

Comprehension spread like a blanket of sunshine across Brandi's face. "No wonder Bentley dashed off like a child with a hidden sweet. He knew."

"He did indeed." Quentin caressed her face, threading his fingers through her burnished tresses. "We never did have those three days alone together."

"No. We didn't." Brandi twined her arms about his neck. "But Quentin, if Whitehall should require your deciphering proficiency . . ."

"They won't. There are others now. Trust me, Sunbeam." He tilted her chin up, his eyes darkening with emotion. "Besides, I intend to be very busy."

"Managing Colverton?"

"No. Filling you with my child." Quentin's lips feathered across her cheek, seizing her lips in an endless, drugging kiss. "Ah, Brandi, I love you so bloody much. I want to watch you swell with my babe. I want to pour myself into you and create a daughter with your spirit, a son with your fire. I want to pervade Emerald Manor with our children's laughter, and its gardens with their joy. Tell me you'll give me that. Tell me you want it as much as I do."

"Want it?" Brandi managed, dazed with the combined elation of Quentin's military retirement and the idea of carrying his child. "I want it more than anything on earth. Other than you." She drew back, staring up at him with wide damp eyes. "Pinch me."

His lips twitched. "Gladly. But you won't awaken."

"Oh, Quentin, I love you so." Finally accepting that her most fervent, impossible wish had been granted, Brandi tightened her grasp about her husband's neck, pressing against him as if to meld their souls as well as their bodies.

A hard shudder racked Quentin's body. "And I love you. With all my being." He swung Brandi into his arms. "Christ," he muttered. "I don't think I can make it to the cottage."

"I think the woods would be an ideal place to conceive our child," she assured him breathlessly. "'Tis, after all, where we mastered all our other skills. We'll master this one there as well."

Already, Quentin was taking determined strides through the trees. "Very well, Sunbeam" was his husky reply. "But I must confess, I believe this is one sport at which we're already proficient."

A joyous smile curved Brandi's lips. "That might be true." She snuggled closer. "But 'tis the only sport at which I have yet to best my instructor."

Quentin's laughter echoed exultantly throughout the gardens of Emerald Manor.

Author's Note

I hope Brandi and Quentin's joy was as contagious for you as it was for me! Also, I hope I managed to capture the lush beauty of the Cotswold Hills within the pages of *Emerald Garden*—it's truly a garden-lover's dream. (Incidentally, I took the liberty of accelerating the carriage ride from London to Colverton. In reality, it would have taken eight or nine hours to reach one destination from the other, not to mention a break for eating, changing horses, and stretching one's limbs along the way. Brandi, Quentin, and I beg your indulgence, as they were most eager for their story to be told posthaste.)

I'm thrilled to share my current project with you. (After all, we've all awaited this spinoff since *Echoes in the Mist* was released two years ago.) You guessed it—at long last, Dustin Kingsley is getting his own book!

Wishes in the Wind is the stuff dreams are made of: breathtaking love, overpowering passion, and a danger that could destroy it all. One thing's for sure: From the instant Dustin sets eyes on Nicole Aldridge, he intends to claim her—for good.

Want to see for yourself?

Enjoy the sneak preview Pocket Books has provided. And remember, some wishes are destined to be realized. . . .

I love hearing from you! Drop me a note (include a legal-size SASE for a copy of my current newsletter) at the following address:

P.O. Box 5104
Parsippany, NJ 07054-6104

With love,

Andrea

Pocket Star Books
Proudly Announces

WISHES IN THE WIND

ANDREA KANE

Coming soon from
Pocket Star Books
Late Fall 1996

The following is a preview of
Wishes in the Wind. . .

"*N*ickie, this is no life. Not for either of us."

Nick Aldridge swerved away from the window, pacing his half of the room's modest floor. "I shouldn't have listened to you. Or to Sully, for that matter. Now I'm imprisoned in a bloody London inn, locked up like a caged rat for Lord knows how long. You and your crazy scheme."

"It isn't crazy, Papa," Nicole murmured, her voice muffled by the blanket they'd strung up to afford them each a bit of privacy. She stepped around it, concentrating on the unfamiliar task of buttoning up a bodice. "The rumor we started makes perfect sense. As far as the world knows, you injured your leg during the last furlong of the Two Thousand Guineas, and are now recuperating outside of Glasgow, at the home of relatives."

"We have no relatives in Glasgow."

A twinkle. "How would anyone know that? Besides, Mama had a Scottish cousin or two. That's why Sully and I chose Scotland. It's a perfectly plausible place for you to visit—and remote enough to keep your pursuers at bay. After all, you can do them no harm if you're away from England, and the turf." Staring at herself in the looking glass, Nicole's twinkle vanished. *"This,* on the other hand, is totally implausible. Impossible, in fact."

"What is?" her father demanded, still prowling restlessly about.

"Me. This gown. I look—and feel—like a fool."

For the first time, Nick focused on his daughter. Abruptly, his pacing ceased, an odd look dawning in his eyes. "My God, Nickie. I'd forgotten . . . you look . . ." He broke off.

"That bad, is it?" Nicole sighed. "Well, 'tis a choice between this and the beige one—they're the only gowns I own. Quite frankly, I don't understand why women submit to wearing these absurd things anyway." She raised her pale yellow skirts, glaring down at the offensive layer of petticoats beneath. "It takes an hour to arrange the bloody outfit, after which you're too exhausted to move, too constricted to breathe, and too unwieldy to collapse in a chair." With a disgusted sound, she released the full skirts, letting them fall back into place. "I'll be grateful when I'm employed, back in the stables—and in breeches—where I belong."

Nick shook his head in disbelief. "You're blind, do you know that, Elf?" He swallowed, hard. "You're beautiful. Dressed like that—you're the image of your mother."

Now it was Nicole's turn to look incredulous. "Papa, I believe a week in seclusion has affected your vision. Mama was a lady—an elegant, fragile lady."

"Which you would be, too, were Alicia alive to see to it. She gave you so much I never could: her quick mind, her love of reading—and that fanciful imagination of hers. Thank God she lived long enough for that. But she died before you finished growing up. You were a girl. Now you're a woman. And I'm too rough around the edges to teach you anything about manners or social graces. I always assumed Alicia would do that."

Hearing her father's voice quiver with guilt and regret, Nicole went to him at once. "Stop it, Papa," she said quietly, taking his hands in hers. "You know as well as I do that Mama's death had nothing to do with the way I turned out. I've been in the stables, underfoot, since I could walk. The only time Mama managed to drag me away was for my studies. When she tried to interest me in more feminine pursuits like baking or sewing, I fled the instant I could, scooting back to the stables in record time." A small smile. "Let's face it. I was hopeless."

"You were also a child."

"Not when Mama died, I wasn't. I was nearly thirteen when she contracted her influenza. And she'd long since accepted that I was, to coin her affectionate words, 'Nick Aldridge-to-be.'"

The sadness in Nick's eyes softened to a whisper of memory. "She was so bloody tolerant. Even though my job meant she could never have the traditional life she wanted."

"What she *wanted*, Papa, was you. She adored you—just as you were." Nicole leaned up to kiss her father's cheek.

"She'd be proud of how lovely you've turned out. And she'd want me to see to your future."

"Fine." Nicole returned to the looking glass. "And you shall. But first we must see to yours."

Nick's lips twitched. "I think you should unbind your hair, for starters." He gestured to her thick sable mane, which was twisted into an expedient but less-than-ladylike braid. "Try to fix it somehow. However it is that women do."

Another sigh. "However indeed. It's nearly dusk.

By the time I finish making myself presentable, twilight will have come and gone and all the newsstands will be closed. I wonder if it's really worth the effort just to fetch a newspaper that will doubtless offer as little in the way of employment as its three predecessors did."

"A job will come up, Elf," Nick soothed.

"Hopefully before we run out of funds." Nicole chewed her lip. "If we had moved to the East End like I suggested, we could have saved half of what we're spending on this room. There's still time to—"

"No." Nick cut her off at once. "As it is, I worry every time you go out alone. But at least we're in a respectable section of Town, not living in a filthy hovel, surrounded by drunks and highwaymen who would do Lord knows what to you the instant you stepped out the door." He shuddered. "No, Nicole. We stay put until you find a position."

Nicole recognized that tone of voice and conceded at once, tugging her hair free and shaking it loose. "Then I'd best finish my chore and fetch today's *Gazette.*"

Two hours later, Nicole was no closer to finding a copy of the newspaper than she'd been at the onset of her excursion. Further, all the newsstands had shut down, as the fashionable world shifted from day to night, abandoning diversions like reading in preparation for a festive evening of theatre and parties.

Nicole halted on the embankment road, her stomach lurching to remind her she'd eaten nothing since breakfast.

Breakfast.

A wave of panic accompanied the more dire realization that the lateness of the hour meant all the shops had closed for the evening. Besides the newspaper, she'd intended to purchase food for her father and herself. They were down to a half loaf of bread and a bit of smoked meat—hardly enough to sustain them beyond tonight.

Beads of perspiration trickled down her back. What was she going to do?

Think. She had to think.

Instinctively, she made her way to the roadside and drew a deep calming breath—one that was instantly thwarted by the stubborn confines of her corset. Dizziness exploded in her head, and she clutched blindly at a nearby lamppost, determined to steady herself. All around her, the sounds of night were unfolding at an alarming rate, a profusion of elegantly dressed people leaving their Town houses for gala rounds of merrymaking. Originally, Nicole had counted on this very occurrence when she'd planned her jaunt, knowing that the throng of aristocrats would swallow up her presence as she made her way back to the inn. But her plan would backfire if she chose this moment to swoon, for amid this crowd someone was bound to notice a woman lying prone on the roadside.

The dizziness intensified as her corset stood its ground. In response, the collar of her gown seemed to tighten oppressively about her throat. *No,* she ordered herself silently, scrutinizing the passing carriages. *You will not faint. You can't risk calling attention to yourself.*

Staunchly, Nicole whirled about, seeking a private spot, her gaze scanning the banks of the Thames. Unthinking, she darted toward the river walk, which stretched between the embankment road and the river itself.

Thankfully, there was a secluded, empty bench behind a marble statue and a row of trees. She dropped onto it, forcing her breaths to become slow and shallow until the dizziness receded. *Damn this bloody corset,* she fumed. *Gown or no gown, I'll never again don one of these lethal stranglers.*

Twenty feet away, couples were milling about, but the lush line of trees acted as a shield between Nicole and the walkway's patrons. Safe and unseen in her tiny niche, she allowed herself to relax. She needed to plan her strategy—and she would—in a moment. But first, her body needed to recoup its strength in order for her mind to function. And, in the absence of food, a brief respite would have to suffice.

Leaning her head back, she stared up at the sky, watching the twinkling of the stars as they appeared, one by one. This onset of night was magic—not just here, but everywhere. Even amid the chaos at the stables, everything seemed to slow at the spellbinding instant that twilight merged with darkness, as if to acknowledge the reverence of the occurence.

A reminiscent smile played about Nicole's lips. This was also the hour of night when, as a little girl, her mother would tuck her in and tell her stories— wondrous, fairy-tale stories that made her heart sing and her imagination soar. She'd hang on to every word, awestruck, somehow believing it could all be. But then, her mother had the power to make one believe. And Nicole knew why. It was because Alicia Aldridge herself believed.

Do you know what stars really are, Nickie? She could almost hear her mother's voice. *They're bits of light offered to us by the magical sprites of happiness. They're reserved for special nights and equally special people, because only those who see—truly see them— can reap their magic.*

What is their magic, Mama? she'd ask. *And am I one of those special people?*

Her mother would smile that faraway smile. *Indeed*

you are. As for their magic, it's an offering. A precious offering to seize and to nurture. So remember, darling. Every time you see a star, you're being offered a miracle. Wish on it—wish very, very hard, and that star, and all its enchantment, will be yours.

Forever, Mama?

Yes, my love, forever.

Two tears slid down Nicole's cheeks and she wrapped her arms about herself, capturing the memory as she studied the sky. This was the kind of night her mother had alluded to: clear, warm, and fragrant, alive with the blossoming buds of spring.

And illuminated by a sea of dazzling stars.

Dreamily, Nicole focused on a star that seemed to call out to her. It wasn't the largest, nor even the brightest of the heavens' offerings. But there was something extraordinary about the way it glowed—as if trying to compensate for its diminutive size—that drew her to it, held her captive.

I'm wishing, Mama, Nicole declared silently. *Like I did on my locket. Only this time I'm wishing for the magic offered by that tiny star. Because, thanks to you, I still believe.*

Her throat constricted, and two more tears trickled from the corners of her eyes.

"May I offer my assistance?"

Nicole froze at the sound of the deep masculine voice, dreams reverting abruptly to reality. She'd been discovered. Someone knew she was here. She had to escape.

Inching to the edge of the bench, she mentally gauged her distance to the road, preparing to bolt.

"Don't run off. And don't be frightened. I'm not going to hurt you."

A hard hand closed over hers, and the bench shifted as her unexpected companion sat down beside her.

"I'm not frightened," she heard herself say, keeping her chin down. "I'm . . ." She broke off. *I'm what? Avoiding detection?*

"I saw you clutching that lamppost. When you fled into the trees, you were white as a sheet. I was concerned you might faint."

"I'm fine." She stared at the tips of his polished evening shoes, feeling the warmth of his palm over hers. "But I'd best be on my way."

His grip tightened, and an instant later a handkerchief was pressed into her other hand. "Try this. I've been told it works wonders. Guaranteed to dry a lady's tears."

Nicole couldn't help it; she looked up, drawn somehow to the husky teasing in his tone.

Her breath suspended—only this time her corset had little to do with it.

He was perhaps the most classically handsome man she'd ever seen, undoubtedly a nobleman, and not only because of his elegant evening attire. He had a bold straight jawline and patrician nose that screamed aristocrat, and thick black hair over a broad forehead and equally black brows, all set off by penetrating eyes the color of midnight—eyes that now assessed her with the practiced skill of a man who knew women . . . intimately.

His perusal was thorough, his approval obvious, even to a novice like herself. She could see it in his smile, his lips curving ever so slightly, and in his eyes, a glint of admiration in their deep blue depths, the dark brows lifting in surprised pleasure.

For the first time in her life, Nicole was grateful to be wearing a gown, outdated or not.

"You're far too beautiful to cry," he murmured, reclaiming the handkerchief and gently drying her cheeks. "Further, you're far too beautiful to be racing about London alone at night. Where were you headed?"

Nicole moistened her lips, her mind totally unable to formulate a reply.

"What's your name?"

She blinked. "Pardon me?"

"Your name," he prompted. "You must have one."

"Oh. Yes. It's Nicole."

He smiled, and Nicole found herself wondering just how long someone could exist without breathing.

"Nicole," he repeated. "It suits you perfectly: beautiful and delicate. Have you a surname as well?"

That snapped her out of her reverie.

"I must be going." She made to rise. "I've already been away too long."

Those amazing midnight eyes narrowed. "Away? Away from whom?" His gaze fell to her left hand. "A husband?"

Nicole found herself smiling. "No. I'm sorry to disappoint you, but I have no husband."

"Disappointed? *Au contraire,* my mysterious beauty, I'm elated." He caught her wrist, stroked it ever so lightly. "Sit. Just for a few minutes. Until the color returns to your cheeks."

She found herself complying. "Very well."

"Since we're exchanging only given names this evening, mine is Dustin."

"Hello, Dustin."

He grinned. "Hello, Nicole." His thumb traced the pulse in her wrist. "Why were you crying? Is it a man? If so, tell me his name and I'll beat him senseless."

She was helplessly aware of the heat his touch evoked, making her wrist tingle and burn. "No, it isn't a man. It's many things. Memories, mostly."

"Sad memories?"

"No, actually happy ones." She swallowed. "I was thinking about my mother."

"You lost her." It was a statement, not a question, and Nicole's eyes widened in surprise.

"Don't look so shocked," Dustin answered her unspoken thought. "I've worn that particular look myself."

"I see." Nicole inclined her head. "Why are you here?" she blurted.

A corner of his mouth lifted. "Is that a philosophical question or a specific one?"

"A specific one. Not 'here' meaning on this bench, but 'here' meaning on the river walk—alone."

"Is going for a solitary stroll so astonishing?"

"For a man like you? Yes."

"A man like me," he repeated. "What does that mean?"

"It means you're handsome, well-bred, and devastatingly charming. Add to that the fact that it's the height of the London Season and countless parties are in progress. So why aren't you there, surrounded by eager, adoring women rather than walking along the Thames by yourself?"

One dark brow arched. "I'm flattered. And dumbfounded. Are you always so honest?"

Nicole considered his question. "I think so, yes."

"Very well then, I'll be equally honest. I was invited to all those parties to which you refer, where I would mingle with all those women you just alluded to. And the very thought of spending another evening like that left me cold—cold and empty. So, instead I'm here, taking an unescorted walk along the Thames. Now, have I shocked you?"

She studied his face, then shook her head. "As a matter of fact, no."

Absently, he leaned forward, tucking a stray curl behind her ear. "What nearly caused you to faint?"

"Exhaustion, I suppose. I haven't slept in several nights. I have a great deal on my mind."

"Obviously." His gaze intensified. "Would you like to talk about it? Perhaps I can ease your distress."

Nicole sighed. "Not unless you can undo events that have already occurred, or right life's wrongs and balance its inequities."

"Only that?"

He was teasing again, in that disarming way of his, and Nicole found herself responding by speaking the emotional truth that had gnawed at her all week. "Sometimes it all seems like too much. Sometimes I don't think I'm strong enough to overcome the obstacles."

Dustin's smile vanished. "But you are. And it's not," he replied, somehow not needing to ask for clarification of her veiled declaration. "I have it on the finest authority that when a problem becomes unbearable, a solution appears. Therefore, the very fact that you're reaching your limit means your answer is near."

She started, taken aback by his profound assertion. "Is that a promise?"

"So I've been told." His forefinger traced the fine line of her jaw. "Let me help you."

"I can't." She eased away, knowing she must.

"At least let me see you home."

"No. It's . . . far."

"My carriage is parked just beyond these trees. My driver will take you anywhere you want to go."

"No."

"Very well, forget the carriage. I'll walk you home." He pressed a silencing forefinger to her lips. "I don't care if it's ten miles away."

"Dustin—please. I appreciate the offer. But I can't accept it."

His fingers captured her chin, those midnight eyes delving deep inside her. "I have one final request, then. A good-night kiss."

"What?"

His glance fell to her mouth, but he made no move to draw her near. "You don't have much experience with men, do you?"

"If you mean romantically, no. None."

"I thought not. You're too honest, too damned refreshing for it to be otherwise." His hand slid around to cup her nape. "If I promise to let you go immediately thereafter—no questions asked—may I kiss you, Nicole?"

She searched his face in powerless bewilderment.

"I realize it's an outrageous request—outrageous and thoroughly improper—a request I have no right to make. But I'm making it nonetheless. And I want you to say yes."

"Yes," she heard herself whisper.

Tenderness and triumph flashed in his searing, midnight gaze. He framed her face between his palms, lowering his head until his lips brushed hers, once, twice, then settled on them for a slow, warm, exquisitely gentle exploration.

Nicole sighed, shifting a bit, unconsciously easing closer to the wondrous contact of his mouth.

He deepened the kiss slightly, molding his mouth to hers, nudging her lips apart to accept the initial penetration of his tongue. She made an inarticulate sound, swarmed by unfamiliar sensations, shivering with the awareness that she hovered on the brink of something new and dark and dangerous.

Slowly, Dustin raised his head. "Where do you live?"

The moment shattered, and Nicole leaped to her feet. "I must go. Now."

"Just tell me where you live."

"No more questions," she reminded him, backing away. "Your promise, if you recall."

Frustration drew his brows into a harsh, dark line. "How will I find you? I want to see you again, damn it."

"That's impossible." Gathering up handfuls of material, Nicole prayed her customary speed wouldn't be hindered by her gown. "Thank you for comforting me, Dustin. As you can see, the color has returned to my cheeks. Good night."

She bolted into the darkness.

Look for
Wishes in the Wind
Wherever Paperback Books Are Sold
Late Fall 1996

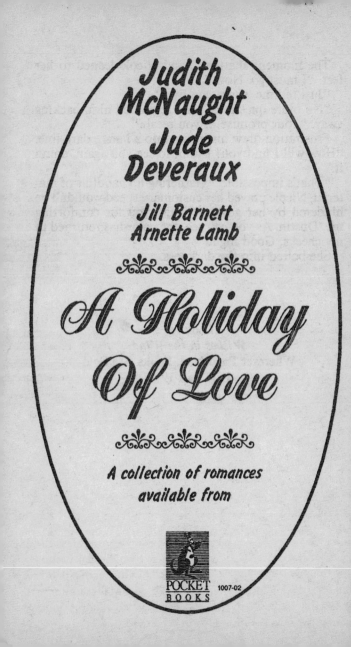

Judith McNaught

Jude Deveraux

Jill Barnett
Arnette Lamb

A Holiday Of Love

*A collection of romances
available from*

POCKET
BOOKS

1007-02